Life ain't
Nothin'
but a
Slow
Jazz
Dance

Also by DH Parsons

from Bliss-Parsons Publishing

1967 San Francisco:
My Romance With the Summer of Love

The Muse:
Coming of Age in 1968

Eat Yoga!

Book of Din

from All Things that Matter Press

The Diary of Mary Bliss Parsons
Volume 1: The Strong Witch Society

Volume 2: The Lost Revelation

Volume 3: Beyond Infinite Healing

All available on Amazon

Life ain't Nothin' but a Slow Jazz Dance

Summer • 1966

D H Parsons

BLISS-PARSONS
PUBLISHING

Life ain't Nothin' but a Slow Jazz Dance

Copyright 2019 by DH Parsons

Illustrations by DH Parsons

Editing, layout, and design by Susan Bingaman, Bliss-Parsons Publishing, Columbia, MO

Disclaimer

This story is an impressionistic account of people and events in the life of the author as recorded by him in 1966. The names of the participants, and certain specifics of some of the events have been altered for the preservation of anonymity and the exercise of artistic license. The work is based on journal entries and, as such, accurately depicts the experiences and thoughts of the author of that time.

ISBN: 978-1-948553-06-3
Library of Congress Control Number: 2019914978

To Annie

1 MONDAY

1 PM • At Home

I promised my friend Manny that I'd come over this afternoon and hang around while his rock band, The Riders, practices. Manny is the drummer and pretty much the leader of the group. Paul plays bass, and Burt's on lead guitar and sometimes sings. Pet, the gorgeous blonde girl with the hot body, plays a tambourine and does most of the vocals. She has a great voice — she could sing real music if she wanted to. She worships Grace Slick and tries to be like her when she's performing with the band — they play a lot of Jefferson Airplane. Actually, she's probably the biggest selling point the Riders have. I think most of the gigs they get are because of her. She's the one they send out to solicit paid performances. I can imagine her walking into some guy's office wearing those crazy short dresses she wears. The gig's probably a done deal even before she opens her mouth to sell it.

The jam session in Manny's garage will probably go on for a couple of hours. Usually after the practice, Manny and I and some or all of the others head to the Royal Scot restaurant to drink coffee for as long as the waitresses will let us take up a table without ordering any food. They usually don't mind 'cause we flirt with them and flatter them into letting us hang there as long as we want. A couple of them even flirt back.

I always look forward to summer, but especially so this year. I graduated from high school last week after spending the last four years of my life locked inside a giant brick womb preparing for a future that's rushing at me like a runaway train. I sit here now in my little bedroom with nothing to defend myself with except all the books I read, all the term papers I wrote, and a head full of bizarre impressions of what life is supposed to be all about.

I'll be eighteen years old in a few days. What the heck do I know about anything? Some of my friends are already declaring their majors in preparation for college next year. Good grief! I hardly know what I'm gonna do next week, let alone for the rest of my life.

I enjoyed high school. I had some decent classes and some good teachers. I loved some of my subjects, and didn't care for others. It usually boiled down to the teacher—if I liked the teacher, I liked the class and did pretty well in it; if I didn't like the teacher, I didn't do so hot. But teachers are history now. I need to move my life forward—get past the past, and even the today—and head on toward the brighter future that my teachers promised I would have. I hope these journal entries help me sort my head out to do just that.

I started keeping this journal a few weeks ago. I'm not sure why; I just thought it'd be fun to keep a running record of my daily stuff—not that my stuff is that exciting—and it seemed like a good idea. I told Manny about it and he said that it might be a kick in the pants to read it again in about twenty years. But even if I never read it again, I suppose my kids—ifI ever have any—will get that kick.

My first semester at Riverside City College (RCC) in September will probably give me a lot to write about. I've got an interesting lineup of classes: literature, astronomy, philosophy, ancient history, art, and a general math class that everybody has to take. I'm looking forward to most of them. I've already studied some ancient history on my own, especially Egyptian and Greek. I read the Egyptian Book Of The Dead while in junior high when all the other guys were still reading comic books. I even did a pretty good job of teaching myself how to translate hieroglyphs. I don't know what got me started on ancient Egypt—probably the desert and the palm trees. I've always been attracted to the desert and it seems like it would've been fun living the life of an ancient Egyptian, even if you were just a regular guy and not a Pharaoh.

I also enjoy learning about philosophy—which is a generic term that seems to take in all the different ways of looking at life. I've been reading some of the writings by existentialist philosophers recently, as well as some of the modernist poets. I think these poets are more philosophers than mere dawdlers who sit around all day thinking of clever lines to rhyme. I mean, look at E. E. Cummings and T. S. Eliot, a couple of guys I learned about in Mrs. Collard's high school English class (more about her later). Their poetry isn't just cutesy rhymey-whymey stuff; there's hidden meaning in every poem. Reading their poems is kinda like an Easter egg hunt—there are hidden gems of thought squirreled away between the lines. I'm hoping that my English class at RCC will include some modern poetry. It wouldn't surprise me if we got into some in philosophy class, too.

I don't know why I signed up for the art class, except that I doodle all the time and I like to look at paintings in art books, so there must be something inside me that needs an artistic outlet. I'm planning to go to the art museum in LA this summer to check out some paintings in real life. A lot of people devote a lot of time to the art business, so I need to look into what all the fuss is about. It takes hours and even days to paint some of the larger, more detailed paintings hanging in museums. I saw a picture in a magazine the other day—a landscape by some American painter I'd never heard of and I can't remember his name right now—but the dimensions of the painting were given in feet, not inches. That had to take some time to paint. It was a beautiful, highly detailed work that obviously had a lot of thought and sweat mixed in with the paint. I doubt that I could ever create paintings like that, but I want to know what it is that makes a man want to even try. I guess that's why I signed up for art. What the heck drives a guy to spend weeks on a painting like that? It can't just be the money. Even more, what is it that drives a guy to paint one of those huge abstract paintings like Pollock whats-his-name? Just dribble colored grease on a bed sheet for hours then hang it up behind the couch? What's that all about?

The literature class sounds pretty interesting. It's taught by a guy named Bill Hunter. I got to meet him when I enrolled last week.

He was sitting at a table in the Quad answering questions about his classes. Somehow we got to talking, and when he started rattling off about the literature class, what he was saying hooked me into it. He said he tries to cover a little bit of everything, from the old English guys like Chaucer, all the way up through some famous authors here in America like Poe and Steinbeck and Jack London. The thing that really grabbed me, though, was when he said he was devoting the last two weeks of the course to some of the really contemporary guys. He rattled off a few of the names. I can't remember all of them right now, but he called them *Beat writers*. One name I do remember is Kerouac—I had to have him spell that for me. Another one was Burroughs. Professor Hunter sealed the deal when he told me he was adding some contemporary poets into the mix with the Beat guys. Allen Ginsberg was one, and Somebody Snyder was another. I just may go down to the local bookstore and pick up some books by these Beat guys.

I love astronomy, but I'm not so hot in other areas of science, or math either. I hated algebra, which was as far as I got in any of the numbers classes. Other kids were into geometry and even tougher things, but algebra stymied me. I got a D the first quarter, and another D the second quarter. Third quarter I got an A, and the fourth quarter I was back to a D. I'll bet you're thinking that there's a story behind all that. Well, there is. The regular teacher got sick at the start of the third quarter and was in the hospital. The substitute teacher was a cute chick with a nice smile, big boobs, and short skirts. I just did what every other guy in the class tried to do—I flirted with her. It got me an A. When the regular teacher came back the last quarter, he was not happy about that. He wound up giving me a D for my final grade. To be honest, he was right. I hadn't earned that A.

I'm off to Manny's now, but I think I'll stop at the bookstore first; that Kerouac book sounds like a gas. Hmm ... *On The Road* ... gas ...I guess I'd better get some of that, too.

Jam Session In Manny's Garage

The band was a few minutes into a long number when I got here at 2:00 PM. Burt had written it, and had given himself the opportunity for a guitar solo about half way through. It's 2:30 now and he's been at it for about twenty minutes. Burt thinks a lot of himself and he doesn't mind sharing his superior gifts with others every chance he gets. He and I are acquaintances only, not really friends. We have very little in common, and he seems to think that since I'm not the fan of rock music that he is, I shouldn't be allowed to attend their sacred practice sessions. Since Manny's my good friend, and it's his garage, there's not much Burt can do about it. If they held their practices in Burt's garage, I have no doubt that I wouldn't be allowed inside. On the other hand, his opinion of me does not prevent him from accepting rides in my VW when we all go somewhere together. Since Burt doesn't have a car and I do, I'm always the one who drives.

The houses in Manny's neighborhood are small and close together, so they need to keep the noise to a minimum. The band is really loud, though, and if I were the next-door neighbor, this sound level wouldn't be minimum enough. The last time I attended one of these little gigs, it took about two hours for my eardrums to get back to normal. To be honest, the only reason I come to the practices is because I don't want to disappoint Manny—that, and Pet is worth the trip across town.

When Pet is singing, she is center stage and all eyes are on her. The piece they're doing now doesn't have any vocals, so she's just swaying to the music and banging on a tambourine while the guys play their instruments. Every once in a while she acknowledges my presence and tosses me a smile. Wait a minute—did she just wink at me?

The bass player, Paul, is a quiet guy who never appears to be stressed out by much of anything. I suspect that he does a little dope and comes to the jams high. Either that, or he's drunk all the time. He and Pet are the oldest members of the band—Paul is over twenty-one and Pet's close to thirty—so they can buy booze when they want. I don't know how Pet fell in with this group, as she's that much older than the others. I'm pretty sure that she and Paul are related—cousins, I think—and she's just doing this as a lark. Burt's the only one who can be difficult. I get the feeling that all of his showmanship and airs of superiority are meant to hide a basic insecurity and that there's a nice guy underneath it all. I keep hoping that one day he'll be more comfortable with his true self.

The music has stopped, and now I just need to sit here for a while and let the ringing in my ears subside. I suppose if the garage were a bit larger the music wouldn't be so over-powering. Even though it's a double garage, it's not all that big. Manny has it set up nicely, though. There is a little portable stage against the wall in the back. All the instruments fit on it, with plenty of room left for Pet to prance and jiggle back and forth in front of the band. I'm sitting in a chair with my back to the big garage door, as far from the amplifiers as I can get and still be inside. The side walls of the garage are covered with posters of rock stars, an American flag, and shelves filled with odds and ends that Manny has collected through the years—feathers, an old baseball jersey, and other bits and pieces of significance only to Manny. Along one wall is a small sink with a large mirror over it. Next to the sink is a refrigerator that the band keeps stocked with drinks and snacks for their practice sessions. Manny lives with his sister, Shanie, and his mother, Hester. He has his own bedroom inside the house, so most of his personal stuff is in there. His mother is kind of a babe in her own right and she loves to let everyone know that. Manny has told me more than once that she likes men too much. I'm not exactly sure what he means by that, but I think I have a good idea.

Burt, Paul, and Pet are busy tuning their instruments and adjusting the equipment. Manny has set down his drumsticks and is heading this way.

"Well, what did you think?" he asks.

"It was loud," I say, shaking my head as if to clear my ears.

"That's what you always say. But did you like it?"

"I thought you had it down pretty good." I always try to give him constructive criticism, and they really did sound like they knew what they were doing. "If you'd been playing at a dance somewhere I think they would have been pretty impressed."

"I thought it sounded pretty good, too. What did you think of Burt's solo?"

I pause before answering. "It was long."

"Too long?"

"Maybe. I know solos are supposed to showcase the guy doing them, but I can't remember ever hearing of one that long. I think five minutes is pushing it, and that one went over twenty."

Manny sighs and says with a frown, "Yeah, I thought it was a bit much, too." Then under his breath he adds, "Try tellin' that to Burt, though."

Pet strolls over and greets me with a big grin, saying, "What's shakin', DH?"

The voice in my head wants to say, *Those incredible tits of yours, Pet.* But wisdom prevails, and I reply with, "Not much, Pet. Manny invited me over to hear your new stuff, so I thought I'd take him up on it."

"You're always welcome, you know," she says warmly. "Did you like the music?"

"Yeah, I thought it was pretty good."

Pet turns to Manny and says quietly, "I thought that solo was a bit long."

"Ha!" Manny and I respond in chorus.

"We were just talkin' about that, Pet," I say.

"He went over twenty minutes," Manny says. "That's too much. I think no more than five ought to be the rule, or people are gonna get bored and leave."

"You gonna be the one to tell him?" Pet asks softly. It seems she has the same opinion of Burt that we have.

"I guess it'll have to be me," Manny says. His face acquires a demonic grin as he continues, "He won't get too mad 'cause it's my garage."

"Maybe you ought to wait till the practice is over before you tell him, though," I suggest.

Pet seconds that thought. "Not a bad idea. He'll be pissy for the rest of the afternoon if you tell him now."

"You're probably right," Manny agrees. "Let's just do music for a while and have fun with it."

"How long are you gonna practice today, Manny?"

"I don't know. Why?"

"Just wondering what the plans are for later."

"Got no plans," he says. "You wanna do something?"

"Can I come?" Pet asks brightly.

"I was just thinking about the Royal Scot for some coffee and fries," I say, falling back on the default answer to the eternal discussion, *What do you want to do? I don't know. What do you want to do?*

"That sounds boring," Pet says.

Manny turns to her and asks, "You got any ideas?"

"We could just hang around here and drink some wine and listen to records," she says.

"Doesn't your mom mind us young folks drinking wine in here, Manny?" I ask.

"She knows but she ignores it."

"Cool mom," Pet says, smiling.

"Yeah, she's pretty cool," Manny says. "Okay, I don't care if you guys want to hang around here after practice. I'm up for records and wine."

"Sounds good to me," I say. "But I think I'm gonna go out in the backyard for a while and do some sketching while you guys finish up in here."

"Sketching?" Manny asks.

"I signed up for an art class at RCC for next semester. I haven't done a heck of a lot of art other than a few doodles here and there, so I thought I might practice a little."

"Is that your sketch book?" Pet asks, pointing at my journal.

"Actually, this is my journal. My sketch pad's in the car."

"What's a journal?" she asks. "Is that like a diary?"

I smile at that. "Yeah, a journal is a guy's diary. I've decided to keep a journal of things that happen in my life, questions and ideas I have—stuff like that."

"How come?" she asks.

"Just for the heck of it. Some day it might be interesting to look back and read about stuff I've done and what I was thinkin' at the time."

Manny says to Pet with mock confidentiality, "He thinks he might do something important."

Pet studies me seriously for a moment. "You never know," Pet says, then she asks, "What are you writing about right now?"

"Just making some notes about this jam session," I say.

"About what a good singer I am?" She grins.

"I did mention that."

"Really?" she asks. "You really did?" She's excited, as if it really would mean something if the quality of her singing was reported in my totally unknown journal.

"I really did," I tell her. "But don't get too jazzed up, I doubt that anybody will ever read anything I write in this thing."

"One thing's for certain," Manny says.

"What's that?" I ask.

"You sure do write fast. I don't know how you can sit there and hold down a conversation with us and take notes at the same time."

I smile. "It's the one thing I did really well in high school," I say. "My teachers all told me that I could be a court recorder without even having to use a stenograph machine."

Manny shook his head. "They might be right."

"Let's get this show on the road," Pet says putting her hands on her hips. "The sooner we get the jam over, the sooner we can chill out with some wine and tunes."

"Other people's tunes," Manny says under his breath.

I went out to the VW to get my sketchpad before heading to the backyard. I settled into a folding chaise lounge under a big tree at the back of the yard where I had a good view of stuff to draw. Besides the weatherworn back of the garage, there were a number of objects on and around the freshly mown lawn between the garage and the house: an old push mower, a clothes line supported by two shiny metal poles, a brick barbecue that Manny helped his mom build last summer, and the large pepper tree.

The yard is surrounded by an eight-foot-high redwood fence, insuring privacy from nosy neighbors. Manny's mom, Hester, spends a lot of time lounging out here in this very chair while wearing a skimpy bikini, so privacy is probably a good thing. Hester is what people call a "full-figured woman" like Marilyn Monroe—voluptuous and round in all the right places. I discovered that for myself one day about a month ago when she was out here putting clothes on the clothesline. I'll never forget the sight. Manny had asked me to come and hang out with him and the band in the garage. The big door in front is bolted shut to keep the expensive band instruments and equipment safe, so the only way to get in is through a gate, down a walkway to the backyard, and around to the back door of the garage. The clothesline is near the fence and in full view of the gate. I saw her as soon as I came through. Hester is deeply tanned, so at first I thought she was stark naked. A second glance told me that she was actually wearing a cream-colored bikini. That awareness did not change the effect of my first impression by much, however. She had her back toward me, so she didn't notice me coming slowly down the path taking in the full view of her backside, fascinated by the sight of her butt-cheeks oozing out of the bottom of her bikini. Man oh man! Then I caught my toe on a crack in the walkway.

Hester turned and smiled broadly at me. "Hi, DH. Here to visit Manny?"

I wanted to say, *No, I'm here to bury my face somewhere in the crevices of your body.* What I really said was, "Yep."

Hester continued with her chore—reaching down into the laundry basket, pulling out the wet clothes, and shaking them vigorously before pinning them to the line, her breasts wiggling and dancing with every movement. She made some small talk, but I was totally flustered and nearly speechless. My replies came out in high-pitched, shaky bursts of two to three words. Although Hester kept grinning like she knew exactly what she was doing to me, I couldn't really accuse her of that. She may well have been simply hanging up laundry with no ulterior motive.

She was done hanging clothes by the time I finally made it to the garage door. I paused with my hand on the doorknob and watched as she turned and walked to the house, her healthy posterior jiggling like jello all the way to the back porch and up the steps. I probably would've just stood there for hours by the garage door with my mouth open if Manny hadn't grabbed me by the collar and pulled me in.

"You know she's teasing you, don't you?" he said.

"She is?"

"My mother has this thing about men. She'd be in bed with one all day long if she could."

"But I'm just a kid," I said.

"I don't think that makes any difference to Mom," Manny said.

Back to reality

I think I'll sketch the back of Manny's house first. I doubt that it will be a perfect replica, but I should be able to do a pretty good job. The whole point is to practice so I don't look like an idiot in the art class in September. I'm betting there'll be several students in the class who've had a lot of experience drawing. Maybe even some with real talent.

In Manny's Garage Much Later

Well, it's been quite a day. I spent a couple of hours out in the backyard and did several sketches of Manny's house and yard, including the clothesline with clothes hanging from it. Hester came out again and added another batch of wet clothes to the line—lots of panties and bras this time. I wondered while she was doing it if she might have been acting on purpose, knowing full well that I was out there and would watch her. I knew that she knew I was out there because I saw her peeking out at me from her bedroom window right after I first sat down. She moved away quickly when she saw me looking and it wasn't long before she came out with her basket of clothes.

"Hey, DH." She smiled at me as she set her basket down under the clothesline.

"Hey," I said.

She was fully clothed this time—at least she had on a dress. It was a short cotton thing that blew around in the breeze, giving me a brief glimpse or two of certain parts of her that should have been covered but were not.

"Beautiful day," she said as she began to pin her panties to the line.

"Yes, it is." I couldn't disagree with her.

She continued to hang her things up without saying anything more, but she seemed to take her time. When she finished, she turned to me, smiled, and said, "Don't make yourself so scarce around here." Then she walked back into the house.

I sketched until the band stopped playing, and then I gathered up my stuff and came back into the garage. The guys were milling around by the refrigerator, pulling out snacks, and Pet had set the wine out on a table by the stage and was busy pouring it into plastic cups.

Manny's a funny guy. He actually asked me once, "If wine is full of alcohol, then why don't plastic cups melt when you pour the wine in?" As if alcohol is the same thing as acid.

I told him, "If that's the case, then why don't you have a big hole in your stomach?" I don't think he ever really figured it out, but he continues to drink wine as often as he can get it.

I honestly believe that Hester buys some of the wine for us; I don't think Pet has that kind of money. Hester never says anything about it, but I think she's one of those mothers who likes to be more of a friend to her kids than a mother. I think she thinks she's buying Manny's and Shanie's love with things like that; that's probably the reason that Manny and Shanie get to do pretty much whatever they want any time they want. Fortunately they're both really good people and never get into any trouble. I know Manny wouldn't even think about getting into trouble. He's the nicest guy I've ever known, and the most laid back. Very little ever bothers him.

Pet spied me as I came in from the back yard. "DH!" she yelled at me from across the room. "Come get some wine."

"What kind is it?" I ask.

She examines it carefully before answering, "Red." Then she grins at me.

"I know that," I say, returning the grin, "but does it have a name?"

"Only the finest, Red Mountain, the nectar of the gods!"

"Then why are you drinking it? You're a goddess, not a god." I can't believe I said that. I've often thought that Pet looks like a goddess, but I'd never say that out loud.

Pet gives me a quizzical look but doesn't say anything. I hope she thinks I was joking. With a comeback like that I could have just been teasing, but her expression makes me think she isn't sure how I meant it.

I take a cup of wine from the table, thank her, then walk over to join Manny.

"Hey," Manny says.

"Hey," I say.

"You get any drawing done out there?" he asks.

"Quite a bit. Not sure it's any good, though. I think I'm gonna have to practice some more."

"Let me see it," Manny says.

I hand him my sketchpad and watch his face as he goes through the ten or so drawings I had done. Manny would be a good poker player—he's hard to read. All I can do is watch his eyebrows go up and down now and then. I assume they go up when he likes a drawing and back down when he isn't impressed.

Finally he looks up at me. "I like some of these," he says as he hands the sketchbook back. "The one of the tree is good. The one of the back of the house is really good. And the one with all the clothes hanging on the line is really, really good. It looks like you actually caught the wind blowing the clothes around."

I'm sure he noticed that the clothes were his mother's panties and bras, but he didn't say anything. He and I had already had several conversations about Hester, so there wasn't much more to be said. She's running hot all the time and Manny knows it. He also knows she'd probably drag me into her bedroom if she could, and I'm sure he suspects that she wouldn't really have to drag me.

Pet comes over and asks, "Can I see your pictures?"

"Sure." I hand her the sketchpad and she starts to slowly turn the pages.

I don't have any problem at all reading Pet's face; she's an open book. Whatever she's thinking shows on her face before she even opens her mouth. I kind of like that open, innocent honesty in a girl. Lots of girls try to hide what they think; they keep you guessing on purpose. Not Pet. She gives it to you at full force, whether you're ready for it or not.

Her eyes widen and her smile grows as she turns the pages. "Wow! I like these!"

"Thanks. I don't think they're all that good, but it's nice of you to say."

"No kidding—these are really cool!" She looks up at me with genuine delight and appreciation showing on her face. "This one of the panties and bras on the line has a kind of Zen quality about it."

Manny rolls his eyes.

"What do you mean?" I ask Pet.

"It's like a koan, but it's drawn, not spoken. It's not moving because it's a flat two-dimensional drawing on paper, but it is moving because the panties are obviously represented as flying in the wind."

"Wow ..." What a mind-boggling critique of my simple little drawing.

"Admit it, DH," Manny says, poking me in the ribs. "You don't know what a koan is, do you?"

Pet comes to my rescue. "It's a Japanese riddle of sorts," she explains. "They use koans in Zen Buddhism all the time in order to provoke thought and contemplation. In a way, they're meant to confuse your head so that you lose all sense of reasoning. It's human logic and reasoning that keep people from becoming enlightened."

Manny looks at her with genuine surprise. "Geez, Pet, when the heck did you become a Buddhist?"

"I'm not a Buddhist, Manny. I've just been reading about stuff. Zen's a fad right now and I wanted to know what it's all about."

"Well, watch it," Manny says with a laugh. "We're not used to you doing things like that around here."

"You mean like using my brain?" Pet's eyes are now shooting daggers at him.

Manny quickly raises his hands in surrender. "Just kidding," he says.

"No kidding from me, Pet," I say. "I'm impressed. I didn't know what a koan was."

"I really do like your drawings, DH," she says warmly.

"Thanks, Pet."

"What's this? A budding artist?" Burt is looking over Pet's shoulder.

"Budding is a good word for it, Burt." I say.

"Can I see?"

"What's shakin' over here?" Paul has joined us now, as well. "Can I see too?"

I give my permission, and Pet hands Burt my drawings. He starts to go through them with Paul looking over his shoulder.

Neither of them says much—just a few grunts and a hmm or two.

Paul looks after a few minutes, and says to me, "These are good, DH. Really good!" Paul's a pretty nice guy who never seems to look down on me for being interested in things other than rock music. "I think you ought to get serious about being an artist," he says.

Burt doesn't say anything when he hands the pad back to me, which doesn't surprise me, but he smiles at me—which kinda does.

"Paul is right," Pet says. "Just keep drawing!"

"I probably will—I sorta like drawing. I want to buy some paints and see what I can do on a canvas. Making things happen on an empty canvas leaning up against a wall is a whole lot different from putting a pencil to a piece of paper in a little book on your lap."

"Can't be any harder than finger painting," Manny says with a laugh.

"I'm not sure I want to get oil paint on my fingers," I say. Squishing oil paint through your fingers might be fun, but probably not the best idea.

"That would be permanent, wouldn't it?" Pet asks.

"It is hard to remove," I say. And that's only one of the problems.

"So, what would you paint first?" Paul asks.

I like Paul. He's sort of an odd looking character, but maybe that's why I like him. I don't trust people that look the way the world thinks people should look. With Paul, though, they broke the mold after making him. He's short and scrawny, with red hair and freckles—kinda like an Amish kid straight off a hay wagon. And he plays a mean bass.

"I'm not sure. I'll probably start small and do something easy, like a tree."

"That doesn't sound too easy to me," Paul says. "Trees have all those leaves on 'em. You gotta paint 'em one at a time, don't cha?"

"True, but that's the challenge."

"You could paint people." Pet is grinning and batting her eyes. I think she's hinting that she could be my first model.

I smile back at her. "I'm sure I will. I think portraits are much better than photographs. When I finally do I'm going to try to paint the personality as well as the face. Not sure how to do that yet, but that's what I've been thinking about lately."

"Do a self portrait," Burt suggests.

"That's not a bad idea Burt," I say. "Might as well experiment on myself instead of screwing up somebody else's face."

Burt would make an interesting portrait himself. He looks pretty ordinary at first glance—medium height, medium brown hair, regular face—not much to set him apart from all the other guys on the street. The features of his face though—his nose, eyes, and lips—all seem large and puffy. In fact, his whole body looks a little puffy. He isn't fat, just a little overweight, and his clothes are always a little too tight so that his belly hangs over in the front, making him look fatter than he really is.

"You have a pretty face," Pet says.

"Thanks Pet," I say. "I'm not sure that pretty is a good word for it, but it's the only face I have."

"I guess I should have said handsome, since you're a guy."

"I suppose. I have a handsome face. You have a pretty face."

"You really think I'm pretty?" Is she blushing?

"Here we go …" Manny rolls his eyes.

"Yes, I think you're very pretty," I say.

"She's definitely the prettiest one in this band," Burt says.

"That ain't sayin' much," Manny says.

"Pretty is a state of mind," Pet says seriously.

"Oh boy. You gonna get all Zen-ified on us again?" Manny says.

"I'm serious," Pet says, scowling at Manny. "Some of the prettiest people I've known have not been the prettiest to look at."

"You're gettin' too deep for me, Pet," Burt says.

"I'll just shut up then," Pet says as she turns and walks back to the table to pour some more wine.

"I hate to be a party pooper," Paul says, "but I promised my mom I'd be home early tonight. I've been out late three nights in a row and she's getting a little disturbed about it."

"That means I have to go, too. He's my ride," Burt says.

"Mama's boys." Manny grins. "Go on home. The night is young, but if you can't handle it."

"Yeah, right," Burt says, giving Manny a friendly slap on his head.

2 TUESDAY

At Home

It was already pretty late by the time Burt and Paul left, so Manny, Pet, and I decided to call it a night. That was okay with me because I need to be awake and aware to teach my yoga class this morning. I only had one or two glasses of wine last night, and I got a full eight hours of sleep, so I feel pretty good right now.

I was just leaving the garage when Pet asked me if I could give her a ride home. She said she was going to ask Paul, but he left before she had a chance. I would never turn down an opportunity to spend time with her, especially time alone without all the others, so off we went, Pet and me, in my little VW Bug. Sitting close to her in the tiny car, I soon became aware of her smell. I don't mind saying that it was a turn on. When I finally asked her what perfume she was wearing, she said she wasn't wearing any. What could I say to that— *You mean you smell like that without even trying?* Or, *You mean you smell like a saint and don't even know it?* Or how about, *Every time I get near you I think I'm coming close to Venus because you smell like roses.* So I said nothing at all and just drove the car.

Since my brother and I were little, our mother had made sure that we knew how to behave like gentlemen, so when we arrived at Pet's house I got out of the car, walked around to open the passenger door, and held out my hand to help her out. She took my hand and smiled up at me like she'd never had anyone do that before.

"I'd invite you in, but my parents are home," she said as we stood by the car.

The invitation sounded interesting, but knowing Pet, she was just being nice. Besides, she has a boyfriend. I don't know how serious they are because she only sees him about once a week, if that much, so I don't really know where she stands in the dating department.

Not that it matters—she's way out of my league. Girls don't get interested in me very often, especially the cute ones, and even more especially the ones with *experience*, as I assume Pet to be at her age.

Anyway, it's Tuesday morning about nine o'clock and here I sit in my little room—The Hole, as I call it—filling up a little time before my yoga class at ten. I got interested in yoga about four years ago. I was born with asthma, which kept me from playing sports and doing a lot of other things that guys do for fun and exercise. For a long time I didn't do much of anything, then one day I was in a bookstore with my mother. I wandered into the section of books dealing with exercise, and there right at eye level was a little book by a guy named Richard Hittleman—Yoga At Home, all about yoga and meditation. Curious, I pulled the book off the shelf and thumbed through it. What I found got me interested—excited, even. It looked like a form of exercise I could do without going into an asthma attack. I ended up buying the book on my way out of the store.

When we got home I went immediately to my room, lay down on the bed, and read through the little book, realizing with every page that I could do this stuff! Every day for the rest of the week, regardless of anything else that might be going on, I made it a point to practice the yoga postures. After four or five days I was feeling really good about it. A couple of weeks later, I heard about a yoga class being offered in Riverside that was based on Hittleman's book, so I thought I would check it out. The class met for a couple of hours once a week. The teacher not only taught us the yoga postures, how to do them, and how they benefit the body, but he also introduced us to a bit of Buddhist and Hindu philosophy and gave us tips on how to meditate. This was all new and interesting to me. The teacher was impressed by both the physical and the mental energy I put into the class. He told me that he thought I would make a good yoga teacher some day. I thought he was kidding—after all, I was just a beginner—but he wasn't. After a while he asked me to teach a couple of his classes. It was challenging and fun, and I felt good doing it—it still is, and I still do. I'm teaching my own class now that meets at RCC every Tuesday morning. I don't make much money, but I like doing it and I figure I'm also benefiting my own health along the way.

Among the perks of a yoga class are the women dressed in leotards and tights and other outfits that cling to every nook and cranny while they go through the poses—some of them can be pretty provocative. A couple of girls in my class are particularly noteworthy. They're beatniks—that is, they talk the slang, dig the jazz, and wear clothes that you'd see on the real thing in San Francisco or New York City. They're both really cute and they both know it. They go through the routine of movements and postures in a way that makes their tights ride up into all the cracks and crevices available. One of them, Abby, wears a large white t-shirt that she ties into a knot at the bottom. That keeps it out of her way, but she ties it high and tight so that her bare stomach shows above her tights. She's also cut the neck hole so that every time she bends forward she shows off the lacy bra that just barely covers her little boobies. I'm sure that Abby and her friend, Mamie, do these things on purpose to tease me. I've caught them watching me, and they just smile when they see that I see them.

Abby's reddish-brown hair is cut up in one of those short beatnik hairdos that's shorter than a pageboy and longer than a pixie. She has big brown or possibly hazel eyes, a Roman nose like you'd see on an old statue, and a pretty heart-shaped mouth that reveals a triangle-shaped gap between her top front teeth when she smiles, which is somehow very sexy. All in all she's nicely put together, with everything about her face, hair, and style creating the finished Beatnik product. But it's her attitude more than her looks that tempts me to get to know her better. She's a little cocky, and a bit wild, but, based on some of the things I've heard her and Mamie talking about, she's also very bright.

Speaking of Mamie, she's not too shabby herself. She's bigger than Abby. Some might call her fat, but I'd say full-figured. The finished puzzle has all the pieces and they all look good together. Mamie's black hair is cut the same as Abby's. Her nose is rounder, her eyes are blue, and her mouth is wider with full lips that she keeps painted bright red at all times. She looks kinda like that Liza chick, Judy Garland's kid, only with more meat on her.

Those two are the stars in my class, but there are several other attractive women, as well. One of them, Bette, is another full-figured woman. She has long black hair and large breasts. Even though she's somewhere between forty and fifty, she looks good in her yoga clothes, and, like Abby and Mamie, she knows it. She wears a white shirt and black tights like Abby, but her shirt buttons up the front and she ties the tails tight around her waist. She also leaves the top few buttons undone so that the tops of her large breasts are visible. The view can become quite spectacular at times during class. She's another woman who likes to tease and then smile at me as if to say, *Whattaya think?* But I don't know what to think—I'm only seventeen. Granted, I'll be eighteen in just a few days, but I'm not about to come on to a lady that old—I'd be afraid she'd jump down my throat and leave in a huff.

Okay, that's the update. I need to cut this off and head to class. This journal thing seems to be going well and I'm determined to keep it up as faithfully as I can. I hope I can stay with it for many years to come, but who knows, I might grow tired of it and just toss it in the trash one day.

Royal Scot Restaurant • Noonish

I'm sitting in my favorite booth—the one in the corner near the swinging doors that go into the kitchen. The Royal Scot Restaurant is a favorite hangout of ours—that is, me and my little group of friends—and we come here frequently. For me, it's almost like going to church in that I do a lot of serious contemplation seated at this table while sipping on a bottomless cup of coffee. I can't afford to buy meals every time I come in, but all the waitresses know me since I come here so often. And since I'm so nice to the people who work here, I can sit here for as long as I want and the cup never goes dry. Sometimes a couple of the waitresses who've been here the longest will bring me a little something to eat on the sly and not charge me for it.

I'm not here alone today, though. I finally got up the nerve to ask Abby if she'd like to join me for a cup of coffee after class and she accepted. Actually, it was more her doing. She approached me after class to ask me to explain what I know about Hindu philosophy. She's been curious about it and she's heard me talk about it in class, so she considers me an expert—which is silly. I doubt that I know much more on the subject than she does. Anyway, I told her I'd be happy to tell her what I know, but we'd have to go somewhere else as a Tai Chi class was scheduled for the yoga room at 11:30. When Abby asked if I knew a place we could go for some coffee, I said, "Of course. Does the Pope know how to get to the Vatican?"

So here we are at The Scot, as I like to call it. Abby's gone to the restroom, so I'm taking this opportunity to bring the journal up to date. The first thing she did was ask me about the little black book I'm always writing in, so I explained it to her. With that out of the way, we can chitchat when she gets back. I promise I'll tell the journal everything we discussed as soon as I can.

Here she comes.

Abby slides into the booth beside me and picks up her coffee and the conversation.

"I've been trying to learn more about the Hindu religion and to understand how it's connected to yoga—if indeed it is," she begins. "All I seem to come up with is more questions. I'm reading a biography of Gandhi now, and that's got my mind wandering all over the place."

"I know what you mean," I say. "I've read some books about Gandhi and about some of the famous yogis, so I can fill you in on some of the facts. The deeper spiritual stuff though, is harder.

I'm not sure there is a single answer—certainly no easy ones."

"Do you think Gandhi was really sincere in what he was doing?" Abby asks while sipping from her cup. "I mean, it takes a lotta moxie to walk around half-naked like that, with not much of anything but a rice bowl and a pair of glasses, but he did seem to have a circle of friends who took care of him. Maybe he was just trying to impress everyone with how humble he was."

"No one can really know exactly what was in his heart," I tell her. "There was a lot that needed changing in India—poverty, oppression, civil and religious violence. I think he believed that the best way to make change happen is for people to peacefully do the *right thing* even when they are up against the threat of force or violence. He wanted to change India for the better, and to do it in a way that would be an example to the rest of the world—to show the world that passive resistance and peaceful demonstrations by ordinary people could cause leaders to make the changes that were needed. Gandhi believed India was the heart of the world, but that the heart was sick and in need of repair."

"So, he wasn't just a bum using all his friends so he wouldn't have to get a real job?"

"I doubt that," I say, shaking my head. "He didn't have an easy time of it, and it got him killed in the end."

"I haven't finished the book yet. When did he die?"

"He was assassinated in January of 1948, six months before I was born."

We are silent for a few minutes, both of us staring into our coffee and lost in our own thoughts. Then Abby looks up at me and says, "Do you believe in reincarnation?"

I return her look with curiosity. "I'm not sure. "I haven't really thought about it."

"I read in the Gandhi book that the Hindu people do. They believe that when they die, they come back in a week or two in the body of a new-born baby. This supposedly happens over and over again."

"It has to do with what they call, *karma*," I explain. "They believe that the human soul is always striving for perfection and it just can't get there in one life. It has to keep coming back until it gets it right."

"Perfection, huh?" She laughs. "I don't think that's even possible. How can anybody or anything really be perfect? Look at the people in this cafe—does anyone here look even close to perfection?"

"I don't believe it's possible either," I agree. "In some cultures, people believe that only the gods are perfect and that people shouldn't even try to be perfect because that would offend them. Some people, like the Chumash and Navajo Indians, always work an obvious flaw into the blankets or baskets or pots they make so that the gods won't get mad."

"Well, nothing I ever do is perfect, so I guess I don't have to worry about that," she says, smiling. "I'm not sure I even believe in the gods."

"It's hard to believe in something you can't see or feel," I say. "How do you wrap your mind around something that you can't picture in your head?"

"Yeah, I know what you mean. My parents were Catholic when I was much younger. My mom's not so much any more, but back then they wanted me to be Catholic, too. I tried for a while, but it just didn't make sense to me. The church kept telling me I couldn't do a lot of the things that I really liked doing. In fact, according to the church, I couldn't do anything—I was doing a lot of stuff, and none of it was on the list of church-approved activities. I couldn't dig that. In all honesty, I was pretty young. It's possible that I was only seeing what I wanted to see and not the big picture. I really don't like being told what I can and can't do, so I don't blame my church for anything. It could be right and I could be wrong."

I nod in agreement. "I know. I'm not a bad person inside—in fact I think I'm a pretty nice guy—but if I were to believe what some of the religions teach, I'd feel guilty all the time. What good is that? Why go around feeling guilty about things you don't know you're doing, thinking you're bad when the religions aren't even clear about it and can't agree on what's really bad and what's really good. That doesn't make sense."

"I read in the Bible somewhere that nobody really knows who God is or how His mind works, so how can a church speak for God like the churches say they do?" she says.

"I wonder about that myself," I say. "I've read the Bible a lot, too, and what I don't get is how people in churches say they love Jesus. If they really love Jesus, and if they really believe what He taught, then why do they act so nasty all the time? Then they tell us we gotta be like them! So I guess that means they want us to act nasty all the time." I smile.

Abby grins. "Makes sense to me," she says.

"It's crazy," I say, quickly adding, "I mean people are crazy, not God. I believe that God exists, but I think people are crazy for trying to speak for God and for fighting each other just because they can't agree on what God is saying."

"I do think some of the Catholic saints might be for real, though," Abby says.

"You mean like Saint Francis?"

"Yeah, and others. But I don't think you have to be a Catholic to be a saint. I think anybody can be one."

"What do you think it takes to be a saint?" I ask.

"Havin' all your ducks in a row," she says, smiling at me.

"Whattaya mean by that?"

She looks me straight in the eye and says without hesitation, "Knowing what you're doin' all the time you're doin' it. If you believe in yourself, and you think what you're doin' is the right thing to do, and you know it isn't gonna hurt anybody but might even make the world a better place, even by accident, and that's the way you live every day you're alive, then you just might be a saint."

"Quite a mouthful. I like that." I smiled. "Maybe that makes us saints."

"I'm not sure about that." Her serious look has changed to a lopsided smile, and there is an odd glint in her eye. "I'm thinking some pretty nasty thoughts right now."

"You are?"

That's when I felt the pressure of her foot against my ankle under the table. I cleared my throat as it moved slowly up my leg.

"I'm coffeed out," I told her. "I think it's time to go."

She smiled and licked her lips. "Where can we go?"

"We can go to my little hovel. My parents are off on a camping trip, so we can have the place to ourselves. We can continue this conversation there."

"Good." She stood up. "Because I have a whole lot I want to 'discuss' with you."

In The Hole • 4 PM

We left the restaurant and drove here to my little room in my parent's garage. I'd been sharing a large upstairs bedroom with my brother, Jim, but as we got older it seemed like a good idea for us each to have a room of our own. Grandad built this one for me in the northeast corner of the large double garage at our house and we named it, The Hole.

It isn't much, but it's perfect for my few needs: one room with a closet for my clothes, a bed to sleep in, a small desk and chair for a place to study. There is a sink and a small refrigerator just outside The Hole in the garage itself—kind of like Manny's setup. There are a few items of personal importance to me on the desk and tucked into various nooks and crannies around the room, and there are stacks of books all over the place in addition to the neat row on the desk. Other than that, it's pretty austere. Most importantly, it's private. The only drawback is that I don't have my own bathroom. The garage is connected to the house by a breezeway, and there are doors from there into both the house and the garage, as well as to the outside. If I have to pee, I go through the garage and the breezeway and into the house to use one of the bathrooms there. I have to confess that sometimes, in the middle of the night, I just step out into the backyard. We have a large patio out back, and

the lawn slopes down from the patio to the edge of a gully. I like
going out there to pee on a clear night. I can stand at the top of
the gully, stare up at the stars, and feel like a million bucks. But
all that has nothing to do with the fact that I'm now sitting at my
desk and staring at Abby, who is lying naked on my bed three feet
away from me. How that came about is another story, but you can
use your imagination.

At this moment, Abby is on her back and apparently sound
asleep. Her top half is exposed, and her bottom half is covered by
a sheet. It's hot, and the big drops of sweat running down between
her breasts form a small river that follows the line of her tummy.
The sweat fills her belly button, then cascades over her right side
and into the sheet bunched up below her hip. I've never had a
totally naked girl in my room before. I wish I could memorialize
the moment somehow. I wish I could film it and store the film away
so that twenty or thirty years in the future I could look at it while
I read the words I'm writing now. Will I know Abby then? Will I
know her in fifty years? Will I even know her next week? She may
wake up in a few minutes, grab her clothes and go running off, and
never come back to my yoga class. She may think, *What have I done*,
get embarrassed, and dump me for good. Even now she might be
dreaming about angels and saints who are telling her, *Run, Abby,
run! This isn't right! You're being nasty again*, and when she wakes
up, it's adios amigo.

I can see her eyelids vibrating and twitching like she's in some
sort of deep sleep even though we haven't been here very long. It's
still early, too, so she shouldn't be tired—not like the going to bed
late and being drunk kind of tired. I'm planning to open up a jug
of Red Mountain when she wakes up, but we haven't had any yet.
The jug was given to me as a high school graduation present. I can't
say by whom—after all, I am under age. I will say that it's from
one of the teachers I grew close to during my senior year—I'll
call her Mrs. Collard, but that isn't her real name. She was always
dropping hints that she might want to teach me more than just

what was in the books. I wasn't sure what to do about that. I knew it was kind of taboo and that she might get into big trouble for it too, so I just kinda smiled at her and tried to pretend that I didn't get it. One day, just before graduation, I walked into the classroom. Mrs. Collard was in there alone. When she saw me, she came from around her desk and motioned for me to follow her. She led me to the back of the room where she slipped behind a black and red folding screen she'd used recently as part of a lesson on Japan. When I looked behind the screen, she pulled me toward her and kissed me deeply. While she was kissing me, she pulled one of her large breasts out of her shirt, put my hand on it, and made me squeeze it almost violently. I was in shock. I didn't know what to do except to ride with the tide and go with the flow until, after about five minutes of playing squeezy-feely, we heard someone entering the classroom. We separated quickly and she put her clothes back to where they should have been. She picked up some books that were on a shelf behind us and made it look like we were back there grabbing books instead breasts.

I'll probably never see Mrs. Collard again, although ….I do have Abby right here with me now, however. This may seem obvious, but Abby's even prettier without her clothes than she is with them. Don't get me wrong, I love her whole Beatnik style, but it detracts from the reality of what lies beneath. She has a sexy little body—I know because I studied every inch of it about thirty minutes ago—smooth, velvety flesh, lightly-tanned with some small moles—one where her neck meets her shoulder, another down a little farther toward her breast, a couple on her right upper arm, one on her forehead over her eye, one on her cheek, several more here and there all over her body—all of which I kissed one by one before she nodded off.

I just saw Abby's left eye open a little and look over at me. Now she has a half smile on her lips.

"Are you staring at my tiny titties?" she whispers.

I smile back at her. "I would if I could find them."

"You dog!" she says as she grabs the pillow under her head and throws it at me. I block it with my arm. "You'd better be kidding."

"Of course I'm kidding," I tell her. "They may be small, but they're terribly cute. I was just thinking you'd make a good model."

"I wouldn't show my titties if I was a model," she says. "They couldn't pay me enough to do that. I don't mind pulling them out for you, but I don't want to display them to the world. Models are the cream puffs of society, but they're like hookers—you pay them and they'll do anything. If I do anything, I do it for free and because I want to do it."

"Glad to hear that," I say.

"Glad to tell you," she says as she sits up and wipes the sleep out of her eyes.

Abby is a couple of years older than me; she hasn't told me, but I'm guessing about twenty. She's already had a year of classes at RCC, and I think she mentioned something about a philosophy class. I'd like to ask her about that one, and about her other classes, as well. I'm hoping she can give me some insight into campus life and culture there at RCC.

"Now what are we going to do?" She stands up in all of her glory, stretching her arms toward the ceiling and her mouth wide with a yawn.

"I think we ought to just hang out around here for a while and get to know each other better."

She finishes her stretching and smiles at me. "I think you know me pretty well after what we just did on that bed," she says.

"I mean, learn about each other's likes and dislikes, philosophy of life, that kind of thing."

"How long are your parents going to be gone? I wouldn't want them to come home and find us out here in our birthday suits."

"They're on vacation. They won't be home till some time next week."

"You mean we've got the run of the place for a whole week?" she asks.

"We do if you want," I confirm.

"Cool."

"They left me a full refrigerator in the house. How about if I pull out some steaks? We can barbecue and drink some wine. Later we can watch the moon rise from the cliff in the back yard."

"You have a cliff in your back yard?" she asks.

"I do. It's not too high, and if you fell off, you'd roll more than fall. It isn't dangerous, but it's kinda neat standing on the edge and looking out over the lights in the distance."

"Really cool." She smiles. "I think hanging around here for a week might be very nice. How about a tour? I want to see that cliff."

"Your wish is my command."

She looks at me with a wicked grin. "Better not tell me that," she says. "Beat girls can have some pretty crazy wishes."

I grin back and say, "I'll take my chances."

◎ ◎ ◎

So I started out by giving Abby the grand tour of the house and property, including my brother's bedroom upstairs—the one we shared until a couple of years ago. She told me I got the short end of the deal because his room is so much bigger and nicer than mine.

"This is like a hotel room," she said, looking around the neat and spacious room. "That Hole of yours is like a monk's cell in comparison. He's even got his own bathroom up here."

"I don't mind," I said. I kind of like being in the garage, and if I start doing art work I can use the main part of the garage as a studio for painting and sculpture."

"You really going to do that? Be an artist?" she asked.

"I'm thinking seriously about it."

"You need to show me some of your drawings while I'm here."

"I'll be happy to."

After touring the house, we went outside. The patio fills a corner in the back of the house that's formed by the garage and breezeway on one side and the living room on the other. It's pretty big, and it's easy to get to either from the kitchen through the breezeway, or from the living room through the two sets of double French doors, so it's great for entertaining—which my parents do a lot of. Abby was quite impressed.

"This is really nice. It looks like something a movie star would own. Your parents must be rich."

"Not rich, but my dad has a good job and so does my mother."

"What do they do?"

"My dad's an aerospace engineer and my mother's the head secretary over at the Sunkist Lemon Plant in Corona."

"Aerospace? That sounds kinda important."

"He helps design parts for things that fly," I explained. "Planes and rockets and stuff like that."

"That's a gas!" Abby said. "You mean rockets to the moon and outer space?"

"I do." I smiled. Even I think it's a gas.

"That's off the wall, man!" Abby was genuinely impressed. "I wish I could do something like that."

"Why can't you?"

"I don't think my brain works that high," she said.

"I think you could do just about anything you put your head to."

"If I get tuned in to something, I can pick up on it quick. But if not, it's like a boat without a motor. I get tired of rowing after a while."

"Well, one day you'll get tuned into something," I said, "and then you'll be able to afford a place like this, or even better."

"In the mean time, I'll just borrow yours." She hugged me and gave me a quick kiss.

I took her hand and led her across the lawn to where it ended at the top of the gully. For some reason, that was the place Abby most wanted to see.

The scene was laid out before us like an aerial panorama. The air was unusually clear for this time of year and the late afternoon sunlight highlighted all the details—the boulders on the hills across the valley, the clusters of trees around the chicken ranches and five-acre ranchos where people kept horses, the band of green that followed the river bottom, and beyond that, the city of Riverside—it was truly beautiful. I guess I've grown accustomed to the view over the years. It's been a while since I've really been impressed or inspired by it. Seeing it with Abby, though, was like seeing it for the first time. Of course, we were both standing there in our underwear, and Abby herself added to the beauty of the scene. Since my parents weren't home and our property is isolated from the spying eyes of nosy neighbors, we hadn't bothered much with clothing before touring the homestead. Abby had put her skimpy little panties back on, so I had grabbed my undershorts and put those on. I was still wearing my t-shirt, but Abby chose to remain topless, her breasts bare and her pretty back naked and smooth as silk to my touch.

"It's really lovely," she said. "I've never seen the city like this before. I stay down there in the flatland too much. I need to get out into nature more often."

"You look tan," I said. "How'd you do that?"

"Sunbathing in my mother's back yard. She lives out toward the orange groves on the other side of town. She's got a big yard with an eight-foot high redwood fence, so I can run around naked most of the time if I want."

"That's neat."

"The only problem is my step-dad. Sometimes he comes home from work early and I don't hear him. He stands at the window and watches me when I'm naked out back."

"That's not so good."

"He's an ass." She frowned and studied the ground for a moment. "He tried to rape me once."

"You're kidding!"

"I'm not. He came home from work one day about a year ago. He saw me naked out in the back yard. He came out to me as bold as can be and with a big smile on his face. He must have stopped off for a few beers on his way home because I could smell them on his breath. He just stood there grinning and looking at me for the longest time, not saying a word. He finally said that he and my mom had a fight and she wasn't putting out for him any more, and that I could help to relieve a lot of the stress in his life. Then he grabbed me, turned me around and bent me over the lawn chair. He was going to have me just like that, but then we heard Mom drive up. He pulled it back in, zipped up, and started into the house. He turned back to me, grabbed my arm, and put his face right into mine. He said 'If you ever tell your mom about this, I'll kill you.' I knew he meant it, so I never said a word." She closed her eyes and shuddered at the memory.

"Good grief." I was dumbfounded. "You should have told your mom any way."

"I couldn't." Her eyes were open now and looking straight into mine. "My mom's a maid at a motel and she just makes pennies. We both depend on his paycheck to pay the rent and keep food on the table. If he were to leave or go to jail, we'd have a hard time making ends meet."

"Still …"

"There's no still about it—we're poor folk. It's the way things are." She gave me a look that matched her words, then said brightly, "I'm hungry. Didn't you say something about steaks?"

I held out my hand to help her up and we walked back to the house.

Sitting On the Edge of the Backyard Cliff • 7 PM

I got the charcoal started in the barbecue then we went inside. Abby stayed in the kitchen to put together a big salad, and I took the steaks out to the grill. Abby brought out the salad, plates, and forks and knives and kept an eye on the meat while I fetched the jug of wine and a couple of mugs. We ate our meal and drank some wine at the patio table, and then we had a little more wine and chitchat before we cleaned up the mess and washed the dishes. When the kitchen was clean enough to meet my mother's standards, Abby suggested that we go back out to sit on the cliff. I picked up the jug and the mugs, and that's where we are now.

I'm seated cross-legged at the edge of the cliff recording the last few hours in my journal. Abby is perched at the edge of the cliff, peeing a great stream over the side. Her aim is not too good and the journal is catching some of the splatter as it bounces off the ground.

"Oops," she says. She giggles as she stands up. "Well, there's a little bit of gritty realism for the old journal. If somebody in the distant future reads that page they're gonna wonder what those little stains are." She giggles again.

I smile at her and say, "You're a mess, Abby."

"I try to be." She smiles back. "Fill me a mug with that red stuff."

She sits down next to me and I hand her a mug of wine. She leans against me, kisses me, and whispers something into my ear. An interesting proposition, but I tell her, "Maybe later after I've had a little more wine."

"So, what do you wanna do then?" She asks. "You got any friends we can call? We could have a little party."

"I've got a few, but I'm not sure I want to share you with anybody else tonight. I think I'd like to just sit here and drink wine and talk about things."

"I'm okay with that." She leans over and licks my ear. "Can we play some jazz tunes?"

"Sure. I've got a stereo in The Hole. I can set the speakers in the window and point them out here so we can hear it."

"You have jazz records?"

"My parents listen to jazz sometimes. I'm not sure it's the same stuff you like, but it's something—Julie London, June Christie, Peggy Lee …"

"Any of those are good—I like June Christie. Keep it low, though, 'cause I also like to hear the bugs making noises when night falls."

"We get a few crickets out this way. They sound kinda nice," I say.

She closes her eyes and her face takes on a relaxed, contented look. "I like to hear the wind in the trees, too," she says. "That's a really sweet sound."

"You must be part Druid."

"Part what?"

"Druid—they were Celtic wise men. Some say they were like priests, but that's not really been confirmed. They spent a lot of time out in nature trying to figure it all out. They studied birds, clouds, weather, animals, vegetation, and especially trees—the word, Druid, has some connection to the oak tree. They lived a very long time ago and were very mysterious. They had no written language and passed along their knowledge orally from one generation to the next. The Romans pretty much wiped them out, and the only evidence of who and what they were comes from a few old Romans who were trying to justify why they should be eliminated.

"Were they all Brits? Can Germans be Druids? My ancestors are mostly German through my real dad's line. I think my mom's Irish, but I'm not sure."

"People today think of England, Wales, Scotland, and Ireland as the Celtic world, but in ancient times there were Celts in Germany, France, and other parts of Europe.

"Maybe I am part Druid. I love nature. I love all that old British stuff too—old castles, knights in armor, swords, Sherlock Holmes, Renaissance Faires." She grinned. "But how come you know so much about all this stuff?"

"I like learning new things. I've read a lot about the Celtic people. One of my favorite things is ancient history. Ancient Egypt is also fun." I pause for a moment before continuing with a laugh, "I like 'em all. I guess my real favorite is whichever one I'm reading about at the moment."

"I love that old Egyptian stuff too," Abby says. "It's really a kick to think about all those crazy gods and goddesses. You think there's anything to that? I have a hard time believing in old gods. If they were real gods, and they were so powerful, why did they disappear?"

"Who knows?" I say, shrugging my shoulders. "There are thousands of religions on this planet and each one thinks they're the only one with the truth. Thousands of wars have been fought because of religion. Personally, I don't believe that there can be millions of gods and goddesses running around up there in whatever it is that heaven is. I believe there's probably one Creator God-type Being, but who the heck knows what He's like? Nobody's died, gone to heaven, and come back to give a detailed report."

"Aren't there a lot of people that claim they did and have stories about angels and heaven?" Abby asks.

"Yeah. That's called a near death experience—an NDE. But near death ain't the same as being all the way dead, and if you aren't all the way dead then you didn't make it all the way to heaven, so whatever tales they tell when they get back into consciousness are either highly exaggerated or they're outright lies. I died once when I was nine. I had double pneumonia and I kicked the bucket while I was in the hospital."

"Really!" Abby gasps. "Did you see anything while you were dead?"

"I did, but it wasn't God or Heaven. When I tell the story, people tell me they think I saw an angel. I guess that's possible. Sounds like the closest thing to truth."

"You saw an angel? How cool is that!" Abby looks up at me, her bright eyes and big smile inviting me to share my story.

"I remember leaving my body and hovering over the bed for a while. I could look down and see my mother, the doc, and a couple of nurses. One of the nurses, a pretty redhead, sat on the bed right by me. Later, when I told everybody what I saw they all said there was only one nurse who took care of me that day, and she had black hair. In fact, no one knew of a redheaded nurse working in the hospital."

Abby pulls her knees up under her chin. "Wow, I love ghost stories!" she says, giving a little shiver as she wraps her arms around them. "I never thought I'd meet one of the ghosts in the story, though. Tell me about the angel."

"Well, he was wearing a long white gown, like a choir robe. I appeared to be standing in a meadow filled with flowers, and he was on the top of a small hill overlooking the meadow. I was just a little kid lying unconscious in a hospital bed, so I didn't know what the heck was going on. I wasn't afraid of him because he looked like a nice guy. I walked up to him, but I didn't say anything because I didn't know who he was. He smiled at me and shook his index finger from left to right like an angry mom when she's telling you not to talk out of turn, even though I wasn't talking. Then he made a motion with both his hands, like he was shooing me away. He was clearly telling me to skedaddle, so I turned around and started walking toward a beautiful forest that I could see in the distance. I looked back just once to see him, but he made that same shooing motion with his hands like I needed to do as he was telling me to do. I didn't want to tick him off, so I went on toward the forest, and BAM, that's when I came back to consciousness. The doctor had already told everybody that I was dead, but like all the other NDE people, I was probably just sort of dead 'cause I didn't stay dead. When I opened my eyes, he and the nurse were standing by my bed looking like they'd seen a ghost or something."

Abby hugs her legs tighter and shivers again. "That gave me goose bumps," she says.

"It was pretty strange. Something I'll never forget."

"There's a lot to this world we just don't get," Abby says. "And this world is just one of billions of other worlds out there in space."

"Yep. A lot of people think they know what's going on, but they really don't. Nobody knows."

"That's one of the reasons the Beats are so Beat," she says, smiling.

"That's another question I have for you, dear Abby," I say. "You call yourself a Beatnik, but the Beatniks kind of died out didn't they? How did you get to be one?"

"They aren't as prominent as they used to be maybe, but they certainly aren't dead. Ginsberg's still around. Kerouac, Corso, Fer-linghetti, Cassady, Di Prima, Snyder—all still alive and still writing. Heck, you're a Beat, you just haven't figured it out yet."

"How did you get into all that Beat stuff?" I ask. "These days, people our age are getting into rock music and hippie stuff.

Not exactly what I'd call Beatnik material."

"I was born to it. My mom, Carrie, she's the real deal. She hung around with some of the big guys for a while — slept with a couple, still sees them when she's up in The City. She even wrote some poetry but never had it published — there's a publisher up there who likes her stuff a lot. I think she could be one of the biggies if she'd let him put her in print, but she keeps putting it off."

"So you're like a second-generation Beat," I say.

"That's me," she says, giving me a cheeky smile.

"Wow. So you're the real thing. All those times I saw you in my yoga class I thought you were just a wannabe. Do you write poetry?"

"Yep, it's in the blood." She smiles again.

"I'd love to read it some time. I'd like to read your mom's poetry too, if she'd let me. I'm not so much into the flowery frou-frou stuff like 'roses are red and violets are blue,' but the kind of poetry the Beatniks make intrigues me. I've actually been writing poetry in a style similar to that for quite a while now. I don't know where I got the urge to write like that, but I didn't know until recently that it was the way the Beats were writing. I'd love to meet those guys and compare notes."

"Maybe you will one day. Just don't call 'em Beatniks when you do."

"Why?"

"Because that's a derogatory word to a real Beat. When you think of the word, Beatnik, what comes to mind?"

"A guy with a beret, a cigarette, sad eyes, black t-shirt."

"See what I mean? Maybe the cigarette's right, but the rest isn't. Lots of the guys wear t-shirts, mostly black, but some are white, and I don't know any guys that wear a beret."

"You wear a beret."

"It's a joke. My mother gave it to me so I'd look like the stereotype. We had a big laugh about it."

"Where'd the whole Beat thing start?" I ask.

"NYC and The City. New York had it's day, but The City's

the heart of the Beat Generation. All the tuned-in cats live up there now."

"What city?"

"San Francisco! You haven't been around much, have you?" she says, flashing me a teasing grin.

"I'm still young, give me a chance," I protest. "I take it you've been there?"

"Mom and I go up there once or twice a year to visit old friends."

"Some of the original Beats?"

"Yep."

"Why did you say that you think I'm a Beat but I just don't know it yet?"

"Because you have all the symptoms of being one. Not a Beatnik, but a real Beat."

"What are the symptoms?"

"You want to be an artist; you were writing Beat-style poetry before you even knew what it was; you have a sharp inquisitive mind that isn't mired down by the clichés of the contemporary society; you're into cool jazz, not hard rock; you're into yoga, not race cars or playing army; you're not into sports, and muscle cats aren't your latest fad romance —"

"Muscle cats?" I ask.

"Rock and rollers."

"So all that stuff makes me a real Beatnik — excuse me, a real Beat?"

"How many guys running around today are into those things? I don't mean one or two of them, but all of them at once? And I could add a lot more to your list."

"Oh?"

"The one thing that really slams it home, though, is probably the most important."

"And what's that?"

She looks at me and grins. "You're hangin' with me. You're dating a real Beat Girl and she's not blowing you off."

"Cool."

"You got it made in the shade, Daddy-o." She leans over and licks the end of my nose.

"I've just been licked by a REAL Beat Girl! I guess that makes me pretty cool."

"You're there, Baby."

We laugh and toss 'Beat talk' back and forth until I run out of words. After a few moments of silence, I ask, "Say, what ever happened to your real dad?"

"He went to Germany and never came back. We don't know exactly what happened to him—just bits and pieces here and there."

"How German was your dad?"

"He was born here but his folks were from Germany. When his dad died, his mom moved back to Germany to live out her days. One day he got up, put on his pants, and walked out the door. Mom thought he was going to work as usual, but he never came home again. She finally got a letter from Grandma telling her that Dad was in Berlin living with her. Grandma said that he'd gone kooky, and would probably never come back to the States. Mom thinks he got into some bad weed the morning he left and it sent him over the top."

You mean marijuana?"

"There was a lotta bad stuff goin' around about that time, tainted with some other drugs. Some people even said it had gasoline residue in it. Dad did it up a couple of times, but Mom didn't know about it till she got the letter. Grandma mentioned that Dad had told her he'd inhaled some poisoned smoke in the States. Mom knew he was acting weird, but she thought it was just his job—he had a lot of stress, but it seemed to be getting worse."

"That's a pretty sad story."

"Yeah. But we got over it."

"So your mom never divorced your dad, and the guy that lives with her that tried to rape you isn't really a step dad."

"Right on both counts. Billy's a turd that fell out of the butt of hell."

"Why did your mom ever get with him in the first place?"

"He's cute, he acted nice to her for a few weeks, charmed her a bit, was good in bed, and he had a pretty good job. It all worked for her at the time, and some sort of hitch up with the guy seemed to strike her as the right thing to do. He didn't start getting real bad, though, until about two years ago."

"Is he violent?"

"He hasn't been, but I think he could be. Now that I'm older and a lot wiser, I'm pretty sure he's starting to be afraid of me. If I were a betting girl, I'd give two-to-one odds that he'll be taking a hike soon."

"I hope so. I don't like the thought of you or your mother living with such a slime ball."

"Like I said, I think he's afraid of me now. One evening just before dinner, I was cutting a roast with a large knife. He walked into the kitchen and all I did was turn to him and look right into his eyes. I didn't say a word, and I didn't point the knife at him or anything, but I think he kinda got the idea that the roast could be him someday if he isn't careful." She smiles grimly at that thought.

I laugh a little to lighten the mood. "If I ever get invited to your house for dinner, remind me to stay out of the kitchen while you're cutting the meat."

"Silly." She licked my nose again. "Hey, where's my jazz music?"

"I'll go put it on."

I got up and walked quickly back to The Hole. I'd forgotten that I was in my shorts and that Abby was wearing only her skimpy white panties. It felt kind of weird to be walking around in the backyard like that—I'd never done it before. I kept thinking that if my parents came home early and found us like this, it wouldn't be pretty. But they're at least a hundred miles away on a week-long camping trip. I talked to them on the phone earlier today—they call me every day—so I know they won't be home for at least this night.

I found the June Christy album and put it on the turntable. I moved the speakers from the floor to the windowsill and set them facing out toward the back yard and the cliff where Abby and I are sitting. I turned the stereo on, and set the volume high enough to hear, but low enough not to scare the crickets away, then hurried back out to Abby.

When I got back, Abby was standing up, looking out over the little gorge below the cliff. She was stretching her arms above her head and wiggling her body like a baby kitten waking up after a long nap. I stood there and watched as her movement morphed into a slow jazz dance. It was getting dark now, but with her silky skin and bright white panties I could clearly see her moving seductively to June Christy's, "Spring Is Here," from her album, *The Intimate Miss Christy*, playing on the stereo.

"Is this turning you on?" she asked without turning around.

"How did you know I was here? I was trying to sneak up on you."

"I could sense the Beat of your heart."

"Is that a play on words?"

"Yes, it is." Then she turned and ran toward me. Leaping up and wrapping her legs around my waist, she held on to me like a starfish on a rock and kissed me.

"You're so cute," I said. Her grinning face was just micro-inches from mine, and she was cross-eyed from looking at me so close.

"Yes, I am, aren't I."

"Conceited, too," I said, grinning back at her.

"It's not conceit when it's true," she said smugly.

She kissed me again, and then slowly slid her body down mine until her feet touched the ground. She looked up into my eyes. "What do we do now?" she asked.

I answered with the time-honored phrase, "I don't know. What do you want to do?"

"We could just dance." Her hips moved with the soft jazz rhythms drifting from The Hole.

"You like to dance, don't you?" I said. She was standing just close enough to me to let her breasts brush lightly against my chest.

"Dancing is the definition of living," she replied.

"It is?"

"Yeah. Life ain't nothin' but a slow jazz dance," she answered as she swayed seductively. "That's the secret to everything."

"How's that?"

"Livin' life's a crazy wild song. Everything's movin' at a million miles a minute, but here we are slowin' it all down. We may be forced to live inside the chaos of life, but we can slow down the tempo just by being who we are—poets, lovers, Beats. If you move like everybody else, life'll wear you down, so you gotta go slow. Go with the poetry. Go with the jazz."

I've never been much of a dancer, but she rested her cheek on my chest and I nuzzled her hair as we swayed together in the moonlight until the mellow sound of Miss Christy faded away.

We stood motionless for a moment, then Abby turned and walked back over to the cliff edge. "Can we get down there? Is there a path? I think it'd be kind of neat to check it out."

"There's a path just over there to the left," I said, pointing in that direction. "It starts there and winds down into the gully. It's nice at the bottom. Once you're there, you can't see any of the houses or trees or anything else for that matter. It's almost like being on the Moon.

"Do we need to wear shoes?" she asks. "Are there stickers or sharp rocks along the way?"

"Nope. I've been going down there barefooted for years and never stepped on anything."

"Great! We don't need these, either," she said as she pulled off her panties and waved them in my face. Before I knew what she was doing, she was reaching over and pulling down my shorts, too. "I want us to be totally naked, just like aliens on the Moon."

"I don't think there are any aliens on the Moon," I said, not knowing what else to say.

"Then we'll pretend its Mars," she said. "There might be aliens on Mars."

"There might be," I said, smiling.

"Wait a minute!"

Abby went back to where we had been sitting and refilled our mugs from the wine jug. "Let's drink these down before we go so we can be really high when we get there," she said as she handed one to me.

"Okay … Anything you say, Beat Girl." Then, against my better judgment, I emptied the mug in one big gulp. It's no surprise that my head was beginning to spin a little.

I'm not sure how much those mugs hold — they're pretty big, maybe sixteen ounces — but Abby chugged down the contents of hers and it didn't seem to faze her at all — at first, anyway. Then she took my hand and we headed off toward the path. "Let's walk real slow so we can make it last."

Two Hours Later

We're back in The Hole and Abby is laying face down on the bed with her little derrière staring right at me with a big smile on its face. I'll swear, every inch of Abby is cute.

We had a great time. It was dark, but the winding path was clearly visible in the light of the Moon. The path is used by lots of people, both on foot and on horseback, and the surface has been ground into a fine powder. The soft dirt felt good squishing up between our toes with every step. We walked slowly to make the experience last.

"I love the way the dirt feels on my feet," Abby said as we started down the path. "It's cool — like my hands feel when I mix up a cake mix."

"There's a place at the very bottom that's all soft powder. It's like a big sandbox you can lie down in. I've never done it naked, but I'll bet that'd feel good on our backs."

"I don't want any bugs crawling up into my ass," Abby said.

"I don't think we have to worry about that," I said.

We continued our walk, dividing our attention between the path at our feet and the sky overhead, which was rapidly filling with stars. The night was crystal clear, and even though the quarter moon in the west was vivid enough to see the individual craters in stark detail, it was not so bright that it diminished the millions of stars above us, or the band of the Milky Way in the east.

"Don't forget, we're on Mars," Abby said. "That's the Moon up there and we can't see the Earth because it's behind it." I could hear the smile in her voice.

"I wonder if any of our friends and family miss us up there on Earth?" I said, playing along with her.

"We haven't been gone that long," she said. "But I'll bet they're all jealous 'cause we're here on Mars while they're stuck there watching corny sitcoms on TV."

"I'll bet they are." I smiled.

We finally made it down to the bottom of the grotto. It really did feel like we were stranded on another planet. There we were, just the two us without our clothes. The walls of the grotto shielded us from visible signs of Earth life around us. It was quiet, too. The sound of June Christy had faded away and the crickets had never started singing. Our bare feet made no noise on the dusty surface of the path and the only sound we could hear was that of our own breathing. We spoke softly, almost in whispers. It just seemed the right thing to do.

"This is eerie," Abby said. "All I can hear is the breeze rattling those dead weeds over there on the left. It's like we're the only two people on Mars."

"Yeah," I said. "I thought for sure there'd be somebody else up here."

"Oh hush." She said, playfully punching my arm. "Get into the moment."

"You mean into the Zen?" I asked.

"I don't think anybody out here on Mars has ever heard of Zen."

"Good," I said. "It would be nice to have at least one planet the occupants haven't spoiled by inventing rules to live by."

"I told you, you're a real Beat." She smiled. "I heard Neal say something very similar to that once."

"Neal who?"

"Cassady."

"The Beat guy who runs around with Kerouac, right?"

"Yep."

"I am amazed that you know all those guys," I said.

"You'd fit right in with them."

"I'd be the only baby in a crowd of adults," I said.

"They're all a bunch of babies at heart," she said. "Just kids really—not in terms of age, but in terms of behavior. If they were with us right now, they'd all be rolling in the dirt and having dust fights with each other. Except maybe for Jack; he's getting fragile up in his head. He's turning into an old man before his time."

"That's too bad. Is he sick?"

She frowned. "I don't wanna talk about that, I wanna roll in the dirt with my new boyfriend."

Abby grabbed my hand and sat down in the dirt, pulling me down on top of her.

"Ooh … I like this," she cooed.

"Then you'll really like this," I cooed back as I fill my hands with the fine, soft dust and smeared it over her breasts and belly.

"You brat!" she cried. So much for speaking softly. "Is that any way to treat a Martian?" Then we lunged at each other and did some serious grappling in the soft dirt. The night was warm and humid, so we quickly worked up a sweat that made the dust stick to our skin and turn to mud. When we finally fell apart, worn out from laughing and wrestling, we were a mess.

"We look like a couple of zombies!" Abby said, catching her breath.

"We're filthy," I said. "We're gonna need a shower when we get back up there."

"You got a hose?" Abby asked.

"Yes."

"That would be more fun," she said, slurring her words. The effects of all that wine had caught up to her in full force. To be fair, we were both more than just a little tipsy.

I wound up half supporting and half carrying her back up the path. She was pretty loopy, but all I could think of was her pretty little body and her sweet little head, and all I could see was cute. When we finally got back to the patio, Abby grabbed her mug and poured herself more wine. I couldn't believe it. I'd had enough wine for a week, but she was still drinking even though she could hardly walk.

That's when I decided that it was time for the garden hose. I leaned her up against the house, found the end of the hose, and turned on the water. Well, that woke her up. She screamed and ran around the yard like a chicken with its head cut off while I chased after her with the hose, both of us naked and covered in mud, our bodies bouncing as we ran, Abby squealing and flailing her arms and me grinning like a maniac.

Finally, we'd both had enough. We were cleaned off pretty good, but winded. Abby collapsed on the lawn by the patio, and I collapsed next to her after turning off the water.

"You're a monster, you know that?" Abby's words were soft and slurred from the wine.

"Yep, I am." I smiled.

She threw her arms around me and I let her pull me to her. Then she kissed me.

"Can you carry me into The Hole, 'cause I don't think I can even crawl right now." She was barely able to hold her head up.

"I just carried you all the way from Mars back to Earth, so I don't think a few more feet will be a problem."

Abby smiled at that and kissed me again. I stood up and helped her to stand, but she couldn't walk if her life depended on it so, I really did have to carry her.

I toted her into The Hole and laid her on the bed. She looked up at me, her expression oddly innocent in spite of being drunk. "You know, you could have your way with me right now," she said.

"You could do anything you want and I wouldn't be able to stop you." She was almost unintelligible by then.

"That wouldn't be any fun," I said.

Then, with a smile on her face, she turned over onto her tummy and said, "Here, make it fun."

So, here I am, sitting at my little desk and catching up on the night's events in my journal while Abby sleeps on my bed.

We didn't make anything fun because Abby conked out completely and started snoring; that sort of took all the romance out of the fun part. I did take the liberty of exploring her backside, brushing off small pebbles and picking grass blades out of her butt crack along the way — that was fun. Overall, we had a heck of a good time tonight. I only hope that our relationship can grow into something stronger than just wine and chit-chat.

3 WEDNESDAY

I'm sitting on a bench outside the bookstore at the open-air shopping mall in Riverside, doing a little writing and watching the people go by. Abby and I got up just a little while ago. Considering the amount of wine we drank last night, though, I am surprised that we didn't sleep longer. Abby hopped out of bed, all sunshine and daisies. She slapped me on the behind and said, "Come on! It's a beautiful day out there." I could see through the window that it really was. The sun was shining brightly, the sky was blue, and all the colors everywhere were intense in the warm summer air.

She leaned over the bed and smiled down at me. "Kiss me," she said, bringing her face closer to mine.

"But I have morning breath," I protested as I turned my face away to spare her the experience.

She smiled and said, "So do I." Then she grabbed my hand and pulled me out of bed. We wound up in front of the window, kissing.

"You know what I wanna do?" Abby asked.

"What?"

"Go to the bookstore."

"Okay …" That was a surprise. "The bookstore? But you said it's a beautiful day—I thought that might mean you want to spend it outdoors in nature."

"I do, but I want to buy some books so that when I go home I'll have something to read to keep my mind occupied."

"Why do you need to keep your mind occupied?" I asked.

"Because you won't be with me and I'll miss you."

"That's very sweet, but we can see each other as much as we want. I like being with you," I told her in all honesty.

"I like being with you, too, but it won't be the same—just doing yoga together, then going home."

"We can do more than that. It is what it is for now, Abby.

We just have to let it play out for a while and see what happens."

"I knew you'd say something like that." She smiled. "That's why I need to buy some books."

"Okay. Let's go buy some books."

So I'm sitting here on this bench while Abby is in the store looking for her books. I'll probably join her there in a few minutes; it's just that it's so pretty out here I thought it would be nice to sit for a while and soak up some rays. I can never get enough heat and sun. I know it sounds funny coming from a guy living in sunny Southern California, but it's never sunny enough for me. If it weren't for the fact that nighttime is so romantic, I could probably do without any darkness at all—although I do love the moon, but that's part of the romance of the night. There's nothing more romantic than sitting outside in the moonlight, feeling the warm, soft air on your face, and talking with Abby … yeah … talking with Abby.

What Abby said is true. It's not gonna be easy going back to normal after being with her these past couple of days, or however many days we're gonna hang with each other, but that's part of life—separation happens now and then. For us though, being completely together is a separation from the norm, since we are both young and have lived separate lives, so separation from the norm is harder than separation from each other for now.

The Mall is a busy place—not crowded, but busy—and that makes it a good place for people watching. I watch all these people pass by and I wonder what their private lives are like. I don't really care what they do for a living or what kind of house they live in; I'm more curious about their hidden lives. How do they act when they get off work and go home at night? What are they going home to? What are their family relationships like? How do they treat their dog? What's rolling around up in their heads? What do they think about when they have the time to think about anything they want? Do bosses lust after their secretaries? Are secretaries having affairs with the paperboy? What kind of secrets do they hide from each other?

Humans are complicated beings. Over the centuries they've developed entertainments, diversions, and religions for the single purpose of uncomplicating their minds — that is, to distract their minds away from their consciences and their guilt trips. The daily life of any given human is always going to be filled with ordinary crap — the information, responsibilities, and experiences that create a complicated web in the part of the mind that deals with the process of just getting by. It's the deeper, secret world of the conscience that humans have tried to uncomplicate over the years, but nothing they have done has worked. In fact, I could argue that many, if not all, of the diversions, entertainments, and religions have actually increased the complication factor. Take religion, for instance. Before humans had religion, things were less complicated. After religion was invented, there were laws, rules, regulations, doctrines, dogmas, rituals, and traditions they had to learn and follow, whether they wanted to or not. They were doing just fine before all those things were pumped into their heads. Where did all those rules come from? Man had been living out in nature for thousands of years, having a blast with his uncomplicated life. Some would say that the rules came from God, but that just isn't the truth; they came from people. I say that because the dogmas, doctrines, and laws are all different. There may be a few similarities between them — some more than others — but each one is going to be different from all the others out there, and every one of them professes to be the right and ONLY religion, which means that all the others are lies. So all the religions fight each other all the time over supremacy in the heavenly and earthly realms. If God is the Intelligent Designer and Creator of such an organized universe as we live in, why in the world would He then turn around and throw all these complicated laws and rituals onto us knowing that they would confuse the hell out of us? All religions are the same. They're all wrong. I have some Buddhist friends who are among the unhappiest people I've ever known. They are so eaten up by all the stuff they have to do that life has become miserable for them, and yet they believe that all of it is necessary in order to reach what they call, Nirvana. I have some Christian friends who are the same way, only they're trying to get to Heaven and if they don't get it right, they'll suffer forever in Hell. At least the Hindus believe in reincarnation—if they don't get it right the first time they come back again and again until they do. Where the heck did they get that idea? God didn't come down and tell them to believe it, some Indian guy made it up. God didn't come down and tell the Jews to follow those hundreds of Old Testament laws, some guy named Moses did. Some guy named Paul took the simple teachings of Jesus and turned them into laws. Who told him to do that? Abby and I were talking yesterday about how Zen is a popular thing with the Beats. I'm reading Kerouac's *Dharma Bums* now, and there's Zen stuff all through it, and another Beat guy, Gary Snyder, is really into Zen big time. I asked Abby why they would want to believe something that is so complicated and adds even more complications to the complications already running around in their heads? Who told them that was a good thing? The writings of Alan Watts, another Zen guy, seem to be a fad right now. I picked up one of his books about a month ago and read it. I thought it was kind of a waste of time, not because I didn't get it—I did, I got it—I just didn't see any need for it. It seems to me that God is a pretty good guy—after all, He did create some pretty cool stuff down here for us all to play with. It also seems to me that God gets along just fine all by Himself without us mere mortal humans adding to the mix. Even so, it looks like there are a whole lot of middlemen claiming to act for God without His permission and without a clue as to what they're talking about. What's the deal with that? Why do I need a guru or a priest or a Zen scholar to tell me how to get enlightened, especially when you look at their lives and see that they aren't any more enlightened than you or I? I think it's a game—a big ego game. It's cool being a guru. Everybody bows to you and calls you Master, but you're the one that gets to sit on the satin pillows and eat gourmet food all day. You're the one that has all his bills paid and money in his pocket while all your followers are busy going gaga over your shadow every time you walk by, and busy complicating their minds with tons more stuff that they'll one day probably regret ingesting. It just doesn't make sense.

I wonder what all these people walking by here in the mall have running around inside their heads. I wonder if they're thinking things like I think, or if they're just content to be like zombies, walking up and down the mall, thinking about the next basketball game, or a new car they want to buy. I wonder what books Abby will buy in the store. I hope she doesn't disappoint me, although 'tis I who is more likely to disappoint her.

Later, in the Bookstore

Abby and I are sitting in a couple of comfy chairs in the reading section of the bookstore. She wanted to thumb through the books she picked out before she paid money for them. Money is scarce for Abby, as it is for me, but I'm sure she has a harder time of it than I do. My parents make pretty good bucks, so I can always fall back on them if I need to. They give me a pretty generous allowance and I've always managed to hold down a couple of part time jobs, but Abby's mom doesn't make much, and Abby won't ask for money from Billy, her mother's boyfriend. He doesn't offer to give her any either, so she's pretty short all the time. Books aren't cheap. I know a person gets a lot out of reading books, but the book market also seems to be one big hairy rip off. Books are just paper and cardboard, so how much can it possibly cost to print one — it can't be all that much — and how much do they cost? Unless you're buying mass-market pulp fiction, you can't find a book for less than three to five bucks, and some of the nicer ones can cost up to ten dollars or more. You'll only read most of the books you buy once and then set them on a shelf and forget about them for the rest of your life. Abby's kinda like me, though; she doesn't just read a book, she studies it, underlines it, and dog-ears it a hundred times. Sometimes I even tear pages out of books and carry them in my wallet. I wouldn't be surprised if she does that, too. If you're into learning, then you're into books, and they become more to you than just things you hold in your lap when you fall asleep at night. Anyway, I brought a little cash with me. If Abby can't come up with enough, I'll make up the difference for her.

I picked a book by Thomas Merton off the shelf, *New Seeds of Contemplation*. I've heard about Merton from several people; he's a Catholic monk and a bit of a rebel in the Catholic Church. People don't seem to know how to take him, which really means that they don't know how to define him — humans like definitions for everything, and Merton doesn't have one. He's another guy who's into the Zen thing. I haven't read much about him yet, but he seems to be trying to find a way to meld Catholicism and Zen together into one happy package. I think that's not gonna be easy; the two religions aren't exactly peas in a pod, and Zen seems to be such an unhappy way of looking at things. I have a friend, Elvis — no jokes, please — who takes part in meditations at a Zen monastery up on Mt. Baldy. He says that if you fall asleep or nod off in any way during a meditation, one of the monks hits you on the shoulders with a board. Where the heck is that written anywhere? I don't think Merton's into that kinda stuff, though. He also writes poetry. He's been called a modern poet, which means his poems don't have to rhyme. His stuff is pretty much like the Beat poetry, telling a story in short blurbs and pauses and with no rhymey stuff — kinda like the poems I write that I will never be famous for. Anyway, I picked up Merton's book and I'm thumbing through it. It's more of a Catholic thing and doesn't have much, if anything, in the way of Zen in it, but it looks interesting in spots. I also want to read his autobiography, *The Seven Storey Mountain*; I hear it's really good. One day in the not too distant future I'll buy it and take it home. Somebody told me he published it in 1948, the year I was born. For now, though, I'm still trying to get through all the Beat books

I bought the other day—a couple of Kerouacs, a Ferlighetti, and a few more poetry thingies.

So, what's Abby reading while she's sitting next to me and playing footsie with me? I was expecting stuff by the Beat Boys up north, but instead she picked up *The Story Of Art*, by E. H. Gombrich, and *My Life and Loves* by Frank Harris. I've never heard of either one of those guys, but that's what Abby snagged and brought out here to peruse.

"What have you got there, little girl?" I ask her.

"Art history books." She grinned. "I figure if I'm gonna be hangin' with a wannabe artist, then I'd better learn something about art."

"Heck, I don't even know anything about it yet," I told her. "Maybe I'll be able to talk art with you after a year or two at RCC, but, if you read these books you're gonna be way ahead of me until then."

"Actually, only one is totally about art, the Gombrich one. It looks a little dry, but it's got a lot of stuff in it that I don't know about."

"What's the other one? I've never heard of Frank Harris."

"My friend, Mamie—you know her from yoga—she told me about this book."

"Oh yeah, Mamie from yoga. I guessed you two would be friends. She's into the Beat culture too, isn't she?"

"She's into it, but she's not a part of it like me and Mom. She's a fun kid to hang with, though. You'd like her if you got to know her better."

"So, what's this book about? Who's this Harris guy, and why are his life and loves so important?"

"According to Mamie, Frank Harris was a real Renaissance man. He knew a lot of famous people, knew a whole lot about art, held all kinds of jobs, and traveled all over the world. He was even a cowboy for a while. Mainly he was a journalist, and he wrote this book filled with colorful accounts of all his escapades. I say escapades because Mamie told me he got around a lot, if you know what I mean. I was thumbing through it and there's a whole lot of sex stuff in here. Very explicit, I might add."

"Sounds interesting." I smile and reach for the book.

"You don't need to read it." Abby frowns as she snaps it shut and puts it out of my reach. "You have me in real life. I can do everything to you his little chicks did to him in this book and a whole lot more."

"What if I get to RCC next year and his book is required reading?"

"I doubt that. It's way too racy."

"Okay, I promise not to read it if you promise to act it out with me along the way."

"Deal. No matter what's in that book, I'll be even better." She smiles, and we shake hands to seal the deal.

Back At My Place • 2 PM

I've been sitting in the swing on the front porch for about an hour now, contemplating the beauty of the day. Abby was sleepy when we got home from the bookstore, so she decided to take a nap on my bed in The Hole for a while. That's okay; I need to catch up on my journal entries.

The swing is nice. I come out here a lot and swing back and forth while watching the birds fly up into the pine trees in the front yard, the butterflies float by, and our little dog, Chico, chase the butterflies. Chico is a feisty little Chihuahua that barks at everything and will bite your hand off if you get near his food. Other than that, he's a pretty cool dog. He's also a philosopher; I'm sure of that, because he sits around most of the time in deep meditation. My mother says he's napping, but I know better. He's lost in a world of wonder behind those big brown eyelids, solving the problems of this world before they even arise.

My mother loves to sit here. When she does, Chico is usually right by her side. He'll play with me and do things with me, but he's pretty much her dog—probably because she's the one that feeds him. I guess that's a primal instinct that all dogs have—never bite the hand that feeds you, and be sure to hang around with the owner of that hand a lot more than you do with anybody else—it's written in the stars somewhere.

I think the reason I like being here so much is because it reminds me of trips up into the mountains. There's a campground in the San Jacinto Mountains where we love to camp. It's filled with giant pine trees, boulders, and steep slopes a guy can climb and get winded on. Our front yard has two big pines standing sentinel that remind me of that campground. I love those trees, and I climb up in them every chance I get. One is easier to climb than the other; it has lots of lower branches that I can hang onto and put my feet on, kind of like climbing up a ladder. I've been known to climb almost to the top, much to the dismay of my family, especially my grandmother who's convinced I'll fall one day.

Behind the pines is a large mulberry tree that has the sweetest mulberries you've ever tasted. Every time I walk by I grab a handful and chow down. I'm not so sure that my parents like the tree though, because mulberries are a bit messy. The berries squish all over your shoes when you walk under the tree, then you bring the purple squish with you when you go into the house. We've all learned to be careful about that since it doesn't look so hot on the carpets. We check our shoes faithfully every time we come into the house during the fruiting season.

It's nice out here today. The air is warm and I can smell the scent of the pine trees being released by the heat of summer. The sun's really hot if you get out from under the porch roof, so it's best to observe nature from the shade of the porch. To me, summer afternoons in southern California are among the most pleasant experiences a person could ever have. There's nothing else like the hot summer breeze hitting your face. I fully believe that there's something built into us that enables us to sense that it's summer, not because it's hot, but because there's an energy about it that's different from the energies found the rest of the year. Kinda like autumn. Autumn has a high, powerful energy you just can't miss when it hits. You can feel autumn when it first arrives; you can feel it in the crisp wind. You can feel summer when it hits, too. The heat makes you sweat; lots of people don't like that, but it re-energizes me. One of my favorite things to do is to take my VW out on the freeway, roll all the windows down, and let the hot summer air hit me full in the face as it is accelerated by the force of the speeding car. The feeling is indescribable. Maybe it's a Taoist thing; a combination of the soft comforting wind and the powerful heat of the sun—yin and yang, yang and yin—happening at the same time. I love it. My left arm is a darker tan than my right in the summer from driving down the highway with my elbow sticking out the window during my Taoist road trips.

I found a small book about Taoism in the bookstore, which is what brought all this to mind. I've been looking for some sort of spiritual path or insight that's less complicated than the others. I've heard that Taoism is so simple that anybody can understand it. One of my yoga students told me that The Tao is The Way. She said that it's a simple path and all you have to do is follow it, but she couldn't tell me how to do that. I thumbed through the book, skimming over the table of contents and reading bits here and there. From what I could gather, Taoism is just as complicated as all the other religions—maybe more so. It has its own abundant share of rules and regulations. I suppose a Taoist would never call them that, but that's exactly what they are. And just as there are a bunch of different Christian denominations, thanks to in-fighting and church-splitting over the years, the same is true of Taoism. That's the one constant I've found in every religion I've studied—somewhere along their historical line, the subtle art of in-fighting has screwed them up. Every religion has it's own denominational problems, which tells me clearly that they can't be the TRUTH. TRUTH, if it is indeed established by God, can't be chaotic and can't be interpreted in various ways depending on the flavor of the denomination. That's why I believe that all religions are wrong, and the only way mankind can get back to the TRUTH is to throw them all out and start over with nothing. The problem is that humans would never do that; they're too jealous of their own ways to dump them. They could never start over because no two people out of the 3.5 billion on this planet can ever totally agree on anything. It just ain't gonna happen. So my search for a TRUE religion will continue for a very long time, I'm afraid. In the meantime, I'll continue to believe in God, but I won't attempt to put any definitions on Him. I'll worship Him in the summer breeze, the stars at night, and those big pine trees over there that make the most wonderful sounds ever heard when the wind rattles through them. Pine tree rattle shall become my own gospel hymn, and the scent of the pine trees in the heat of the day shall by my incense, wafting up to the very gates of heaven, and into the very presence of God. An object of nature is sacred, and far more valuable than any gold medallion or pendant on the face of the earth. I choose to wear a simple seashell on a leather cord around my neck. The sea itself is a holy place, and all things associated with it are precious objects representing the sanctity of the sea.

◎ ◎ ◎

Abby has just emerged from the breezeway, yawning and wiping sleep crusts from her eye with her fist. Even though it's the middle of the afternoon, all she's wearing are her little white panties. She sits down next to me and puts her head on my shoulder.

"Good morning, again," I say.

"I think I could have slept all day," she says without opening her eyes, "but I don't wanna be without you that long." She snuggles closer to me, like a sleepy puppy.

"Aww, what a sweet thing to say." I kiss her gently on the forehead. "It's a lovely day. The summer air feels so good."

"It does," she murmurs. "I like the wind hitting my skin on a hot summer day."

"I was just writing about that very thing."

"Really?"

"Yep. Driving on the freeway with the windows down and the

hot air streaming in."

"I like doing that, too."

"I guess we're a couple of summer freaks."

"Always have been."

"We oughta drive down to the beach and lay out on the sand some time today," I say.

"It's getting a little late in the day for that. Besides, I think I'd rather stay here. It's just as sunny and warm, and I can be naked. I can't show my tits on the beach—I'd get arrested."

"Yes, you would. We're pretty secluded here, so you'll be safe," I assure her.

"I oughta call my mother sometime today," Abby says. She's wide-awake now and sitting up straight. "She'll be wondering what I'm doing."

"Doesn't she know where you are?"

"Not really."

"Won't she be worried that you didn't come home last night?"

"I doubt it—it's not the first time. If Billy's there and I sense that he's got some nasty ideas in his head, I split and go over to Mamie's house. I've spent a lot of nights with her."

"Well, you should call your mother just to let her know you're okay."

"Where's your phone?"

"In the kitchen, on the wall behind the door."

"I'll be right back."

Ten Minutes Later

"I'm back," Abby announces as she returns to the swing.

"Well? Was your mom okay with you being here?"

"No prob. I told her a little about you and she wants to meet you."

"That'd be nice. I'd like to meet her, too."

"I told her that you were a fellow Beat. She was real happy about that."

"Really? I hope I don't disappoint her."

"You won't," Abby says. She pulls me close and kisses me. When she's done kissing me, she leans back and tells me, "She's going up to The City tomorrow and she wants me to go along."

"San Francisco?"

"Of course. I have an aunt up there that we haven't seen in a long time and she wants us to come visit. My Aunt Emily — I know, Auntie Em, so don't say it — she owns a little motel. She calls it Auntie's Motel. Original, huh? It's a cute little place hidden off one of the main streets and surrounded by big old trees. Very rustic. Some of the Beats stay there from time to time because it's so peaceful. It's kind of a secret getaway and they never tell people when they visit. The courtyard sorta reminds me of your front yard here, only it has a big fountain in the middle."

"How long would you be gone?"

"Not sure. A few days I guess." She looks into my eyes. "What's the matter? Don't look so sad." She smiles and licks the end of my nose.

"I'll miss you."

"It's only a few days. You can come with me if you want."

"Not this time," I tell her. "I doubt that my parents would like me leaving this place without somebody here to watch it. They're paranoid about burglars."

"Well then, next time, cause I'd really love to show you off up there."

I laugh at that. "Show me off? What's there to show?"

"You're cute, you have a good head on your shoulders, you love all our Beat friends, and you write poetry. That's more to show off than any other man I've dated."

"How many other men have you dated?" I ask.

"Two. One for a month and the other for about two weeks."

"That's all? Just two?" I am astonished.

"That's it. Sorry to blow your image of me."

"No," I say quickly. "I'm delighted."

"I know, Beat girls have a racey image. They aren't known for their celibacy."

"I just thought that a girl as cute and smart as you would be in high demand out there in the world, especially among the Beats. Didn't you ever have a boyfriend when you were hangin' around up in The City?"

"Not really. A lot of my Beat friends are airy-fairy, remember? And the ones who aren't fairy are too wrapped up in their work, or they're already taken, or they're too old. Besides, I'm not one of those girls who feels like she has to have a guy to date all the time. I kinda like my independence."

"Well, it looks like you're gonna be independent for at least a couple of days then," I say rather sadly.

She looks at me seriously. "I would never have said this last week, but right now I think I'd rather be with you than be without you up there," she says. "What will you do while I'm gone?"

"Probably not much. Maybe hang around with my friend, Manny." Then I smile at her. "It's more likely I'll just stay around here drawing and reading and thinking about you."

"Can you draw me from memory?"

"You bet I can." I tell her truthfully. I've memorized every detail.

"Then I'll expect to find some nice drawings when I get back."

"You will."

"So, now what do we do? It's still early and we have the whole evening ahead of us."

"Your wish is my command." I smile. "Just name it and we'll do it."

"Better not tell me that." She smiled back.

"Oh, really?"

"I do have an idea. Why don't I call Mamie and get her over here. We can call out for pizza, drink some wine, and write some poetry. She'd like that, she's into Beat poetry."

"Sounds fun to me. We can do a long group poem."

"That would be cool." Abby smiled. "But Mamie drinks even more than we do—she's liable to be too drunk to drive back home. Can she crash here if that happens?"

"Sure."

"Be right back!"

Abby is up in a flash and running, presumably to call Mamie, her little pantie-covered bottom bouncing all the way to the breezeway.

In The Kitchen • 6:30 PM

While Abby was calling Mamie I stayed in The Hole to look for something that Abby could wear — she said she was tired of wearing the same thing for two days. When she was done with her call, she came bouncing back. I don't have a lot of clothes — mainly Levis, t-shirts, a couple of pairs of shorts, a sweater or two — she wasn't very impressed. She finally settled on a pair of tan shorts and a white sleeveless t-shirt.

"I don't really like shorts," she said, frowning as she held them in front of her. "They're so normal looking."

"I'll bet your little behind will look pretty good in those."

"They're too loose for that," she said. "Do you have a pair of scissors?"

"I can find a pair. Why?"

"You'll see," she said with a sly smile.

I came back with the scissors and Abby proceeded to cut along the line of the crotch seam in my shorts. She opened them up, trimmed up the legs, and voila, before my eyes she had created a scandalously short skirt.

She held them up and examined them. "Not too neat to look at, but at least I'll be able to breathe down there," she declared. Then she gave me a grin and said, "It'll be convenient for other things, too."

◎ ◎ ◎

Mamie arrived with a large sausage pizza and two gallons of Red Mountain — she's obviously older than I thought if she's able to buy wine. She set the pizza on the dining bar between the kitchen and the family room, then came over and hugged me hard.

"Is it okay to hug my yoga teacher?" she asked with a big smile on her face.

"Of course. Tonight I'm just another guy."

She opened up one of the jugs, found some glasses and filled them up, and then we started to eat. We decided it would be more fun if we just sat on the family room floor to eat so that we could have a better conversation.

"This is nice," Mamie said. "Thanks for having me over."

"You're welcome. It was Abby's idea," I said, smiling at Abby.

"Oh? So that means you didn't want me to come?" Mamie looks hurt, but I know she's kidding.

"I tried to talk Abby out of inviting you, but it didn't work." I grinned.

"Yeah, right," Abby said.

Mamie really is a pretty girl. Some might say she's a little hefty, but that's just the illusion one gets when first meeting her. Her stomach is trim, her legs are slim and firm, but her boobs are large, giving the impression that she's overweight. She looks good tonight. She's wearing pretty much what she wears to my yoga classes: a short black skirt, black nylons, and a low-cut, stretchy black shirt, similar to the sleeveless undershirt Abby is wearing. The shirt really accentuates her breasts—I'm going to have a hard time not staring.

"So, what's the occasion?" Mamie asks.

"I'm heading up to The City tomorrow with Mom, and DH and I just thought it would be fun to have you over for a night of merriment." Abby smiles.

"How cool is that?" Mamie says. "How long will you be there?"

"A few days."

"Man, I wish I could go with you," Mamie says.

"Why can't you? Mom would love to have you come along."

"I have to work tomorrow and I can't afford to take off. My boss tells me just one more day and I'm canned," Mamie explains.

"Where do you work, Mamie?" I ask.

"I work at a shoe store in the mall. I squat and fit shoes all day."

"Sounds like good exercise."

"Not really, it's just enough squatting to make my legs sore. But it has its perks." She grins at Abby.

"Come on, Mam, you aren't gonna tell him about that, are you?"

"Why not?" Mamie asks.

"Tell me what?" I ask.

"Some days, Mam doesn't wear panties to work so that when she squats down to fit the shoes on certain guys, they get a real show," Abby explains.

"Oh … that." My mind wanders as I consider the prospect.

"Like they haven't seen one before," Mam says. "They get really uncomfortable, but they don't dare say anything. I act like there's nothin' goin' on — cool as a cucumber."

"I can see why they might be a little taken aback by your exhibition." I smile. "But I'll bet that image springs into their heads every time they tie their shoes after that."

"You know it does." Mam winked at me.

It's time to change the subject. "Abby thinks we ought to write a group poem."

"That sounds fun!" Mam says. "You mean like we take turns writing a line?"

"Yep," Abby says. "Let me pick up the pizza stuff first, then we'll fill our glasses and do the poem."

"I brought in one of my new sketch pads. We can write the poem in it,"

We ate a lot of pizza and wrote poems — probably twenty or so over the course of the evening. I think they were all pretty good, but the more we wrote and the later it got, the drunker we all got and the more mangled the poems became. Here is one of the better ones, I think. I figured I'd immortalized it here in my journal:

Two Beat Girls
Girls on floor
pizza breath
two bad Zen Beat girls
plastic bracelets on the girl with
the red lipstick
bright red on hot sunny day
heat streaming through the shut
glass window
one girl is sweating big drops
down into
grand canyon cleavage
says she wants to be a poet to
the only
man in the room who
watches air come out of the
Beat Girls mouths and
wishes
for
time alone with at least one
of them
before
this night is over and
before the
June Christy album ends
because that's when the
rubber meets the road
proverbially speaking
taoist hindu baby speak
solitude's gonna hit hard then
because
wine kicks in
late at night
wine

lays foundations for bigger
things
one Beat Girl screams
"I
WANT YOU IN ME" the
one with the
swollen breasts
"WHY
WON'T YOU QUIT BEING
SUCH A PHILOSOPHER! AND
ENTER?"
philosophy is dead the
man tells her
"I don't want any part of
philosophy
I just want to feel
warm
flesh
and
be
content"
and that would be with the smaller
girl
Beat Girl number
2
(who offers the man the
sacrifice of her
levis
sliced open in the right
places) and
the last piece of pizza she
saved just for
him
My Name Is ABBY she

tells him,
the guy with the golden
hair
and the sketchbook.
"I
want you more than she does." And to
prove her point she
covers up her breasts that were already completely
bare.
"You want these but
you can't have them 'cause they're for
someone else . . .
the
man that doesn't take them
by force
—broken citadel—
stick with cleavage girl who
will
kill you with her breasts if
you enter her."
that's not Zen
but it feels right
today
because of the
heat
and the hot wet canyons found
in this part of the
world.
"smell me." The small-breasted Beat
girl says. "Smell me." Roses . . .
roses and more roses and pink salmon
underneath
the bluest sky ever. "Smell me."
"taste me." I'm not shrinking, neither

are you, so
why the sad face?
Somewhere oh somewhere there is
a large wide oak tree
a protector defender and hider of
those
who wish to be
passionate and not be seen and
that
would be dearest
ABBY
the queen of the Beats
the zen of the zen
and the
golden haired man
she
chooses
because she knows he
knows what she has in her
heart
and
what awaits him under
her
ill-fitting skirt

I'm not going to put all the poems in here because a lot of them are pretty bad, but I'll save them in my sketchpad just in case one day we need to show them to prove just how bizarre we really were at this age.

The evening wore on as we filled up the sketchpad and emptied the pizza box. Finally, after a few minutes of silence, Mam said, "I really need to get some air."

"You wanna go out on the patio for a while?" I suggested.

"Let's take her out and show her the cliff," Abby said excitedly.

"The cliff?" Mam asked.

"Just one of the many features DH and his parents have here," Abby explained.

"Really?" Mam said. Then she turned to me and said with mock sternness, "And where are your parents, DH. How is it we get this place all to ourselves?"

"They're off in a tent somewhere. They do a lot of traveling, mostly camping trips and the like."

"Camping? I love camping! Where do they like to go?" Mam asked, genuinely interested.

"Pretty much anywhere they can pitch a tent, but we do have a family favorite spot."

"Where's that?"

"A private campground in the San Jacinto Mountains out past Hemet on the way up to Idyllwild. We go there all the time."

"You're kidding! That's Joe and Leona's place."

"Yes. Do you camp there?" I was totally surprised. I'd never have taken Mam for a camper.

"Joe and Leona are good friends of my mom's. She and I go there all the time just to visit Leona. Boy, I've had some times up there. I really need to get back soon. It's been a while, and Leona's probably thinkin' I left the country." Mam smiled.

"Well, I'll be. Small world," I said, shaking my head. You just never know what's gonna come out of the people you meet.

Mam stood up and grabbed the jug of wine. "Tally ho, campers!"

she cried as we filed out the kitchen door, through the breezeway, and into the back yard.

Mam stopped on the patio and looked around. "Nice patio," she said. "Mine looks pretty chintzy compared to this."

"DH's parents have good jobs," Abby said.

"Don't rub it in. I wish mine did," Mam said. "You can't have nice things if all you do is answer the phone for a plumber."

I guess I looked confused, so Abby told me, "Mam's dad's a plumber. Her mother is his secretary."

"Honorable jobs," I said. "Nothing wrong with those."

"They just don't make much money," Mam replied. "We barely make ends meet."

"I thought Beats weren't supposed to be concerned with materialism and possessions," I said.

"We aren't," Mam said. "But it would be nice to buy a little something special now and then. Girls like to be spoiled."

The thought occurred to me that Mam's gonna marry some guy someday and he's gonna have a mess on his hands, but I didn't say anything. I just smiled and led the girls out to the edge of the cliff. It was pitch black except for the lights of the city twinkling in the distance, and waning moon that gave off just enough light to see the outlines of the grotto below us. We stood in silence for a moment, admiring the view.

"Wow! That's really cool," Mam said in a hushed voice.

"If it were lighter we could walk down there and check it out, but it's a bit dark for that," Abby said.

"We could fall off the path," I said.

"That's okay. We can stay up here and look. It's nice enough up here." Mam smiled and took a long slow breath. "That air feels so good."

"It's so quiet out here," Abby said. "I can't hear any traffic, dogs barking, kids yelling—nothing."

"It's like that most of the time," I said.

"There's something kind of magical about silence," Mam said.

"I often wonder what silence really is."

"What do you mean?" I asked.

"When the air's filled with sound you know the air is really there, but when it's totally silent, how can you be sure? Silence is invisible and so is air."

"An interesting thought," I said.

"And just because you can't see silence, doesn't mean that it isn't a physical thing. If sound is a physical thing, then what is silence? The opposite of a physical thing? Is it something on another plane of existence, or is it something on this plane that we just can't see? But if it's invisible, that doesn't necessarily make it non-physical, does it? Do invisible things have mass?"

"Whew … is that the wine talking or is it something you've been wondering about for a long time?" I asked her.

"My mind's a mess." Mam smiles and shakes her head. "I can't shut it up. I think about crap like that all the time."

"Well, it's something worthy of thinking about," I said. "Why do all the monks in the world seek silence all the time? They say they need silence to meditate. They claim that silence helps them to empty their minds of clutter. But if silence is a physical substance like you just implied, Mam, then meditation can be just as disturbed by silence as it can by cluttered thoughts."

"Hey, that almost makes sense." Abby laughs. "It's like something one of my buddies in The City would say."

"Can we sit down right here?" Mam asked. "It's so pretty looking out over the gorge. Look at the moon out there."

"Are you wearing panties, Mam?" Abby asked.

"No, I came straight from work," she answered. As she looked at Abby, a grin appeared on her face. "Why?" she asked.

"You might get a bug crawling up your crotch," I told her.

"Lucky bug," Mam turned her grin on me and winked.

"It's okay, I'm not wearing any either," Abby was grinning, too.

We sat on the ground about a foot from the edge of the cliff. Abby and I settled in to enjoy the view, but Mam was feeling the ground around her with her hands.

"What's the matter?" I asked.

"Did it rain while we were inside writing poems? The ground seems damp here," Mam said.

Abby started to laugh, and then she fell back onto the ground, rolling with laughter.

"What's the deal Abby?" I asked.

"That's where I squatted to pee last night," she said, gasping for breath.

Mam jumped to her feet. "Eww!" she said, trying to wipe her hands and bottom off with the end of her dress.

"If we move over about three feet we'll be out of the danger zone," I said, trying to control my own laughter.

After checking first that the ground was dry we sat down again in a little line at the edge of the grotto. Abby was still snickering, and Mam was muttering something like, "My ass is gonna be cold all night now. Nothin' worse than a damp ass." I just kept my mouth shut.

"Shh … listen," Abby said. An owl was hooting in the distance.

"I love that," Mam whispered. "What do you think that means?"

"Huh?" I ask.

"In nature, everything has meaning," Mam said. "It's a quiet night and suddenly in the middle of the solitude an owl hoots. It has to mean something."

"It could be he's just horny," Abby said, smiling.

"How do you know it's a he?" I asked.

"The deep voice," Abby said as her smile widened to a grin.

"You guys are silly," Mam said. "I'm serious. Nature's a very mysterious thing. It's a force, not a word, and everything interconnects and gives meaning to the whole of everything."

"Where did you learn that, Mam?" I asked.

"Books, mainly, but something inside me tells me that it's true."

"You sound like one of those Druids DH and I talked about last night."

"I've read all about Druids," Mam said. "There's something to those old beliefs and practices."

"Is there?" I asked. "Or are those beliefs and practices just man's way of trying to understand things as he evolves throughout history?"

"Maybe a little of both," Abby said. "I think humans accidentally trip over the truth every now and then as they move forward along the line of history. They knew about the forces and energies of nature hundreds of years ago, but they didn't see them as principles of physics. They figured them to be gods and goddesses."

"They personified them," I said.

"But you have to wonder if that really makes any difference," Mam said. "Just because they personified them, it didn't in any way change the fact that those principles of physics still worked. I don't think man can change anything just by claiming it to be so. Do you know what I mean?"

"I think so," I said. "There's the old saying that history is written by the victors, not the vanquished."

"What does that mean?" Mam asked.

"It means that the guys who won the battles and kept the land can write and rewrite history the way they want it to be, regardless of the truth. Nevertheless, no matter what anyone says about history, or claims to be so, the truth can't be changed. Abby and I talked about this too. We have no idea what the Druids really believed, or what they were capable of doing. Some say they worked magic, and modern day Druids embellish the historical tidbits in ways to make them look hip and mysterious so they can wear their costumes and fulfill some sort of identity crisis, but they don't have a clue about what they're doing. All anyone can do is guess. But just because we guess, right or wrong, it doesn't change the fact of who and what they really were."

I paused to check to see if the girls were following what I was saying. When I was sure that I hadn't put them to sleep, I continued. "Man has always lied about the truth and still does. Abby and I talked this one into the ground, but look at all the religions we have today—every one has it's own written record of what the truth is for that religion, and none of them match. Catholics are different from Protestants, and they're both different from Buddhist, Hindus, and Taoists—and they're all different from each other, as well. But wait—there's more! All the Protestant denominations are different from each other. All the Hindu denominations, all the Buddhist denominations, all the Taoist denominations—all are different from each other. They aren't just different in small things, either; they're different in large ways that can never be resolved by any form of compromise. Some of the Protestants and Catholics have been trying for years to find some sort of commonality to bring them together into one body of believers, but they haven't been able to do it. I just wonder what archaeologists will think a million years from now when they unearth all the confusing, conflicting reports of what religion was like during our time. It's going to be a nightmare for them to sort out."

"What does all that have to do with silence?" Abby asked.

"Not a damned thing," Mam said. "It's just fun to talk about. Although you could make the case that silence is one of those large differences between all religions. Just think, if silence is a real substance with mass, then all monks everywhere and of every faith who spend hours meditating are getting short circuited by silence and their meditation doesn't count for squat."

"Maybe that's the one thing they all have in common that could bring them together," I said. "Meditation doesn't work for any of them."

Abby frowned. "I think the only thing all the denominations have in common is that they don't get along with each other. That's the one thing they believe. They ought to just forget about a formal joining 'cause it ain't gonna happen"

"So, now we have two points upon which every denomination can agree: number one, meditation doesn't work; and number two, we don't get along together," I said, holding up a finger to tick of each point. "If we drink enough wine tonight we just might be able to solve a problem that's been around for hundreds of years. We might even fuse the Catholics and Protestants back together into one happy family."

"What would you call them then?" Abby asked. "Protelics?"

"Lick what?" Mam asked.

"Protelics ain't bad," Abby said. "That's better than Cathostants."

"Where's the vino jug?" Mam asked.

I handed her the jug of Red Mountain. In one smooth motion she raised it to her lips and took a big gulp.

"I hope nobody's afraid of my cooties. There aren't any cups out here and I'm thirsty. I plan on killin' this whole jug before the night's over."

"The alcohol will kill the cooties," I said.

"And the wine will kill us all," Mam replied.

"But we'll go out happy," Abby said, smiling.

"To peace, love, joy!" Abby took the jug from Mam and drank deeply. "That's what Jesus taught."

"Yep. That's pretty much all He taught," I said. "Humans added a ton of stuff to His teachings later on."

"What do you think about that guy? Was He the real thing?" Mam asked.

"You're asking me?" I said.

"An open question for both of you."

"I think He was the real thing," I said. "There's no question that He lived and there's no question that He taught the things He taught. It's what people did when they got hold of His teachings and twisted them all around."

"Was He the Son of God?" Mam asked.

"Why not?" I said. "Again, every religion has their beliefs. The Hindus believe Krishna is the Hindu Christ, and there's even a similarity in the spelling of the names. But Krishna's only a person-ified god—he never existed. Jesus is a real person with historical validation. There are hundreds of eyewitnesses for every miracle He performed and for all the sermons He preached. That's the big difference between Jesus and all the personified gods and goddesses out there. But in the end it all boils down to faith. That's what faith is, believing in something you can't prove. While most of the gods of history are made up and have become more like cartoon characters than gods, Jesus has somehow managed to retain a powerful, validated presence among His followers, so maybe He is the Son of God." I smile. "He certainly is to millions of believers."

"To me, faith is based on logic." Abby said. "To be honest, if I were to put my faith in someone, and I haven't as yet, the number one thing I'd ask is that the someone be a real person with historical validation. I could never believe in a god that has no foundation in historical evidence. You know, Jack Kerouac believes in Jesus. I don't think he goes to Mass any more, but he's actually a very religious guy and he gets a bit testy when someone slams Jesus or Christianity."

"I've got a theory about that." Mam said. "I think that Jack put a lot of the principles of his own personal, disjointed faith into his books when he wrote them. He also salted his stuff with a lot Buddhism. His observations went beyond Buddhism, though, because Buddhism is basically an atheistic religion and Jack never has been able to totally buy into that. He was raised a Catholic and he's still a Catholic."

"Jack once said that everything he writes is about Jesus," Abby said. "I'm not sure exactly what he meant by that, but it seems pretty profound."

"I don't know much about Kerouac yet. I haven't met him like you have, Abby," I said. "But I think the man is a whole lot deeper than people give him credit for — maybe even deeper than he believes himself to be. From what little I have read of his stuff, I can see a very complex and complicated soul being revealed between the lines of his books, far deeper than what his outer person exhibits. I hope he pulls it all together and writes another book that sorts it all out."

"I just wish he'd stop drinking so much," Abby said. "Mother wants to talk to him about that the next time she sees him. We're hoping to run into him when we go up tomorrow. He's pretty reclusive these days, though, and he's not always in The City. He can't seem to stay in one place for too long."

"I think he's a saint in the making," Mam said.

I smiled at that thought. "You may be right, Mam. If I were a Catholic, St. Francis of Assisi would be my favorite saint. What a nut-job he was—just like me. A real nature freak, and that's a point in his favor. Francis wrote down some stuff later on in his life, but not the kind of stuff Kerouac writes. I've read a few things attributed to old Frank, and they're more along churchy lines than they are about the real lives of people and how people relate to this crazy world. Kerouac writes about the crazy stuff. That ought to earn him some brownie points upstairs. Anyway, I'm lovin' Jack's stuff. The more I get into it, the more I like it. Hand me that jug."

The conversation lagged and we sat there on the edge of the cliff just listening to the silence.

"There goes that owl again," Abby said softly.

"Such a mournful sound," Mam said. "Kinda spooky, really."

"You believe in ghosts?" Abby asked her.

"Are you kidding?" Mam replies. "My grandpa owns a little ranch not too far from here, in Hemet, just under Mount San Jac. A woman was found dead in the barn there about eighty years ago, just before his dad bought the ranch. He swears his barn is haunted by the ghost of that murdered woman. I think we ought to go out there sometime and spend the night in it."

Mam's face lit up with excitement at the thought of spending the night in a haunted barn, but Abby looked at her with something like horror. "You gotta be kidding," Abby said. "Why would we want to do that?"

"Just for the heck of it," Mam said. "I've been there a few times, and it did feel kinda eerie inside. Every time I went in there I felt like somebody was watching me. Only I always thought it was a man ghost, not a woman. Of course, how would I know about that—I haven't had a man watch me do anything in a long time."

"What are you talkin' about, Mam?" Abby asked. "Men look at

you all the time."

"Lookin' and touchin' are two different things, Abby." Mam frowned. "I guess I'm just kinda lonely. Haven't had a male friend in three years. Two guys I dated recently were jerks and I walked out on them mid-date. I don't like being alone."

"Aww, I'll be your friend." Abby reached over and took Mam's hand.

"Holdin' hands with a girl ain't the same as doin' other things with a man." Mam frowned. "It's been three years since a man's been down there where he belongs."

"What about all the guys at the shoe store?" I reminded her.

"Very funny," she said sharply. "They're too wimpy for me. If they were really interested in me after I flashed them like that, they'd attack me right there between the shoe aisles."

"Are those the type of men you'd really like to date? The ones that attack you?" I asked her gently.

"Of course not. I was just kidding." Tears were forming in her eyes. "It's just the wine talking. If I drink more I'll be happier." She tried to smile.

"What kind of man are you really looking for, Mam," Abby asked.

"Like the one you found, Abby," Mam said, nodding her head in my direction.

"Don't judge a book by its cover." I throw up my hands in mock defense. "You probably wouldn't like me if you really knew me."

"Baloney," Abby said. "She'd love you. You're one of the good guys."

Smiling, Mam asked her, "Can I rent him from you while you're up in The City?"

"How much?" Abby responded, going along with the joke.

"I've got twenty bucks," Mam said.

"I'll think about it," Abby replied.

"Hello! I'm sitting right here," I interjected. This conversation was getting out of control. "Give me the jug," I said.

"Get him drunk enough and we can both have him tonight right here on this cliff," Mam said, and both girls giggled.

"That would certainly add a new twist to things," I said.

Just then, Mam sat up straight and held up a hand to silence us. "Shh!" she said.

"What's the matter?" Abby whispered.

"I thought I heard something."

"What did you hear?" I hissed.

"I'm not sure," Mam said softly. "It sounded like somebody walking on dry twigs, right behind you, Abby."

Abby looked cautiously over her shoulder.

"I think you're hearing things, Mam." I said.

"Yeah, we were talking about ghosts and you got spooked." Abby sounded like she was trying to convince herself as much as Mam.

"No, I heard it." Mam insisted. "But I do believe in ghosts. I went to a séance once, and a girl there got to talk with her dead uncle."

"You mean literally?" I asked.

"Through a medium," she explained.

"Most of those people are frauds," I said.

"I think she was the real deal. She told this girl things that only she and her uncle would know. Very secret things that the girl didn't want to come out in public."

"Like what?" Abby asked.

"Like how her uncle was having sex with her all the time, and she wasn't a little kid. The girl was twenty-something, and she was doing it with her uncle because she wanted to."

"You're kidding," I said.

"Not kidding," Mam said. "She and her uncle had been doing it for years and never told anybody. She said they were in love, but he died and that was the end of it."

"Well, they were both adults. I guess they weren't breaking any laws." Abby said.

"And they were happy," I added.

"Yeah ... but her uncle?" Mam shook her head. "It was really weird. All that information came out through the medium, and the girl was really upset that everyone at the séance heard it."

"I'll bet she was," I said.

Suddenly, Abby let out a big yawn. "I'm getting sleepy," she said.

"It's the wine. It's not that late," I said. "Wanna go to bed?"

Mam gave me a sly smile and said, "Who you askin'?"

"Better watch it, Mam, Abby's tough. She might punch your lights out," I warned her.

"Naw," Abby said. "That's just Mam bein' Mam. Besides, I'm too tired to punch her lights out."

"Well, as nice as it might be for me, we can't all sleep in my little bed in The Hole."

"Mam can sleep on the floor in the family room," Abby said.

"No way!" Mam objected. "You mean alone? By myself in that big house?"

"Are you scared of spooks?" Abby teased.

"If I'm all alone I am." Mam admitted.

"Why don't we all sleep in there on the floor? The carpet is nice and thick." I suggested.

"That's sounds much better," Mam said happily. "I may not be through drinking wine — glub glub glub — that way I can just pass out knowing that you're both there to protect me."

And that's exactly what we did. The family room is pretty large and by pushing some of the comfy chairs out of the way we easily made room for the three of us in a row with me in the middle. I think I was the first to go to sleep and Abby would have been the second. Just before I fell asleep, I saw that Mam was sitting cross-legged and upright, meditating and drinking wine — which I think is kind of an oxymoron. I mean, how many true seekers meditate and drink wine at the same time? I can just hear a Zen master teacher telling his disciples, *Okay, lets all chant Om for a minute or so, then we'll take a big gulp of Red mountain, then back to meditation for five minutes, then we will repeat the process. Ready? Begin.*

It was a long, odd night. I would have slept soundly until morning had it not been for Mam. I woke up three different times to find her snuggling close to me and kissing me. At first I thought it was Abby, but the kiss was different. The second time, I opened my eyes fully and saw that it was Mam, not Abby. I jumped a little, but Mam reached around my chest and held me down to the floor and whispered, "Quiet, this won't hurt a bit."

I glanced over at Abby on my other side and saw that she was fully asleep and facing away from me. I didn't know what to do, so I let Mam kiss me—just a kiss, that's all. When she was finished she sighed, pushed away, and went to sleep on her back. The third interruption came around 3 AM. Mam rolled toward me and started kissing me again, but this time she grabbed my hand, and placed it on her breasts. She had pulled her shirt off at some time during the night, and I found myself fondling her fully exposed, massive, squishy breasts. She wouldn't let me stop; every time I tried to pull my hand away she'd bring it back, forcing my hand to rub hard all over both her breasts. At some point she must have decided it was time to stop and go back to sleep, but not before whispering to me, "When Abby leaves tomorrow I'll come back over, that is if you want me."

How do you answer a statement like that? So I didn't. I just smiled, rolled over on my side so I was facing Abby, and dozed off.

4 THURSDAY

Abby was up and out of here before 9:00 this morning. She said that it's a little more than an eight-hour drive to San Francisco, so she and her mom needed to hit the road before 10 AM to make it there by 6 or 7 this evening. Now Mam and I are here alone in this big house.

I have to confess that I was more than a little apprehensive at being left here with Mam, considering how she'd come on to me last night. Abby was fully aware that Mam was flirting with me, even before we went to bed—the message was plain as day. Every time anyone said anything even remotely suggestive, Mam gave me a sly smile and a wink. Her quick brain turned even the most innocent remarks into sexual innuendos—always accompanied by that wink and a smile. So why would Abby leave me here alone with Mam? There are lots of things in this world that I don't get, and how a woman thinks is way up at the top of the list.

After Abby left, Mam and I whipped up a tasty little breakfast of toast, kipper snacks, cheese, and grapes. My mother had left me some of the pound cake she had baked to take on their camping trip, so Mam and I had some for desert. Mother's recipe has been in the family for generations going all the way back to England. We spooned strawberry jam and Devonshire cream over the cake, making it especially delicious. My Mother loves everything English—the old manor homes, the castles, afternoon tea, you name it. She really likes "playing castle," so the pantry is always filled with goodies to put together an afternoon tea that would be a credit to the best of British manor houses. I have inherited her love of all things English. According to our family tree, almost all the branches go back to England, Scotland, Wales, and Ireland, so I suppose the Anglophilia is in our blood.

We had all the food laid out on the dining bar and were getting ready to fill our plates when Mam said, "Well, here we are, all alone in the castle." There was that sly smile again.

"Yes, we are." I didn't smile.

"So, what are we gonna do for the rest of the day?" she asked.

I said the only thing I could, "I have no idea." I wasn't expecting to be alone with her today. I thought she would leave when Abby did, but she's still here, in my kitchen helping me make breakfast. She was still wearing the short black skirt from yesterday. She had put her shirt back on, but left it unbuttoned so that it hung loose, barely covering her ample breasts.

While we were cleaning up after breakfast Mam said that she wanted to check out The Hole. I guess Abby had told her all about it, so now she had to see it for herself. I'm not sure why, though; there's not much there that can be of any interest to anyone, but I took her out to show her anyway.

"How sweet!" Mam said as she stepped through the open door. She could see all there was to see from where she stood just inside the door—my bed along the east wall, my desk on the south wall at the foot of the bed, and my bookcase next to the desk. A floor lamp stands next to the bed, and the wall behind the bed is bare. I keep my clothes in the large wardrobe-style closet that Grandad had built along the west wall to the left of the door. I also store three or four gallons of Red Mountain in there, just in case someone pops in for a visit. Besides the two windows that let in a lot of light and fresh air, that's all there is to my little room in the garage. Really, what's so special about the place?

"You're probably wondering what girls find so special about this place," Mam said.

"I have—many times. There's not much to see here."

"It's like an artist's garret," she said. "While a girl is inside this room she can pretend she's back in time somewhere—Paris or Amsterdam or a village in southern France—inside the garret-studio of Van Gogh, Monet, or any other struggling, not-yet-famous artist. It's very romantic in here."

"Well, I'm not an artist."

"Abby told me you're gonna take some art classes at RCC in September. Doesn't that make you a budding artist?"

"I suppose it does in a very loose sense of the concept, but so far all I've done is draw pictures in my sketchpad."

"Do you draw pictures while you're lying on your little bed there?" she asked.

"Sure. I do most of my drawing on that bed."

"Then you fit the image of every artist ever born. You're no different than Van Gogh, or Picasso, or Kandinsky, and this is your garret—your studio—where you come to drink wine, create masterpieces, and pine away after all the women you fall in love with."

"I haven't painted many paintings—just a lot of sketches—so I don't have any masterpieces."

"Do you know how much a little pencil sketch that Cezanne did of his young son brought at a major art auction in Los Angeles last year?" Mam asked.

"I have no idea."

"It was thousands of dollars. It was just a simple little line drawing on a piece of paper five inches square, but they called it a masterpiece."

"But he was a great artist and he's also dead. Artists don't get famous until they die."

"You're missing the point, Pablo," she said. "Every artist starts out the way you're starting out. I don't know of one artist who was famous after painting only one painting. They may paint for decades, living in poverty for years choosing to buy paint instead of food. Then, one day, someone discovers them and the rest is history. But in the mean time, they're living the life of one of the most holy of all professions—the life of an Artist."

"Holy?"

"Think about it, DH," she continued passionately, "what is it that artists do? They create colorful landscapes on paper and cloth. What did God do when He created the universe? He created landscapes and seascapes out of dirt and plants. Granted, He creates out of nothing, and an artist needs the raw materials to begin with. An artist can't create anything literally like God does, but what an artist can do is copy the act of creation—make beautiful copies of God's real creations for people of this world to enjoy; make natural landscapes that people can take indoors. In a sense, artists are God's ambassadors. They represent God and His creations by copying them onto the canvas."

"I never thought of that before," I said. "That's a pretty impressive lecture you just gave. Are you saying that artists are like priests?"

"Yes! But only those artists who paint what God would want them to paint. There are a lot of false artists out there these days who are painting some pretty crude stuff, and I'm sure God wants nothing to do with that."

"I agree with you there," I said. "Young artists in particular seem to think that they have to make some sort of shocking political statement with their work. That's really just a bunch of nonsense."

"Yes, it is," Mam said. "And their art isn't all that shocking, anyway. Their young minds just think it is because their brains are still fairly immature and empty. They don't know what real life is yet."

Mam moved into the center of the room and stood there, hands on her hips, a smile on her lips, and a glint in her eyes as she analyzed everything in the room.

"So, what now? You've seen The Hole—what more could there possibly be to life?" I asked grandly.

She turned to face me. "I can think of all kinds of things we can do," she said while sliding her hands around my waist and pulling me to her.

I gently removed her hands, took a step back, and explained, "Mam, right now you are indeed a very tempting woman, but it would be wrong for us to do anything while Abby is away. She and I have become kinda close and it just wouldn't be right for us to do anything behind her back."

"Didn't you notice?" Mam said. "I dropped hints all night that I was trying to seduce you and she went right along with it."

"I think she thought it was a game you were playing, but I believe that if you and I got naked and spent a few hours together on the bed, Abby would not think that was okay."

"What she doesn't know won't hurt her." She smiled coyly. "I won't tell if you don't."

"I find you very attractive, Mam, but you're Abby's best friend. If you were just another girl I met who didn't know her, I might take you up on it. After all, she and I aren't engaged or anything like that—heck, we haven't even known each other that long—but since you guys are friends, I just can't do it. Besides, I think I'm really getting hooked on Abby. The three of us had a lot of fun last night, and I want there to be more nights like that."

Mam made a pouty face like a disappointed little girl. "Spoil sport," she said. "You don't know Abby very well, do you? If that's your wish, then you and I can just be friends. But mark my words, DH, one of these days Abby's gonna disappoint you. When that happens, ring me up—I ain't goin' anywhere."

Mam buttoned up her shirt and went back into the house. When she had gathered up her things she kissed me goodbye. "Don't forget what I said—you've got my number. When it happens, I can be right over to comfort you in your loss," she said. She smiled, kissed me again, and then headed out to her car to drive back to the real world.

A small part of me regretted turning her down—heaven knows, she's extremely attractive and it would have been most pleasant—but going down that road with her is not a good idea, considering my recent and still undetermined relationship with Abby. Her words will haunt me for a while, though: *Abby's gonna disappoint you. When that happens ....* Not if, but when. Mam does know Abby a lot better than I do.

Should I be worried? What kind of best friend is Mam if she's trying to seduce me as soon as Abby leaves town for a few days? I don't get any of it. Maybe there's something about Abby I need to know.

Now that Mam has gone, I'm all alone here. I'm planning to attend a poetry reading in the Quad at RCC later this evening, but I think I'll use the time until then to catch up in this journal and do more sketches.

The Quad is the oldest building on campus, and down in the basement there is a large multipurpose room with a snack bar/ cafeteria. One wall of the room is glass with doors that open onto a sunken patio in the inner courtyard of the Quad. Although you can access the area from inside the building, most people enter from the courtyard by way of the steps built into one end of the sunken patio. I'm not sure what the official name is for this com-plex, but it is generally known as The Pit, although I have heard it called the Concrete Womb and a few other things too colorful to mention here.

The Pit is a popular gathering place; this is true even in the summer as a lot of students attend summer classes. The snack bar serves typical snack bar food—burritos, hot dogs, burgers, fries, etc.—but it's pretty good and it sells well, so they keep it open into the evening and for special events like the poetry reading. There are tables inside should anyone wish to eat there, but lots of people like to eat outside at the big green picnic tables on the patio unless it's too cold or rainy. There are a few tables at the far end of The Pit that are sheltered by an overhang, so you can sit outside and enjoy it even if it's raining, if you like that sort of thing—as I do. I have a feeling that I'll be making The Pit my home away from home when I start classes in September.

It's about 5:30, and I'm down in The Pit waiting for Manny. I called him earlier today, and his mother, Hester, answered the phone. She told me he was in the garage with his band practic-ing for a gig at the high school next week. School's out for the summer, but lots of organizations rent out the gym for special events year-round—politicians, labor unions, religious organizations, just to name a few, have all held events at the high school. This time, Manny's band has been hired by a local men's benevolent group to headline a shindig to raise money for sick children, or orphans, or some worthy cause like that. The Riders played this gig last year; they were a big hit and the group raised a ton of money, so they were invited back this year. This event is a pretty big deal here in Riverside. Hundreds of people show up to dance, or just sit around and chat with each other. No alcohol is served, and no fistfights ever break out like they do at some venues. Quite a few members of the group are cops, so it would be really dumb if anyone tried to start any trouble.

Hester said she would give Manny the message to meet me here by 6:30.

As usual, I'm early; I like to get to things like this well before they start so I can get the best seat for watching the people in the audience, as well as for seeing the event itself. This evening I've found the perfect spot in The Pit to sit unobserved while I write and watch the people—girls, especially—go by. There are a ton of girls down here this evening, and judging by the way they are dressed, many are here for the poetry reading. There are lots of faux Beats here tonight—the ones the real Beats call beatniks, according to Abby—both guys and girls. Nearly all of the guys are wearing brand new Levis, t-shirts, and either tennis shoes or shiny black motorcycle boots that look like they've never been worn before tonight. A lot of them are also wearing big medallions on thick chains around their necks—what's that all about? I don't believe I've ever come across a picture of any of the real Beats, like Kerouac, Snyder, or Corso, wearing big gaudy medals like these. They're all working hard to look cool—to look like Beatniks. Kinda funny, really; according to Abby, real Beats would never try to act or look like Beatniks. In fact, they would avoid it.

Girls have more choices of what to wear than guys do, and they are making the most of that advantage here this evening.

A lot of the girls are going for the beatnik look and are wearing pants—either tight with ankle-length legs, or looser and rolled up to the knees—and loose white or blue man-style shirts. Stripes seem to be popular, too. Their shoes are mostly sneakers. Some of the girls are wearing short dresses or skirts and tops that are simple in style, but with bright colors and patterns—I think it's called the mod look. Many of these girls are also wearing go-go boots. There are a few girls in the crowd trying to look cool in very tight skirts or pants and bullet bras under figure-hugging sweaters. When I say they look hot, I mean that literally.

This corner of The Pit is a great place to sit and write poetry—but not this evening. Since I'll be attending a poetry reading here later, I don't really want to be seen writing poetry before it begins. I don't want people to think I'm showing off, or trying to let the world know I'm a poet, like whoever it is that will be reading tonight. Besides, I haven't been writing poetry for very long and I don't want to risk having strangers read it over my shoulder. I'll just continue to record my observations of the humans walking by. That way I can truthfully say that I'm writing in my journal, if anyone should ask. That's not the same as writing poetry.

The poets who are reading tonight are not anybody that anyone has heard of. They are all local people, mostly students, who were recommended for this event by their teachers, either here at RCC, or at the university—UC Riverside.

I have no idea what styles of poetry will be read; I'm sure there will be at least one rhyming poet like Robert Frost, but probably most will be free verse like the Beat poets—that seems to be really popular these days. Who knows, one of the poets might even recite haikus. I like some poetry, but not all of it. Poetry seems to be a big fad right now and everybody on Earth seems to think they are a poet, but it takes more than just calling yourself a poet and whipping out a couple of rambling free verse compositions. What makes a real poet and a good poem is the same thing that makes a real artist and a good painting—the Art Spirit that resides within the true artists, poets, and creative people, but not in everyone who paints or writes poems. I'll probably sit toward the back so that if the program is really bad I can buzz out quick without disturbing anybody.

Speaking of poetry, I just saw Mrs. Collard at the top of the steps—yes, that Mrs. Collard, the one who lured me behind the screen in the back of her classroom three days before graduation. All the guys in her English class were in love with her. She really is easy to look at, as they say, but whatever she has goes way beyond just her physical appearance. I wasn't really in love with her, but I certainly enjoyed watching her and letting my imagination run crazy with thoughts about her. Now she's coming down into The Pit. Every step she takes into this giant concrete womb makes her boobs jiggle and bounce like jello above the low-cut neckline of her very short yellow-print dress.

Damn, I was trying to keep my head down, but she's spotted me and now she's coming my way.

The Pit • 9:30 PM

There were several other tables where she could have sat, but she sat down next to me and made herself at home, sliding closer to me on the bench than necessary. The light scent of her rose perfume and the clear view that she was offering of her ample cleavage brought those moments behind the screen vividly to my mind.

"How are you DH?" she asked. "Are you here for the reading tonight?"

"Yes, I am." I smiled at her, hoping for an expression that was pleasant without being too friendly. "My friend, Manny, is supposed to meet me here, but he's kinda late."

"Are you enjoying your summer so far?" she asked.

"I'm loving it. I'm not doing much except for a few fun things with friends."

"So, what does a young man like you do for fun before you start your first year of college?" She smiled.

"No plans, really. So far I've watched Manny practice with his band, and we've had a couple of get-togethers at my house."

"You mean parties?"

"Not really, just a few friends getting together, sitting out in the back yard, drinking wine, writing poetry …"

"Wine? Aren't you too young to buy wine?"

"I am, but one of my teachers gave me a gallon for graduation." I gave her a knowing look, and she, understanding my meaning, smiled back coyly. "Besides, I figure I can drink it on my own property as long as I don't go out and do something stupid like drive to town drunk."

"That wouldn't be good," she agreed.

"No, it wouldn't." I smiled back.

"And you're writing poetry? That's great! What kind are you into these days?"

"I've been experimenting with some contemporary styles — not too long-winded and mostly free verse."

"I hope you got a few things out of my class last semester."

"Actually, I did," I told her truthfully. "You introduced me to a couple of writers that made my head spin."

"Let me guess — E. E. Cummings and T. S. Eliot," she said with a smile.

"Good guess," I said.

"So, tell me about that black book you're writing in," she said.

"I'm sorry. I guess it's kind of rude to write while you're trying to have a conversation with me."

"That all depends on what you're writing. If it's worthwhile, I would certainly want you to continue. I am an English teacher, remember?"

"It's my journal," I said as I closed the notebook and laid my hand on the cover. "I started keeping it a few weeks ago. I want to keep track of what's in my head and how it develops over the years."

"Very interesting, and very wise for a man your age. I don't believe any of my students have ever started a journal like that. I have no doubt that when you go back and read all the entries, you'll be amazed at the things you've done, the ideas you've had, and how it all focused in on your future life without you even being aware of it."

"I remember what you said once in class — that we're all living books. We write about ourselves by what we do with our lives. One experience leads to another, over and over again, until they come together to be an autobiography of a life well-lived."

"You remember that?" She smiled, looking both surprised and pleased. "That's almost word for word what I said. You must have a photographic memory."

"Not sure about that, but I do remember things that impress me."

"I feel honored that you were so impressed," she said while moving closer to me, her body making contact with mine.

"You've impressed me a lot, Mrs. Collard," I told her looking down at my hands as the words came out of my mouth.

"You're thinking about me kissing you that day aren't you?" She looked at her own hands. "I'm sorry if that made you uncomfortable, and if I could take it back I would. I worried for a week that you'd turn me in to the principal and I'd get fired."

"It did make me a little uncomfortable — not so much because of our age difference, but because it came out of nowhere like a bolt of lightning and I wasn't expecting it." I looked up into her eyes. "I went home that day and wondered over and over, what in the world does a beautiful creature like Mrs. Collard see in a young cat like me who doesn't even have a future yet. I wasn't mad in any way. In fact, I was honored that you, the prettiest teacher on campus, would let me do that to you. I mean — I played with your tit. Do you know how many guys on campus would have died to do that?"

"No guy on campus has ever done that, DH. I don't know what got into me, but I just had to let you do it. You didn't force it on me, I'm the one who grabbed your hand and put it there."

"That's what surprised me the most, and just for the record, I would never have turned you in to the principal. You're a great teacher, and I like you very much," I said.

"I like you too," she said, smiling warmly. "And thinking back on it, I'm not sorry about what I did."

I smiled back at her. "I'm not either. My only regret is that I didn't get a chance to do it again."

"It's never too late to try for seconds." Then she reached behind my head, pulled me toward her, and kissed me. This time I wasn't worried about the consequences; she's no longer my teacher, I'm no longer in high school, I have no real relationship with anyone right now, I'll be eighteen soon, and I'm getting ready to go to college. Quite frankly, Mrs. Collard can do anything she wants to me.

"Aren't you afraid someone will see you kissing me?" I asked when we separated.

"Why should I be?" she said. "I don't know anyone here at RCC, I'm not your teacher any more, and there isn't that big of a distance between our ages — I'm only twenty-nine."

"But why me?" I asked hoarsely, still wondering what in the world attracts such a woman to me.

"Because you're different." She smiled and patted my cheek.

"What do you mean?"

"Look at your friend, Manny," she said. She dropped her seductive manner for a more conversational tone. "He was in one of my classes last semester. He's a great guy, but look at what he holds dear in life — a rock band? What kind of conversations do you have when you two just sit around and talk?"

"Usually we talk about his band, or some of the famous rock stars."

"What does Manny read when he isn't reading assigned school books?"

"I don't see him reading much, but when he does, it's usually comic books."

"What's his biggest goal in life?"

"I suppose he wants to be a rock star. He's a great drummer."

"Doesn't he play classical piano?"

"I'm not really sure about that," I said. "He never talks about it, and I've never seen a piano in his house."

"Well, he mentioned it to me, and he also told me he'd rather be a rock star." She shook her head. "You see, that's what I'm talking about. Look at all the guys you hang with, what do they hold up as the gold standard for personal development and achievement for their lives? You don't have to answer that." She grinned and held up her hand to stop me from speaking. "Then look at yourself. What do you dream about? What do you like to talk about? What books are you reading?"

I thought about that for a moment. "I'm reading several books. One about Florentine art during the Renaissance; another about the possibility of interstellar communication that got me thinking about utilizing light as an energy source to send messages beyond our solar system; another on Egyptian mysticism and how it interrelates with the various hieroglyphs in the Pyramids of Giza, I'm starting to get into Jack Kerouac and some of the Beats …"

"See what I mean? Do you realize that most of the guys graduating from high school today are mental midgets? If you were a girl, who would you rather go out with, one of those guys, or a DH?"

"But what about our age difference? You say it isn't much of a difference, but isn't there a problem with that? Doesn't age make a difference? You have eleven years of experience on me."

"And how old are those pyramids you're studying?"

"Thousands of years. No one knows for sure," I told her.

"Do you really think then, that eleven years means all that much in the whole scope of all eternity?"

"Well, since you put it that way …"

"I could give you a hundred reasons why I'd rather hang out with you than with men my own age. It doesn't really matter what their ages are, they're just children who like to play children's games, like football and basketball. They like to cuss and go to bars and laugh at dumb jokes, and at the end of the date, all they want to do is come into my house and have sex."

"I guess I get it." I was still a bit baffled by her candor. Unable to think of anything else to say, I asked lamely, "So you don't like having sex?"

"Of course I do!" She laughed good-naturedly. "Why do you think I pulled my tit out for you? I would have let you bend me over the table behind that screen if somebody hadn't come into the room." She seemed lost in that thought for a moment, then she shook her head. "But I don't want to have sex with a guy who'll be thinking about who's gonna win the next basketball tournament while we're doing it. The reason I let you grab me that day was because of who you really are—the person I see you to be on the inside. I wanted to get the first move over so that maybe you and I could get together more often. The next move would have been to ask you out for coffee. If that went well, we would have gone to the park for a chat."

"You had all that planned out?" I asked.

"I did." She smiled. "Usually I wait till the fourth date, after I'm sure I'll be doing it with a guy who's paying attention to me and not to the LA Lakers. But in your case, I knew right away."

"Well ..." I didn't know what to say.

"Besides just sex, I think you'd be a lot of fun to hang around with. I guess that's really the bottom line." She smiled again, and this time it was an offer of genuine friendship.

"This is certainly something I wasn't expecting."

"I wasn't expecting it either, that's why it feels so right to me. And I'm not talking about living together or anything like that. Just hang together when we get a chance. Doing things together."

There was one more thing that bothered me, though. "I have to ask you one question."

"Ask away."

"Mrs. Collard, aren't you married?" I asked bluntly.

"Ha! I wondered when you'd ask that, and I would have been disappointed had you not. No, I am not married. I've never been married. Whenever I get a job, I sign on as Mrs., not Miss, because I don't want all the guys hitting on me. If they think I'm married, most of them stay away."

"Very clever." I said. "I'll bet you get your share of guys."

"I do, but it's only because of my looks and not my mind. I don't like that and I don't want that."

"It's a guy thing," I told her. "Guys always see the surface first and sometimes that's all they really care about." I raised my hands in self-defense. "Just being honest."

"Still one more reason to like you," she said. "And you like poetry! Most guys don't. They make fun of it."

"Speaking of poetry, I wonder why Manny's not here. He's late."

"If he doesn't show up you and I can sit together." She grinned at me. "It can be our first date."

"One thing I need to clarify before we get any deeper into this bizarre little liaison," I said.

"What's that?'

"Do I keep calling you Mrs. Collard?"

"No way. My name is Jan. Call me Jan from now on, and I hope you call me often." She kissed me on the cheek. "I have a feeling you and I can learn many new things from each other."

"You might be right about that. I'm afraid I'm new to all this relationship stuff. I've only dated a couple of girls and they were totally different from you."

"I hope that's a compliment."

"It is. But as far as a woman's body is concerned, and her likes and dislikes, I'm afraid I'm really a novice."

"That may be one of the things I get to teach you. After the reading maybe you and I can go somewhere and explore a few possibilities." For a brief moment, the seductive smile was back.

◎ ◎ ◎

Manny never showed up. I have no idea where he was or why he couldn't make it; he probably just forgot. I'll bet he calls me tomorrow and begs my forgiveness.

Jan and I went to the reading and it turned out to be exactly what I expected it would be. There were three readers reading their own poetry. The first one was a girl from RCC. She was dressed like a beatnik and her poetry was terrible. It was a mixture of styles and themes that came out sounding like something Edgar Allen Poe and Allen Ginsberg might have collaborated on and thrown away.

The second reader was another RCC student. He wore Levis and a black t-shirt and tried hard to look like James Dean. A number of people in the audience found that comical and could barely control their snickering during his reading. His poetry was better than the first girl, but I found it a bit boring. He was going for Beat, but it just seemed like a hodge-podge of stuff he might have thrown together at the last minute.

The third, a girl from UCR, was the best of the three, but she spoiled it—in my opinion—by throwing a curse word or two or a lewd reference into every line just for the shock value. That seems to be a popular game in poetry and art these days—it ain't about the message or the talent any more, it's about the shock and politics and each artist or poet is trying to be more shocking than the ones before. Ho hum … boring.

Jan and I are seated back at the same table we occupied before the reading. The reading was the last event of the evening, and the campus has shut down, so The Pit is deserted.

Jan's looking over my shoulder and reading every word as I write. She seems to be getting a kick out of my determination to relate all the details of a simple encounter with a woman in a college eating area. To me, though, there's nothing simple about it. Bizarre would be the best word I can think of to describe the situation.

"So you think I'm bizarre," Jan says after reading that line.

"No, this little scenario we find ourselves in is bizarre."

"What's really bizarre is that you just wrote down your own words as you spoke them to me." She grinned. "You sure can write quickly."

"It's a talent of mine." I smile.

Jan leans against me and reads more. "So, do you think that first girl from RCC was really a Beat?" she whispers into my ear.

"Well, it might surprise you to learn that I've had some experience with the Beat Generation recently, and my best guess is that she's not the real thing, just a wannabe. Her poetry sucked. If she were to take it up to San Francisco, the real Beats would call her a beatnik and probably order her out of The City."

"She was pretty bad," Jan agreed. "How do you know so much about the Beat Generation?"

"I've been interested in it for a while now, but I recently met a girl who seems to be the real thing. She's told me a lot about it. Her mother's a real live Beat who knows all the famous Beat personalities up in San Francisco."

"Really? You mean Ginsberg and all those guys?" Jan was impressed.

"Yep, all the biggies. In fact, she and her mother left for The City earlier today. They may be up there right now having dinner with Jack Kerouac for all I know."

"Wow! Wouldn't that be something," she said. "So, is this girl a serious interest in your life?"

"Do you really want me to be honest with you?" I ask.

"Of course I do."

"I like her a lot, and I can almost see a long term relationship as a possibility with her, but at the same time I'm kind of scared of her."

"Why's that?"

"She's been around the block a few times. She's had some pretty wild experiences in her life, and known some pretty wild people. I also believe that if I don't agree to jump headfirst into the Beat scene up north she'll just evaporate from my life and look for somebody else. She's never told me that to my face, but I have a sense it might play out that way."

"It's hard to hang on to someone like that," Jan says. "It's not like you're dating them—it's more like you're trying to keep up with them so they don't trot off into the sunset without you."

"That's exactly what I feel. I'm sure she doesn't think this, but when I'm with her, I'm always concerned about what I say, or how I react to what she says. It's just not as comfortable as I'd like it to be."

"So what are you going to do about her?"

"I'm not sure. She may never come back, Her mother's boyfriend is a real jerk, and they don't have much to come back here for."

"How long have you known this girl?"

"Just a few days, really. That's why I hesitate to call it a true relationship."

"A few days isn't a relationship. Weeks maybe, but not days." She smiles sympathetically. "You know, I remember you once mentioning in class that you're interested in art. Is that still a thing in your head?"

"Yes it is. I've been seriously contemplating all the possibilities of what I want to be when I grow up." I smile. "Art is on the list, but I doubt it'll be a real profession for me — it's a difficult scene to break into — but there's something about it that really intrigues me. I signed up for a few art classes here at RCC, and I bought a sketchpad. I'm drawing every chance I get."

"Have you drawn any pictures of your Beat Girl?"

"A few, but I didn't keep any of them. They just weren't any good so I threw them all away."

She smiles. "Maybe that's a sign. I'll bet you can draw pictures of me and not end up throwing them away."

"I'm pretty sure I can."

Jan pulled me over and kissed me. She made me put down my pen for a while so my hands could roam around on her body. "You need to memorize every inch of me if you expect to paint my portrait," she told me.

"Are there any inches that are off limits to me?" I asked?

"None, and I expect you to explore all of them very carefully, very slowly."

I was considering the possibilities when she whispered, "Have you ever gotten intimate with a girl in a public place?"

"You mean go all the way with them?"

"Yes."

"No. I haven't."

"Follow me."

5 FRIDAY

Catching up

Jan took my hand and led me up the steps of The Pit and into the tree-filled square at the center of the Quad.

"I noticed a secluded spot over there when I was crossing the courtyard earlier this evening," she said as she pulled me along. We soon left the walkway and cut across the lawn toward a thick clump of trees and shrubs in a dark corner opposite The Pit. It was, indeed, very private, and she got right down to the business of teaching me a lesson that I've never seen on any English class syllabus.

After "class" we found our cars in the parking lot and Jan followed me back to my house. I showed her into the family room where we could sit and talk in comfort, and then I went out to The Hole to get the jug of wine I keep out there.

"Do you have any big glasses?" Jan asked when I came back with the wine.

"Yep," I answered from the kitchen. I passed over the wine glasses I had been reaching for and pulled two large mugs out of the cupboard instead.

I handed her a mug and watched amazed as she downed at least half of it in one swallow. She let out a little sigh of satisfaction and said, "That's better—I haven't had any wine all day. This'll loosen me up a bit." She smiled.

"You seemed loose enough back there in the Quad behind the bushes," I said.

"I don't mean that kind of loose," she said. "For talk about the deeper things in life. A glass or two of wine loosens my brain—opens me up to new ideas and makes me more creative."

"Wine does that for me too, although I have a limit."

She took another deep drink of her wine and looked around the room. "So, your parents are away on a trip and you have the place to yourself for a few days," she said.

"They are, and I do."

"What can we do that would make the most of that time and opportunity?"

"You could strip naked, and I could put you up on a pedestal and just sit and stare at you," I suggested.

"You know, for someone who professes to be so young and inexperienced, you can say some of the cleverest things." She smiled. "You haven't really seen me naked, though—just a part of me here and there."

"It was dark back there under the trees."

"Well, where's your sketch book?"

"Out in The Hole." I smiled.

"The what?"

"I'll tell you about it when I get back," I said on my way out the door.

I returned to find her standing stark naked in the middle of the kitchen, her magnificent figure illuminated by the bright lights of the overhead fluorescent fixtures. Every part of her—her full pink-nippled breasts, smooth stomach, wide hips, strong shapely legs—in perfect proportion to every other part. As I stood there gawking at her, she began to turn slowly so that I could see all of her. The back was as beautiful as the front.

"I thought the light would be better here in the kitchen." Jan smiled as she came around to face me again. "Don't start drawing yet. Just watch."

She then began to pose for me, moving gracefully from one position to the next, opening up all of her hidden chambers and sharing every part of her with me. I told her to bring her mug and follow me. I led her into the large living room and settled down to draw her while she continued to pose. She turned out to have quite an imagination. I wound up with sketches of her in front of the fireplace, on top of the fireplace, sitting in the window, laying on the floor, sitting in chairs, and in a few creative and challenging positions that I would probably never see in a college art class—but I can't be sure of that since I haven't had any of those classes yet.

The whole time though, I'm thinking of Abby—I'm still crazy about her. I know I told Jan that I wasn't sure about her, but even with Jan dancing naked in front of me, I wondered what Abby was doing, what's she thinking, who's she with. I wished I was there with her. I should have gone with her. Damn. She promised to call me when she got the chance, but she's gonna be movin' around a lot up there, and I'll be in and out down here, so it'll be hard to touch bases by phone. When is somebody gonna invent a portable phone that you can put in your pocket and carry with you everywhere you go? We've got battery-operated razors, radios, even vibrators. It just doesn't make that sense we're still using these clunky old black things plugged into the wall.

The evening got later, and the level of wine in the jug went down. I drank my fair share, but it seemed that for every two or three sips that I took, Jan drank a mug full. At about one o'clock when I was finishing a sketch of her lying on the floor I realized that she wasn't posing—she had passed out. I got a blanket from my parents' bedroom and covered her up. Since there was nothing else to do, I got a blanket for myself and went to sleep on the floor next to her.

The moaning awakened me at around eight o'clock this morning. I opened my eyes just in time to see her rush into the bathroom, her disappearance followed by further sounds of distress. I went into the bathroom to make sure she was OK, and found her buck-naked on her knees in front of the porcelain throne.

"Ooh," she moaned, her head wobbling. "I never could take red wine."

"You took quite a bit last night," I said. "But if it's any consolation it looks like most of it's in the toilet now."

She reached up and flushed it, "Can you hand me a towel?" she said weakly.

I did better than that. I ran cold water over a washcloth, rung it out, and handed it to her.

"Help me up," she whimpered after she had wiped her face.

I took her arm and lifted her nearly dead weight up to a standing position. I held onto her to keep her from crumbling to the floor, led her to the sink, and turned on the cold water. She bent over to splash water on her face and to drink from her cupped hands while I stood behind her with my arms wrapped around her to support her. She made a small noise and snuggled against me like a sleepy puppy. "Don't let go of me," she said. "Just stay right there for awhile. It makes me feel much better."

So I stayed right there for a while. And when the while was over I helped her back to the living room where she sat down cross-legged in front of the fireplace, holding her head in her hands as if it would fall off if she let go.

"I guess I'm not making a very good impression this morning," she said. "And I probably ruined the evening by passing out like that."

"It was late—one in the morning," I told her.

"And I was beyond drunk." She took a deep breath and looked at me sadly. "I guess now you know my darkest secret. I'm a pretty heavy drinker."

"We were having a party," I said. "People drink at parties."

"I know, but I'm like this even when there isn't a party. You remember that day I kissed you in the classroom?"

Do I ever. "I'll never forget it."

"I was drunk then, too. That's probably why I took that chance I took to kiss you. My guard was down."

"You mean it wasn't my good looks?"

"That too." She smiled. "But just before you came into class I'd already had a goodly amount of vodka from a flask I keep in my purse."

"Wow, at school? How come I didn't smell it on you?" I asked.

"There are ways to cover up the odor. I ate a couple of mints when you weren't looking, and had you noticed it, I would have said that I used some mouth wash just before you came in. Besides, a student like you doesn't expect to smell alcohol on a teacher like me, so you are less likely to notice."

"Are you telling me that you were drunk in that class all last year?"

"I was drunk in every class — not stumbling drunk, obviously, but I drank enough throughout the day to keep up a good buzz. I'm what they call a functional drunk. I've been drinking so long and I drink so much that it almost looks like I'm normal when I'm three sheets to the wind."

"I never would have guessed," I told her honestly.

"Nobody has ever guessed. I've been drunk at teacher meetings, school activities — you name it. I even got stuck in a few meetings in the principal's office when I was higher than a kite. It's a miracle no one has ever noticed. I would have been canned for sure."

"Well, your little secret is safe with me."

"Thank you." We sat there without speaking, each of us lost in our own thoughts for a moment. Then she kind of shook herself and said, "You know I think it's best I go right now."

"Don't you want to hang around and have some breakfast first?"

"I'd love to, but my senses are telling me I need to go home and straighten myself out." She tried to get up off the floor but seemed to have some difficulty getting her feet under her, so I stood to give her a hand.

"Are you sure you can drive?" I asked. I was genuinely concerned.

"Are you kidding? I'll just swallow a little mouthwash and hit the road. I haven't gotten a ticket yet."

We wandered back into the family room where we found her clothes still laying in a rumpled heap where she'd tossed them last night. I had to help her put her clothes on because her balance was pretty much nonexistent. When she got herself together we walked through the kitchen into the breezeway. Before she went out to her car, she turned to face me. She took both of my hands, guided them around her and placed them under her skirt and firmly onto her bare bottom. Then she kissed me deeply. "I hope this is not something that finishes our relationship. I'm really pretty embarrassed by it," she said as she released me.

"Of course not," I said. "Don't be embarrassed for being who you are. But you might want to be careful driving like that."

"I'll be very careful," she said as we continued out to her car. She opened the door then paused before she got in. She looked up at me and said, "Can we get together again sometime, and maybe make up for this?"

"I think so," I assured her. "You have my number."

She dug into her purse and pulled out a crumpled piece of paper. Handing it to me, she said, "And here's mine. I wrote it down for you last night and almost forgot to give it to you."

Then she got into her car, and drove off to get herself back together. She said she was going home, but I'm not sure about that.

So, that's that. Jan is, in all probability, history for me. The way she asked me if we could get together again—her eyes downcast, avoiding mine—made it seem like a Dear John moment. In a way, though, I'm kind of relieved. My entire experience with Jan going back to that classroom kiss has been a little too bizarre, even for me. I think it's a good thing that I'm probably never going to see her again. We did exchange phone numbers though, so maybe ....

I don't know what to do. The whole time I had my hands on Jan's bottom back there in the breezeway, and the whole time she was kissing me, I was thinking not of her, but of Abby, and wishing it was Abby's bottom that I was fondling.

Manny is supposed to call me, so I'm catching up on my journal entries while I wait for the phone to ring. The band has a gig coming up at the auditorium downtown and Manny wants me to sit in while they run through the tunes they'll be playing. The event will be open to the public so it'll be good exposure and an opportunity for some much needed publicity. There might even be a scout or two in the audience. Riverside is halfway between Hollywood and Palm Springs, and you never know who will be stopping off along the way looking for fresh talent. Just look at the Beatles — I think they started out in a bar in a basement. They were nothin', and they seem to have worked out okay.

I still haven't heard from Abby; I wonder what she's doing right now. She said she'd only be gone for a few days, but I'm afraid she'll love it up there and want to stay. It's gotta be like home for her there with all her Beat friends and family, especially compared to her depressing situation here in Riverside — that slimy worm of a man, Billy, her mother's low income, and Abby out of work. Besides Mam, she has few friends that she's really comfortable with. She told me that there was very little here for her.

But that was before she and I really got to know each other. Was that only a few days ago? I feel like I've known her forever. I like to think that I mean something to her, but that's probably a pipe dream. When I stack up all the pros and cons of San Francisco against all the pros and cons of Riverside, I still come up with, *Don't hold your breath*, even with me on the Riverside end.

I can see her face even now as I write these words. Sometimes, Abby wears this black, crocheted beret. Her bangs hang out from under the front of it, and her big, heavily-mascaraed eyes peek out from under the bangs. The way she looks up at me with a tiny bit of a smile on her lips and a hint of a dimple on her soft cheeks drives me wild. I can see her as clearly as if she were here with me right now.

I happen to be sitting out here on the porch swing where Abby and I sat before she left. The weather is almost identical to the way it was then — of course it is; it's summer in Riverside. The touch of the warm breeze brings my memory of Abby to life; I can almost smell her as if she were here right beside me. Have I mentioned how Abby smells? I'm not sure I can describe it. I know it's a cliché to say a girl smells like flowers, particularly roses, but I have to come up with something — maybe not roses, but some other flower. I don't really know much about flowers though, other than that they're pretty and colorful and I love them, and I certainly couldn't tell you what kind of flower Abby smells like. Just think of the sweetest, best smelling flower you ever smelled in your life and call it that. The odd thing is, though, Abby says she never wears any perfume. She doesn't wear any scented products at all, not even deodorant. Could it be her underarms that I'm smelling? Could it be that she's so perfect in every way that even her armpits smell like flowers. Wow! That's what I call a saint! Saint Abby. I wonder if the Catholics already have a St. Abby? I'm pretty sure there's a St. Abigail, I think she's Irish, but I'm not sure if Abby's short for Abigail … hmmm … and Abby's at least part German, not exactly sure what the rest of her is, whatever it is, it's Beat Hot.

RIIIIIIIING!

Could that be Abby?

It was Manny. Damn. I was hoping it was Abby. I still haven't heard from her. Manny and the band are ready to start practicing and he wants me to be there from the beginning so that I can give them a full critique. But if I'm gone from my phone Abby's liable to call and I'll miss her call. I don't know what the heck to do. Damn. Here's where that porta-phone would come in handy.

Manny's Garage • 5 PM

I'm sitting in a folding chair in the middle of the garage—an audience of one. The guys told me not to move the chair because it's in the perfect spot to appreciate the performance. I look like a real big shot, like a band scout. I just need a cigar and a glass of champagne to complete the picture, but the tuna sandwich and cup of Red Mountain that Manny just handed me will have to do. He's up on the stage turning some screws on his drum heads—I guess that makes them taut or something. Paul's tuning his bass and Burt's playin' riffs on his guitar. Pet, who does most of the lead singing, is in front of the stage doing a little jazz dance to Burt's riffs while sipping wine from a cup. She looks good when she dances. She looks good when she stands still. It really doesn't matter what Pet's doing, she's gonna look good. She's wearing one of those tank top things — low cut and tight so that her boobs burst out at the top. Her boob skin is very white, almost blinding to the eye. A guy can't help but stare at those things even at the risk of losing his sight. She just looked over and threw a big grin at me. I think she noticed that I was staring at her. That's okay; I'm sure she's used to guys ogling her.

"Let's go!" Manny yells from the back of the porta-stage. "We got a lot to do here tonight. Tomorrow night's the biggie."

"You really think it'll be a big deal?" Paul asks, apprehensive as usual.

"A bigger deal than any other deal we've had," Manny replies.

"We're not only getting paid," Burt says, "but the audience will be huge and there just might be a scout in the crowd."

"You never know," Manny says, optimistic as usual.

"Money!" Pet yells, then sings out a line from the Beatles' song,
"Give me mooooney
That's what I want, yeah."
"Let's do it!" Manny says and starts pounding out the beat to a song he's just written. Pet bounds up onto the stage, wine cup in hand, grabs the microphone off its stand, and starts belting out the tune.

She sounds good — a little like Lesley Gore, only I think she has a bit more range. Pet's delivery is smoother and her transitions are a little cleaner. Not that Lesley isn't good, but she's a pop singer. Manny's band is all about rock. I think the hottest female singer out there is Helen Shapiro. She's a pop singer, too, but no one else has that deep, rich voice. Pet is every bit a rock singer, and she's right here in front of me bouncin' her stuff in my direction with a big smile on her face. I have no idea where Lesley or Helen are, but I'll bet neither one of them know I exist.

Pet goes on and on, singing and prancing around the stage, slurping wine between lines when she can, spilling half of it down into her cleavage. She follows that up with a weird gyration that looks like she's trying to lick the wine off her boobs, never missing a beat. I'm telling you, they could make a fortune selling tickets just to watch Pet. The song is really good, too, which makes the show even better. I wish that Manny had more original tunes for the Riders to do at their concerts. It's okay to do stuff by other guys, but you don't make it big unless you write your own. The songs that Manny has written are pretty good, but so far he's been reluctant to perform them in public. Maybe tomorrow night? It's too bad he can't bring in a portable piano. I've not heard him play yet, but his mother, Hester, says that he's incredible. The band does have a little keyboard, but it hasn't worked in months. They should get it fixed. Pet knows how to play it, and it would really add to the professional look of the band.

They've finished the song and the guys are chatting about the performance. Pet hopped off the stage and headed over to get more wine, passing by me along the way. She's stopped in front of me and stooped over, putting her boobs in front my face.

"Lick the wine off, little boy," she says in a little girl's voice.

I look up at her face and smile, accepting her dare. I take one lick, burying my tongue in her cleavage. She smiles back at me and walks away to refill her cup. Pet can be a nut job sometimes, but I like that; you never know what to expect out of her.

"How'd it sound, DH?" Manny asks, raising his voice so I can hear him from the stage.

"Once you got into it, not bad."

"Whattaya mean?" he asks.

"You didn't have a smooth kickoff. You all started off at different times and had to struggle a bit to bring it all together," I explain.

"I noticed that, too," Pet says, walking back to join the others.

"Okay—" Manny says.

Before Manny can say anything about how to deal with the issue,

Burt speaks up. "They're right. We do that a lot. We need to get it together from the very beginning. We need to concentrate and come together as a group, an organism, and quit doing our own thing all the time."

Actually, Burt is the one most likely to be out of sync.

"Alright," Manny says. "I agree. We're way too loose. Let's do it again, and tighten it up this time!"

Manny's Backyard • 8 PM

They played that song over and over until they got it right, then they rehearsed the rest of the songs they'll be playing tomorrow night. They've got a pretty good program lined up, and I think that Manny's original will be a stand out number — the highlight of the show.

They're just hanging around now in the garage, relaxing after their hard work and going over some of the final details of the show tomorrow. I enjoy Manny's company when it's just him and me, and I'm flattered that he thinks enough of my opinion to ask me to sit in on these rehearsals, but I just can't get into all the details of the music, the performance, what the other bands are doing, who's hot and who's not — I'm just not into it and all that chatter gets on my nerves. These guys live it and breathe it and I guess they really have to if they want to make it to the big time. I hope they do make it big. At least then they would be able to afford a better place to practice. They've got the garage set up as best they can, but they have to keep the big door closed, and there are no windows, so it can get pretty stuffy in there, even when they leave the small back door open. It doesn't help that they all smoke. Sometimes it can get pretty thick in there — like now — and my asthma kicks in. When that happens, I step out to the back yard so I can breath.

So I'm sitting on a lawn chair out under Manny's big tree, suckin' up the (relatively) clean California summer air. It's a warm evening, and I can smell orange blossoms, or possibly honeysuckle or maybe it's jasmine — they all kinda smell the same and I haven't got a clue which is which, I just know it smells sweet and I like it.

The moon is up and there are a few clouds in the sky. I heard a weather report on the car radio while I was driving over here that said we might get a little rain tonight. That would be nice; it hardly ever rains here in the summer. I wish it would. The trees get really dusty through the summer months and a good storm can clean them all up and make them sparkle like new. Rain also helps to wash some of the smog out of the air. I've noticed that the smog is getting worse every summer—that bothers my breathing, too. Sometimes I have to use my inhaler two or three times in the course of any evening. So far I've only used it once tonight. I'd like to see those clouds build up and give us a good downpour.

It's quiet out here. It's amazing how even an active neighborhood like Manny's can seem perfectly quiet and calm after sitting in a small garage for a couple of hours listening to a rock band. I think I've written this before somewhere, but I can't imagine living next door to one of these bands. I'd go crazy if I had to listen to this stuff all the time, yet, these little groups pop up all over the place these days and nobody seems to object—at least not effectively. There are two or three in Manny's subdivision alone, and I can't even guess how many are in Riverside all together. I'm just glad my parents bought their house out in the country away from all the cacophony.

A light just came on in the house. Manny's mom, Hester, and his sister, Shanie, are both at home. Shanie's a year younger than Manny, so she's got one more year of high school. I have no idea what she wants to be when she grows up. She seems pretty smart, makes straight A's and is involved in a lot of school stuff like the science club, interclub council, and student body government. I think she's even in the concert choir. She's one of those girls who wants to do it all, and I think she's got a good chance to get what she wants one day.

Shanie's a cute little thing—blonde, kinda thin with long lanky legs, and a really nice face. The face is what makes it for me with a girl. If the face is nice I don't really care what the rest looks like.

Notice that I say a nice face and not a pretty face. That's because I don't necessarily agree with our current culture's definition of a pretty female face. Just look at the typical beauty pageant contestant—long face, big mouth, with perfectly straight teeth, long oh-so-elegant nose, eyes that are so perfectly sized, matched and placed that they could have been made by a machine and then pasted onto the woman's face. They all look the same. Even the hairdos are the same, just different colors. How boring is that? I think a few flaws and a little asymmetry make a girl a bit more intriguing. Abby has that space between her front teeth that forms a kind of triangle; I like that a lot. And her eyes are huge with the outside corners tipping downward giving her a kind of mystical look. I've heard that people with large wide-set eyes are often psychic. Is that true? Saints usually have large eyes don't they?

Where is she? Where is my Abby?

The light that came on a few minutes ago is in Hester's bedroom. The curtains are open and I can see her walking back and forth like she might be getting ready to do something. It's still early, so I doubt she's going to bed. The window is large, so she is plainly visible all the way down to about her mid-thigh. She's stopped in front of the mirror—one of those large, round ones like you see on antique dressers. She's doing something with her hair—fluffing it up in the back, combing it down, fluffing it up again. She's put down the comb and now she's fiddling with something in front of her—I can't make out what it is. She's turning around now. Oh boy, she was apparently unbuttoning her blouse. She's taking it off and it looks like she's laying it on her bed. She seems to be making quite a project out of the simple task—leaning over, smoothing it out, folding it up—her large boobs hanging heavy in front of her the whole time, oozing out over the top of her white bra. My reward for sitting through all that loud rock music?

I don't know about Hester. Every time I come over here she manages to present me with some sort of titillating surprise—a skimpy outfit, an exposed butt cheek, or a breast about to escape from a bra or shirt. Are these all accidents? Does she know where I am at all times, and wait for the perfect moment to spring them on me? She never really goes all the way, like letting a total breast fall out, nipple and all, or walking around completely naked in the back yard while hanging up her clothes. It's always just an entice-ment of sorts. A tempting. A teasing. If she's doing it on purpose she's damn good at it.

She's turned her back to the window and is facing the mirror again. She's reaching up in back and unhooking her bra. This could be it! The bra is off, but she's not turning around. She's looking at herself in the mirror but she's positioned herself so that I can't see her full reflection. Suddenly she turns left and walks away, briefly showing me her profile including a glimpse of a large white tit before the light goes off. See what I mean? So close! She had to know I was out here. She had to have planned that little scenario.

The back door just opened and Hester is standing there yelling for Manny. She's holding a towel in front of her so she must be naked behind the towel. "Manny!" she yells again.

"He's in the garage. I don't think he can hear you." I call out to her.

"DH? Is that you?"

"Yes. Hi," I say.

"I don't really want Manny," she says. "I want you."

"Really?" I reply, with just a little apprehension.

"Yes. You need to come in. You have a phone call."

"What? A phone call? From who?"

"Some girl named Abby. She said she's calling from San Fran-cisco. Do you want to take it or not?"

"Yes!" I say, knocking over the lawn chair in my haste to get to the phone. "Yes I want to take it. How'd she get your number?"

"I don't know," Hester says with a smile like a Cheshire cat.

Hester held the door open and I rushed past her into the living room. The phone with the receiver lying beside it was on a table next to the couch.

I picked up the receiver, and as I turned to sit down on the couch

I caught a glimpse of Hester walking slowly back down the hall. She was holding the towel around her so that it flapped open in the back with every step she took, flashing full views of her butt like images from a time-lapse movie. An accident? For me, at that moment, it wasn't even a minor distraction. All of my attention was focused on a face four hundred miles away.

"Abby?" I say.

Ten Minutes Later

It was long distance so we didn't talk long. Also, Hester kept walking in and out of the room. I couldn't tell if she was trying to distract me with her little show, or if she was eavesdropping. Either way, she made it difficult for me to tell Abby some of the things I really wanted to tell her. It was good to hear Abby's voice, though. She actually said she missed me! That was nice. I was worried that she'd get up to The City and fall back into her old Beat life with all of her old Beat friends, and that I'd be just a fading memory. So far, though, she's seen very few of the old crew. Her mother has been busy helping her aunt paint some of the rooms at her motel and Abby's been hanging with them all this time. They've been having a lot fun listening to jazz music and drinking, as Abby put it, "good wine". Allen Ginsberg popped in on them a couple times. Abby's aunt wanted to paint all the walls white so they'd show off all the crazy art she's collected over the years, but Allen wasn't having it. He called her some sorta Jewish name and told her she needed to break out of her birdcage, or something like that, and left in a huff. He came back in about an hour with three gallons of paint, one each of red, yellow, and blue, and instructed her aunt to, "Paint the damned walls white, but do the trim with these!" Then he went out to his car and came back with a grocery bag full of popcorn. He turned on the TV in the motel lobby, sat down, and watched an old movie while the three ladies painted.

Abby told me that she not only misses me, but she misses me a lot and she wishes I'd have gone up to The City with her. I told her I wish I had too, and I meant it. It would have been a whole lot better than hanging with Manny. Even better than watching Hester flop around half dressed, since there's nothing I can really do about that any way.

I told Abby how much I miss her, then she said she thought she might be falling in love with me cause even though we were hundreds of miles apart and she was doing fun things with her family, all she could think about was the times we already had together down here. She told me she wanted to wake up in bed with me with her legs wrapped around my waist and her arms around my chest. I told her that would be nice, and after I told her that, I realized how simplistic my words sounded.

We had reached that awkward point in a conversation where you've said just about all you can say, but you don't want to stop talking. I finally said, "I miss the hell out of you, when are you coming back?"

"It's gonna be another two or three days. Mom wants to help Auntie finish painting the motel."

"Three days?" I moaned. "That long?"

"Auntie has fifteen units and we're doing seven of them. It takes time to paint just one."

"I'm sure it does." I tried to put a smile in my voice. "That's okay. I'm not going anywhere. I'll be here when you get back."

"What have you been doing while I'm gone. Did you sleep with Mam?"

"What?"

"You know one of the reasons I'm falling in love with you?" she asked.

"Tell me," I said, just a little worried.

"I called Mam yesterday, and she told me all about her coming over to your house and trying to get nasty with you. Don't worry, I'm not mad about that. She does that all the time. But she told me she spent the night there, and when she came on to you the next morning, you turned her down and told her you missed me.

Did you really tell her you were getting hooked on me?"

"I think those were my exact words," I said.

"Well, I'm getting hooked on you too." She sounded sad and so far away.

"I can't wait to get you back here," I said.

"Soon," she told me. "I need to get off here now. This is long distance."

"I know. Okay. Please take care, have fun with your Aunt, but get home safe to me."

"I will," she replied in a sweet whisper. "Bye."

And that was the end of the call. I hung up the phone and started to walk back out to the garage just as Hester whipped back into the room. She was now wearing a short skirt and the bra I had seen her take off earlier.

"Oh my!" she said, making a token effort to cover her cleavage. "I didn't know you were still in here."

Fat chance. "I just finished. It's getting late. I thought I'd say goodnight to Manny and head on home. Tomorrow's the big night for the band." I smiled.

"I hope they do good." She smiled back, this time with motherly pride in her son's talent and achievement. "I'm really pulling for them."

"It's nice of you to let them practice in your garage all the time," I said.

"I don't mind parking my old bucket out front, and who knows, maybe they'll become famous some day and buy me a bigger house." She laughed, relaxing and dropping her arms, no longer pretending to hide her bra-covered breasts.

"I hope so." I smile and turn toward the door.

"Here, I'll get that for you, it sticks sometimes," Hester said.

She reaches over for the door, making sure her breasts brush my arm as she does. It's a long reach, so I get one heck of a view of those great globes when she places them right in front of me. She pulls the door open with almost no effort. Sticky door, huh?

"Come back soon," she said as I squeezed past her. "I think you're a good influence for Manny. I like having you around." She smiled, and not in a motherly way.

A good influence for Manny, or someone she can have around to practice on? Surely she isn't really interested in me — I'm her son's friend from school. I think she likes putting me in uncomfortable positions and watching me sweat. It may be just a game, but she knows exactly what she's doing.

I opened the small back door to the garage and poked my head in to yell good-bye to the band. They all still had their heads together talking over everything for tomorrow's performance. Manny was the only one to look over at me.

He waved and yelled back at me, "Don't be late tomorrow! Be at the auditorium by six so we can get set up."

I told him I'd be there, then I got into my little Bug and headed off for home.

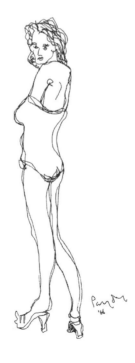

6 SATURDAY NIGHT

The Big Concert

The night of the Big Concert has passed into history; a rare chance for the Riders to receive the notice they so justly deserve. They really did make an impression—I'm just not sure what kind. Just kidding. It was a real hoot.

We arrived at the auditorium right at six, and immediately started to set up. There were lots of wires to unwrap, string out, and plug in; amps to set up, guitars to tune, and drums to assemble, but they've done this dozens of times at smaller venues so everyone knew exactly what to do. The biggest challenge was placing the amps and adjusting the volume levels for the big auditorium. Manny also insisted on bringing along the broken keyboard and setting it up as well. It did help fill up some of the space on the big stage.

By 6:45, I was seated in a chair on the main floor of the auditorium, listening to the band warm up and watching the people trickle in for the show that was due to start in about thirty minutes. The band looked great. The guys were all dressed in that Carnaby Street style like the Beatles wear. It looks kinda corny when you see people around here just wearing it out on the street, but I have to agree with Manny that it makes the band stand out and look bigger than life, as he put it. Pet had disappeared after all the equipment was onstage and set up. When she showed up again, she was wearing a long, bright pink satin dress and she looked like a million bucks. The top was cut low—almost down to her belly button—and outlined with a wide white frill, and the skirt was slit up to her thigh on one side. No matter which way she moved, something was gonna hang out somewhere before the night was over. I decided to move to a seat in the center front row while I still could.

I had dressed as I always do: in a black t-shirt, old jeans, and tennis shoes. At Manny's insistence, I was also wearing a faded black sport coat of his. He said it made me look cool. Since I'm not in the band, I figured it wouldn't make any difference what I looked like.

About twenty minutes before show time, Manny came down to talk to me.

"Okay, we're on in a few minutes. You ready?" he asked.

I looked up at him and smiled. "I'm pretty comfy down here in front. If you start doing anything stupid I'll toss out some hand signals, so keep an eye on me every once in a while."

Manny grinned devilishly. "Oh no. We have other plans for you."

"What do you mean?"

"We took a vote. We decided that you're gonna be up on stage with us as a member of the band tonight."

"Huh?" He was kidding. I knew he was kidding. He had to be kidding. "Yeah, right," I said.

"You heard me. Tonight you are one of the Riders." He smiled.

"Come on. I don't play anything," I argued. Manny just kept smiling. "Oh, I get it, you want me to do the tambourine."

"No, Pet's doing the tambourine. You're doing"—he paused and made a sweeping gesture toward the stage, like a game show host revealing the grand prize—"The Keyboard!"

So, he really was kidding. "Ha! Good try, Manny," I said, relaxing back into my seat.

"I'm not kidding. Get your ass off that chair."

"Manny, I don't know how to play a keyboard." Has he lost his mind?

"Shh, not so loud. You don't have to know how to play it. It's broken, remember?"

"Geez, are you wacked up, or what?" I asked.

"Just get up there, move around a lot, and act like you're hitting the keys."

"But no sound's gonna come out." I told him.

He hushed me again. "Of course not, but nobody's gonna notice. It'll be too loud to tell one instrument from another."

When I looked up at the stage again, the guys were lined up along the edge, looking down at me and grinning. Pet was doubled over with laughter in the middle of the stage. What the heck, why not? Manny might be right. The crowd wouldn't be able to tell the keyboard from the guitars if they crank up the amps. Besides, it might be fun.

"Okay. I'll do it." I said reluctantly.

"Good!" Manny said, slapping me on the back.

"But I don't have an outfit! I'll look weird up there next to you guys."

"You look fine. The audience will just think you're odd."

"Thanks, Manny," I said, rolling my eyes.

We took to the stage at 7:15, and fiddled with the instruments and settings one last time while the crowd settled down. From his position at the drums, Manny could keep a close eye on the audience. Just when everyone was paying attention and before they could get restless, Manny waved his drumsticks over his head and shouted, "Uh-one-two-three-four," brought his sticks down hard, and the band launched into their first number in perfect unity. They started off with a bang, and it only got better as the night went on.

As for me, the first beat pulled me into my performance and I hit that keyboard like I was born to it. My hands and fingers blurred as they flew over the keys, and I was the epitome of the hard-core master rocker — what Abby would call a real Muscle Cat. I never stopped moving. I've never been much of a dancer, but Manny's drumbeat took possession of my hips and shook them from side to side. I spun around on one foot at random times during the music, first in one direction, then in the other. Near the end of the last set, I got really carried away. At one point, I stopped in mid-spin and pounded the keys behind me, my fingers never missing a beat. My back was to the crowd and I could hear them going wild. When I turned to face them, still caught up in the music, everyone was on their feet with their hands in the air applauding ME! They were all looking at me and going crazy. I turned around again and slammed my butt down on the keys, bouncing from one end of the keyboard then back again. Energized by the whoops and hollers from the audience, I turned back to face them, kicking my right shoe off and out into the crowd as I spun around. I lifted my bare foot to the keyboard and started playing it with my toes! They went bananas! It was nuts, man! As loud as the band was, the broken keyboard couldn't be heard over the combined noise of the crowd and the music.

As the last note of the last set vibrated out into the room, the crowd rushed the stage yelling things like: *Who are you, really;? You're somebody big, aren't you? I recognize you, and They brought in a ringer—it's what's his name!* The only thing between me and the mob was the keyboard. People were pounding me on the back and asking for my autograph, but I just stood there and smiled, occasionally giving a nod of my head or a wave of my hand in acknowledgment of the adoration of my fans. When I had a chance, I looked around to see what the rest of the band were doing; they were watching me, barely able to control their laughter over their little joke.

And what a stunt it was. I was the star of the night even though not a single note came out of that machine, and the reaction of the crowd to my keyboard pantomime had energized the band and boosted their performance over the top. We started packing up the equipment as soon as we could before anyone in the audience noticed that the keyboard was not plugged in.

I had lost a shoe, but it had been a heck of a lot of fun. Later, Burt confessed that Manny had been planning my part of the performance for a week. He didn't want me to dress up like the rest of the band and had made sure that I looked different and a little mysterious. Also, he knew that if I practiced acting like a keyboard player, my performance would be stiff and obviously phony. He wanted the crowd to think that I was a guest star making some sort of cameo appearance. By springing it on me at the last minute, he left me only one option—the only thing I could do was let the wild spirit of the music inspire my performance, and the enthusiastic response of the crowd and my own ego urge me on to see how far I could take it. Manny can be smart sometimes. He nailed this one, and I had a blast.

7 TUESDAY

After the Concert

Even though I've been lazy the past couple of days just sitting around the house doing nothing, there's been a lot of activity so I thought I'd better bring the journal up to date.

Manny invited a couple of girls to come back to his garage after the concert Saturday night to help the band unload and hang around — faux groupies I suppose — drink some wine, listen to some records, that kind of thing.

Both girls are very pretty. The brunette, Stef, is slender but not skinny. Her long hair is feathery and curls around her face, giving her a sultry look.

"That's Stef, with one *f*," she informed me as we were introduced.

In contrast, Candy is short, blonde, round but not fat — more like what some people might call compact — with big round boobs and a round face with pink cheeks. Cute and perky rather than exotic and slinky. The first thing I thought of when I saw her was cheerleader. Come to find out, she and Stef were, indeed, both cheerleaders at their high school last year (not my high school).

I was sitting by myself sipping some wine when the girls came over and sat down, one on each side of me, and started to chat. Candy did most of the talking and it was mostly all about their cheer-leading escapades. As the evening went on the stories got raunchier. I'm not sure I believed half of them, but every time Candy came to a big point of emphasis Stef backed her up with, *Yeah, it happened*, or *Exactly*. I just nodded in agreement and went along with it like it was the gospel truth.

Candy described how the cheerleading squad had their own game going on with the guys in the bleachers while the teams were out on the field playing football. The outfits they wore had really short skirts and some of the girls would pull their panties up into their butt cracks. When they jumped around during the game the boys up in the stands would have a clear view of their little bare bottoms—which, of course, is one of the most exciting sights a young guy can experience. Candy then confided that she'd even gone to some of the games totally bare under her skirt, with no panties at all. That really got the guys going.

"I swear, it's all true," Stef said, raising her right hand and crossing her heart with her left.

"Yeah," Candy said. "We'd try to get the guys in the bleachers turned on, then when the game was over, we would take them out behind the bleachers and do the nasty with them.

"She got caught doing that once," Stef said. "One of the deans was walking by the cheer line and got a peak at her short, curly blonde stuff just as she was jumping up in the air. He about dropped his teeth!"

Stef dissolved into laughter and Candy picked up the story. "When I came down out of that jump, Mr. Herbert was standing there watching me. I knew my goose was cooked. Or at least I thought it would be."

Stef had recovered from her giggles and continued, "Mr. Herbert took Candy back to his office after the game to 'discipline' her." She gave us an exaggerated wink and handed the narrative back to Candy.

"When we got into his office," Candy continued, "he locked the door, turned around, and asked me, 'Do you want to stay a cheer-leader, Candy?' I told him, 'Sure I do.' Then he said, 'Well then, how can we make that happen?'"

Stef snorted and said, "What a line!"

"I knew right away what he was getting at," Candy said. "So I bent over his desk, flipped up my skirt, wiggled my butt, and asked him, 'Will this work?' And he said, 'That'll do.'"

"When he was done with her, she came right back out and kept on cheering!" Stef said. "About fifteen minutes later we saw

Mr. Herbert sitting up in the stands with a big old smile on his face like he'd just kissed the queen."

With that, both girls collapsed into laughter. On the face of it, it was a funny story, but it made me uncomfortable and I didn't want to believe any of it. School administrators are supposed to be above all that. At least that's what I thought. Stef and Candy were so busy laughing at their story that they didn't notice my discomfort. When they had calmed down, I asked, "So, are you guys still in high school?"

They grinned at each other and Candy answered, "No, we graduated. We're gonna go to RCC in September." That set them off laughing again.

"What's so funny?" I asked.

"We flunked our classes last semester—" Candy started.

"—but we got to graduate anyway," Stef finished.

"How'd you manage that?" I asked.

"We took Mr. Herbert out to lunch," Candy smiled sweetly at me and Stef wiggled her eyebrows like Groucho Marx.

"Okay," I said, obviously confused. "Are you telling me he fixed your grades because you took him out to lunch?"

"We were the lunch, stupid," Candy laughed. "For dessert we told Herbert that he'd better fix it so we graduated, or else we'd go to the principal and tell him all about how he seduced us. I mean, neither one of us is stupid. We just got carried away that last semester and our grades went down."

"Oh," I said.

"Everything worked out good," Candy went on. "I saw Herbert a few nights ago at the Mall and we got to talking. He's really not a bad guy. I took him out to my car for a little private 'conversation' and now we're good friends." She sounded like she could have been talking about the weather.

◎ ◎ ◎

While the girls and I were having our little chat, Manny and the guys were busy putting their instruments back on the porta-stage and getting them ready for the next practice. The part of my mind that was not listening to Stef and Candy was following their commentary on the success of the concert. Every once in a while a loud *DH*, would catch my attention and I'd look over to see one of the guys grinning and giving me a thumbs-up sign. Then he'd say, "Right on," and I knew they really appreciated me being there for them on stage earlier even though I was only playacting.

Candy and Stef didn't seem to care that I wasn't a rock star; in fact, I don't think they thought anything about me. They'd just come to the concert so they could get picked up and party all night. I wasn't really sure what Manny planned on doing with them that night as he didn't seem to be all that interested in what they had to offer. Quite frankly, I've often wondered about Manny. Sometimes he's so serious that he completely ignores girls. I thought for a while he might be of a different persuasion, if you know what I mean; that he might like guys instead of girls, but that's not the case. Manny just gets so inside his own head — really deep sometimes — that he can't think about anything else. But at that moment those two cheerleaders there in Manny's garage, well … and I seemed to be the only one paying any attention to them. It's like they were invisible to the rest of the guys.

"So where do you live?" Stef asked me.

"Over on the other side of town," I replied.

"Have you got anything to drink at your place?" she asked.

"Just some cheap wine."

Candy said, "Why don't we go there. This place is dull." I don't think she's used to being ignored by members of the opposite sex.

"It's gonna be dull at my place, too. Not much to do there. I just have some wine, some jazz records, and a big yard."

"Hey, that sounds nice!" Candy said. "I love jazz."

"And I love sitting outside at night," Stef added.

"You know it's getting kinda late," I said.

"It's only ten-thirty," Stef said. "We can drink wine and fall asleep on the grass outside looking up at the stars."

"Come on, DR!" Candy said.

"It's DH," I said.

"I promise we'll be good," she said. "I'm just wound up and this place is dead. I need to talk for a while."

"What would we talk about?" I asked, thinking I'd be able to talk them out of coming over, since we probably had absolutely nothing in common, and that I'd bore them even more with the things I like to talk about.

"What kinda stuff are you into?" Stef asked.

"Well, I'm into art, particularly painting. I like contemporary poetry, Egyptian mysticism, Astronomy …" I was trying to discourage them with my huge intellect, but it backfired on me.

The two girls suddenly showed more genuine excitement and interest than they had all night.

"I love astronomy!" Stef said, her eyes sparkling.

"And I love Egyptian stuff," Candy said, grinning. "I just got through reading the Book of the Dead. Have you ever heard of that?"

"You're kidding," I said. "I read it a few years ago. It was fascinating."

"You see," Candy said coyly, "we do have something to talk about. Can you read hieroglyphs?"

"As a matter of fact, I've been trying to teach myself that skill for quite some time."

"I have too," Candy said. "I'm getting pretty good at it."

"Well I'll be." I shook my head.

Stef looked at me sternly and said, "I know what you're thinking."

"What am I thinking?"

"You thought you bagged a couple of whores tonight because we're cheerleaders and we put out. You thought we'd be ditzy and dumb. Am I right?" she asked.

"No, you're not right," I told her. "I try never to judge a person until I've known them for a while."

"You're sweet," Candy said, and smiled at me.

"We're more than just cheerleaders," Stef continued seriously. "Candy wants to be an archaeologist and I want to be an astronomer. I'm gonna be working at Palomar observatory for part of the summer. Just getting my feet wet." Her expression had shifted from defensive to a mixture of modesty and pride.

"Wow. How cool is that?" I said, genuinely impressed and maybe a little envious. "Okay. You talked me into it. You can follow me home and we'll sit outside and talk about mummies and comets."

We said goodnight to the guys — I don't think they noticed — and I got into my little Beetle and the girls got into theirs and they followed me back to my house. I began to have second thoughts on the way home. I mean, who are these girls, really? What if their plan is to trick innocent men into taking them into their homes where they could tie them up at gunpoint and rob them? What if we sit out drinking wine for a couple of hours, and then they pull butcher knives out of their purses, stab me, and rob the house? All sorts of scenarios played out in my head on the drive home. None of that stuff happened, of course.

The first thing that did happen was a tour of The Hole — which impressed the heck out of them. What's with that anyway? I don't care what Mam said about it being romantic and all that, I still don't get why girls are so impressed with it. Then we got some wine and I grabbed a blanket. Instead of going out into the back yard — which I kind of consider to be a spot sacred to Abby and me — I led the girls out to the front yard where we spread the blanket on the lawn in front of the porch swing.

The three of us lay there side by side, gazing up into the night sky. As it turned out, neither Stef nor Candy had a butcher knife, and they were both great conversationalists. Over the course of several hours we drank a lot of wine and talked about a lot of things. Every time we seemed to have said all there was to say on one subject, one or the other of them would come up with another really amazing topic.

"Have you ever heard of the Duat?" Candy asked.

I was impressed. That was the first time anyone had asked me about that. "You mean the underworld realm of the Egyptian dead that some people believe is also mirrored in the sky by the constellation Orion?" I replied.

I guess Candy was impressed, too. "Wow," she said. "You do know about that. That's cool."

"I think it's pretty cool that you just came up with a subject we can all talk about that combines archaeology and astronomy at the same time," Stef said.

And that's exactly what we did. We talked on for quite a while about the ancient Egyptians and about how their entire society was based on the position and movements of various stars and constellations. Such things as the orientation and location of temples and tombs, prediction of the annual floods, and the determination of times for planting and harvesting—the entire rhythm of life in the Nile Valley—were all in the hands of the powerful astronomer/priests.

"Look," Candy said, pointing up into the night sky. "You can see that the stars in the belt of Orion are a map of the Pyramids of Giza." Stef and I looked in the direction of Candy's finger and could see that, indeed, the stars picked out the arrangement of the three big pyramids near Cairo.

The three of us lay there in silence for several minutes contemplating the connection between us, the ageless stars, and a civilization that thrived several thousand years ago.

That moment of quiet contemplation served to emphasize just how full of life the girls were. There was nothing dark or delirious about either one of them. Yes, they were indeed sexually attractive. In fact, Candy was hotter than hot, and she had dressed to accentuate her hotness. She was wearing a tiny red skirt that looked like it might have been part of her cheerleader outfit, and a piece of cloth kind of like a scarf covering her breasts. It was tied in a bow in the back and it was all I could do to resist pulling the end of it to reveal those lovely orbs to the entire universe, including the Egyptian gods above.

Stef was also wearing a short skirt. Hers was light green, and her top was a simple, flimsy tank shirt that clearly showed the shape of two large nipples poking through from the inside.

Both of the girls seemed to be naturally happy and exuberant; I guess that's what led them into cheerleading. Both of them spoke with their entire body, waving their arms and hands about with each word, their breasts bouncing and jiggling with each gesture. Needless to say, I found myself losing concentration several times during the course of our conversation.

As the night wore on and the nectar from the succulent grapes of Red Mountain exerted its influence, Candy and Stef became even happier and more animated, if that's possible. They kept their voices down and were not loud, but their conversation became increasingly physical to the point of incorporating movements from their cheerleading routines. Suddenly, Candy jumped up and went into full cheerleader mode, minus the yells, right there on the lawn in front of me. The yard lanterns were on so I could clearly see every movement of her athletic dance. She kicked high in the air and shook her hips from side to side kind of like a hula dancer does, then she turned around to show me how it looked from the back side. With each thrust of her hips to one side and then the other she managed to take a step backward, and soon she was waggling her bottom just inches from my face. For the finale she flipped her skirt up to show me her panties, which had by this time ridden up quite a bit. It was some view.

Stef had been watching the two of us, and now she was rolling with laughter. "Look out DH," she said. "She's gonna do a Mr. Herbert on you!"

Stef's words and laughter encouraged Candy to greater efforts. She got even closer to my face while working her compact body like a dynamo, every once in a while leaning forward to plant a kiss on my lips or cheek. Rivulets of sweat ran down her neck and into her cleavage, emerging below her halter top to join the streams of sweat pouring down her bare tummy. She danced with wild exuberance and glowed with the joy of it. She finished with a final leap that threatened to send her into orbit. When she came back to earth, her feet were together, and her arms and hands were straight up. Her back was arched, her head thrown back and her face turned up toward the stars. She stood like that for a moment, her chest heaving and her body glistening with sweat, before she threw herself down beside me on the blanket. I've been to a few ball games and I've seen a few cheer routines, but none like this, and never this close.

We played around a bit on the blanket in the front yard, but it wasn't long until we finally just gave up and went to sleep right there on the lawn. We were awakened the next morning by Ra, the summer sun, rising slowly in the East. The shadows shortened until the full force of its heat was upon us and we could ignore it no longer.

"Gawd, my head," groaned Stef as she tried to rise up from the blanket.

Our three bodies and the blanket had become tangled and inter-twined in the course of our play the night before and during the few hours we had been asleep. Our clothing was mostly intact. The girls still had on their skirts, but their tops were buried in the blanket somewhere.

Candy's head was in my lap, and my legs were on top of Stef. When she lifted them up so she could move, she issued her second praise to the gods of morning, "Jeez, I think I'm gonna puke!" She tossed my legs out of her way, got up quick, and ran a few feet toward the eucalyptus trees on the west side of the lawn where she emptied the contents of her stomach onto the carefully mulched flower garden next to the trees.

"Oh Gawd, I'm gonna die," she said.

The sound of Stef puking woke Candy. When she looked up and saw me staring down at her head in my lap, she made a noise kind of like a purr. She sat up slowly and looked over at Stef, who had quite a mess of stuff on her face. "What happened to you?" she asked.

"I drank too much," Stef moaned. She made another sound—something like geeawww—then she squatted right where she was and emptied about a gallon of pee onto the lawn.

"Washing away the evidence?" Candy smiled.

"Don't ever let me do that again," Stef moaned.

On the other hand, Candy was remarkably cheerful. "Good morning," she said. She smiled up at me, and her incredibly white teeth sparkled like diamonds in the sunlight.

"Good morning," I answered. My own head was reasonably clear as I hadn't drunk anywhere near the amount the two girls had.

"How'd you sleep?" Candy asked.

"Pretty sound, but I think we only slept about three hours," I said.

"That's all I ever get," Stef moaned as she came back and plopped down on the blanket next to Candy and me.

"Eww …" Candy made a face. "You smell like vomit."

"Kiss me!" Stef said as she leaned over to try to kiss Candy. Candy dodged and Stef wound up planting her kiss squarely on my lips. When she realized what had happened, she settled in and kissed me for all she was worth.

"Okay," I said as I managed to pull myself away. "That's something I'll probably never forget."

"You know what I want to do today?" Candy was lying flat on the blanket and was stretching herself like a cat in the patch of sunlight.

"What?" I replied.

"I want to just lay around out here in the sun and read," she purred. "Whataya think, Stef?"

"I don't care," Stef said listlessly. "Might as well. I don't really feel like doing much of anything right now anyway."

Candy rolled onto her side and propped her head up with one hand to look at me. "Is that okay with you, DH?" she asked. "Can we hang here today and just be mellow?"

"Fine with me. We have the place to ourselves. My parents won't be here for a couple of weeks."

"Where are your parents?" Stef asked.

"They're on vacation up in the mountains. They have a camper and they'll stay in that most of the time and do a motel when the mood hits them. They had originally planned to be gone for a couple of weeks, but they called yesterday and told me they've decided to add a couple more onto their trip."

"Wow, cool. Sounds fun," Candy said.

"Food sounds fun to me. I need some protein," Stef said.

"I've got a frig full of stuff and a freezer in the garage packed with all kinds of frozen meat and veggies. We can whip up a pretty good breakfast if you want," I offered.

"Sounds good," Stef said. "If you've got bacon and eggs and potatoes, I can do the cooking. It'll keep my mind occupied."

"I want to read something new," Candy said. "I'm ready to move on from Egypt to something more contemporary. What kind of books do you have, DH?"

"I've got a bunch of books, mostly art and philosophy. Some poetry. A few Beat books."

"What's a Beat book?" Stef asked.

"A book written by one of the Beatnik writers," I answered.

"I've heard of them," Stef said. "They wear berets and say daddy-o all the time, or something like that."

"They're a little deeper than that," I said wryly.

"My English teacher mentioned one guy a few times—Jack Kerouac. Doesn't he write poetry?" Candy asked.

"I'm not sure about poetry, but he's written a couple of novels. Have you heard of *On the Road*?" I asked her.

"Yeah, that hitchhiker guy. He went all over America with that other crazy guy writing about his experiences."

"Yep, that's him."

"So why is it called Beat? What's the beatnik bit?" Stef asked.

"I think the term is more of a statement about how they perceive the world around them. The beatniks are a group of poets and writers mostly up in San Francisco. Somehow, they got the idea that society just isn't the way it should be. To them, it's all screwed up. Nothing's right about it and nothing's really fair, and the common man on the street is growing tired of the stress and ennui of the world around him. He's just beat — tired, worn out, and maybe a little frustrated and depressed about the whole thing, and he's worried about how it might all turn out in the end."

"Interesting," Candy said thoughtfully.

"I'm gonna go into the kitchen and fix breakfast," Stef said. "You two can talk about the depressed guys all you want out here. I need protein." She stood up and wobbled off toward the house without bothering to put her shirt on, her rather pendulous boobs keeping time with her every step.

"Let us know when it's ready!" Candy yelled after her.

I turned my attention back to Candy, "I have a couple of books by Beat poets," I tell her. "Would you like to read those?"

"I would," she answered. Then she smiled at me playfully and said, "But I'd like you to kiss me first." So I did.

That pretty much set the stage for the rest of the day with Candy and Stef here at the house. We wound up eating quite a lot before the day was over, which was all Stef's doing. Apparently, she has this thing about cooking, almost a nervous habit. She can't sit still for very long doing nothing, and when she's not doing something, she turns to cooking. "It's what I do. I don't like being idle."

So we ate, and then we ate, and then we ate some more. All day we ate. A great big breakfast that was not just bacon and eggs. Stef served up a huge omelet with bacon crumbled up inside, lots of veggies and some cheddar cheese. It was delicious.

For lunch, Candy and I helped her barbecue several pounds of pork ribs with some sauce she made from scratch that was just about the best I'd ever had. She also whipped up some potato salad and we found a couple of cans of baked beans in the pantry. We emptied them into a big bowl and all ate them straight from there.

The ribs were messy, as all good ribs are, and a great deal of sauce wound up in places other than our mouths. Candy reached over to—I thought—wipe some sauce off my chin. Instead, she spread an even bigger glob across my face. Naturally, things escalated and soon all three of us were covered with the sticky red stuff. Stef led us to greater heights when she yelled, "I'm a human spare rib. Lick me." So, of course we did, which led to even more fun and games. Eventually, full of food and worn out from laughter, we returned to our earlier discussion about Beatniks and Beatnik literature.

As we were talking about Allen Ginsberg's poetry, my mind wandered back to the phone call from Abby the other night. Allen Ginsberg had actually been there in her aunt's motel, eating popcorn and watching TV. What disturbed me though, was the image of Abby in my head while I was playing around in the yard with two semi-naked girls. I feel a little guilty about that, like I'm being disloyal, but at the same time I still have a bit of doubt about Abby. I'm not sure where she truly stands in our bizarre little relationship. Heck, I'm not even sure any more about who Abby really is. I don't know that much about her; only what she's told me over the short time we've been together. And now we've been apart almost as long as we were together. I haven't heard a thing from her since the phone call at Manny's house the other night. She told me then that she thinks she's falling in love with me. She also told me she'd have to stay in The City for a few more days helping her aunt, but I haven't heard anything more from her. I've been home a lot over the past couple of days and the phone's only rung once, and that was when my parents called to tell me they were extending their vacation.

So, I'm in a bit of a quandary. I have some serious questions that need to be answered before I commit to anything with Abby, or with anyone else for that matter. The bottom line is that I need to take care of my own emotions before I get tangled up with someone else's.

◎ ◎ ◎

Candy and Stef left here yesterday afternoon. Our whole time together had been great. We spent the rest of Sunday after the barbecue reading and talking and playing games. Sunday evening found us back out on the front lawn, staring up at the moon shining down through the tall pine trees and telling ghost stories.

At one point between stories, Candy shivered and moved closer to me.

"You're not cold, are you?" I asked, putting my arm around her shoulders.

"No," she answered. "It's just that the shadows of the trees in the moonlight is kinda spooky."

"I think it's romantic, "Stef said. "I just wish I had a man to share it with."

"I can share DH with you Stef, if you want," Candy said. "We're all family now."

I liked the sound of that. I was feeling kinda lonely—maybe a little sorry for myself that night. My family was away. Abby was gone and maybe not even coming back. Candy and Stef had been welcome company. They had treated me nice and we had spent a very happy couple of days together. I think that sort of defines true family, what family should be—nice and happy. So, Candy and I laid down on the blanket in the front yard and played and watched the stars for a while until we fell asleep.

We woke up yesterday morning and made a big breakfast together, then Candy and Stef got into their little VW and rode off.

"I need to check in with my own family—my other family," Candy had said. "They'll be worried about me."

"Yeah, me too," Stef said. "My folks probably think I dropped off the planet."

We exchanged phone numbers and promised to get back together real soon, then they drove off into the midday sun. I seem to be making a good start on a collection of girl's phone numbers.

◎ ◎ ◎

So here I am on Tuesday morning, alone again, which is not a bad thing since it's been a busy couple of days. I spent most of yesterday tidying up after the weekend and thinking about recent events—the success of the concert Saturday, and the great time with Candy and Stef. In spite of all the fun, I can't ignore a feeling of uncertainty growing deep inside me. What now?

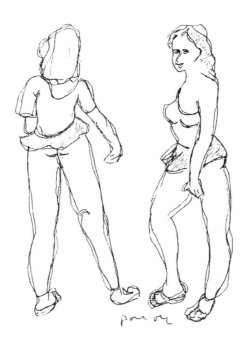

Phone Call From Abby

Well, the other shoe finally dropped—Abby called a few minutes ago.

She won't be coming back to Riverside. In fact, she can't tell me anything about where she and her mother, Carrie, might be going next because she has no idea, and even if she did, she couldn't tell me or anyone else. It's complicated.

It seems that Carrie's boyfriend, Billy, drove up to San Francisco looking for them. He is familiar with The City and knows most of the places they hang out when they are there, so they were easy to find. He went straight to Auntie's Motel where he left his car in the front parking lot, got out, and stormed up the walkway, a gun in his hand, and fire in his eyes. Luckily, Auntie Em saw him coming and locked the front door. She found Abby and her mom and told them to hide out back in the woods. Billy barged in, breaking the door in the process, but before he could find Auntie, she managed to get a call off to the cops. When she hung up, Billy was right in front of her, waving his pistol and shouting at the top of his voice. He told her he was gonna kill Carrie, and run away to Mexico with Abby. He had to be high on something. Auntie told him they weren't at the motel, and that they were staying with some friends over in the Tenderloin. Tenderloin's a pretty rough area and she thought that if he went over there brandishing a loaded gun, some really tough guy might just send him to his Maker. Billy kept threatening Auntie Em, but she swore that's where they were. She gave him a fake address and told him that they weren't coming back to the motel, and that they're headed back to Riverside after they get through visiting relatives in the Tenderloin. She lied to him just so he'd get outta town fast and be far, far away.

Billy believed her. He ran out, got in his car and drove off. He had just disappeared around the corner when three cop cars pulled up from the other direction. Auntie had told them on the phone that Billy was armed, so when the cops got out they drew their guns and ducked behind the car doors. One of them brought out a bullhorn and called for Billy to come out. Since Billy had gone, Auntie Em opened the door a few inches and waved a white napkin so the cops wouldn't shoot her. As soon as she was out the door, she stopped and yelled to the cops that Billy had just driven off. They all relaxed, came out from behind their car doors, and put their guns away. They escorted Auntie, who was scared to death and crying, inside where Abby and her mom were waiting in the living room afraid for their lives.

After the cops took the report, they said they'd cruise over to the Tenderloin to look for Billy, but that it would be like trying to find a needle in a haystack. They also warned the women that Billy might figure out pretty quickly that Auntie Em had lied to him, and if he did, he might come back with a vengeance. They left a cop there at the motel just in case. They said they would have someone on guard at all times for a few days.

Abby was calling me from the police station. She was still scared and upset and was barely able to get her story out. "I can't come back. Mom and I can never come back down there as long as Billy's on the loose. He's gonna kill us."

I did my best to project my love and concern over four hundred miles of telephone line. "The cops will find him, Abby. They know where he lives by now and they'll just go pick him up when he gets back to Riverside."

"Billy has a lot of really bad friends down there. Not only can he hide out with some of them, they'll even help him get to Mom and me."

"Great," I said. "So, what are you gonna do? He can find you up there, too."

"Mom and I are gonna hit the road. We have some relatives we can stay with in various places in several states. That's what the cops told us would be best right now, and we think they're probably right."

"You mean like go into witness protection?" I ask.

"Sort of," she said. "But we won't really be protected. Mom and I will just go off on our own and not tell anybody where we are."

"Will you be able to call me once in a while?"

"That's the bad news, DH. I have no idea. I may not be able to call you. I may not be able to ever see you again." Then she started really crying.

"Surely this'll all blow over soon," I told her, trying to remain positive even though my gut told me that this is not gonna work out okay.

"The only way it's gonna work out is for one of us to die." Abby was barely able to get the words out. "Either Billy kills me, or somebody kills him first. But I'm not gonna be taken by him."

"Do you have to talk like that? You're not gonna get killed."

"You never know. I might. Would you still love me if Billy killed me?"

"How would I even know you were dead? You're hiding out somewhere; if you die, nobody's gonna know who the heck I am. I won't get notified, I'll just never hear from you ever again. I'll never know if you're alive or dead ... ever."

"Yes, you will. I'll make sure of it."

"How would you do that?"

"If I die, I promise I'll come back somehow and tell you." She's not crying any more, and her words seem to convey a kind of certainty or even authority.

"You mean haunt me?" I shake my head in disbelief at what I'm hearing.

"Or I'll come back in a future life so you can meet me all over again."

"What are you talking about?" I'm lost.

"Mom and I both believe we all live more than one life."

"You mean reincarnation?"

"Something like that."

"So, you get killed, then thirty or forty years later you come back as some guy named Ralph, and that's supposed to make me feel good?"

"I believe that when we die we can control how and when we come back. Maybe fifty years from now you'll be teaching your yoga class, sitting around chatting with your students, and I'll walk through the door."

"You honestly think I'll still be teaching yoga in fifty years?" I laugh.

"Why not? Yoga keeps you young. But that isn't the point. I'll come and find you. I will. I promise. Our love can never die."

"But how will I know it's you? How will you even know it's you? Reincarnated people don't have a clue they've even been reincarnated from what I've read."

"I'll make sure that the person I reincarnate into will have certain things about her that you'll recognize immediately. Physical features like eyes and teeth, the certain way I walk, the way I talk and form sentences, even the way the future me thinks will be similar to how I think now. She'll have similar views and opinions in her philosophy of life. She may not know who she really is, but you will."

"Then what? What happens when I find her? What if she doesn't believe in reincarnation? What if she turns out to be a lot younger than me? What if she doesn't like yoga and never comes back? There's a lot of what ifs involved here, Abby."

A deep sigh comes down the line. "All I can do is make the effort through her. If she can't be so brave as to think deeper than the superficial ways of society, then there's little you or I can do. But you will know that I still loved you … always."

Then I could hear someone telling her that it was time to go. We said our goodbyes and that was it.

I may never hear her voice again. I feel like a huge chunk of my life has been forcibly taken from me. I know we hardly ever knew each other and only for a short time, but our time together was pretty intense. I really don't know if or how this is gonna affect me. I do know that it'll take me quite some time to stop missing her. Could this be the greatest love story ever? All of the elements are there. Will I ever get to hear her voice again, in this life or in another? Will she really come back one day as someone else? Will I ever kiss her again? Will I go through my life constantly crying out, Abby! Where are you? Abby … where are you? This would make a great movie.

8 FRIDAY

I got up this morning still feeling depressed after Abby's call last night. If I just knew that she was alright up there in San Francisco, I could live with that, even if I never saw her again. But to never know where she is, or even if she's alive … what kind of terrible destiny is that?

Things have been quiet here at my house since Candy and Stef left on Tuesday. No one has visited, and I haven't gone out. I don't know about this summer vacation crap. I had always imagined that the summer between high school and college would be a constant parade of activity and laughter, but the parade needs to be meaningful to me. I've had some of that, but so far this summer has been more like a roller coaster ride than a train ride. I'm finding that happy times and stimulating experiences come as high points or peaks separated by valleys of solitude.

I'm in a particularly deep and dark valley right now. The peaks have been a kick in the pants, but they've been jumbled and confused with no feeling of stability or permanence, or even any real connection to me. The parties and concerts and nights on the lawn with naked girls have been fun — I am a young guy, after all — but what kind of stimulation is that for the deeper brain cells where true comfort lies? I love the word, comfort. The world needs more comfort. People need more comfort. To be comfortable means to be content. To be perfectly content with everything and everyone around you, and even though I'm content with my physical surroundings — The Hole, my parents' house and property, even my little Beetle Bug — I'm not content with my friends, and I'm not completely comfortable with the relationships I've been forming lately. They make me uneasy. Why is that?

Los Angeles County Museum of Art

What am I doing here at the museum looking at art? It occurred to me this morning that if I think I might wanna be an artist one day I'm gonna have to start studying what art really is. I need to go look at some real art and not analyze it for how it looks, but to try to feel the energy of what it represents—try to understand the heart and soul of the artist who created it, and what the artist was trying to say with it.

I've never been here before, to the L A C M A. The only other museums I remember ever visiting are the Will Rogers Museum back in Oklahoma, and the Riverside Museum, which is a kind of eclectic and disorienting place that I would have forgotten about had it not been for the Egyptian mummy in the basement—that was pretty cool. This museum is in a whole nother league. There's something about the place that draws me to it and excites me. I can see myself spending a lot of time here in the future.

The outside is pretty spectacular. There are fountains and reflection pools out in front, and lots of beautiful landscaping. I'll probably take a break from the art inside and go back out to walk around the exterior. The place looks brand new. I should have looked up its history before I came, but I'm sure somebody in here can fill me in, or at least point me to a brochure. The buildings are shiny and clean with no brown watermarks on the outer walls and no pigeon crap on the sidewalks, sculptures, and lamp posts. It sits like a glistening diamond in the middle of the concrete and blacktop forest that is LA.

I can't even begin to comment on the contents of these beautiful buildings. Maybe in a couple of years I'll know enough to be able to write glowing and/or scathing critiques of the lot, but right now I don't, so I won't. I'm taking pictures of all the works that I can with my little instamatic camera, and writing down all the details in the pocket-size spiral notebook I carry with me all the time. I want to be able to look at the slides and remember who the artists were for each work; the titles, styles, dates—stuff like that. Some of the paintings are off limits to photos for some reason. I think it has to do with the flashbulbs harming the paint, or something like that.

There are some incredible paintings on these walls. I suppose that so far, I'm most impressed by the huge landscapes. They're massive—like twenty feet long. Of course, I'm pretty young and inexperienced so I may be exaggerating their size and importance, but man, they're impressive to me. I think the one that moved me most was a landscape by an artist named Moran. Geez Louise, it was beautiful. The painted light was so realistic I could almost feel the warmth of it—almost like I was standing there under the sun on top of a cliff looking down on the real scene below. It's stuff like that that jazzes me up and makes me wanna be an artist. I don't know where the heck that emotion comes from.

Some of the abstract paintings are very cool in that they have pretty colors and I like them, but they don't trip my trigger like some of the more realistic paintings. My mellow spot falls somewhere between real and abstract, along the lines of what they call Expressionism or even Folk Art. I love the Impressionist stuff, too. Those paintings are kind of whimsical, in a way. The figures aren't really all that realistic when you look at them close up; you have to stand back a little and see them from a distance, The farther back you stand, the more real they get. I love Monet and Degas—pretty romantic stuff—but Renoir, holy moly! His naked ladies are amazing, and not because they're naked. They look so warm and cozy. Renoir knew how to paint the feeling of flesh, not just the shape of a thigh or a breast. He knew how to reproduce the true color of a woman's, warm, nude skin, as if she'd just stepped out of her clothing moments before the viewer sets eyes on her painted form and she's still warm from the clothing she had on.

Man, I wish I could paint like that! If I could paint like Renoir, I wouldn't have any problem deciding whether to be a writer or a painter—I'd be a painter. Of course, I have no idea how well I can paint because I haven't really painted much yet. I did a couple of small pieces a few days ago; one was a bullfighter and the other was a tree. I didn't really take my time on them, so they were pretty bad. I also did them while balancing the canvas on my lap. I don't own an easel and I'm using an old plate my Mother gave me for a palette. I only have a couple of small, cheap paintbrushes and some tiny tubes of paint. I need to go out and buy some stuff. You can't be an artist without stuff. In the meantime, I'll faithfully keep this journal goin'. At least it's free.

I stumbled across the museum cafeteria. It's quiet and pleasant, so I'm taking a break. I picked a good day to begin exploring the art scene—there's not very many people here today. I don't care for crowds anywhere, let alone in places where I need to study stuff that's gonna make something happen inside of me—like an Art Museum. They ought to limit the number of people they let into a museum at any one time. Museums are places where you need to just sit and watch. Soak it all in. Pictures and sculptures aren't just cloth and boards and metal and stone; they're energies. I believe a work of art has a piece of the artist deposited within it. When a guy paints something with all the senses he uses to paint whatever it is he paints, some of the energy from his own soul surely must be released into the energy of the paint, mingles with it, and becomes a part of the finished piece. I don't know if it's true or not, but I read somewhere that electrons revolve around atoms, or is it molecules—whatever—and they can be revolving way out there, several feet from their host atom/molecule. So why can't an artist's electrons actually bounce around with the electrons from the atoms of the paint and the canvas, and mix around with them till they're tight buddies together? Maybe a whole lot of a painter's electrons get caught up with the paint electrons and join with them to become one with them. Is that the process that makes it green when you mix blue paint with yellow paint? Is that what happens? The bonding of electrons? Well then, why can't artist electrons bond with paint electrons? Heck, I don't know. Sounds good. The one thing I do know is that artists put a lot of themselves into their work, and whatever they put into a painting should radiate out and into the head of whoever is looking at it. Maybe the electrons of the painting jump into people's heads when they walk around museums looking at the art works. Maybe that's what keeps everybody coming back. Electrons are like drugs. People get hooked on the feeling of the energy of the art. Whataya think? It's like a drug and the more you come back to the museum the more of the drug you ingest. It builds up in your body and your soul, like lead poisoning, and it keeps you wanting more art.

If I'm gonna just sit and think I might as well head outside and find a bench somewhere. I'd rather be sitting out there in the sunshine and fresh air than in here smelling the hot dogs and fries — although they do smell pretty good.

I'm sitting on a bench outside the museum and watching the people go by. I think there are more people out here than there are inside, lots of them elderly, strolling around slowly, smiling and looking content with what they see. The bench is perfectly positioned so that I can overhear conversations without anyone noticing me.

"You think they'd mind if I took off my shoes and wade in that big pool down there?" one old fellow said to his wife.

She slapped him gently on the shoulder and said, "You'll be arrested if you do that."

I don't think he has to worry about being arrested; he's just having some fun. He's a cute old guy — a real sharp dresser. He's wearing a bright blue suit with a yellow tie, a dark blue vest, and shiny black shoes you can see your reflection in if you get close enough. He has a slight limp and is steadying himself with a silver-handled cane made of dark wood. Everything about him says class. He's not in any hurry, and he appears to have not a worry in the world, but he seems to be looking at everything — his well-practiced, squinting eyes, really seeing it all, the inside as well as the outside, analyzing everything his gaze touches. He may look old on his outside, but it's clear that on his inside he's as young as me.

I can't resist. I feel that I must talk to him. I call out, "Sir!"

He turns slowly to face me and smiles. When his sharp eyes meet mine, I feel like he is looking right into my head. Before I can speak, he says "I'm an artist, too, young man. Just like you." Then he winks, then turns and walks away without even letting me ask him what I was going to ask him. His wife never even acknowledged our short conversation. It was like she wasn't even there.

How did he know? How did the old man know I was going to ask him what he did for a living before he retired? How did he know that? I look up from my journal to catch another glimpse of the man and his wife, but I don't see them. They couldn't have reached the museum doors yet; they weren't walking that fast. Where did they go?

An attractive girl just hustled by, creating a breeze that I could feel on my face. I could smell her perfume in that little wind burst—real sweet, something expensive. She was kinda sweet looking too. She was wearing a short, light blue summer dress and scuff-free white shoes with heels just high enough to make her calves bunch up in the back when she walked. I think that's kinda sexy myself. She looks like she might be somebody, meaning she's probably got a rich boyfriend. She seems to know where she's going and she's moving fast, heading into one of the side doors. She must work at the museum, or maybe she's one of the artists. Could be anybody, I guess. Nope. She's coming back out and she's got some guy on her arm. They're both grinning like they just got married. He's a good-looking guy. He's not wearing a suit, but what he is wearing sure looks expensive. His shoes look Italian, maybe hand-made, and those cost big bucks. Anyway, they both seem pretty happy. I guess I'm happy for them, even though they're off to somewhere I'm not—someplace where the sun shines just a little brighter than it does on me. Maybe some sort of penthouse apartment with a city view and room service. Who knows? I ain't complaining though, 'cause I got the world on a string right now. I'm doing exactly what I wanna do.

Later • About 2 PM

A lot has happened since my last entry. While I was at the Museum just sitting on the bench and enjoying the sun, another chick walked by. I didn't think she noticed when I looked at her and smiled, but then she changed course and came over to me. She grinned like a Cheshire cat, stuck out her hand and said, "I'm June. What's up?" Then she sat down on the bench beside me.

June is about my age I guess, maybe a little older. She's tall—about my height—with brown hair pulled back in a ponytail, brown eyes, full lips, and a nice round nose. She was wearing tight Levis that she had cut the legs off years ago to make shorts. They were full of holes, nearly white from years of washing, and the edges where they were cut off were fringed with soft white threads. What caught my interest though, were the multicolored paint stains that decorated the ancient denim—some old and faded, others bright and fresh. Could she be an artist? Her shirt was a man's blue work shirt with the sleeves rolled up. It, too, was quite faded and covered with paint stains. She must be a painter. She sat down on the bench beside me, leaned back against the wall, and stretched her legs out straight in front of her. They were long, tanned, and muscular. I noticed that she had a dimple in her left knee. Then I noticed her feet—they were encased in well-worn, scuffed black leather motorcycle boots.

She started talking almost before she sat down, telling me stuff about herself. LA is a strange place. I'm experiencing all kinds of things I've never encountered before, and I'm seeing people in an entirely new light. I never realized that my life in Riverside had been such a sheltered one. I don't know how to react to much of what I'm experiencing. I'm not sure I know how to communicate with LA people, they seem quite different from those I've known up till now. I still hadn't figured out the dapper mystery man who disappeared from the face of the earth, when this girl named June sat down and began sharing her life story with me. How normal is that?

"I live about two blocks from here. I'm a painter and take classes at UCLA. I'm here today just checking out the latest exhibits. They're gonna have some German expressionist paintings coming soon—in fact they might already be here. I need to check on that." She paused, and her attention momentarily focused inward, as if it took all of her concentration to make that mental note. Then her brightness returned, and she asked me, "Are you an artist?"

"Do I look like an artist?"

"As a matter of fact, you do. And you're wearing the same clothes I am, so you must be a pretty good one. Besides, I could see that one blob of paint on your pants from clear over there." She grinned and pointed toward where she had come from. "That's why I came over to talk to you."

I was, indeed, wearing pretty much the same things she was—Levis (mine were not cut off) and a blue work shirt. I looked down at my pants and sure enough, there was a small glob of yellow oil paint. It must have gotten there when I was juggling paintings on my lap earlier.

"Well, I'll be," I said, shaking my head. "Aren't you something? To be honest, though, if you ignore the paint blob on my pants, you'll find that I'm just a guy struggling to find out who and what I really am in this life,"

"What's the problem?" she said earnestly. "Maybe I can help."

"I'm torn between two paths, art and writing. I like to do both, but I need to pick one to focus on and I'm not sure which one. And even if I pick one, neither one of those things is a real job that'll make money and give me a future."

June smiled sympathetically. "First of all," she said, "art isn't a job, it's a lifestyle, an inner drive. Once you discover you have it, you can never break free from it."

Wow! This girl was talking like I think.

"Second, why can't you be a writer and an artist at the same time?

Writing is a form of art, words are the paint, paper is the canvas. There's no reason you can't paint and write all you want. They won't cancel each other out."

I nodded and said, "You may be right. But I'm getting ready to start college and the college demands that I declare a major. I'm not sure what that should be."

"Simple. Pick art. You can write anywhere, and it's almost free, But making art costs money and you need facilities and machines and material to make it happen. If you declare an art major, you can use the college for all that stuff and you won't have to pay anything, or at least, not much — maybe some studio fees and such, but not like doing it on your own. I've been an art student at UCLA for four years and I'm nowhere near getting a diploma. I'm just using their stuff so I don't have to buy my own."

"You're smarter than I look," I said.

She laughed and said, "I am smart." Then she smiled and looked at me. "I'll bet you're smart, too."

"Why would you say that?"

"Because you're young and instead of spending your day goofing around watching TV or throwing footballs around in the back yard, you're down here at the museum studying art in the middle of summer. School hasn't even started yet, and you're here preparing for your first college semester. Most guys would pack in all the partying they could before buckling down to college. They wouldn't even think about getting a head start on schoolwork. That makes you smart."

"I suppose," I said. "But I wasn't thinking about all that. I was just curious about what makes art tick, because it has to be the same thing that makes me tick, or art and me aren't gonna successfully tick together."

"You see? You have to be smart to think like that. You're thinking about things deeper than textbooks and pencils."

"Well, thanks for having that kind of faith in me, June, even though you don't even know me yet." I told her.

"Yet is the operative word. I don't know you *yet*." She gave me a speculative look. "And what shall we do about that?" she asked.

"I don't know. Play twenty questions?"

"I have a better idea. Are you hungry?"

"I'm always hungry. It's two o'clock and I haven't had lunch."

"Come on then."

She got up, grabbed my hand, and pulled me after her as she started walking away from the Museum.

"Where are we goin'?"

"We're goin' to my place. It's only two blocks from here and I have a ton of food. We can eat a real artist's lunch."

"What's a real artist's lunch?"

"In all of recorded history there has always been one meal that just about every artist survived off of at one time or other during their life. Picasso ate it, Van Gogh ate it, I know for a fact that most painters today still eat it. It's a classic and it's a staple of life for all artists everywhere."

"I hope you don't say something strange like caviar and puffed pastries."

"Nope. You'll see when we get to my place."

Back in real time

I've heard of studio apartments, but June's place is literally an apartment that's been made into a studio. The building appears to be two stories from the outside, but on the inside, it looks as if the second story floor has been removed.

One corner of the large open space has kitchen stuff in it—a refrigerator, stove, cupboards and a sink, plus a table and a couple of chairs. Another corner is occupied by a king-size bed, a wardrobe and a dresser, making it the bedroom. There is a closet next to the kitchen area that turned out to be a bathroom just big enough to hold a sink, a toilet, and a shower with barely enough room left over to turn around in. The rest of the room is filled with easels, small tables laden with tubes of oil paint and jars filled with paint brushes soaking in turpentine and there are paintings — more than I can even guess — in all stages of completion on the easels, hanging on or leaning against the walls, even lying flat on the floor. The best thing about the apartment, besides the cheap rent, is the light. The ceiling over the main part of the studio is a giant skylight. There are windows on each side of the door at the ground floor level, but the second floor level of the north wall is almost all glass. With no nearby buildings to overshadow it, the light is perfect for doing art. I'd give anything to have a place like this.

The studio is beautiful; all light and color. Something inside of me tells me that I belong in a place like this; that this is not the first time I have experienced such an atmosphere, even though I can't recall anything like it from my own lifetime.

We pause for a moment in the small space that acts as an entry hall while June closes the door behind us, and my senses adjust to this wonderful space. Then June heads across the cluttered studio towards the kitchen. She obviously has the position of every obstacle memorized, as she moves swiftly across the room without even glancing at her feet. I don't want to knock over a table or step on a wet painting, so I follow her slowly.

I arrive in the kitchen without incident to find her already busy pulling things out of cupboards and rummaging through the old refrigerator. "Have a seat," she says, without taking her attention from her task.

I look around and see two mismatched chairs, one on each side of a green Formica table with shiny steel legs that doesn't match either one of the chairs. In fact, nothing in her apartment matches anything else. She doesn't have much in the way of furniture, and what she does have looks like it was acquired over a period of time from various flea markets and thrift stores as the need arose and funds provided. The whole colorful, eclectic assembly comes together in a way that is comfortable, relaxing, and artistically stimulating, all at the same time.

She pauses in her preparations and watches me curiously for

a moment. "Are you gonna tell me what you're writing in that black book?"

"It's my journal. This is something you have to get used to if you want to keep me around." I smile up at her.

"Like a diary?"

"Bingo. I've been keeping it for about a year now."

"Do you write every word people say?

"No. I'm fast, but not that fast. I just write down key concepts of conversations and sometimes I draw little sketches. I go back later to fill in the details — usually at the end of each day."

Then she asks the next question in the familiar catechism, "And why do you do such a thing?"

"I've been asked to explain this so many times that I feel like a broken record."

She raises her hands in mock surrender and turns to continue the meal preparations. "You don't have to tell me if you don't want."

"I'll be happy to tell you," I assure her. "I keep a journal of important events in my life so when I get older I can remember the major highlights of my life and ponder my existence, so to speak. I figure that one day I'm gonna write an autobiography and this journal will come in mighty handy for that."

"And you consider that sitting here in my studio talking to me is a major highlight of your life?" She turns to look at me again, her eyebrows raised in an expression of amused disbelief.

"I have a sixth sense about such things. It may not seem like much right now, but I have a feeling that one day it'll be very important."

She gives my response serious consideration. "Wow — that sounds to me like you're psychic."

"I've had people tell me that, but I'm not really sure. When I was nine I had double pneumonia and actually died. A minute or two after being declared dead, I woke up. When I came back, I felt different. I've read that near-death experiences bring out psychic abilities in some people."

"You're kidding. You died?" June's big brown eyes have become even larger with amazement at this revelation.

"While I was dead, my Spirit left my body and went up to the ceiling. I could see my body lying there in the hospital bed below me. I watched my mother crying and the doc shaking his head. There was a nurse with red hair sitting on my bed holding my dead hand, and another nurse with brown hair standing beside her and crying. Later I found out there were no redheaded nurses on the staff. The doctor said it must have been an angel that was there holding my hand, because that nurse didn't exist. After floating around up near the ceiling for a while I must have lost consciousness or something because I wasn't in that room anymore. That's when I saw what looked to me like an angel wearing a bright white robe standing in a beautiful meadow filled with flowers."

"You mean you died and went to heaven? Is that what you're telling me?"

"I'm not sure if it was heaven, but I do believe it was an angel. I was only nine, and he let me know I didn't belong there yet. He kinda shooed me on my way, and shortly after that I woke up in my hospital bed. I've told this story a lot, too."

"Well, it is a crazy wild story. People like to hear about things like that, though."

"That's it," I say, shrugging my shoulders. "People tell me I got my psychic stuff from that experience, although my mother was also psychic before all this happened, so it could just be a genetic thing."

"What am I thinking now?" She's closed her eyes tight and put her fingers to her forehead as if she's really concentrating.

I roll my eyes. "Here we go with the parlor tricks."

"No, I'm serious." She's laughing in spite of her protest.

"You're thinking that you're really hungry, and you wish that I'd just shut up."

"Wow, you're good—at least about the hungry part. I'd never tell you to shut up. I like you too much."

"And I liked you the first time I saw you," I reply. "Of course, since I'm psychic I can pick out the winners."

"So, how do you like my studio, Mr. Psychic?" she asks as she returns to pulling stuff out of the fridge.

"I don't like it," I tell her flatly.

June turns to look at me, slack-jawed and with her hands full of bags and containers from the refrigerator. "You don't like it?" she asks with equal parts disbelief and disappointment.

"No, I don't," I tell her, maintaining my deadpan face. Then I grin and say, "I love it. I'd give anything to have a place like this."

She lets out a sigh of relief as her smile returns. "You don't know how happy that makes me," she says as she throws her arms around me in a hug.

"Really?" I ask as a cold bag of grapes hits me between the shoulders.

"You may not believe this, but you're the first person I've ever brought into my studio," she explains as she returns to her preparations.

"You're kidding. How long have you lived here?"

"Five years."

"Five years? And no one besides me has ever been in here?"

"No one."

"What about plumbers and repairmen?"

"So far I've only had a couple of small problems and I've been able to fix them quite nicely without any help."

"What about your family? Your parents?"

"They live in New Mexico. They've never been here."

"But—"

"I know what you're gonna ask. Why you? After five years of guarding my studio sanctuary, why in the world would I let you, a complete stranger, come in without a second thought."

"That's exactly what I was gonna ask. You must be psychic."

"I have no idea." June shrugs her shoulders. "Something from somewhere deep inside told me that I needed to bring you here."

"Wow. I'm honored."

"I thought you were hungry."

"I can be honored and hungry at the same time," I reply.

Without further conversation, June arranges the provisions on the table while I watch. There are grapes, apples, apricots, pears, two or three kinds of cheese I don't recognize, and a couple of long loaves of French bread joining the stack of canned sardines that was already on the table.

She steps back to survey the bounty. "We need one last thing," she says as she then heads to the refrigerator. She pulls out a gallon jug of red wine and places it in the middle of the table. "There, now we're ready."

One thing I'm learning about life as I live it is that where there are two or more art people gathered together in one place, there will be wine. It never fails. It's a Law. Art people can't have any type of get-together without at least one jug of wine, and that jug is almost always a gallon of Red Mountain. For some reason, that seems to be the bad wine of choice for this generation of artists. They don't smoke dope, they don't do speed, most of them don't even smoke cigarettes, but they all, without exception, guzzle Red Mountain wine like it was water.

"What you see here is the most artistic meal ever created," June announces. "It's been the sustenance of artists for many centuries. Simple but savory, filled with lots of protein and who knows what else, giving the artist energy and life to paint a thousand paintings, not to mention the subject matter for still life paintings. Fruit, bread, cheese, sardines, wine, and the occasional salami when the artist has a few extra coins in the pocket."

"Oddly enough, I've discovered this on my own. I usually eat like this all the time in my own little room, but sometimes I don't have any fruit."

"Your little room?" June asks.

"My little room. I call it The Hole." I smile. "I still live on my parents' property, but not in the main house. I used to bunk upstairs with my brother in a large bedroom, but as we grew older, we both came to need our own space. My grandfather measured out a corner of my parent's double garage and built me a bedroom just big enough for a bed, a closet and a desk. It's pretty cool really."

"That's a small Hole, so it can't be your studio, can it?"

"My parents park outside so I can use the rest of the large garage for my studio."

"That is nice of them. It's so cool you have parents that support your art." She's smiling, but her gaze has turned inward. I wonder what her story is.

I let my questions go unasked and continue. "I'm just getting started so I haven't really done much art, but the fact that they've given me the space to do what I want is encouraging."

"You'll do it," June says. "You've got the Kunstwollen, I can tell already."

"The what?"

"Kunstwollen. It's a German word. I'm not sure anyone really knows how to translate it, but from what I gather, it means something like having the will to create art. It's a driving force inside certain people that makes them want to do art all the time."

"Sounds like it could be a sickness." I'm only half joking.

"Like an addiction maybe," June says thoughtfully. "Most of the artists I know just call it the Art Spirit. They like to treat it as an inner Muse of sorts that forces them to work all the time."

"Doesn't forcing it take all the fun out of it?"

"I suppose it can, although being forced to do art is a whole lot better than being forced to do a lot of other things I can think of."

"You got that right."

While I'm talking to June, I'm becoming increasingly aware of the abundance of art that her Art Spirit has been forcing her to create. From what she had told me about herself at the museum, I expected to see large canvases covered with drips and blobs of muddy color, or fields of white minimally decorated with a slash or two of isolated color, or possibly pop art-style paintings of sardine cans or celery stalks. I was wrong. Her paintings are powerful, and they certainly aren't abstract. In fact, they're very much like what

I'm attempting to do myself, more like the Expressionists or the Impressionists, or a blend of the two. Her studio is filled with beautifully designed landscapes and seascapes, people and things, all in wild vibrant colors that bring intense light into the paintings. I love what I see. I'd hang one over my couch any day.

"Do you like my stuff?" June asks.

"Are they all yours?"

"Every one of them. Whattaya think?"

"Quite frankly, I'm stunned. They're beautiful."

"Why are you stunned?"

"I thought you might be one of those new minimalist or pop artists trying to make the art scene in LA these days. I'm surprised to find all these lovely creations."

"I'm not into that stuff. To me, it's all a cop out. I guess the min-imalists and such are gonna have their place in the history books someday, but as far as art's concerned, I don't see anything of true value. Their paintings are without soul. There's no inner fire. No—"

"Kunstwollen?" I offer with a grin.

She grins back. "Exactly. The Kunstwollen gives us the will to do art; the resolve to create soulful works that reflect an inner drive to represent the cardinal emotions and forces of a Spirit that exists somewhere far above our superficial, mundane minds."

"You are incredible. I've had those very thoughts. I remember mentioning in my journal not too long ago almost exactly what you're talking about."

"Birds of a feather?" She smiles at me, and I sense a glimmer of something deeper in her eyes.

"Maybe." I look at her closely, studying her face. There's some-thing about her that baffles me. She blushes under my scrutiny, so she uses the activity of unwrapping the cheeses and opening up sardine cans to avert her eyes.

She clears her throat and makes conversation. "We can just rip hunks off the bread. I never slice it, that's the way real artists do it."

I follow her lead and reach for the bread. "I'm sorry. I was staring at your face. I didn't mean to make you nervous."

"No, you didn't. I liked it," she said, still looking down at the sardines.

"I didn't mean to be rude, it's just that there's something about you that feels—"

"Familiar?" Her eyes reconnect with mine and she finishes my sentence before I have a chance to.

"How did you know? I'm beginning to think you really are psychic."

"When I saw you sitting on the bench at the museum and you smiled at me. Had you been any other man, I never would have come over to say hi. I wouldn't even have smiled back. I certainly would never have drug you back here to my studio. But the second I saw you, something felt really good inside my gut that I'd never felt before. I didn't come over because I wanted to meet you, I went over because I was compelled to meet you."

I held her gaze and said, "I also read somewhere that people who are psychic have an energy about them that draws people to them, like bugs to a bright light."

The silence between us was filled with a deep, reverberating rumble of thunder rolling up from somewhere outside the studio, and the skylight flickered with distant lightning.

"What they heck?" I look up at the skylight just in time to see a brilliant bolt of lightning directly overhead, followed immediately by a loud boom of thunder. We both half-jump, half-duck in reaction.

June laughs. "Why do I feel like I'm in the middle of an Agatha Christie novel?" she says.

"Where'd that come from?" I ask. "There wasn't a cloud in the sky when we got here.

"I have no idea," June said, grinning with delight, "but I love it. We don't get enough real storms here in LA. I've thought about moving somewhere back east just so I could experience them again."

"You aren't from LA? You said your folks are in New Mexico—is that where you're from?

"No, my parents moved there almost the same time I moved here, but I grew up in Tulsa—Tornado Alley."

"You're kidding. I grew up in Tulsa."

"No way! You're an Okie?" Her expression is a combination of astonishment and delight.

"I was born in Winfield, Kansas, right across the border, but we moved to Tulsa when I was only one year old. Lived there for eight years, then moved to Ponca City where we lived for two years."

"I knew that accent of yours sounded familiar."

"Can't seem to shake it." I smiled.

"Please don't; I love it. It sounds just like mine." She smiled. "Come here and give me a hug."

I stand up and she pulls me into a bear hug with surprisingly strong arms. She loosens her grip, but we don't break our hug. We stand there like that for a long moment, looking into each other's eyes.

"So, what is it about me that looks familiar?" June asks.

"I'm not sure," I reply. "No idea. But I do know that I belong right here, right now."

"I think you might be right," she says softly.

She puts her hands on each side of my head and pulls my face down to hers. Our lips meet, and we kiss. There was another long rumble of thunder.

"I kinda hope this is an Agatha Christie story. I've always loved those things," June whispers.

◎ ◎ ◎

Our little party made its way from the kitchen table to the floor of the studio where we are now sitting on cushions under the skylight, surrounded by the remains of one of the best meals I've ever had. I've had cheese and bread and wine many times before, but never has it tasted this good. It must be the company. June is a doll.

"You like the cheese?" She watches me smear the soft, buttery substance on a crust of bread.

"It's wonderful. What is it?"

"Port Salut. It's French. Goes well with wine. The other one's just the local market's yellow cheddar, but I like it a lot."

"I like them both a lot. Very cheesy."

"Just like you."

"Ha."

We talked a lot about art; not so much about what's going on in the world of art, as about our own art—the styles we're each working on, trying hard to develop something unique, something true to our own Kunstwollen. We both believe that there's much more to a painter or a painting than the simple process of smearing colored grease onto a piece of cloth.

Our conversation drops to a companionable silence as we each savor another mouthful of bread and cheese. After washing it down with a sip of wine, June asks me, "What do you think of my paintings? Do you see anything in them that causes you to ponder and reflect?"

I take a sip of my wine before answering. "To be honest, you must have around fifty paintings in here in various stages of development, and I don't see anything I don't like. In the ones that aren't finished I see the potential of what they will become under your guided and gifted hand. The ones that appear to be finished are lovely. The purity of the colors and the inner light you've managed to place within every brush stroke gives them elements of both Expressionist and Impressionist style. The thing I really like about them though, and where I believe your Art Spirit truly shows in each and every one, is your composition. Your compositions don't look like the results of mathematical calculations, as those of so many artists seem to. Your landscapes all have odd and challenging points of view, like the one over there by the bathroom door." I point to it. "I feel I'm actually on a cliff looking out over the sea. I get a sense of vertigo, as if I'm standing right on the edge of a deep drop off and am about to fall onto the rocks below. I can almost hear the waves rolling in, and feel the cool damp wind against my skin."

"Wow, what a critique. You describe it so perfectly," June says solemnly. "That's exactly what I had in mind when I painted it."

"It's magical," I say. "Where did you get the idea for it?"

"All in my head. I've felt a deep connection to the sea all my life. I don't know where it comes from. Maybe having been raised in Tulsa, not able to be near the sea, I manufactured one in my own soul." She laughs. "The connection is there, though, wherever it came from. I can't go a week without driving down to Laguna or Malibu and spending some time on the beach watching the waves. Not when a lot of tourists are there, but at night, or in storms, or in the winter when it's deserted."

"I feel that same connection. Maybe it is the prairie — people do compare it to the ocean, and they sometimes call covered wagons 'prairie schooners,' like the ships. It could be a primordial thing. Some people think that life began in the sea, and that even humans are remnants of the sea creatures they once were millions of years ago. Maybe our desire to visit the sea and to paint it is some sort of genetic memory that got stuck in our DNA and came on down through the line of our own history."

"That's an interesting thought," June says. "I've pondered on a similar idea. Maybe in a past life I was a girl who lived by the ocean, maybe an Indian girl on the northwest coast a couple of centuries ago, or even up in Alaska. Or I could have lived in England or Ireland. Could've been a fisherman's daughter, growing up to love and respect the sea."

"I've thought about the British Isles thing, too. I have a couple of relatives who have traced our family tree back to England, Scotland, and Ireland — to seaport towns and fishing villages. We inherit our physical traits from our ancestors; who's to say that other things aren't passed along, as well. It's been known for a while now that DNA is the key to all of that, but they're only just beginning to figure out how it works. What if some of it doesn't have anything to do with physical stuff? What if it has to do with spiritual stuff? Or even stuff of an inter-dimensional nature? What if some of our

DNA turns out to be remnants from people who aren't even of this world but of worlds many light years away?"

My ramblings have carried me across space and time, and I can tell from her expression that June has traveled right along with me. "Wow," she says, "I'm sure glad I drug you here today. This is fun stuff."

"It is. There's so much in this world that no one knows a thing about."

"Yet, everyone has an opinion about everything."

"And they're always right," I say wryly.

"To hear them tell it," June replies, matching my tone.

Returning to Earth, I ask, "So, what's with the motorcycle boots? I have a pair just like them at home."

"These?" She stretches her feet out in front of her and waggles them. "They go with the motorcycle out back."

Why am I not surprised? "You have a bike?"

"Yep. A brand new Harley FLH Electra-Glide. How about you?"

"I don't actually have a bike yet—just the boots. I wear them because they're tough, especially with steel toes like mine have. You can do anything in them without hurting your feet. I figured they'd be good for an artist-type guy."

"Plus, we look cool wearing them," June says smugly.

"Yep, I do look cool wearing them," I say, grinning back at her. "When I visited RCC at the beginning of the summer, I noticed a lot of the guys in the art department were wearing steel-toed boots. It makes sense working around the kilns and welding areas, and they do look cool. I have to admit, though, they look a lot cooler on you."

June stands up and strikes a pose like Betty Grable in that famous picture. "I think I look pretty sexy in these boots," she says, turning slowly like a New York model, only prettier because she's got more meat on her. Her tight, ragged Levi shorts show off the perfect heart shape of her butt. The soft denim covering her left cheek is worn thin enough to show her beautiful pink skin perfectly complimented by the light blue cloth—something that should be painted? When she moves, her butt crack comes into view.

"Yes, you do. You look very sexy in those boots."

Suddenly, she reaches down, grabs my hand, and starts pulling me toward the kitchen.

"Come on. I want to show you my bike."

She pulled me through the kitchen and out the back door. The brick patio is surrounded by a tall wooden fence and contains an abundance of potted plants, some of them very impressive specimens. In a corner sheltered by a small roof is a brand-spanking new Harley bike. Very nice. Sleek. Black. Lots of chrome.

"Wow, gorgeous. A very hard-core biker bike."

"My dad bought it for me," she explained. "He always wanted a son, so he picked out a macho bike for me. But I love it."

"I thought your dad had never been here before. How'd he get you the new bike?"

"He mailed me a photo of the bike he wanted to buy for me, I picked out the closest thing to it here in LA, and he sent me the money. He said, 'I don't want my daughter buying a sissy bike. Get the real thing.' So this is what I came home with. He loved the picture I sent back to him."

"What happens when it rains? Aren't you afraid it'll get wet?" I asked.

"Water won't hurt it silly," she said, punching my arm lightly. "It's under a roof and I also toss a tarp over it when I think the weather's gonna be really, really bad."

"Judging from that sky up there, it looks like it might be building up to some heavy rain pretty soon." I think that thunder we heard earlier was a precursor to a storm. The sky was almost as black as June's bike.

"Well, come on then. We need to hurry."

June kicked back the kickstand and started moving the bike out from under its little roof. I could tell by the way she was hanging onto it that it had to be pretty heavy. I wondered if she would be able to pick it up by herself if she ever dropped it.

"Open the gate." Since she needed both hands for the bike, she pointed with her chin. "Over there."

"What are you doing? What are we doing?" I unlatched the gate and flung it open. I had a feeling I knew what we were about to do and I wasn't too sure I wanted to do it.

"We're going for a little ride. Hop on."

"I've never been on the back of a bike before," I protested.

"There's a first time for everything," she countered.

I tried again. "I'm not wearing my boots."

"You're not a sissy, are you?" she challenged.

"Of course not. At least I don't think so."

Her look told me that further resistance was futile, so I got onto the back of the bike. She laughed in triumph and I laughed in resignation. She kicked the bike into life, and we headed out into the streets of LA.

"You left your studio wide open back there," I yelled as we roared down the street.

"Don't worry, I do it all the time."

I'm not that familiar with LA streets so I have no idea where we went. She took it easy at first. There seemed to be a cop on every street and she didn't want to get a ticket for hot-rodding. I noticed that the first cops we passed were smiling—or maybe laughing—at us, so I started waving at them. They smiled and waved back. They probably thought it was funny that the girl with the boots was driving the hot Harley and the sissy guy in tennis shoes was on the back. Or, just maybe, they were a bit jealous. There I was with my front side pressed up tight to June's backside and my arms wrapped around her pretty little waist, and there they were, standing on the street watching us go by. I enjoyed every moment.

Eventually June picked up a little more speed. I was immersed in the sensations of the ride—the wind in my hair, the vibration of the bike beneath me, the warmth of the girl in my arms—when June hit a bump in the road a little faster than she should have, causing us both to loose contact with the seat. I instinctively tightened my grip around her waist only to find that I was now grabbing her breasts instead. I returned my hands to her waist as soon as I felt steady enough to loosen my grip.

"Enjoying the ride?" she yelled over the sound of the engine. Was she angry, or making fun of me?

"Sorry. You're the one that hit the big bump back there."

"So, you thought you'd grab my tits to get even?" I didn't know what to say. Then she laughed. Yep, she was making fun of me.

We rode like that for about an hour, up and down streets, and in and out of alleys all over town. June would yell something back at me from time to time, and I would just yell back something like *Yeah*, or *Really*, because I couldn't understand her over the noise of the engine. Once I even let out a loud *Yahoo!* That made her laugh.

After a while, she pulled over to the side of the road and let the bike idle. She twisted around on the seat and wrapping her arm around my neck she pulled me to her and kissed me.

"It's gonna get dark and stormy soon. I've got an idea," she said when I had been thoroughly kissed.

"What's that?"

"Let's go back to the studio, pick up some wine, and take your car to the beach so we can watch the waves roll in during the storm. We'll have to hurry though, cause storms never last long enough for me."

"I'm game," I said.

Her face lit up like a little kid's on Christmas Eve. She gave me one more kiss, then revved up the engine and headed back to the studio.

Laguna Beach • 6 PM

I love Laguna. It has to be one of the prettiest towns in America, and the beach itself is even prettier. Here I am now, in that pretty town, sitting on that pretty beach with one of the prettiest girls in the world. It doesn't get much better.

By the time we got back to her studio, we could once again hear the rumble of distant thunder, but we decided to take a chance and head off to the beach anyway.

"That's the point," June said, barely able to contain her excitement. "I want to be there in the storm."

She found an unopened jug of Red Mountain wine, we filled a shopping bag with bread, cheese, and a couple of cans of sardines, and headed out the door to my Bug.

June was about to lock the door when she said, "Wait a minute," and went back into the studio. She returned a few minutes latter with a large heavy plastic tarp trailing behind her. "If we have to, we can wrap up in this during the storm."

I looked at it with some apprehension. "What about the little metal holes along the sides? They could attract the lightning and we'd be fried."

She answered, "Come on, sissy," and off we went.

We decided on Laguna over Malibu as it's more familiar to me and I was doing the driving. We passed the time on the freeway by telling each other stories about our experiences on the beach — plenty of good ones and a few strange ones. June had more to tell than I did, LA being closer to the ocean than Riverside, and her time being more flexible than mine. Even so, I've visited the beach a lot, often with Manny, but a few times by myself when I just wanted to be alone on the beach to listen to the tide and write poetry. One night I sat on the beach at Laguna and cranked out about twenty poems, then watched the sunrise. I kept about a half a dozen of the poems and tossed the rest.

"That's probably the best time I've had at the beach, so far," I said, wrapping up my story.

"Spending the night on the beach until dawn is one of my favorite things, too," June said. "I've had some odd encounters, though. You might even say they were close calls.

"One time I was sitting on the sand watching the sun set and this guy comes along and starts talkin' to me. He seems nice enough at first, but then he sits down next to me — and I mean right next to me. He keeps talking, but I don't say much, just 'uh-huh,' and 'oh, really,' once in a while. Even though I try to ignore him, he just keeps scootching closer, and I just keep scootching away. He finally leans right up against me and whispers into my ear, 'I just got out of prison,' like that's supposed to turn me on or something.

"At that point, all I want to do is get away from him. I don't want to do anything to make him mad — I wouldn't stand a chance against him if he got physical — so I come up with a plan. I cozy up to him as much as I can stand and tell him that I sure would like a little wine to loosen me up. 'I get real friendly when I've had something to drink.'

"Well, this guy's face lights up like he actually is the brightest bulb in the box, and he tells me he just happens to have a jug of wine in his car. As soon as he heads for the parking lot, I go around the other way and get on my bike. I'd like to have seen his face when he got back to the beach."

"Wow," I said. "You got lucky. That could have turned into a serious situation. I hate to think what he could have done to you."

"Not lucky — smart," she said. "I spend a lot of time alone and go a lot of places by myself. I've gotten into the habit of always being aware of my surroundings and reading the people around me. A part of my brain is constantly coming up with and revising escape plans for every situation."

"I'm glad to hear that, but still ..."

She gave me a look that I'm not sure how to interpret and then started in on another story.

"You'll like this one." She had to control her laughter before she could continue. "A bunch of college-aged kids were playing volley-ball on the beach not far from where I was sitting. A couple of them saw me and invited me to join them. I love volleyball in the sand, so I did. It was a good game at first, but after a while things started to get a little loose. They had been passing around paper bags holding bottles of some sort of hard booze, and it was beginning to have an effect, especially on the girls. Their play was getting sloppy, and everyone was getting silly. Finally, the girls decided that it would be more fun if they took their tops off and let their boobs flop in the breeze while they jumped around after the ball.

"Now, I'll be among the first to admit that it does feel real good to just 'let 'em fly,' so to speak, but there are laws against public nudity. There's a cove about a mile up the coast that's reserved for that sort of thing. It's quite nice, too. Maybe I'll show it to you someday."

"Sorry about that," I said. I had jerked the steering wheel a little too quickly to make the turn off I had almost missed.

"Anyway," she continued, "the party was rapidly deteriorating, and I didn't want to be associated with all their nonsense. I went back up the beach and found a rock where I could spend the rest of the afternoon watching the waves in quiet solitude. It wasn't too long before I noticed a change in the activity back at the beach party. The cops had arrived, and they were rounding up the revelers. It looked to me like the only ones being arrested were the topless girls, and they were being held under close arrest, if you know what I mean. It seemed pretty clear to me, even from where I was sitting, that the cops were having a fine afternoon. Each one had his arm around a girl as he guided her to a squad car, while the boys were left to find their way on their own.

June and I finally arrived here at Laguna. I think the coming storm is keeping the "normal" people away, so I was able to find a place to park not too far from my favorite spot, Rocky Beach or Rock Pile Beach, depending on who you're talking to. The cove is separated from the main beaches by rocky points on either side of it, and there are some large boulders scattered along the strip of sand at the water line. Unless you knew the cove is here, you wouldn't know the cove is here.

We spread the tarp on the dry sand in a little alcove between some big rocks that have rolled down from the low cliff at the back of the cove. The sidewalk and street are directly above and behind us, but there is a hedge of oleanders at the top so no one can see us. The rocks on either side of us frame an impressive view to the west. The ocean is rough, and the waves are huge. Both the sky and the sea are nearly black except for the glowing foam of the waves and the flickering of distant lightning. The line in the distance where the ocean meets the sky is blood red with the light of the setting sun, which gives just enough light to see the rolling waves and the roiling movement of the heavy black clouds. The wind is blowing pretty hard; I can see some palm trees out at the other end of the cove, their tops whipping back and forth in the strong gusts. I can only imagine what it must be like up in the clouds — an invisible Force, powerful enough to push the mass of water through the heavens with ease. The sky is ominous, but June and I are cozy down here, sheltered from the wind by the rocks that surround us on three sides and eagerly awaiting the coming storm.

"Beautiful, isn't it?" June says.

"Yes, it is. In all my visits here in the past, I've never seen the beach more beautiful. Look at the power up there in those clouds."

"There's a lot of rain up there if it lets loose."

I turn to look at June. As compelling as the sky and sea are at this moment, I only want to sit here and stare at her beautiful face where every emotion brought on by the scene before us is on display. Her full lips quiver with the excitement of watching the powers of nature play out in the waves, the clouds, and the wind. Her bright brown eyes sparkle, amplifying the waning light of the ever-darkening sky. The sun has hidden itself away, but June has an inner light that is uncontainable in her excitement. Her body may be totally still at times, but that glow refuses to be suppressed or subdued.

I move closer to her and kiss her on the cheek.

She turns to face me and smiles. "That was a sweet kiss."

"I couldn't resist. You're so beautiful in this light, I wish I could paint you right now."

"I'd like that." June kisses me, then wraps her arm through mine and lays her head on my shoulder. "Listen to those waves. I love that sound," she says.

"It's more than just a sound, it's energy. You can feel the vibrations through the sand beneath us. And just think, all the waves of this world have been crashing their energy onto all the beaches on Earth since the beginning of time."

"I'd live on the beach if I could."

"Me too, if I had the money."

"It's all about the money isn't it?" June says. "Everything in the world seems to be about money. I read a poem a while back by one of the Beats—I can't remember which one now. He made a strong case for the idea that the heartbeat of the world is the almighty dollar."

I pause for a moment as her last comment sinks in. "You read Beat poetry?" She's an interesting girl who has just become even more intriguing. I've been missing Abby and had found myself replaying in my head the conversations we used to have about the Beat writers. Now, here I am, sitting on the beach on a stormy day in summer with this beautiful motorcycle-riding art-girl telling me she reads Beat poetry.

"I love Beat Poetry," June continues. "I don't always agree with it, but I love the newness of it."

"What do you mean by the newness of it?"

"When I was in high school, and even in college, the only poetry anybody ever taught me was the flowery stuff like 'Trees,' by Joyce Kilmer, or 'Ode To A Grecian Urn,' or some of the English sonnets, or the really romantic stuff like Byron, Shelley, and Yeats. Even Emerson and Thoreau—for as much as they seemed to think outside the box with their philosophies and such, their poetry still slides around on flowery language and rhymes. Don't get me wrong, I love most of it, but when I came across the Beats and their stuff, I found something I could sink my teeth into. None of it rhymes, and it's certainly not flowery. It's raw and edgy, like the poet is having a conversation with himself about the world and what's going on in it right now."

"I take it you've read *Howl*, by Ginsberg, and some of Ferling-hetti?" I ask.

"Sure. *Howl* is pretty incredible. It's like, a book long. It's terribly disjointed, pornographic in places, and in other places it just doesn't make any sense at all, but I still love it. It's open and honest. Ginsberg's got some nuts to write something like that."

"He got in trouble for writing it, or at least Ferlinghetti did for publishing it and selling it in his bookstore. I think he was actually put on trial for obscenity, wasn't he?"

"You're right. I think he was."

"So, have you ever met any of them? The Beats, I mean."

"No, I never have," she replies. "I'd like to, though, and see what they're like in real life."

"They can be pretty crazy at times."

"Have you met them?"

"No, but the mother of a friend of mine knows them well. When Abby, my friend, was growing up in San Francisco they were in and out of her house all the time. Her mother is still good friends with some of them."

"Wow. How neat would that be."

"I'm not so sure. I've read Kerouac's book, *On the Road*. Those guys are bananas."

"I started reading that a while back. It almost put me to sleep."

I nod my head. "It could have that effect if you were already tired when you started reading it."

"Parts of it were entertaining enough, but some of it just didn't interest me. And that Dean Moriarty character—I can't believe the way he treated women."

"Neal Cassady, in real life. According to Abby's mother, he's a real lout. He's like a little kid, immature, always doing silly things and never getting called on it. Not really a bad guy, just incredibly self-centered. Even the girls he slept with in the book—he was just using them, and they all knew it. He was going to bed with all of them at the same time and they didn't seem to care, or didn't let on if they did. I feel sorry for his wife, Carolyn, she got a bum deal when she hooked up to Neal. You gotta hand it to Kerouac, though. The detail he puts into his sordid tales about trippin' around the country is amazing. I hope he writes another book similar to *On the Road*. Maybe a sequel."

"Well, I'll wait for the movie," June says wryly. "Then you and I can see it at a drive in and make out during the boring parts."

"I like that idea."

As we sat gazing out to sea, the quiet was split by a loud clap of thunder directly above us. Then another bolt of lightning struck the water not too far from the shore, followed by an even louder peal of thunder.

June recoiled from the explosive sound. "Wow! That's crazy."

"Incredible! Did you see the lightning blow the water up into the air?"

"I'm glad we're not out there swimming." June's voice carries just a little bit of fear. I put my arm around her shoulders and hug her to me.

"Me too. We would have been barbecued."

"More like poached," she says. "Instead of us eating the fish, the fish would be eating us."

I check out the beach below us. "There's nobody out here today. The beach is deserted."

"There's probably a weather warning in effect. They put up signs when that happens. Could be people are afraid to be out here."

"But not us," I look at her and give her what I hope is an assuring squeeze.

She looks up at me and puts on a brave smile. "I'm not afraid."

"I noticed a couple of palm trees at the top of the cliff, and we're sitting right under them." I'm the apprehensive one now. "Lightning always goes for the trees."

"I'm still not afraid. We won't get struck. I think when we're together things become magical, Mother Nature protects us." It's her turn to give me a reassuring squeeze.

"I hope so." But I continue to scan the sky nervously.

The sky is getting darker, but June's face is even brighter with her own glow.

"So, we ride out the storm." I know it won't be long, but I can feel the hair on my arms standing up.

"No matter what comes." I can tell from her voice that June feels it, too.

◎ ◎ ◎

The skies opened up and June and I tumbled off the tarp and dove under it, pulling the wine jug and the plastic bag containing our picnic in after us. We laid there for a few minutes, catching our breath and listening to the rain pounding on the tarp, then I had an idea.

"Wait here. I'll be right back," I yelled to June over the noise of the rain. I remembered seeing a pile of driftwood behind a rock not far from us. I slipped out from under the tarp, ran over to it, and found a long sturdy stick. I ran back to the tarp, lifted the front edge, and put the stick under it to keep it up. I took my shoe off and used it to hammer the stick down into the sand a bit, then took the shoelace out of the shoe, threaded it through a couple of holes along the edge of the tarp, and tied it to the top of the stick.

"Here, hold this steady," I told June. Without waiting for her response, I went to the back of the tarp. I spread it out as much as I could, then used rocks and sand to anchor the back and sides. I was drenched when I returned to the front and entered the little lean-to I had made. It was cozy—just big enough for us to sit cross-legged under the front edge and watch the world go by.

"You're quite the Boy Scout, aren't you?" She really did look impressed.

"I guess I must have learned something from those two months

I spent in the Cub Scouts." I was rather proud of what I'd just accomplished. "But I'll bet you would have thought of it if I hadn't."

"Maybe, but what I am thinking now is that some wine would make this little tent even better," she said, reaching for the jug.

"That's just what I was thinking." I found the plastic bag and started digging through the contents. "Where are the cups?"

"Oh no," June cried. "They're on the kitchen counter back at the studio. Darn."

"We can use my shoe." I handed her the laceless shoe I had used to pound in the tent pole. She looked at it and wrinkled her nose.

"I appreciate the romantic gesture, but this isn't a fairy tale. We'll just have to drink from the jug. That's why they put these glass rings on them."

She twisted the metal cap off the jug, put her finger through the handle and hefted the full gallon up to her mouth, the weight of the jug causing her biceps to bulge. Wow, she is fit. Her biceps are the size of baseballs — that must be from stretching all her canvases herself. I don't think I'll challenge her to an arm-wrestling match.

She swallowed several hefty glugs of wine. She handed the jug to me and I followed her example, then paused to wipe my mouth on my sleeve. "You can't beat Red Mountain," I said.

"You'll get red stains on your shirt," she warns.

"I don't care. They'll remind me of the good time we had today."

"The day's not over."

June unbuttoned her shirt, leaving it on, but pulling it open so that it framed her breasts. They are beautiful, of course. Perfectly proportioned twin mounds the color of ivory tipped with rosy-tan nipples, erect like soldiers at attention. I'm spellbound.

"Well?" she asked.

"You mean, what do I think?"

"No, I mean what are you waiting for?"

I continued to stare dumbly at her.

She let out an exasperated sigh, took the wine jug from me, and set it aside. Then she laid back on the sand and pulled me over on top of her. She placed my hands on her breasts and squeezed them. "Start with these. I'm sure you can figure out the rest."

One Hour Later

The initial energy of the storm has passed, but it's still raining hard. It's impossible to see more than a few feet through the darkness and the downpour, but June and I are snug and dry in our little tent.

June, completely naked now, is on her hands and knees with her head just inside the shelter of the lean-to, watching the storm. I'm sitting directly behind her, watching her wiggle with excitement at the display of Nature's power.

"It's beautiful out there!" She has to yell to be heard over the loud drumming of the rain on the tarp.

"The view's not so bad from here, either," I yell in reply.

"Oh silly." She looks back over her shoulder and sticks her tongue out at me.

My response is as much of a surprise to myself as it is to her. "Your lips drop sweetness as the honeycomb … milk and honey are under your tongue." I recite sincerely.

"Wow." June's eyes grow soft and her pupils expand. Her mouth opens slightly as the tip of her tongue explores her lower lip. "My lips … huh? What a truly lovely thing for you to say."

"I can be sweet when I want to be," I say, smiling at her. She turns her back on the storm and leans in to kiss me.

She doesn't pull away when we're done. Instead, she snuggles up against me. "I've never met a guy like you before," she says. "Certainly not any other artist. They all seem to be so weak and helpless and full of themselves. I can't be around them for very long at a time."

"Artists do tend to be a bit egotistical," I agree. "I don't know how they justify it. Most of them are dirt poor, their work is mediocre, and their lives are dull. I really think that a big ego is a privilege that a person has to earn the right to have. I've always wondered how any guy could come on so big-headed when he's still so young and he hasn't really done anything with his life yet—kinda like me. What's he got to be big-headed about?."

"A lot of guys just think they're hot. They've got handsome faces and hard stomachs and that gets them a lot of mileage in life. I think that's one of the things that gets Kerouac noticed. He's kinda hot. So's Cassady."

"I guess that leaves me out. My face is quite ordinary, and my stomach is far from hard."

"Well, I disagree with you on your first statement, and I'm delighted about the second."

"You mean about having a soft stomach?"

"Yes, I don't like muscle men. I like men I can use as a pillow."

"Then you don't like rock 'n roll?"

"What?"

"Muscle cats. Muscle men. That's what the Beats call rock 'n' rollers."

"You're kidding."

"Nope. But to tell you the truth, I think only the wannabes use that term, not the real Beats. Kinda like 'far out.' I don't think any of the real Beats ever use that term any more, either."

"Well, that's not what I meant," she says, somewhat defensively.

"I know you didn't." I grin. "I was just funnin' you."

"But since you brought it up, to be honest I've never been all that fond of rock and roll, especially the stuff being played today," June says. "Actually, I'm not too sure if very much of what we hear these days can even be called rock 'n' roll."

"Me neither. I don't think music can be called rock 'n' roll unless you can dance to it like the kids on American Bandstand, which is pretty silly in itself. Some of the Beatles' songs can be classified as rock and roll, but they've really gone beyond that lately with what people are calling psychedelic sounds. Not much you can dance to there."

"Some of the other artists I know like to have loud music bouncing off the walls of their studios while they paint, but I like it quiet," she says. "I have a stereo that I play sometimes, but it's usually a little quieter; Helen Shapiro if I want something bouncy, or June Christy if I'm in the mood for cool and jazzy. I like Renaissance chamber music, too—both madrigals and instrumental, especially the English. I love those tight little ensembles with all those intricate parts weaving together.

"I'm impressed. Not too many people know who Helen Shapiro is. She only has a few albums and they're not easy to find. I have a couple and I play them all time."

"She's the best rocker out there—more pop rock with a little jazz than rock 'n' roll. I love her stuff."

"I like English Renaissance music, too. I have a couple of albums at home. The Music of The Court of King James is my favorite. I can listen to that all day."

"Then there's Russian music. I love all the Russian composers—Mussorgsky, Rachmaninoff, Prokofiev, Stravinsky, Tchaikovsky—there are so many. Why is that? It doesn't matter; I love the energy they put into their pieces. I think the blood of a distant Russian relative way out on a limb of my family tree draws me to it."

"I love Russian composers, too, and I have a Russian relative out on a limb, as well. We were fated to meet."

"Do you really believe in fate?" she asked.

"Sort of."

"What does that mean?"

"It means that I believe that everyone has free will to do whatever they want to on a daily basis, but I also think there's a Great Plan behind it all. I don't believe we're set down here willy-nilly just to wreak havoc and play games. I think everybody has a purpose in life and it's up to each person to figure out what that purpose is."

"And that purpose is planned out for us? Does that mean that regardless of whatever comes, we'll all eventually satisfy the original purpose, whether we like it or not?" June asks.

"Possibly. It could be that the purpose is already set, and free will is what can either speed us along to fulfill our purpose, or it can put up detours that slow us down."

"Interesting. I never thought of life that way. I wonder if it's true."

"If it is, there's not much we can do about it. How can we move toward fulfilling our ultimate purpose if we don't know what it is? We don't know what we can or should do to get there; and that means that the things we do every day are totally random. Some things might help us along, and others might hold us back or even hurt us. Can we really be held responsible if we screw up because we don't know what the goal is?" This is something that I've thought about a lot.

"Where does our purpose come from? Who makes it up? God?"

"I guess. Who else could it be?"

"So, if God gives us our purpose but doesn't tell us what it is, and expects us to fulfill it any way, isn't that kind of cruel of Him to do that? I mean, if God punishes those who don't fulfill their purpose, even though they don't know what it is—" She throws her hands up as if in surrender as she finishes her statement. "The whole thing really confuses me."

"It confuses me, too. I was brought up in the Baptist church, and they taught me that my only purpose was to be a Baptist. If you join the church, your purpose is fulfilled. Simple."

June had been leaning against me, but now she sits up to continue her argument. I think she's thought a lot about this, too. "Then what? What do you do after that? And what if you were brought up in the Hindu religion, or any one of the hundreds of other religions on this planet? They're all taught something completely different." June picks up the wine jug. "My head is spinning," she says, raising the jug to her lips.

My head is spinning, too, and I don't think it's from the wine. "If there's only one true religion on Earth, then the assumption is that none of the others will get you into Heaven. But which religion is it? Christianity? Judaism? Something else? God doesn't really give us any hints as to which one is correct. The Bible was written by the people living during Biblical times. The Jews back then didn't, and still don't, believe that Jesus is the Messiah. They still follow the Laws of Moses to this day. What if they're right? Buddhists are pretty much atheists, and Hindus have millions of different Gods in their religion. Catholics do everything through Mary, and the Protestants think that's wrong. Protestants don't believe half of what the Catholics believe. Picking a religion is kinda like playing Russian Roulette." I take the jug from June and down my share.

"You're right. I was raised a Catholic and you should hear the stuff they teach. I think a lot of Catholics believe it because they're scared not too. If God is truly a loving and understanding God, then I'd think His religion would be a happy, simple one, not the complex, dogma-loaded, depressing thing it is today. I don't hate the Catholic Church, I just don't understand it sometimes."

"It's not just Catholicism, all religions are the same. I actually kinda like parts of the Catholic faith and I wouldn't mind chatting with a well-seasoned priest some time, one that's been around the block a while. Right now, though, I'm sorta leaning in the direction of not professing any religion—just believing in God and trying to be the best man I can."

June changes the subject by stretching out full length on the sand, belly down with her perfect bottom shining up at me.

"Let's quit talking about religion," she says. Then, packing each word with sweetness she asks, "Will you rub my back?" How can I refuse?

"Does your back hurt?" We had been hunched over under the tarp for quite a while. My own back was feeling a little stiff.

"My butt's sore from sitting. Brush the sand off and start with that."

"If I start there, it won't be much of a massage. Kneading your butt is gonna lead to other things pretty quick."

"I hope so," she purrs. "You said you wanted to be a good man. Here's your chance."

30 Minutes Later

Just as I predicted, June's butt massage rapidly evolved into something more. It's gotten really dark outside, not just because of the black clouds filling the sky in every direction, but the last of the sunlight has gone and it's full-on night now. The good news is that the rain has stopped.

The beach is totally deserted, not even a loose dog roaming around looking for dead crabs to pick at. We folded the tarp back so we could see around us. The sand where we are sitting is mostly dry, having been protected from the rain, but I can feel the chill of it through my briefs. I'm perfectly warm though, because my arm is wrapped around June. The night is almost pitch black except for a little bit of light filtering down from the street lamp at the top of the cliff behind us. It is just enough light for me to see my notebook.

The major part of the storm has rolled through but there are still some serious clouds whipping by overhead. The glow of lightning ripples through the thickest clouds in the distance, and the muffled rumble of thunder is almost continuous as the storm continues along its way. Imagine, if the power of just one storm could be harnessed, it would provide enough energy to run a large city for years. But humans can't even cure the common cold. They're too busy spending money on worthless nonsense like TV sitcoms and sports. Just think of what society could do if everyone got serious about something for just a few days. If every person on Earth gave one week's paycheck to a fund dedicated to curing asthma, or cancer, or even the common cold, maybe that would be all it takes to do it. But that will never happen, though, because people are selfish at heart. That's why nothing ever gets done fully, because people are greedy. They always have some excuse why something won't work or isn't enough, but the real reason is that they're too selfish to do what it takes to get the job done.

June's voice breaks into my thoughts. "What are you thinking about?"

"The state of the world."

"That sounds depressing."

"It is."

"So, let's change the subject," she says brightly.

"Fine by me." She's right. Enough of this doom and gloom.

"It is getting late," she observes. "We could head back to the studio if you'd like."

"It's up to you. I'm content to sit here with you all night if you want."

June looks up at me and smiles. "Really?"

"Yep. I'd sit all night with you anywhere, any time."

She snuggles even closer to me and sighs contentedly. "Just hold me for a while. I want to enjoy this as long as I can."

9 SATURDAY

10 AM

We cuddled on the beach for a while, but it wasn't long before the damp chill of the night overpowered our shared warmth. We decided to head back to June's studio where we could shake the sand out of our clothes, take a shower, and sleep away the remainder of the night on her king-sized bed. On the way back to LA, I told June more about where I live—The Hole, the yard and the trees around the house, the view from the top of the ravine, and the grotto at the bottom—and she decided that we had to come to Riverside right now, so we did.

We stopped briefly at her studio to pick up a few of what she called essentials. She tossed them into a green army tote bag and then proceeded to gather up all the fruit, cheese, and sardines that we hadn't packed for our picnic at the beach.

"I've got plenty to eat at home," I said.

"You can never be too prepared," she replied. "Besides, this stuff needs to be eaten soon or it will spoil." She grabbed a couple of jugs of Red Mountain and put all of it into the backseat of my VW. Then she went around the back to get her motorcycle and wheel it around to the front.

I got into the VW, June got on her bike, and off we flew at record speed for Riverside. We were both tired, and no doubt I shouldn't have been speeding like that. June certainly shouldn't have been going that fast on her bike behind me, but she was anxious to get here so that I could give her a tour of the place before we crashed from total exhaustion.

When we pulled up the long driveway at around 3 AM, I breathed a sigh of relief with our safe arrival and for the fact that my parent's car wasn't here. They've been on an extended camping trip and have been rather vague about when they are coming home. It would be hard to explain the presence of a drunken, half-nude — albeit drop-dead gorgeous — girl at 2 AM. Did I mention that June had neglected to button her shirt before mounting her bike for the race to Riverside? She rode the whole way with her shirt flying out behind her like Superman's cape, creating a spectacular view for anybody heading into LA. Fortunately there wasn't much traffic at that hour.

◎ ◎ ◎

It's Saturday morning, about 10 AM. I'm sitting in my desk chair in The Hole staring at the beautiful body of June as she lays nude in my bed on top of the sheets. It was a pretty warm night, especially with the two of us trying to get comfortable in my small bed. We were pressed together as close as the stones in the great Pyramid of Giza and were falling out of bed when we rolled over. June slept deeply, never once waking up. I, however, woke up every time one or the other of us tried to change position. I finally gave up around 9 AM. I can either take a nap later or go to bed early tonight and catch up on lost sleep. I heard June make a cute little moaning noise as I sat up on the edge of the bed. When I looked down, she was smacking her lips gently and running her hand over the spot on the bed where I had been laying. I couldn't tell if she was awake or just having a little puppy dream about me.

Anyway, I got up and went through the breezeway and into house. I stopped in the kitchen to put on a pot of coffee on my way to the bathroom. When I finished in the bathroom, I poured myself a cup of coffee and returned to The Hole where I've been pleasantly reviewing the memories of last night and the fun we had while planning what we'll do today. Even though it was late when we arrived, I was able to give June a decent tour of the house including the front porch with the swing. It was too dark to see the big pine trees and the little orchard out front as more than shadows.

We went out to the patio and back yard through the big doors in the living room and crossed the yard to where it drops off into the grotto. There wasn't much of a moon so, again, we couldn't see much more than shadows, but she wants to go down there today. Even though the night was dark, it was clear. The view overlooking Riverside was beautiful with all of the lights of the city spread out before us and twinkling like stars. We stayed there on the edge of the ravine for several minutes, June entranced by the scene while I stood behind her, my arms wrapped around her and my nose close to her hair.

There wasn't a hint of the smell of shampoo. It was just her personal smell. "Why doesn't your hair smell like shampoo?"

"Because I never wash my hair."

"You're kidding."

"Of course I'm kidding. I never wash my hair with shampoo. I use soap some Amish friends of mine made for me. It doesn't have any perfumey stuff in it—just plain old soap, no scent at all."

"Well, they do call them the Plain People. So, you know some Amish?"

"I do. There aren't any Amish communities around anywhere, but there are several Amish families in the foothills north of LA. I think they moved here from the Midwest to get away from the cold weather."

"Maybe they moved here to get away from the other Amish."

"Maybe. They are renegades in a way—just the fact that they're here makes them different—but they still follow the rules and dress the part even though there's nobody around to pass judgment. They follow very strict rules about owning and operating machinery. They do all of their plowing and hauling by hand or use horses. Their English neighbors—they refer to anyone who is not Amish as English—give them lifts into town and help them get their produce and crafts to the Farmers' Market. I guess it's OK to ride, but not to drive. The Amish are generally good neighbors, and trade things like fresh eggs and homemade soaps in return for favors. I got to know one family pretty well. Even had dinner at their house a few times."

"Really? I'd love to see the inside of an Amish home."

"There's not much to see. Mr. Miller—that's the family, the Millers—made all of the furniture himself. It's solid and functional; not fancy but beautiful in its own way. They don't have any electricity. They use homemade candles and kerosene lamps for light at night. They also use kerosene and wood for cooking, and they raise most of their own food. There's a huge garden, and they keep chickens for eggs and meat, and goats for milk and cheese. They even raise a few pigs for the lard and tallow, as well as for the meat. They eat as much fresh food as they can, and what they don't eat is either preserved for storage or sold to their neighbors or at the farmers' market. Mrs. Miller's pantry is full of canned home-grown fruits and veggies, soups and sauces, and cured and canned meats. Mr. Miller even built a contraption to keep things like milk, eggs, cheese, and other things fresh for a while. It's kinda like a big swamp cooler with shelves on the inside. Water evaporating from burlap bags hung on the outside keeps the inside cool. It works well in the dry climate here, but I don't think it would be of much use in Missouri—too humid there.

"The most impressive thing about their home is the cleanliness. The kitchen and bathroom—they do have indoor plumbing—are spotless, and there is not a single item in the entire house that is out of place, even in the bedroom that is shared by their three daughters. Each of the girls has a bed, one drawer in the single three-drawer chest, and a row of pegs on the wall. The beds are made perfectly, and each girl's clothing is in her drawer or hanging from a peg unless it's being worn. June smiled. It's really something to see. Not at all like the typical American family with three kids in the typical American home."

"Wow," I said "Like monks and nuns in a monastery, only no crucifixes on the wall."

"Kinda like that," June said.

"All that simplicity and cleanliness is tempting. There's something appealing about such a regulated life. You wouldn't have to worry much about making decisions—just follow the rules. Would you ever consider becoming an Amish woman?"

"No, not really. It's a tempting lifestyle indeed, but I'm too sloppy to be an Amish woman. I'd have paint dripped on the floors, junk stacked against the walls, dirty panties and bras laying all over the house, the kitchen sink would be full of unwashed dishes, the frig would be full of cheese and fish and beer and left-over pizza, and I'd have a jug of Red Mountain in every room. Besides, while mindless obedience might be nice break, it would get old real fast.

"I get the picture," I said. "You and I are a lot alike."

She looked at me and smiled fondly. "I noticed that," she said. "We dress alike, like the same things, we both paint, we like cheese and bread and Red Mountain, storms and the wild roaring sea, and neither of us seem to care where our dirty panties are tossed."

"Huh?"

"Look in your left pocket," she said.

I put my hand into my left pocket and felt something smooth and silky. "What they heck?" I said as pulled her panties out of my pocket. I held them up to get a closer look at them. "These are dirty," I said. "I can smell you on them."

"Of course they smell." She grinned. "I wore them for two days." "I stuck them in your pocket when we stopped at my studio earlier. You didn't even notice."

"Why'd you do that?"

"Just funnin' you. You can keep them if you want. Kind of a souvenir of conquest."

"I don't consider you a conquest," I protested. "If anything, you're the victor for having captured me. I was just sitting there in front of LACMA, minding my own business, when this gorgeous girl comes along and starts flirting with me."

"And the rest is history." June laughed. "You're right. I was the one coming on to you. Are you sorry I did?"

"Are you kidding?"

I turned her around, pulled her as close to me as possible, and kissed her.

"As beautiful as this view is with all those sparkling lights and the fresh night air, I think we need to go inside." She looked up at me and winked. "A little birdie tells me you want to put me to bed now."

"That little birdie would be right."

And with that, our long, busy day finally came to a close

While I've been using half of my brain to recall and record the events of last night, I've been using the other half trying to figure out how to spend the rest of this day with June. I want to do something special. I don't want to just hang around here doing nothing, or talking about Amish people. I'm not sure I really want to go anywhere, either. After yesterday, I'd like to do something a little closer to home. It would be fun to paint a painting together, but my collection of paints and brushes is barely adequate for myself, and, frankly, after seeing June's studio, I'm a little embarrassed to show them to her. At least I have a couple of descent canvases. I got tired of painting on those little canvas boards they sell three for a dollar down at the art mart, so I bought some real stretched canvases last week. I also have a few large sketch pads—I suppose we could draw some stuff together. I don't know. Nothing I can think of sounds right.

I sense a movement from the bed. "Good morning," June says in a sleepy little voice.

I turn in my chair and smile as I watch June yawn and stretch her perfect form like an oblation to the morning. "Good morning to you, too."

"Wow, I slept like a log," she says.

"A very pretty log, I might add."

"Aww." Without rising up, she lifts her arms toward me in invitation. "Come here."

I shift my seat from the chair to the edge of the bed—I told you The Hole is small. "Are you hungry?" I ask after giving her a morning kiss.

"Yes, but I don't want sardines for breakfast." She grimaced at that idea.

"How about sausage and eggs?"

"Yum, that sounds good."

I stand up and head for the door. "Come with me. I'll cook."

"Can I pee first?"

"You probably should."

Back in The Hole • 4 PM

During breakfast we went over a variety of possible activities for the day, and we decided on a tour of Riverside. June only knows about it as a town on the way to Palm Springs from LA, so everything about it is new to her.

I took the scenic route to get from my parents' house into town—up Van Buren to Victoria Avenue. It's a beautiful road lined with eucalyptus, palm, and pepper trees, with other flowering trees and rose bushes down the middle. It runs through the orange groves from the hills at one end to downtown at the other.

Our first stop was the city museum—I wanted to show her the mummy in the basement. It had been quite a while since I last visited the museum, and a lot had changed. What had been an almost random collection of artifacts and treasures had been dusted off, neatly labeled, and properly displayed in freshly renovated spaces above ground. Seeing all the old stuff cleaned up and presented in a logical fashion was almost like seeing it for the first time. Even the old dioramas depicting the lives of the local Indians seemed brand new. We couldn't find the mummy, but we did spend a lot of time at the geology display turning the black light on and off and watching the specimens glow in the dark.

When we left the museum, we walked all around downtown—back and forth on Seventh, Eighth, Ninth, and Tenth; and up and down on Lime, Lemon, Orange, Main, and Market. A lot of the bigger stores have moved out to the new shopping mall, but there are still some smaller shops tucked in along the side streets. One of my favorites is a cramped and dusty used book store, and there's a health food store with a lunch counter where they serve soup, sandwiches, and health drinks all made fresh right there and amazingly delicious. Our last leg took us up Market Street past a pretty little park to the Fox Theater. The Fox is a beautiful Spanish-style building, with an interior to match. It's showing its age, but back in the day it was magnificent. In the 30s and 40s the Hollywood producers used it for sneak previews of their latest movies, including *Gone with the Wind*. It was not uncommon to plan to see one movie and wind up seeing something else, or to catch glimpses of various Hollywood "royalty." From there, we headed back along Seventh Street to Main Street.

Exploring the Mission Inn was the highlight of our expedition. It was built in stages as a hotel starting around the turn of the century until the mid 1930s. It's really more of a complex than a building, and it's huge. At first glance, the style appears to be mission or Spanish, but when you get to looking around, you can see stuff from all over the world. The Inn has fallen on hard times in recent years though, and now it is practically deserted. I think some of the rooms have been rented out as apartments to students, and there are a few shabby offices and shops tucked in, but the place is a mess. I've even heard rumors that it could be torn down soon; what a loss that would be. In spite of the neglect, there are some stunning features, like the St. Francis Chapel. I'd like to see what a little TLC could do for the place.

The hotel is big, beautiful, and complicated. Nothing is in a straight line or on the same level—there are twists and turns and steps and stairs everywhere. It wouldn't be hard to get lost. I don't think we were really supposed to wander around in there like we did, but there was no one around to tell us not to. We had a great time exploring all the passages, poking our heads into various rooms, and racing up the spiral staircase at top speed. I let June win. The only time we came close to getting in trouble was down in the catacombs. We had been there for a while, and I was just beginning to think we might be lost when I turned a corner and bumped into a security guard. He sucked in his belly, pulled himself up to his full height, and glared at us.

"And just what do you two think you're doing here?"

I think we may have seen a sign back a ways that might have said something like, *Keep Out*. We put on our most innocent faces and I answered meekly, "We're sorry, sir. We must have taken a wrong turn somewhere."

He grunted like he'd heard that line before and showed us the way out.

Outside on the street again, we recounted the wonders of what we had seen inside and laughed about our close encounter with The Law.

◎ ◎ ◎

We were heading in the direction of the Royal Scot for some much-needed refreshment when I happened to glance up and see a familiar figure approaching from the opposite direction. I waved at him and hollered, "Hey, Manny!" June and I were about to enter the restaurant, so we waited on the sidewalk while he closed the distance between us. As he approached, it became obvious that he was quite depressed about something.

"What's up, Manny? You look like you just lost your best friend."

"You're close," he said glumly.

"Manny, this is June," I said, drawing her forward. "I've been showing her the sights of Our Fair City, and we're ready to sit down and have some coffee, or iced tea, or something. Why don't you join us, and you can tell me all about it?"

We went inside and seated ourselves at my favorite booth, then Christa, my favorite waitress, came and took our orders. Manny wasn't ready to talk yet, so I filled in the few minutes before Christa came back by telling June a little bit about Manny.

Christa served us our drinks and we sipped them in silence, June and I enjoying the cool refreshment of our iced teas, while Manny seemed lost in a mood as black as his coffee. Finally, he set down his cup and said to no one in particular, "I dissolved the band this morning."

"You did what?" I said, nearly choking on my tea.

"I broke up the band." This time he was looking straight at me.

"Why? You've been together forever."

"We had an early practice this morning 'cause we're supposed to play at a dance next Friday. I couldn't get the guys to focus on the music. They were goofing off or talking about nonsense all morning, not concentrating on what we were there to do. Even Pet was kinda crazy. It didn't take me long to figure out that they were all high. They'd been at Paul's house smoking pot before they came to practice."

I shook my head in sympathy. This wasn't the first time I'd heard that story.

"I've told them over and over that I didn't want anybody high during the practice sessions. They used to do it all the time and the doped-up jams were chaotic and silly. I finally laid down the law and they stopped doing it for a while, but today, with this really important gig on Friday night, they come over like that, acting like a bunch of giggly little school kids during recess. I couldn't get them to do anything right."

"So, what did you do?" I asked.

"I told them I was through, and to get out of my garage. If they want to start their own band without me, fine, just do it in someone else's garage, not mine."

"And they left? Just like that?"

"They tried to talk me out of it, and for a minute I almost gave in. Then Burt got the giggles and he wouldn't stop. That got the others all going again, so that was it for me. I told them to take their stuff, get out of my garage, and never call me again. We're through. I can find other band members and I certainly don't need friends like that."

"Wow." I glanced at June to see how she was taking all this. She had been listening intently, and her face bore an expression of sympathy and understanding even though she had just met Manny.

I looked back at my friend. I don't think I've ever seen him that down in the dumps. I couldn't think of anything to say except, "I'm so sorry, Manny."

He heaved a sigh and waved his hand dismissively. "Don't worry about it, DH. I should have done this a long time ago. You even told me not too long ago that I should dissolve the band. You were right."

"Yes, I did," I said wryly.

"I didn't like the way the guys treated you either, DH," he said, more indignant than angry. "The only one that gave two cents about you was Pet."

"So, did you break with Pet, too?"

"Not really. The others just grabbed their gear and left as fast as they could. She kinda took her time even though she didn't have much stuff. I was able to tell her before she left that I didn't mean all of that for her. She smiled at me, but I'm not sure where that leaves us."

"Well, this is quite a development." I told him.

June broke her silence and asked, "Do you have other friends you can ask to start up a new band, Manny?"

"My buddy, DH, plays a mean keyboard." Manny grinned at me.

I laughed. "Only when it's unplugged."

June looked first at me, then at Manny, then back at me. "What?"

"It's a long story for another time," I told her. Turning to Manny, I said, "So how about that? Do you have a couple of other guys you can talk into it?"

"I have a couple in mind."

"I can't believe Pet would go with Paul and Burt. I'll bet if you lined up two more guitar guys she'd be back in a flash. I can talk to her, too, and see if I can get her to help you find somebody."

"Would you?" Manny brightened up a little. "Pet likes you a lot, she might just do it if you asked."

"I'll give it a shot."

"So, let's change the subject," Manny said. He turned his attention to June put his elbow on the table and rested his chin in his hand. "Who are you, June? Where did DH find you, and what are you all about?"

"Wow—a lot of questions." She smiled at him warmly while she thought for a moment before answering. "I'm an artist, I have a studio in LA, I like the ocean, motorcycles, storms, and puppy dogs. And DH didn't find me, I found him."

"Okay," he said slowly, looking to me for clarification.

"I was sitting on a bench outside LACMA. She came over and said, 'Hi.'"

"What's a LACMA?"

"LA County Museum of Art."

"Oh, that LACMA." When he realized what had happened, Manny sat up straight and looked at me. "What were you doing there, and why didn't you call me to go with you? I might have avoided the whole band thing if I went with you instead of holding the practice," he said with mock indignation.

"Sorry. I thought about you, but I knew you had a practice so I figured you wouldn't be able to go. It was supposed to be a quick trip in and out of the museum, then back home."

"Then I happened," June said.

"Yep. She happened. Spoiled my whole day." I looked at her and smiled.

"What did you two do all day?"

"We went to June's really cool studio down the street from the museum, we ate the best lunch ever, we rode around LA on June's Harley, we went to Laguna and sat on the beach under a tarp in the middle of a monster storm—"

"Okay, that's enough." Manny shooed my words away with his hand. "I'm going to be mad at you forever. That all sounds like a whole lot of fun that I missed."

"It was, Manny. I'm really sorry I didn't call you, but had you come with me we might have done something entirely different and I might never have met June."

"There's that." June smiled.

"I guess you're right," Manny said. "So, what are you going to do for the rest of the day?"

"I have no idea. I'm getting kind of hungry, we could order some food here at The Scot."

"I don't know. I'm not in the mood for greasy stuff right now," Manny said, making a face that mirrored his mood.

"We could go back to your place and barbecue," June suggested.

"Am I invited?" Manny looked at each of us in turn with an expression like a lost puppy.

"Of course!" June said, looking at me.

"Of course!" I said. "We could make a party out of it, play some jazz, eat some food —"

"Do some drawings, write some poetry —" June added.

"Really?" I asked.

"Why not?" She said.

"No reason. It just brought back some recent memories."

June studied me for a moment. "Good memories, I hope," she said.

"Sometimes." I was thinking about the night Abby and Mam and I wrote poetry in the family room of my parents' house. I didn't want to mention it because June might want me to go into details.

I turned to Manny to deflect more questions. "How did you get down here today?" I asked.

"Mom dropped me off. I was so pathetically maudlin she couldn't stand to have me around the house, so she brought me down here and turned me loose."

"It's a long walk home," I said.

"She's gonna pick me up in about thirty minutes."

"Go ask Christa if you can use the phone. Call your mom and tell her you're going to my house."

"Can you take me home later?"

"Sure, but tell your mom you might be spending the night just in case we've all had too much wine to drink."

"Okay. She won't care."

Manny headed over to find Christa.

"Do you have any other friends you can call? We could make it a real party," June said.

"I might think of a few."

"It can be an Art Party." June was really getting excited by this spur-of-the-moment gathering. "We'll have a contest. Everyone can draw a plan for a large, group drawing, then we can have someone judge the plans and come up with a winner. Or maybe we can all vote on which plan is best."

"What's the prize?"

"The winner gets to keep the big group drawing."

"What if the drawing sucks?"

"With you and me contributing? How could it?"

Manny came back and said that everything was squared away with his mom, so we left The Scot and headed back to my place. On the way we talked about who we could invite to our impromptu party. I really didn't want to mention Jan Collard, Mam, or Steff and Candy. Just the thought of all of them together at the same small party made me uncomfortable, especially with June there. The problem is though, I really don't know a whole lot of people. I decided to check out my yoga students — I keep their names and phone numbers in case of schedule changes and emergencies. I went through the list and picked out several I felt comfortable with.

The first one I called was Bette, the forty-something woman with long black hair who is always trying to impress me. I remember her talking about the art classes she takes at RCC. She's nice and it might be good to get to know her, considering I'll be taking art classes there next year. Then I remembered a couple of others who had expressed an interest in art.

One of them, Mary, looks like a pretty little girl at first glance, but she actually is an adult with a job and everything. She really is little — no more than five foot one or two, with bright blue eyes, and long red hair that always looks like it needs to be washed.

The other one, Diane, is a real stunner in my book. Think classic Italian — large Italian nose, dark close-set eyes, full lips, and the thickest head of black hair I've ever seen. Her hair doesn't end with her head, either. In yoga class, you catch glimpses of things you don't usually see otherwise, and I've noticed that Diane doesn't shave her armpits. I've never seen anything like it. Let's just say that her armpits are well insulated for the cold winter months. Her most notable features though, are her boobs. I hate to sound like the only thing I notice about a woman are her breasts, but Diana's breasts definitely deserve notice. They're not just large, they're also pendulous. They hang way down, kind of like you'd see on a much older woman but they aren't saggy or flat, they're full and heavy. I think elongated is a good word to use for them. It's difficult to describe such things without sounding like I'm writing for a porn magazine, but they still need to be mentioned. When you see Diane, you'll know what I mean. The image is quite startling.

The last call I made was to my friend, Elvis. I think I mentioned him before — his family's Jewish but he visits the Zen Monastery up on Mt. Baldy from time to time. We've known each other a long time and have had a lot of fun together, especially the last few years in high school. Manny is a good friend, but he tends to be quiet and serious. When I want to have a really fun time, he's not the guy to turn to, Elvis is. He and I have spent hundreds of hours together playing guitars and singing folk music — he sings, I don't — going to movies, drinking coffee at The Scot, and talking about girls for so long we almost got tired of it. Almost. Actually, Elvis does bare some resemblance to his namesake — you know the one — in a bizarre, hairy sort of way.

◎ ◎ ◎

Everyone's been called and they all agreed to come. Manny and I are out here in The Hole and June is in the kitchen in the house putting final touches on the food we bought for the party. We had decided that even a simple barbecue with burgers and wieners was too much trouble, so we stopped at the store on the way here and picked up a ton of different lunch meats, bread, cheeses, pickles, condiments, and chips so everyone can build their own plate of goodies. Then all we'd have to do afterward is throw away the paper plates.

On the Patio • 6PM

Elvis was the first to arrive. He's usually the last, or just doesn't show up at all. It's nothing personal, it's just the way he is. He drives a beat up Oldsmobile, at least I think it's an Oldsmobile. It's old, late forties or early fifties, green-faded-to-gray except where it's rust. The engine sputters and coughs like it's on its last breath, but somehow it always gets him from point A to point B. I heard him coming when he was still a block away, so by the time he got here I was over the surprise of his arrival.

Elvis thinks of himself as a man-about-town and likes to dress up for any occasion, even if it's a spur-of-the-moment thing like this evening's gathering. Tonight he's wearing a pair of tight black corduroy pants, a white turtle-neck shirt, and some kind of medallion on a gold chain. The most striking feature about him is his midnight-black hair. It's thick and wavy, and long enough in the back to curl over his collar and it extends in front of his ears in long sideburns. I've seen pictures of Roman helmets that look like Elvis's hair. His luxuriant growth of hair is not confined to his head, either. It's not unusual for Elvis to shave two or three times a day. In high school he was actually suspended for growing a beard. He wasn't trying. He had just forgotten to shave that morning.

Diane, the Italian bombshell from yoga, arrived while I was still outside greeting Elvis. We turned to watch her climb out of her little red fiat and walk toward us. My first thought was, *Holy Moly.* My second thought was, *With that hair of theirs, I wonder what the kids would look like if she and Elvis ever hooked up — Sasquatch?*

But back to the first thought, which was prompted by her attire. Diane is wearing a very short, tight-fitting white dress that actually looks like it might be a man's t-shirt. The fabric is thin, and every highlight and shadow shows through, including the large, dark patch a few inches below her navel. As short as the dress is, we'll be seeing more than just shadows if she's not careful. She's tied what I think is a man's neck tie around her waist as a belt, making the stretchy t-shirt follow the shape of her body even more closely, accentuating the size and shape of her odd elongated breasts

Bette was the next one to arrive. She was dressed pretty much like she always does for yoga; a white shirt with the tails tied at her waist and the top buttons undone enough to show off her assets. Instead of black tights, she's wearing tight black capris that hug her curves from her waist to just below her knees. She's a big woman, nearly as tall as me. There's a lot to her, and all of it in the right places. I'm trying to think of who she looks like and Jane Russell comes to mind.

The last to arrive was Mary, looking more than ever like a little girl as she stepped out of her bright yellow VW Bug. She had dressed her five-foot-two-inch, ninety-nine-pound body in tight, light green capris that fit her little butt as if they were painted on. She's wearing a light blue tube top that covers her small breasts while leaving the milk-white skin of her belly and shoulders bare. She looks a lot like Twiggy — round face, big blue eyes, full lips, and a slight dusting of freckles across her nose. Today she's pulled her stringy red hair into two pigtails, one on either side of her head. I had to look twice when she got out of her car, because she looks like she's about ten years old and not the nearly thirty she had told me she is.

Manny and I are both wearing our uniforms of Levi's and t-shirt — my shirt is navy blue, and his is green. June is wearing her cutoffs, and one of my white t-shirts. She also has one of my long-sleeved flannel shirts tied around her waist so that it covers the holes in the back where her naked butt shows through. I didn't like the idea of sharing that view with Manny and Elvis.

After a few minutes of chit chat, June invited our guests to help themselves to the buffet she had set out. When everyone had filled a plate, I directed them out to the patio where I had set up a circle of chairs. I had decided that it might be fun and enlightening for each of us to take a turn to tell the others a little about who we are. I'm the only one who knows all of the others, but except for Manny and Elvis, I don't really know the others, and although June and I have shared much, there's still much about her that I don't know. This should be interesting.

I reveal my plan to the group, and then I turn to Bette, who is sitting to the right of me. She has a half-smile on her face and is pushing her food around her plate, avoiding eye contact with the others. "Why don't we begin with you, Bette?"

She lets out a breath that is as much of a laugh as it is a sigh and begins to speak. "There's not much to tell, really. I'm one of DH's yoga students. I love yoga, it's a nice, gentle way to stay in shape. I'm not much into sports or going to gyms to get fit, those things are too aggressive for me." She laughs, a little more relaxed now that she has begun.

"Do you work?" June asks.

"Yes, at Harris' in the Plaza—in women's clothing. I've been there for about five years."

"Can we get discounts since we know you?" Diane asks. She has a thick east-coast accent—New York, or maybe New Jersey.

Bette laughs and shakes her head. "I'm afraid it doesn't work like that," she says.

"Wow, Harris'," I say. "Pretty posh. That's where all the rich folks shop."

"We have a very, um … interesting clientele," she says

"How do you mean, interesting?" I ask.

"Let's put it this way, lunacy isn't just for the middle class. Just because someone has a lot of money, it doesn't make them any more pleasant to be around. I get some nut jobs on a daily basis down there."

"When you're rich you're not crazy, you're eccentric." I say.

"You could say that."

"Got any stories you can tell us?" Manny asks.

Bette pauses for a moment before speaking. "Well, just the other day one of the richest women in Riverside walked in, grabbed about twenty pairs of very delicate, very expensive women's panties. Now, customers are not supposed to take panties into the dressing rooms, but she did anyway. I kept an eye on the door and about ten minutes later she came out with nothing but her purse. I checked inside the dressing room she'd been in, expecting to find all those panties, but there was nothing there. I called for a female security officer who was able to stop the woman from leaving the store. She wasn't too happy about it, but we got her back into the women's department and showed her the empty dressing room. The guard asked her what happened to the panties. The woman said she had no idea, but we weren't buying it. The guard looked in the woman's purse and found all the empty panty packages. Then the guard lifted up the woman's dress, and lo and behold, she was wearing all of them! She had put them on, one on top of the other, and planned to walk out of the store like that."

Murmurs of astonishment and disbelief come from everyone.

"Really. This woman's a millionaire. One of the wealthiest, most influential families in town, and she was shoplifting panties. Don't think we didn't get a laugh out of that!"

"So what did you do with all those panties?" Manny asks.

"She wore them, so she had to pay for them. Panties aren't like shirts and dresses that you can just put back on the rack. The woman was arrested, but I think she must have something wrong upstairs to do something like that when she's so well off."

We are all pondering the afflictions of the rich when Diane asks, "So, what about your hobbies?"

"That's easy." Bette is beaming now, and even has a sparkle in her eyes. "I love photography. I was a model for a few years and when I saw how good other people could make me look, I thought I'd try it for myself."

"A model? How cool is that?" June smiles. "Where did you do your modeling?"

"I'd rather not say, if you don't mind." Bette's smile dims and she goes back to playing with the food on her plate.

Her reaction only piques Manny's curiosity. "Oh boy, a mystery," he says, with a Grouch Marx waggle of his eyebrows. I give him a look to tell him to back off.

"That's okay, Bette," I say, "We don't need to know. It doesn't matter in the scope of all things eternal."

"Wow ..." Turning to the source of the exclamation, I find Diane looking at me as if seeing me for the first time. "What a wonderfully metaphysical thing to say," she says.

"I was just telling the truth," I responded.

"Yeah but, when most of the people I hang with say things like that it don't come out soundin' like that," she says rather harshly. "It's usually corny and dumb."

Diane is beginning to look a little different in my eyes, too. It's hard to size up a person based on seeing them in a yoga class once a week, but I like what she just said; it sounded very much like something I would say — the sarcasm, the frankness, the truth. I hate beating around the bush when talking about things I have an interest in, and I hate people who agree with everything everyone says just because they know they'll be criticized if they disagree with the majority.

I smile at her. She meets my gaze and smiles back. "Thank you, Diane," I say. "You might as well be next since you're already in the spotlight. Tell us something about yourself."

"I'm just me," she says without taking her eyes off mine. "I like music, art, pasta. And sex." If the others weren't paying attention before, they are now.

"Well … um … that's interesting." The back of my neck just got warm. Am I blushing?

She finally breaks eye contact with me and includes the entire group as she continues. "I also like just sittin' around thinkin' about things that people don't ordinarily like to think about."

"What kind of things?" June asks.

"Just things. Every day it's a different thing with me. I don't know where it comes from. It just does."

"You mean like science, or politics, or what?" Manny asks.

"Sometimes. Sometimes things that are simpler, like I watch a leaf fallin' from a limb. I think I know where it's headed, but then it suddenly takes a turn and lands a couple of feet from where I thought it was gonna land. What the hell made it do that? There wasn't any wind, not the slightest breeze. Why did it turn to the left all of a sudden? Why didn't it float down to where it was goin' in the first place? What made it change its mind like that? Can a leaf think? Did it sense fear? A predator on the ground? If a leaf is the prey, then who's its predator?"

The rest of us are speechless as we digest what she just said. I can tell from their expressions that the others are having the same thoughts as I am, *This chick is really different.*

"I also write," she says.

Diane has just upped my interest a notch or two. "What do you write?" I ask.

"Poetry. I've written a couple or three books."

Murmurs of surprise, appreciation, and curiosity come from the group.

"You've written books?" Manny asks incredulously.

Diane nails Manny with a look. "Is that a problem?"

Manny responds by backpedaling.

"Uh, no … just asking. What I meant was, are you published?

Where can we buy your books?"

"No, I'm not published. I haven't got a publisher yet. I'll probably have to sleep with one to get my stuff on the market."

Diane is one tough chick who obviously didn't grow up around here. The streets of New York, maybe? Once again, the group is at a loss for words.

"What kind of stuff do you write, Diane?" I ask.

"All those things that I mentioned. Things that I like. It all comes out in poetry form. Each book is one long poem, maybe three or four hundred pages long."

"Wow, four hundred pages—that's one heck of a poem." June has just said what we all are thinking.

"From your accent it's clear that you're not from around here," I say. "Do you mind telling us where you are from?

"New York City."

"I thought so." I smiled. "What brought you out here?"

"I didn't have no choice. Life in New York got to be hell. It was either freeze to death in a rat infested tenement, or get raped and murdered while walkin' the streets tryin' to drum up enough money to buy some bread and wine."

"Geez, Diane," Bette said. "You've had a rough time of it."

"You haven't heard the half of it, but that's as much as you're gonna get. Hand me that jug of wine." Diane looks at me and I hand her the jug. She looks me in the eye and smiles like she really means it, but her gaze lingers just a little longer than I thought it should have.

"Where do you live, Diane?" Manny asks.

"I got an Aunt livin' in a trailer here in Riverside. She's sick, so I'm stayin' with her right now, helpin' to take care of her. I'm probably leavin' town soon, though."

"Well, it's good to get to know you for the time you're here," I tell her.

"Yeah, you too." Then she turns her head away from the group to let us know that her part of the conversation is over.

Before the pause becomes awkward, Manny shouts out, "Mary, you're up next."

This should be interesting. I know absolutely nothing about Mary expect that she's in my yoga class, and that she's been able to drink an incredible amount of wine since she arrived. For such a little thing she can sure put it away.

"Hi, I'm Mary." Even her voice is like a little girl's. "I don't know much about my own background, I'm adopted. I've been told my real parents were from Scotland. I suppose that's why I have a bit of an accent. I don't even know if I was born here in the states or brought here as a baby, or if my parents are dead or alive either here or in Scotland. No one seems to know anything more about me."

I certainly picked an interesting bunch of people to attend this little gathering.

"Do you work Mary?" June asks her.

"Of course I work. If I didn't work I'd starve, but I don't mind." Then she smiles the first smile I've seen her smile in ... well, ever, "We Scots are hard workers."

"What do you do?" June tries to gently prod her into revealing what she works at.

"I've been doing office work part time at the college, but I just got a full-time job that starts in two days. I'll be a waitress at the Royal Scot."

"You're kidding!" Manny exclaims.

"No, really," she responds.

"We go there all the time, DH and I."

"So, I'll see you in there sometime."

"No doubt," I say. "We practically live down there."

"How about hobbies? Likes and dislikes?" June asks.

Mary looks at her and smiles. "I study people. Waitressing is a perfect job for that."

"I guess it is." June grins. "You're certainly gonna get some weirdo's in The Scot." She gives me a look and I blow her a kiss.

"I imagine I will. Other than that, I enjoy history, astronomy, and, like Diane, I love to think about things."

"And what do you think about?" I ask.

"Eternity—where it all began, where it will all end. I like to ponder all the magic out there." Mary waves her arms in a sweeping motion to include all of the world beyond herself. "There's more in nature and in how humans relate to it than meets the eye. It's not just science, there's much magic behind it all."

I am truly amazed by everything I've heard here this evening. "You know," I say, "I never thought when I asked all of you to come here tonight that I'd end up with such a group of philosophers and seekers. I'm blown away."

"Don't worry, DH," Manny says, grinning. "We haven't gotten to Elvis yet. He'll bring us back down to Earth." Turning to Elvis, he continues. "We haven't been friends long, but I have known you just long enough to know you aren't really a philosopher."

"How can I be a philosopher? I'm Jewish," Elvis deadpans.

"You got a point," Manny says, playing along with the joke.

"What's wrong with being Jewish?" June asks, looking genuinely concerned by the exchange.

"Nothing, June." I tell her. "They're just kidding. These two guys really love each other."

"Not in that way," Elvis says, putting his hands up to halt further speculation. "I just want to clarify that I'm all male and that I like girls."

"Elvis, with all that hair and the deep voice, I'm pretty sure we're all aware of the testosterone." I smile at him, and the signs of repressed amusement from around the circle tell me that at least several of the others had the same thought.

"So, tell them about yourself, Elvis," I said.

"Well, I just told you, I'm Jewish. I don't spend a lot of time being Jewish, but I was born with it and I like to keep my fingers in it as much as I can. I'm also into Zen, as I'm pretty sure DH has already told you all. I spend a lot of time at the monastery up on Mt. Baldy."

"Are you a monk?" June asks.

"No. That's way too much trouble. I just like to go up there and meditate now and then. It kinda keeps my head straight. I don't care too much for what's going on in this world right now and the monastery evens it all out for me."

"Do you have any hobbies?" Bette asks.

"I play the guitar, mainly folk music. I'm not much into Manny's kind of music. Rock doesn't do anything for me, and it's way too loud. There's enough noise in this world without adding to it."

"Since you and DH know each other from high school, I assume you just graduated, too. What do you plan to do now?" June asks.

"I'll be going to the community college in the fall. I'm planning to major in some sort of science and maybe get a teaching credential. I've got a part time job lined up at one of the junior high schools. They're experimenting with teachers' aides in the science classes, and I'm to be their guinea pig. The district wants to make learning science a more hands-on process where the kids actually do stuff rather than just read books and watch demonstrations. It means a lot more work for the teachers, so I'll be helping them set up and supervise experiments.

"That sounds fun," Bette says.

"I've attended a couple of staff meetings already and I'm not sure what to think. They got pretty rowdy. Let's just say that teachers in the teachers' lounge are not as they appear to be when in front of a classroom — think Dr. Jekyll and Mr. Hyde. I'm not sure how long I'll last at this, but at least it will give me the opportunity to see if I'm cut out to be a teacher while I still have time to change my mind."

"What do you mean?" I ask.

Elvis takes a deep drag on his cigarette. He's the only heavy smoker in the group and he's been at it since junior high. "After listening to a few of the teachers tell their tales of woe, I'm not so sure I want to get anywhere near a classroom, unless it's an empty one."

"It can't be all that bad," Bette says.

"The way the teacher's tell it, the kids are mostly a bunch of out of control monsters with parents that don't give a damn about their education, but who all have a lot to say about how to run the school."

"I've heard that from others," June says. "I have a friend who teaches in LA, and according to her, the teachers can't do anything right in the eyes of the parents. If a kid does something wrong it's always the teacher's fault and never the fault of the rotten little kid."

"That's what I'm hearing here in Riverside. Maybe not all the kids are bad, but about 50% of them are real turds," Elvis responds.

"Well, as you say, this job sounds like a good way to find out if you're cut out for it. Who knows, you may discover that you have a talent for making kids sit still and learn," June says.

"I'll tell you one thing, if I get one little turd giving me any back talk on the first day, I'll walk out before noon. I don't need that kind of crap in my life."

"Sounds like you already have some other crap in your life, Elvis," Diane says.

"That I do, but don't ask me about it because I don't even want to go there."

Diane smiles knowingly. "That means one of two things, either parents or lovers."

He gives her an appreciative look before responding. "You must be psychic," he says. "It's both, but let's leave it at that."

"Well, that leaves Manny, June, and me. You guys already know a lot about me. I teach yoga. I want to be an artist when I grow up. I love astronomy, ancient Egypt, thinking about the afterlife—having died when I was nine and come back to tell about it, I often reflect on what comes next after we leave this mortal frame."

"Are you kidding me?" Diane says. "You've had a NDE?"

"What's that?" Mary asks.

"Near Death Experience," I told her. "I was in the hospital with double pneumonia. I slipped into a coma and died. A few minutes after the doctor pronounced me dead, I came back, woke up, and told the doc and everyone in the room all about a time and place out of the realms of this physical world or dimension."

"Wow." Diane is bug-eyed with amazement. "I wanna hear about that."

"Half the people here already know the story and I don't want to bore them with it again. Maybe later when everybody else is busy you and I can find a corner somewhere and I'll fill you in."

Uh-oh. The look June just gave me when I mentioned that Diane and I might find a corner somewhere was not a good one.

"Well," I say brightly, trying to cover my discomfort, "I guess it's either Manny's or June's turn to spill their stories."

Manny and June each took their turn. I won't go into detail since I have already recorded both of their histories previously in this journal. I know that June is a terrific story teller based on our trip from LA to Laguna yesterday, and Manny's no slouch either. Manny may seem quiet and somewhat shy, but he's a born entertainer; just give him a stage and stand back. And June … well, June's an artist. Needless to say, they both had the group in stitches.

I had never hosted a party like this before. Everyone listened with interest to what each of the others had to say, and I think we all had our view of the world changed just a bit by hearing what the others had experienced in life and that the seven of us now share the beginning of a bond of friendship. I was hoping we'd do a group poem or drawing or something, but that didn't happen. Maybe next time.

At the far end of the Grotto • 11 PM

The gathering broke up much earlier than I had expected. Most of the people were a bit pooped by 8 PM and they were afraid that if they stayed and drank any more they wouldn't get home at all. So, one by one they took their leave and headed out. Bette was the first to leave after thanking me profusely and telling me she'd see me in yoga. She was followed by Mary, then Diane. I wasn't surprised when June left. She had told me this afternoon that she would be leaving fairly early because she had to be at the museum in the morning for a meeting. It seems she has a good chance at a small art show there if the timing is right, and the judges cooperate. We kissed and she promised to call after she heard more about the show. Then with a rattle and a roar she was on her bike and kicking up a cloud of dust as she sped down the long driveway.

Manny was the last to leave. His mother had called earlier to ask if she could pick him up so he could help her hang some drapes before going to bed. Apparently, Hester had washed and dried all the curtains in the living room and the bedrooms, and she was having a tough time getting them back up by herself. The curtain rod hangers kept coming unscrewed and she had a real mess on her hands. She needed to get the drapes back up unless she wanted the whole world looking into her house at night while the lights were on. The story made me smile because, knowing Hester the way I do, I thought it would be just like her to enjoy teasing the neighbors by walking around naked in her living room with no drapes. I got the impression from the look he gave me that Manny had the same thought. Anyway, Hester picked up Manny at about 9 PM. Of course she had to get out of her car and come over and say hi to me before leaving. She also gave me a very, shall we say, warm, hug, sliding her hands along my shoulders and down my arms before turning and walking slowly back to her car.

I watched the tail lights of Hester's car disappear around the bend in the drive, then turned to go inside with thoughts of watching TV for about an hour before hitting the hay. I had just reached the breezeway when I heard the sound of a car engine headed back toward the house. At first, I thought Manny had forgotten something and was coming back for it, but when I turned to look, lo and behold, there was Diane in her Fiat.

She pulled up next to me, rolled down her window, and asked, "Can I visit with you for a while?"

"Sure," I told her, my face betraying my surprise. "Is everything alright?"

"Everything is fine," she said as she climbed out of the little car.

"I just couldn't go home without talkin' to you some more. It was eatin' at me the whole way, so I turned around and came back." She paused and looked around at the mostly-dark house and the empty driveway. "It looks like everyone's gone."

"Yep. Manny just left. He was the last."

"Do you think we can go back out on the patio and have a conversation for a while? If you don't want to, I'll leave."

"Sure. We can do that." I motioned for her to follow me through the breezeway.

When we got to the patio, Diane just stood there looking ill at ease.

"Is something wrong, Diane?"

"It just feels strange here. I can still feel the presence of all the people that were here. Is there a different spot out here where we can sit that doesn't have the memory of others etched on it?" She shivered briefly and rubbed her arms with her hands as if she were cold, even though the evening was still quite warm.

My mind went into double time, part of it registering just how weird this chick really is, while another part tried to think of somewhere we could go. There have been people all over the back yard, even the cliff at the edge of the grotto had been well used by several, including Abby and me before Abby left for parts unknown. The only place I could think of where no one had been in a very long time was a small clearing at the far end of the grotto. I could grab a blanket out of The Hole to give us something to sit on, and I could get one of the camping lanterns from the garage. There's a small one in there that puts out just enough light to see by, but not enough to blind us to the night sky.

I told Diane to wait while I got the blanket and lantern. When I returned, I found her waiting patiently with an unopened gallon jug of Red Mountain in one hand and two mugs in the other.

"You don't mind, do you?" she asked, raising the jug and the mugs.

"No, I'm always up for a little wine. It helps the conversation flow. you'd better be careful, though. If you drink much more it won't be safe for you to drive home."

"You got a problem with me stayin' here for the night if I drink too much? You never know, we might just talk all night."

I didn't know how to answer that, so I just said, "Follow me." I led her to the path down the cliff edge to the hidden clearing at the far end. I spread the blanket over the soft ground, lit the lantern, and invited her to sit.

She sat on one side of the blanket and pointed to a spot in front of her, "Sit here, right in front of me," she said, "so I can watch your face. Expressions reveal a lot of information that the voice hides."

I did as she instructed, and sat down Indian fashion facing her. She, too, was sitting cross-legged in front of me. Her short dress had ridden up and the lantern light revealed the true nature of the dark shadowy patch I had noticed earlier.

I was momentarily at a loss for words. Finally, I cleared my throat and asked, "So, what would you like to talk about?"

"Can we just look up at the sky for a bit?" Diane asked. "It's so beautiful up there — out there — in deep space. So many stars. So many planets."

"How about I turn the lantern off for a while?" I asked. "There's a pretty big moon tonight, so there's plenty of light."

"Just think of how much light each sun up there gives off in it's own solar system. Can you imagine all the energy, all the power this entire universe produces? And maybe this isn't the only universe. There may be thousands more out there beyond this one." Diane's upturned face was radiant as she contemplated the splendor of the universe. I'm pretty sure it was just reflecting the moonlight, but it might just as well have been her own inner glow.

"I've wondered about that same thing. If that's the case, then there are more suns and planets than humans have a number for."

"Googolplex."

"I beg your pardon?"

"That's the word for a number so large it can't be named or described."

"Cool. Does that have anything to do with what you want to

talk about?"

"Possibly, but not directly. Are you in a hurry to get rid of me? You seem impatient."

"I'm just curious as to what you want to talk about, but I think I can guess—My Near Death Experience, am I right? And no, I don't want to get rid of you. I'm actually quite happy you're here. I thought the party would go on longer, but it seems I called together a bunch of party poopers for this one."

"Yeah, you're right. I want you to tell me about your NDE. I've had one myself and I thought we could share notes."

"Really? Wow, that's neat!" I smiled, excited by the thought of finally meeting someone who has had a similar experience.

"You're happy I died?" I think I could see her smiling in the moonlight.

"No, I'm happy we can share a common experience. I'm not happy you died, but I am happy that you came back to life so you could be right here where you are, sharing my blanket after all the others deserted me."

"Well then let's get this over with …"

Diane stood up. She moved toward me so quickly that, before I knew it, she was standing over me with my thighs between her feet. She placed her hands on my shoulders, and in one smooth motion lowered herself to my lap, slid her hands to my cheeks, and pulled my face toward hers to kiss me as hard as she could.

She finally broke away, both of us panting hard, and said, "You've wanted that for a long time, haven't you? Don't look so surprised. I've wanted it too." Then she locks onto me again, longer and stronger than before, if possible.

"Diane …" I couldn't find any words then, and still can't find any now, several hours later.

"We're not through yet," Diane whispers. "I'm gonna make you forget all about those other people, but we need to talk first."

Diane rose from my lap, slowly reversing the motion that had placed her there. She stood with her body only an inch or two away from my face, looking down at me still positioned between her legs and feet. When I looked up at her, the moon was directly behind her head turning her hair into a wild halo. That image of her combined with the scent of her body to take my breath away. She was like a wild woman. An untamed creature of nature standing in her element in the light of the moon, the ultimate symbol of romance and beauty being washed in pure white rays of splendor and power—an indescribable power that was at the same time both enchanting and terrifying.

The moment passed. Diane stepped back and returned to where she had been sitting on the other side of the blanket. Her lips, slick and swollen from our kissing, glistened in the light of the full moon and reminded me of the scene in the movie, Dracula, where the vampire has the blood of his victim on his mouth and dripping down his chin. I didn't know whether to return to our conversation, or to run like hell.

Grasping at normality, I said, "Why don't you tell me about your NDE, Diane."

"It happened about five years ago, right after I moved from New York to San Francisco."

"How long did you live in The City?"

"You know The City?" she asked. "You wouldn't call it that unless you'd been there."

"I haven't been there yet, but I want to go. I have a connection there, of sorts."

"That means one of two things—drugs or a girl, and you don't strike me as the drug type."

"I don't do drugs."

"A love interest?"

"Not any more. I have no idea where she's at right now. I think she's history."

"Too bad for her," Diane smiled. "So, do you know much about the Beat scene up there?"

"A little. Abby's mother knows a lot of the Beat writers personally.

Abby pretty much grew up around them"

"Abby, huh."

"Yep, Abby."

"I know some of the Beat writers too," Diane said. "I've slept with most of 'em. But that's not my NDE story."

"I hope not," I smiled.

"I was really poor, and the only neighborhood I could afford to live in was the Tenderloin. You know what that is?"

"I've heard of it. It's a pretty rough place isn't it?"

"Rough ain't the word for it. I lived in a one room apartment with no air conditionin' or heatin'. Air conditionin' is no big deal in San Francisco, but winters can get pretty cold, not to mention damp. It's not a killin' cold like back in New York, but it wears you down. But that's not the story, either. The Tenderloin's full of all kinds of riffraff. There are thugs that roam the streets at night and beat up people just to get a watch or a wallet or even a pair of shoes, or just because they feel like it, and they don't care if their victims live or die. That neighborhood is so mean that the cops won't even go into parts of it, and I lived right in the middle of all that."

"I suppose you were broke. Did you have a job?"

"I tried working at a fast food joint for a while, but it was two blocks from my apartment and I worked late. I got attacked on my way home almost every night. They all wanted somethin' I didn't wanna give 'em. Don't get me wrong, I'll give it away for free, but not to somebody I don't know who grabs me on the sidewalk while I'm walkin' home."

"I get the picture."

"One night I was walkin' home and it was pitch dark. I always tried to take different routes when I got off work 'cause those guys watch for girls who have a pattern. It's easier for 'em to grab a girl and haul her into an alley and do what they want with her when they get to know the routine."

"I always thought The City was a really peaceful place," I said.

"Only in the magazines, and it's gettin' worse. There are a lot of drifters moving up there from other cities and states. A lot of young people just layin' around in the parks, doin' nothin', and they're easy marks for the bad guys that prowl at night."

"Wow … and you lived in the middle of all that?"

"I died there too."

"How?"

"I needed money bad. My rent was due, my utilities were turned off, and I was gettin' sick. I quit the fast food job, so I couldn't steal burgers no more and I was gettin' thinner and weaker. One night I passed out while walkin' down the street. I hit my head on a dumpster on the way down to the sidewalk and I just laid there on the cement, unconscious and bleedin' like crazy from my head."

"Is that how you died?"

"No. I was out for about fifteen minutes. When I started to come to, I felt somebody grab my ankles and start pullin' me into the alley, no doubt to rape me and then run off."

"You're kidding! You've been knocked out, you're bleeding like crazy, and some guy wants to rape you?"

She shrugged and said, "Whataya gonna do? That's how it works up there. He pulled me into the alley, ripped open my shirt, and started squeezin' my tits — hard. When he grabbed my panties and started to yank 'em down, I heard a really deep voice yell, 'Hey! Get off her!'

"Who was he?"

"I don't know, but he had a gun."

"Seriously?" I can't imagine where this story is going.

"The guy that grabbed me let go, but he yelled some obscenities at Deep Voice and that made Deep Voice mad."

"What did he do?"

"He started firin' his gun at the guy on top of me."

"And?"

"He shot me. He shot the other guy too, but one of his bullets hit me in the side, right here." She lifted up her shirt to show me a large, ragged dimple on her left side.

"Good grief."

"Between the knock on the head and the bullet in my side, I was in pretty bad shape. I don't think I had much blood left in me."

"Then what happened?"

"The guy he shot was layin' on top of me, dead. I was pinned down and couldn't move — actually, I don't think I could have moved even if I hadn't been pinned down. Deep Voice came over and rolled the dead guy off me. I heard him say something like, 'No! I'm so sorry,' and then I passed out. Somebody must have called for help after they heard the shots — cops, ambulance, whatever. Anyway, they took me to a hospital. The doc said I died at 3 AM, but just when they were all ready to leave the room, my heart started up again and I was back in the show. The doc thought I was dead for three or four minutes."

It took me a minute to digest what she had told me. Finally, I shook my head and said, "Man ... what a story. What a life. You ought to write a book."

"I have. It's one of the books I got at home that I've never published."

"Well, it ought to be published."

"Some day."

"Did you experience anything when you were dead? See any angels?" I asked.

"I knew I was dead as soon as I died. Suddenly, I was up by the ceilin' lookin' down at my body lyin' on the bed. There was blood all over the sheet and on the floor. My head was a mess, with blood in my hair and a big bruise on my forehead. The doctor and the nurses were standin' around lookin' at me, then the doc said, 'She's gone.' Everyone got real still and quiet, and I could actually see tears on the face of one of the nurses. Later, I was able to describe the whole scene perfectly — the cryin' nurse and everything. That's how everyone knew I was tellin' the truth about dyin' and being up over the bed. All those years livin' in New York, the roughest city in America, and I have to come all the way to San Francisco to get killed! It's a sad joke, ain't it?"

"Did you go anywhere else while you were dead?" I've heard of other people having similar experiences, but this was the first time I've actually spoken with a near-death survivor and I wanted to hear every detail.

"I really wasn't up by the ceilin' for very long. I had no sense of time while this was all happenin', so I can only guess about it. It seemed like hours."

"Me too. That's how I felt, that time had slowed way down."

"Probably only about twenty seconds passed when I felt this kind of explosion inside my body and a really bright light filled the room. I thought I'd been blown up or somethin'."

"Wow! That's almost exactly like my NDE. I was just floating around, and then, BAM, the hospital room was gone, and I was in a beautiful summer meadow."

"Well, I didn't go to a meadow. I don't know where I was, but I was in a buildin' I'd never seen the likes of before. It was amazin'. I was standin' in what looked to be a huge reception room, like the lobby of a hotel, kinda. The whole buildin' was made out of glass. The whole place sparkled, and I could see through everything. All the people walkin' around were wearin' white clothes, and lookin' really happy, like they were all doin' somethin' special that was important, but also fun. You know what I mean? I'd never seen anything like it in my life. I was used to tenements, and brick and mortar, and alleys and blacktop, and then I get tossed into somethin' like that. I felt like I was inside the most beautiful Christmas tree you could ever imagine. Like I was one of the ornaments just standin' there takin' in the scene."

"It sounds lovely. What you saw was totally different from what I saw, but it was the same because it was so beautiful and fantastic. Did you get to talk to anybody?"

"I did. The prettiest woman I think I've ever seen walked up to me. She was tall—well over six feet—and had beautiful long, blonde hair. She was wearin' a flowin' white dress and a diamond necklace that must have cost a fortune, and she smelled like flowers."

"What did she say?"

"She took me in her arms and hugged me real tight. When she pulled away, she kept her hands on my shoulders and looked at me — no, she looked *into* me. She told me she was sorry, but it wasn't time for me to be there yet. I asked her if we were in heaven. When she said we weren't, I told her it sure looked like heaven to me. And that was that. She smiled at me and kissed me on the top of my head, then she told me she'd see me again someday. There was another flash of light and somethin' like an explosion, and I was back in my body in the hospital bed and in serious pain. All the nurses were really excited and the one who was cryin' before was raisin' her hands in the air and cryin' even harder now. Then I passed out again."

"Incredible. What a neat experience you had. I'm afraid mine pales in comparison to yours. Imagine, a building made out of glass!"

"Yeah, and it sparkled like crazy. I could see a bright light outside kinda like the sun, only more blue-white than yellow-white, and as the light came through the glass walls, the walls sparkled in colors like I'd never seen."

"Like a prism effect?" I ask.

"I don't know what it was, but it was beautiful. I didn't want to come back here."

"Well, my NDE was a lot different. I found myself in a pretty summer meadow surrounded by a forest of gigantic trees — bigger than any that grow here on Earth. A tall man met me there. He was dressed in a white robe and he had a glow about his face."

"Was it Jesus?"

"I don't think so — more like an angel. He didn't say a word to me, he just shooed me away from the meadow and pointed me toward the forest. I got the impression that I wasn't supposed to be there. He seemed nice and he had a kind smile, but he made it clear that I needed to go. I was only nine years old, just a little kid, so I think he was being gentle with me. Anyway, as I turned to head back toward the forest, I felt the same explosion that you felt.

I was engulfed in a bright light and the next thing I knew, I was back in the hospital. They couldn't believe I'd come back to life. I'd been in a coma with double pneumonia, I'd died, and they figured that was that. But I came back and told them what I'd seen when I was up in the air over the bed. All the details were exactly right, but when I told them about the redheaded nurse who sat on my bed and held my hand, they said there was no one like that on the hospital staff. So, I figure I got to see two angels."

"So the redhead was an angel?"

"That's what I think. I mean, she was dressed like a nurse and everything, had a white apron, nurse's hat, everything. Really pretty face and long, thick red hair going down her back, just beautiful."

"But they told you they didn't have no nurse at that hospital lookin' like that with red hair and all?"

"It was a small place. Not a lot of nurses on staff, and everyone knew everyone else."

"Well, she had to be an angel. I guess we both saw angels then."

"What does that tell us about the afterlife?" I asked her.

"That's easy. First of all, there is an afterlife, and second, they got angels there. That's about it." She smiled and shrugged her shoulders.

"Smarty pants. But why did you go to a really cool heavenly building like that and I went to a meadow. It sounds like you got a little closer to heaven than I did. Maybe there's different parts of heaven people have to work their way through before they get to the top."

"I don't know 'bout that. But if heaven's inside a buildin', I'm not sure I wanna go there. Not even that pretty buildin' the tall lady had me in. I'd rather be outside in nature for my eternity."

"Yeah, buildings are a bit Earthly aren't they? You'd think heaven would be more advanced than that."

"They were made out of glass, though," she pointed out.

"I guess that's pretty cool. But I'm with you, I'd rather be outside. Like we are right now." I had been gazing at the stars, but then I looked at her and smiled. "It's really beautiful out here tonight."

"You have a cute smile," she said. "I can barely see it in the moonlight, but it's there."

"Do you want me to turn the lantern back on?"

"I think you should, at least for a while. I have a few things I wanna show you."

I lit the lantern but turned it down so that it was just enough for us to see each other clearly. "How's that?"

"That'll do."

The soft lantern was enough to illuminate Diane's smile and emphasize her unusual beauty. Her face is like that of a Madonna. That's probably her Italian blood, aren't all Madonna's Italian girls painted by Italian guys? If Diane is representative of most Italian women, then the painters of old were wise to choose them.

Diane and I had been sitting cross-legged on opposite sides of the blanket. Now, she scooted toward me until her knees were almost touching mine. After slowly untying her man's-tie belt she took hold of the hem of her skimpy tee shirt dress and pulled it upward over her head and laid it aside. Sitting up straight and puffing out her chest, she said, "You've been starin' at these all night so I thought I'd give you a good look at em."

Her breasts were enormous. They hung down nearly to her lap and were tipped with long nipples surrounded by dark brown areolae the size of silver dollars. She placed a hand under each of them and waved them back and forth in front of me like a game show hostess showing off the grand prize. I'd never seen anything like it—like them.

"Careful, you might catch a fly," she teased.

"Oh ... sorry." I closed my mouth.

"I have my mother's tits, and my nonna's—my grandma. Big tits run in the family. Plus they got even bigger when I had a kid."

"A kid?" I took a long look at her while digesting that latest tidbit.

"I have a daughter back in New York. She's with my nonna."

"You're just full of surprises, aren't you?"

"I haven't seen her in a long time. She was fifteen on her

last birthday."

"How old are you?"

"I'm thirty."

"Wow ... I thought you were about twenty." I meant it.

"I was thirty yesterday."

"You're kidding! Your birthday was yesterday?"

"Yeah."

"If I'd known that, we would have made you a cake and had a party."

"You did have a party," she said. "Just no cake."

"But cake would have been nice. Did you have a nice birthday? Did anybody else give you a party?"

"I just stayed home and spent it alone. I don't have any real friends. Can't seem to keep 'em long."

"What do you mean? Why not?"

"I don't know. There's somethin' 'bout me that turns people off after a while."

"I can't imagine what it would be," I said honestly. "I haven't known you that long, but I haven't noticed anything about you that would turn me off in any way."

"I believe you." She studied me intently for a few moments, then her expression changed, as if she had come to a decision. "I think I turn you on, don't I?" she said.

"Yes ... you do. In more ways than one."

She gave me one more long, appraising look, then stretched out on the blanket, her face to the stars. "Why don't you turn that lantern off now and lay down on top of me," she said. "I'm tired of talking."

I turned the lantern off.

10 SUNDAY

I just got through talking on the phone with Manny. He told me that he's got a couple of guys lined up for his band and he wants me to come over and listen to them for a while, just to get my impression. I asked him if Pet was still gonna be his lead singer and he said she hadn't made a commitment yet. He called her last night and tried to talk her into it, but she hemmed and hawed, and the conversation went nowhere. For now, at least, he'll have to do without a female singer.

The only reason I heard the phone ring this morning was because I had gone back out to The Hole about an hour ago to get a fresh Bic pen. My other one ran out of ink last night just as I was finished recording the conversation Diane and I had about her kid back in NYC. Bic pens hardly ever run out, so it must have been providence.

Diane and I had spent the night on the blanket, down here at the end of the grotto. To be honest it was one of the most peaceful night's sleep I've had in a long time. The night was warm, and Diane's body was hot, but it felt good and was all perfect for the moment. Plus, she exudes a natural odor that I can't really describe. It seemed to work some kind of magic in my head, lulling me to sleep like a baby. It was like a drug, both erotic and soothing at the same time. So much for the ramblings of a nineteen-year-old guy attempting to describe the indescribable while under the enchantment of a real woman. Such is the stuff of romance.

I'm sitting on the edge of the blanket so that I can watch Diane sleep while I write. I wish I could paint her as she is at this moment.

She's starting to wake up now. She's lying on her back, legs bent with her knees in the air and about twelve inches of space between her feet that are placed flat on the blanket. Her back and shoulders arch, thrusting her chest upward as she clasps her hands behind her head and stretches. There are probably a lot of guys who would find the thickets of black hair marking the corners of the inverted triangle of Diane's torso a bit too much for their taste, but they work for me. It all comes together to make Diane who she is, a woman of nature untouched by the conventions of society and the silly morals of a culture that only gives them lip service. Diane is a Beat woman, not a Beat girl. She is a woman of thirty years, with a child and everything that comes with that package. If anyone has any reason to be Beat about anything, it would be Diane, who's had a rough time her entire life. If I look carefully, I can see that her beautiful face reflects the pain she has experienced, and the few fine lines barely visible between her brows is evidence of the worry that never leaves her. She never looks totally at ease or even happy.

She relaxes from her stretch, opens her eyes, and turns her head to look at me. "Whatcha writin'?" she asks.

I return her smile. "I'm writing about how pretty you look lying there and how I wish I could paint you right now."

"Will you paint me one day?"

"I'd sure like too. I don't think I've ever seen a more beautiful woman." I've seen a lot of girls my age and they've been quite pretty, and yes, in my youth and immaturity I've been a bit infatuated by them all, but never have I seen a real woman like Diane. I could sit and stare at her for hours.

"I'll bet you say that to all the girls."

"No, I don't."

"Well, why not? It's a great pick up line," she teases.

"Because it wouldn't have been true until now," I reply honestly. "And I would never have tried to pick you up, Diane. A woman like you is way out of my league. I'm still trying to figure out why you're with me right now."

"Because I picked you up. I've seen how you stare at me in yoga when you think I'm not lookin'."

"Yes, you did. And I do. I admit it."

"But I was also starin' back at you. You have somethin' 'bout you that I've been lackin', and I wanted to experience it. Somethin' I haven't seen in many years."

"I do?"

"Yeah. You have innocence. And I'm not talkin' 'bout how many girls you've laid or whatever else you've done. I'm talkin' 'bout all the things you haven't done, all the things you haven't experienced that I have, and I wish I hadn't. That kind of innocence." She sits up and reaches for her dress that is lying beside her.

"And that made you want to know me better?"

She pulls the dress over her head. When her face re-emerges, she pauses and looks at me seriously before speaking. "It made me want to sleep with you so I could be close enough to have some of you soak into me, so maybe I could change a little."

"I don't think you need to change at all, Diane. From what you've told me, all the crazy things you've done haven't made you into a bad person, they've made you into the experienced, wise, forward-thinking woman you are right now. I can't see anything wrong with that." Her eyes are glistening with unshed tears. "I'm sorry if I've said something wrong, Diane."

"No … you said everything right." She blinks and the tears spill down her cheeks. "You just proved my point. You're so innocent that you can't see what a terrible person I've been all my life. I've broken every rule in the book and you still don't see it in me."

I set my journal aside and take Diane into my arms.

Manny's Garage • 9 PM

We sat like that for a while — Diane crying and me trying to comfort her. She really has no reason to feel bad about herself. When you get down to it, everyone on this planet has done things they aren't proud of, and some have done terrible things and gotten away with them. Diane hasn't done anything any worse than most, and her honesty puts her way up on the list of people I want to hang around with. I know people who have been absolute jerks and they've gone through life without ever admitting it to themselves or to anybody else. Diane ought to be canonized just for admitting her faults, if they really are faults. Most of her problems resulted from the actions of other people, and then her being forced to alter her lifestyle just to survive what others did to her. I don't find fault with that.

It didn't take long for Diane to recover. We sat for another hour just talking before we went back to the house where we took a shower. When we were squeaky clean, we headed out to The Hole where Diane struck poses while I drew pictures of her and we both sipped on wine. After a couple of hours, we started feeling hunger pains, since we hadn't eaten anything since early the evening before.

"I'm startin' to get kinda hungry, Diane. Why don't we check out the pantry and see what we can whip up?"

"That sounds good," she said as we crossed the breezeway and entered the kitchen. "Ya got any pasta?"

"I'm sure of it. My mother loves pasta, so there's bound to be some in there."

Sure enough, we found a ton of pasta—linguini, spaghetti, rigatoni, you name it and we had it. We also found several jars of sauce, but Diane wrinkled up her nose at those and opened the refrigerator.

"There's a bunch of fresh veggies in here. I'll use those," she said as she pulled things out and laid them on the kitchen counter. She reminded me of a magician pulling flowers and doves and rabbits and who-knows-what out of a hat.

She worked quickly and efficiently. Her hands seemed to know what to do without her thinking about it, which left her head free for talking. "I haven't eaten sauce out of a jar in years. In New York I knew an Italian market where I could always get fresh veggies of some sort, even in winter. The market owner was a kind old paisan who felt sorry for me. He'd sometimes give me stuff he had left at the end of the day, and whatever vegetables he had that day, that's what I put in the sauce.'

"What if he didn't have tomatoes?" I asked.

"Sauce doesn't always have to have tomatoes. Sometimes the best thing to put on pasta is nothin' more than olive oil with sautéed garlic, covered with whatever cheese you got around."

"I always thought Italian food meant tomato sauce."

"I've made sauce just by boilin' celery and garlic in water and then pourin' that on linguini. It's mostly the garlic and cheese that makes the food good.

Diane bustled around in the kitchen, turning the found objects from the fridge — tomatoes, celery, mushrooms, garlic — into a meal. I mostly stayed out of her way on the other side of the counter, but once I snuck up behind her and started smelling her and kissing her. I went all the way up and down her back and legs, her bottom, and even her armpits.

"What are you doin'?" She turned, and the look she gave me could have meant that she was amused, curious, flattered, or annoyed — or all of the above.

"I'm smelling you. I just want to make sure you still smell like you and we didn't wash it all away in the shower."

"Well?"

"You do. That same scent is there just as strong."

"My BO?"

"Call it what you want, it's part of you and I like it."

"Does it make you wild and crazy?" she teased as she looked over the assortment of pasta. She settled on the linguini and pushed the others out of her way.

I nuzzled her hair and took another deep breath. "Yeah," I said. "It sorta does."

"Sounds like catnip," she said, "but I'll bet it's garlic. I've eaten so much garlic in my life that it's gotta be part of me by now."

I gave her another hug, then returned to the safety of the other side of the counter. She found a large pot, filled it with water, and placed it on the stove with a high flame under it. She turned her attention back to the sauce, which had been simmering gently. She gave it a stir, then lifted the spoon, bringing it first to her nose to inhale the aroma, then touching it to her tongue.

"You got any anchovies?" she asked.

"I doubt it, but I'll look."

"It's really best with anchovies, but we can do without if you don't have any."

I returned the rejected pasta to the pantry and then dug a little deeper to see if we had the requested anchovies. Lo and behold, I found two cans of the salty little fish pushed back into a corner along with some cans of tuna and mackerel.

"Eureka!" I shouted as I emerged from the pantry. "Two cans of anchovies. There's some tuna, too if you'd like."

"No tuna, but I'll take both cans of anchovies. Your mother must be part Italian. I don't know many non-Italians who like anchovies in anything."

"Well, actually, she does have some Italian blood in her," I grinned.

"No kiddin'?" Diane grinned at me and said, "That makes you part Italian!"

"A small part," I said

"It don't matter how small your part is. My Zia Sophia once told me that it only takes one drop of Italian blood to make you full Italian. That one drop makes the rest of your blood call out for the old country."

"When my mother went into labor with me in Winfield, Kansas, her doctor realized early on that she was going to need a cesarean if either of us was going to survive. She was pretty anemic to start with, so she needed a blood transfusion before they could even begin. They didn't have any blood on hand, and it was something like 4:30 in the morning and they couldn't find anyone who could come in to give blood. One of the nurses told the doctor that there was a family staying with one of her relatives that might be able to help. She said they were a really nice Italian family — the nurse was Italian, too — and that they would be up and around at that hour because they were heading off to New York later that day. She thought they would be glad to come in because the man was really sweet and loved doing things for people and it was on their way out of town. The only catch was that the guy didn't want anyone to know where he was, so she made the doctor and the other nurses swear to secrecy. I found out later that this family was on the run from the law or maybe somebody else, I never quite figured out who or what. When the nurse was satisfied that their identities were secure, she called the family and they showed up at the hospital a few minutes later—a man, his wife and a couple of big guys the man simply introduced as part of the "family."

Diane had been listening with her back to me while she tended to the sauce and pasta on the stove. Now, with the spoon in her hand, she turned to look at me. "Oh, yeah? So this guy and his wife gave blood to your mother?"

"Yep. I guess they had to give quite a bit because she was really having a hard time of it."

"If they gave blood to your mama, then that blood runs in your veins, too. My Zia Sophia would tell you that with that much Italian inside, you oughta have an accent." Then she turned serious. "Ya know, technically, you became a part of the Italian family that gave the blood."

"I guess, but I won't complain about it. They were really nice to my mother and I wouldn't be here today if they hadn't come along and helped her. Mother said that the whole family hung around for my birth even though they all seemed a bit nervous. When the doctor pulled me out into the world, he somehow cut a big gash in the top of my head. The first time Mother saw me I was covered in blood. See, I still have the scar up here." I leaned forward and parted my hair to show her.

"He didn't cut your brain, did he?"

"No, just the skin, but it really made me bleed. Later, when they showed my little body with the bandaged head to the Italian guy, he asked the doctor what happened. When the doctor told him he cut my head, the Italian man started to come unglued a bit. He wanted to hurt the doctor, but the two big guys with him grabbed him and told him to cool it because he couldn't afford to be involved in something like that. The man told the doctor, 'That baby has my blood now. He's one of the family. He's my new nephew. You be careful with him. You hurt him, and I hurt you.' The wife just said, 'Low profile, Giuseppe, low profile.'"

"This all sounds very odd to me," Diane said.

"What do you mean?"

"I know a lot of Italians. I've been around Italians all my life and I know what a family is. A regular Italian family is a mother, a father, and a ton of kids, with maybe an aunt and an uncle or two or three hangin' 'round. It sure ain't some guy and his wife and two big Italian guys lookin' nervous and pullin' a guy off a doctor. That don't make sense."

"Well, they were Italians for sure. Mother told me the two big guys hardly even spoke English. The man that gave her blood had a high-pitched voice and a heavy accent that was a bit hard to understand, and a real Italian name."

"Do you remember their names?"

"I remember the guy's name was Giuseppe, but Mother said the big guys kept calling him Don Peppino, or something like that. I don't remember his wife's name, I'd have to ask my mother, although she doesn't like talking about it. Her name was something short. I think it might have been Fay, or something like that. They had a couple of kids with them too, boys I think. One was real small."

Diane looked like she had just seen a ghost. "Do you remember what their last name was?" she asked slowly, almost like she was afraid of what I might say.

"I can never remember it. It started with a B. Don't ask me how to spell it."

"*Stai scherzando!*" Diane turned white.

"What's the deal? What's the matter?"

"*Cavalo!*"

"I don't know what you just said, but it didn't sound good."

"*Madonn'!* Didn't your mama ever tell you any details about all this?"

"Not much. She doesn't like talking about it."

"*Porca miseria* …" Diane palmed her forehead.

"You know, I don't speak Italian," I said.

"I think the head guy of one of the five biggest crime families in America gave you his blood. Mafia. You got it?"

"Well … there are lots of Italians around. That doesn't mean that particular family was Mafia."

"But the guy's name was Giuseppe—Joseph—Joseph B. And he's got two big gorillas hangin' around him, guardin' him, and he's on his way to New York. Do the math. I'm tellin' ya, that was Joe Bonanno. *Svegliati!* Wake up! Why do you think your mama doesn't wanna talk about it? She's been sworn to secrecy. Now you let the cat outa the bag. That might not be so good." Diane shook her head.

"Why isn't it good? That means I'm more Italian than I thought I was 'cause I know I've got at least one great-great-whatever that's pure Italian." I smiled.

"Don't you get it? If you have Bonanno blood in you, then you're a part of the Bonanno family. *Per il meglio o il peggio*—for better or worse. That's how it works. For cryin' out loud, he called you his nephew!"

"Does that mean I have to go into hiding? I'll be arrested?"

"No, *stupido!* Jeez … it just means that you need to be proud of your Italian family blood and never do anything to disgrace it. If you're true to your family then you'll be okay, but if you screw up, the cops won't get you, the family will."

"Great." I really didn't know what to do with all that new information.

"Help me fix this pasta now. I'm starved." Diane smiled and put the linguini in the boiling water. We might as well have been discussing a baseball game.

I helped Diane fix the pasta, only now it seemed we had a common bond between us, so it was a lot more fun. Granted, I'd just learned that I was a part of a notorious crime family, or at least that's what Diane thinks, but the fact—and it is a fact—that I have some Italian blood flowing through my veins kinda brought Diane and me closer together. So the two of us made one heck of a linguini with a sauce that was to die for—hmm … do I really want to say that?—and some toasted garlic bread that was out of this world. We didn't have any Italian bread, so we used slices of Wonder Bread. We topped it with butter and olive oil, chopped garlic, and a thick layer of canned, crumbled Parmesan cheese and toasted it under the broiler until it bubbled and turned brown. Man, oh man, it was good.

After we ate, we headed over to Manny's to hear his new band. Diane needed to get back to her aunt that evening, so I drove my VW and she followed me in her little Fiat. Manny's house is actually closer to her aunt's house than to mine, so it made sense to do it that way, but I missed having her beside me even for that little bit of time.

It was about 4 PM when we arrived at Manny's. He was excited to see me and surprised to see Diane. He hadn't expected us to hook up in any way, since the last he knew, June and I were a thing. To be honest, I'm surprised at how all this is turning out, and I haven't got any idea what I'm gonna tell June when I hear from her. I still haven't gotten a call from her. I'm not really sure that Diane and I are gonna become a couple or anything like that, after all we've only known each other for two days, and it was her that picked me up, not the other way around, kinda like June did. Hmm … do I see a pattern developing here? I've never picked up a girl in my life. Not that I'm complaining, I'm just not sure I feel comfortable enough yet to do that.

Anyway, Manny introduced the two guys on the stage with him in his garage as Fred, the new bass player, and Teddy, the lead guitarist. I'll tell you one thing, if Manny is ever gonna make it big in the music world, he needs to start picking some better-looking guys for his band. Fred is a string bean who looks like he just came off a potato farm, and Teddy is short and kinda plump with about three thousand pimples on his face. I'm sure they'll mature eventually and grow out of their awkward physical facades, but I don't know if Manny has that much time to wait on them. He needs to get this band thing going pretty soon, or go out and find a job somewhere and start living life as an adult. His mom, Hester, is pretty proud of his talent and his band endeavors though, so she might not care if he stays here for years to come. I think she lives a kind of second childhood through Manny's doing what he's doing. That, and I think she likes flirting with the guys in the band, although these two guys are a real stretch, even for her.

The band members were not the only change that Manny had made. He has taken the opportunity to use his own original tunes instead of just copying the latest rock stuff. The songs they played for us were all his own compositions and they sounded really good. The two new guys may not be pretty, but they are much more talented than the last ones. The only thing missing is Pet—I really do like her. She adds not only a touch of sex appeal, but she's also just fun to be around and she livens up the crew, although these guys are pretty lively on their own. They're focused on the music, and when they joke around, it's always about the music and not the irrelevant, anal stuff Paul and Burt got into. They're having a lot more fun than Paul and Burt ever did. But, again, they're not much to look at. Manny really needs to get Pet back. He needs a hot babe out front to be the visual center of the band. That would help a whole bunch.

After sitting through three or four numbers—or was it five or six?—Diane and I started getting restless and wanted to do something else.

"Having fun?" I asked her.

She looked at me and smiled. "As long as there's wine I'll have fun, but I'm more into Louis Prima and Sinatra than rock."

"I am, too," I admitted. "I love Sinatra, Prima, and most of the more romantic, late-night jazz."

"Prima's a real *pisan*. He's the guy the Italians hold up above all the others," she said.

"I can believe that. He's kinda raw and crude when he does his thing. I can imagine a big Italian family gathering with everybody be-bopping to Prima songs."

"Been there, done that." Diane smiled and nodded her head. "But these guys are pretty good, and Manny's a nice kid. I don't mind it."

"Said the thirty-year-old woman to the kid sitting next to her."

"Yeah ... to the kid who's eighteen goin' on thirty." She reached down and squeezed my thigh.

"Cradle robber," I grinned.

"Such a pretty baby." She leaned over and kissed me on the cheek. "So, what do we do here, just sit and watch the boys play? How long does this go on?"

"It all depends. Sometimes they go all night, sometimes they break off early and we go over to the Royal Scot and have coffee, sometimes we just all go home."

"You lead an exciting life, don't you?"

"Do I detect sarcasm in your voice?"

"Probably." She smiled again. "I do sarcasm well."

"That's not all you do well."

"Naughty boy." She batted her eyes. Then she looked around the garage and said, "I don't suppose there's someplace we can go to be alone for a few minutes."

"Why? What do you have in mind?" Knowing full well what she had in mind.

"You know ..." She squeezed my thigh again.

"We could go out in the back yard and get some air. But it's still pretty light out there," I told her.

"Isn't there a nook or cranny we can find where we can't be seen?"

"Manny's back yard is big but it's pretty wide open, although there might be a place around the side of the house. I think there's a space between the house and the fence. We could check that out."

Manny laughed when I told him we were gonna sit the next couple of songs out so we could get our ear drums back in shape. Actually, it was a good idea. Even though he turns the volume down because he doesn't want his neighbors calling the police, it's still loud enough inside the garage to leave your ears ringing after a tune or two. Manny waved to let me know he heard me, Diane and I made our way out to the back yard as he and the band broke into another tune.

It had been hot in the garage, and it was still hot and bright outside, even though it was near sunset. "I'm sweating already, and we haven't even gotten started," I said.

Diane giggled. "Good. That means there will be plenty of my body scent that you love so much."

"Shh! Not so loud, there are neighbors."

"The hell with the neighbors," she said.

"You really are a tough little Italian Tessie, aren't you?"

"I'm tougher than you'll ever know." She pointed to a corner of the yard. "There! That'll be perfect. Come on."

She grabbed my hand and pulled me around the side of the house and into a small passage between the house and the tall redwood fence. The space was in deep shade and there was absolutely no way anybody could see us. I wasn't worried about anyone coming around the corner of the house and stumbling upon us, since we could hear what the band was doing, and I knew for a fact Hester wasn't home.

"This looks pretty good doesn't it?" Diane said, leading me to the farthest end of the house. "Here. Right here."

Real time, again

It's about 9:30 PM, and the band is wrapping things up. Teddy's over by the fridge filling a cup with wine from the jug; Fred's on the stage tuning his bass before he puts it in its case; and Manny's sitting on the edge of the stage sipping wine from a mug. Diane and I are sitting in chairs on the opposite side of the garage from the stage in order to get as far away from the loud noise as possible.

I'm not sure if Manny is staring at us, or just gazing out into space while he replays the session in his head.

I'm trying to reconcile myself to being alone again when Diane goes back to her aunt tonight. Her aunt has been sick for quite some time, and Diane hasn't left her for more than one night since she came down here from The City to take care of her. Another night with me would be one night too long for her aunt. Diane's other aunt, Francesca, is coming from New York in a day or two and she'll take over watching Maria, the Riverside aunt. That'll free Diane up for a lot of things, which I would like, including the possibility of her heading back to San Francisco, which I wouldn't like.

"Well?" Manny yells from across the room.

"Well what?" I yell back.

"Why are you two yellin'?" Diane asks, straight faced and in a normal voice, but she does it in that cute, heavy New York accent, and somehow that seems funny to me.

"What are you laughin' at?"

"You're just so cute," I tell her. "I love your accent."

"So, you're laughin' at a good thing and not a bad thing?"

"You don't have any bad things, Diane."

Diane smiles and pulls me over and kisses me.

"Hey!" Manny yells. "Remember me?"

"Hey Manny!" I yell back.

"Whata ya think?" he asks. "What's the final verdict? How did we sound?"

"You want the truth?"

"That bad huh?" He grimaces in anticipation.

"The truth is," I begin severely, "that you sound ten times better than ever." I smile. "These new guys beat the old guys by a mile."

Manny's face goes from glum to glad in an instant. "Really? You're not kidding me, are you?"

"No, I mean it."

"Hey guys! Did you hear that?" Manny yells at Fred and Teddy who are looking at me for confirmation.

"Really?" Teddy asks. "We're better than the old band?"

"You leave 'em in the dirt." I tell him truthfully.

"Wow." Teddy smiles.

"Yeah, wow!" Fred says, matching Teddy's pleasure and incredulity. "That's pretty cool."

"And what did you think, New Lady?" Manny asks Diane.

"I prefer easy jazz, but I've heard a lot of rock, and I'd say you guys are as good or better than any I've heard before."

"That's her way of saying she likes you a lot," I tell the guys.

"Yeah, what he said," Diane smiles and nods in my direction.

Manny is beaming. "Actually, I take that as a compliment, Diane. If you don't even like rock, and you've heard professional bands before and you think we're as good or better, then those are pretty high marks, to me. Thanks."

"You're welcome. I didn't mean nothin' bad an' all. You muscle cats had some good stuff goin' on up there," I think Diane's just being nice, I don't think she's into the band at all.

Manny stands up and crosses the space between us. Offering his hand to Diane, he asks, "Where the hell are you from?"

"She already told us at the party, Manny," I remind him.

"I must have missed it. I was worried about the band thing all that night and I tuned out half the party."

"Diane's from New York City." I smile.

"Of course! I must have been drunk not to hear that." Manny gives himself a slap on the forehead, followed by an embarrassed grin. "I knew you weren't from Riverside, but I've never met anybody from New York, so I didn't make the connection. Sorry."

"I was raised in Little Italy, up in the corner by Greenwich Village, but I've lived all over the place," Diane says.

"I love the way you talk," Manny says, still grinning, but no longer embarrassed.

"Can't help the way I talk," Diane replies.

"So, are you here just for a little while?" Manny asks.

"Don't know. Depends."

"Aren't you one of DH's yoga students?"

"Yeah, I've been that." She smiles at me. "Not sure I'll do it much longer, though."

"You headin' back to New York?" Manny asks.

"Nah. If I head anywhere it'll be up to The City. I got some people up there now. But I'm probably stayin' here for a while."

"The City? You mean LA?"

"She means San Francisco, Manny," I inform him.

"I'd love to get up there some time." Manny's grin has turned into a kind of far-away look. "They got some music stuff starting up there that I'd like to check out. Not sure what's going on yet, but it sounds kinda exciting."

"The only good music in The City is jazz," Diane says matter-of-factly.

"Isn't there any good rock up there?" Manny asks.

"Not so's you'd notice. 'Course, I don't pay no attention to rock."

"Who's your favorite jazz musician?" Manny asks.

"Don't really have a favorite. I like 'em all. Maybe Dave Brubeck, he's got a smooth, cool piano. Stan Getz is cool."

"Manny plays the piano," I tell her.

"Really?" She looks at Manny, reappraising him.

"But I don't do any jazz. I'm more into classical. I don't play very often." Manny has gone back into sheepish mode.

"I've never actually heard him play, but his mother brags about him all the time" I tell her.

"I don't even own a piano. I have to borrow one at school if I want to screw around. There's a church nearby that lets me use theirs, but I stick to classical when I play there."

"You oughta teach yourself some jazz," Diane says. "You could get a job up in The City for some big bucks if you meet the right people."

"I might think about that." Manny says. "Right now, I'm just tryin' to get this rock gig goin', you know what I mean?"

"No, I don't."

"He means the competition's pretty tough," I explain. "There are a lot of these garage bands, and very few of them make it to the top. Manny wants to be one of the few."

"Well, you're pretty mean on those drums, but it's a heavy mean and not a cool mean. You don't wanna box yourself into that one thing," Diane advises. "Smooth it out. Get some Brubeck records and drum along. June Christy's got some late-night stuff you oughta get the beat on. All that oughta wire ya pretty good for The City."

"I just might try that. I've been so focused on rock that I don't know much else. It would be good for me to branch out a bit. Thanks for the advice." I can see that he's already considering the possibilities Diane has suggested.

"Don't mention it," Diane says, "Now I'm gonna get some more of that wine over there."

"Boy, she's somethin' DH," Manny says as he watches her walk over to the fridge. "She's a little rough around the edges, but I like her a lot. I hope you hang with her for a while."

"We'll see," I say, my gaze following his. "She's already talking about heading back up north. I seem to have trouble hanging on to any girl these days."

"Speaking of girls, where's June?" Manny asks, turning to face me.

"I don't know. She said she'd call me, but it's been a couple of days, and nothing. Last I knew, she was lining up an art show in LA. She's probably just too busy to call right now."

"Seems odd to me. I like June though, she's pretty cool."

"Yep, that she is."

"But this Diane chick—she's probably the most entertaining girl you've ever dated." He grins. "I could just stand here and listen to her talk for hours without even caring what she was saying."

I smile. "It's the accent."

"And she's hot. Don't forget that." Manny says. "Is it my imagination, or does she not have the biggest—"

"—breasts in the world?" I finish his sentence for him.

"Yeah, that. I mean, she's not carryin' something around inside her shirt, is she?"

"Manny, you've got a one-track mind. No, it's all her. She said her mama and her grand-mama were both built like that."

"Has she got any sisters?" he asks, using his Groucho Marx impression.

"I don't think so. She hasn't really said much about her family, but if she does, they're probably back in New York."

"Well, carry on, DH. She's a keeper."

"I know it."

Diane comes back taking sips from her cup along the way. "What are you guys talkin' about?"

"Oh, nothin'," Manny says.

"Just silly stuff," I say at the same time.

She gives us a look that says, *Yeah, right*, and then tells us, "I learned a long time ago that when a girl walks away from a conversation, the men automatically start talkin' about her, and it's usually nasty stuff, not silly stuff."

"You're smarter than I look," I respond, smiling at her somewhat sheepishly.

Then she pins Manny with a sharp look and warns him, "Manny, just remember that I ain't yours, I'm his, and if you ever try to move in on his territory, I'll pound your ass."

Manny looks at me with wide eyes, like a wild deer in caught in headlights. I smile at him reassuringly, then turn to Diane and say, "Don't worry, Manny's my best buddy. He wouldn't even think of doing that."

"Well, give me some credit," Manny says with a cheeky grin. "I might think of doing it, but I wouldn't actually do it. Besides, I don't have time for girls right now. I've gotta make this band work or else I'll have to give it all up and get a regular job."

"Never give up your dream, Manny," Diane says, smiling at him warmly. "If you give up your dream, life ain't worth livin' anymore."

"And what's your dream, Diane?" he asks.

"A kind husband, a little white house on Primrose Lane with a pretty flower garden in front, and a white picket fence around the whole yard."

"For real?"

"Whatta you think?" Diane smiles somewhat ruefully before turning away to take a deep swallow of her wine.

"Well, it sounded a little sarcastic, but I do hope you get your dream, whatever it really is," Manny says gently.

Diane nods without looking at him, then turns to me and says, "I think I'm gonna have to head outta here and get back to my aunt. She'll be havin' a cow if I don't come back tonight."

"I know, I've been expecting that. Are we gonna be able to get together again soon?"

"No way to know right now. I'd like to, 'cause I think I'm kinda crazy about you." She smiles and places her hand over mine. "We got a bond now, remember." She pulls me over and with Manny standing right there next to us, she kisses me.

"Okay … I think I'll just mosey over and get some more wine." Manny winks as he turns and walks away.

"I think you're right, Diane." I look deeply into her dark brown eyes. "I think I'd miss you a hell of a lot if I never saw you again."

"I know I'd miss you." Diane says softly, tears forming in her eyes.

Tears … here we go again.

11 TUESDAY

Yesterday, Monday, I received two phone calls that marked the day as one of the blackest so far in my personal history.

The first call was from June. She apologized for not calling sooner and then proceeded to tell me what had happened. When she checked in with her contacts at LACMA, they told her that the museum wouldn't be able to work her in for a show. They were extremely impressed by both her and her work, though, so they reached out on her behalf and located half dozen galleries that said they would love to have her. The drawback is that they are all a long way from LA. One of the closest is in Taos, New Mexico, not far from where her parents live, so guess what she chose to do.

June cried as she explained that the gallery has a tight schedule and she won't be able see me before she heads out. She had spent the entire weekend packing up her work with the help of a couple of people from LACMA for expertise, and a handful of fellow art students for muscle. Now, about thirty of her paintings are on a truck headed for Taos.

"I didn't call you sooner because I didn't have the time until now," she said through her tears. "Mostly, though, I didn't call because I didn't know how to tell you."

"I understand. As much as I hate to see you go, I honestly believe that you're making a good decision." It was an effort to keep my voice sounding light when I felt like my stomach was full of rocks. "Be sure to keep in touch."

"I will," she said. "I don't know how long I'll be gone, but I'll call you."

The second call was from Diane to tell me that her other aunt, Francesca, had arrived from New York, and that she's going to be staying with her sister, Diane's Aunt Maria, in Riverside.

I had a bad feeling about this call from the beginning and my mind was busy with all the negative possibilities, so I didn't really hear her words until she said, "… so, that'll leave me free to head back up to The City, to see some people and to get some stuff done that has to be done." I could only imagine what she meant by that.

"Oh, DH, why don't you come with me?" she pleaded. "I could show you around and introduce you to people. It would be so much fun."

"I would love to, Diane, but I can't just take off on the spur of the moment like that," I explained. "My parents could be home any day now, and I doubt they would be real happy to find out that their youngest son had run away to San Francisco with a wild Italian Beat woman, twelve years his senior." I didn't even mention the fact that I have absolutely no money at all to make such a trip. "It just wouldn't work for me."

So, we said our good-byes amidst a complex mix of emotions and promises to stay in touch.

Well, it seems I have done it again — begun a relationship with a woman, or women, only to have them leave for parts unknown. Well, not exactly unknown, but you know what I mean. It's not like they don't like me and they're splitting up because we don't get along any more. They DO like me. Besides, when people split up they don't move to other states, they just stop seeing each other and that's that. These girls like me, maybe even love me, it's just bizarre circumstances that pull them away. Damn. You can't make this stuff up. I think I'll just lock myself away in The Hole and never come out again. My parents can open the door and push food through a couple of times a day. I can read and draw pictures and pee out the window if I have to.

I sound like a teenage girl writing in her diary about "boys and things," only I'm writing about girls and things. Silly. Everything is silly really. I'm not going to suffer because a couple of girls moved away. I'm still young and there's still a lot I need to do if I am to be molded into a productive, normal, adult, citizen of society.

Blah blah blah. Baloney.

Who wants to be normal? I don't. I want to make something of myself, but I want it to be unusual. I don't want to be everyday ho-hum mundane and cliché. I don't even want to be eccentric. Being eccentric is just riding along on an ego trip trying to charm people into thinking you're something you're not. I want to be me, the real me, whatever that is. Artist? Writer? Poet? Maybe plumber?

I know for sure that I'm going to be spending a lot of time living within the confines of my mind and my imagination. This contemporary culture bores the heck out of me, and I'm afraid that it always will. I just can't get into the things other people get into — the fads, fashions, music, sports, politics — they all seem to be so silly, immature, and so primitive to me. Quite frankly, I see little worth in anything produced by this current society, era, historical-drop-in-the-bucket.

History has only produced a half-dozen or so golden moments in which the human species has produced anything of merit, and even during those moments, there were other things going on that almost canceled out the worth of what humans had stumbled upon. I say stumbled upon because humanity has never invented or created anything in and of itself. A few individuals have accidentally stumbled upon truths and laws along the way and revealed their findings to everyone else, but mankind didn't create anything. Man didn't invent the Law of Gravity, he tripped over it one day. The Golden Age of Greece wasn't golden because humans did anything special. All of the raw materials for what humans stumbled on in Greece were already there. It was like a big jigsaw puzzle of thought and organic material laying around in the mind, and on the ground, and the budding accidental philosopher-artists-whatevers, just tripped over it all and put the pieces together. Those pieces were themselves just things and stuff. They were the original created pieces of the puzzle. They were not created by humans. Humans merely acquired them and linked them together into things that appear to be whole, but are in reality simply bigger pieces of a bigger puzzle.

The same is true of the Renaissance. Mankind was nothing special at that time. People were filthy and mostly illiterate. They still peed in the streets and crapped in the woods, but a few of them discovered more pieces to the puzzle and put them together. The puzzle grew, revealing more of the bigger picture. Someone came along and thought that all the stuff that had been learned, discovered, and built in the previous two or three hundred years was pretty fantastic, and decided to call that time period, the Renaissance.

I want my life to be a renaissance of sorts. No, actually, I want it to be more of a rising above than a rebirth. I want it to be different, and I don't think I want other humans messing up the works. Maybe monks and nuns have the right idea. They squirrel themselves away in monasteries and convents, where they are able to mentally and spiritually rise above the rest of the world without anybody else screwing around with them. The only problem is that monks and nuns don't produce a product that can be seen or felt, bought and sold, or used—except for fruitcakes and cheese. Nothing useful, though, like a toilet, or a refrigerator, or a car. So, within the scope of all things, are monks and nuns really important? For that matter, is anything really important in the grand scheme of all things? This journal—who really cares what I write? The English romantic poets, the Bauhaus architects, abstract painters, the Impressionists, Edgar Allan Poe, Dr. Who, The Beat writers—is their stuff really all that important? Maybe Beat poetry will still be around fifty or a hundred years from now, but is it really important? What is importance? What does that mean? Okay, a bunch of guys painted some paintings during that so-called Renaissance. So what? They put some colored grease on some old boards or rags, and the finished products looked good behind the couch in the cathedral. But other than being a form of reporting at the time, a way of recording current, historical, and legendary events, so that rich and influential people could have their faces immortalized as those of saints and heroes and gods and goddesses, to be ogled at in years to come by people who would marvel at them and wonder about how things used to be. Other than that, what the heck good was the Renaissance?

Things are important when some people tell other people that they should be important. But just because a thing is important to one guy, it doesn't mean that it's important to everybody else. And quite frankly, I see very little importance in anything today. Everything rusts eventually. Everything decays. Don't molecules and atoms eventually break apart and form brand new things that are completely different from the things they once were? Logs and fire become smoke and ash. A 1957 Chevy can be melted down and become the fender on a Mexican battleship, as my father once said to me in jest. But maybe that's one of the most brilliant observations ever made. Maybe none of us should become so dependent on anything this current culture has to offer, or on anyone who stumbles into our life and then moves away. Maybe we need to stop thinking about ourselves as being '57 Chevy's and ponder the thought that we might one day become battleship fenders. Maybe that kind of thinking would produce within us a desire to stop copying the childish ways of this world and to mold our own little worlds to suit ourselves, making each of us the center of our own universe. Ego talking? I don't think so. Survival maybe, but not ego.

12 FRIDAY

After the bad news phone calls of Tuesday, the rest of the week passed uneventfully. I stayed home alone and spent the time reading, sketching, and contemplating my future. On Friday, I decided I needed to get out, so I went downtown to the health food store. The day turned out to be most interesting, but the evening that followed was long and restless. Now it's three o'clock in the morning and I still can't sleep, so the only thing I can think to do is bring my journal up to date.

I went to the health food store early afternoon yesterday, Friday, to buy some vitamins. I don't think the store really has a name. I've always just called it the Health Market downtown, and everybody knows what I'm talking about because it's the only one in town. Anyway, my diet of late kinda sucks, and I need something to supplement it with. I like the atmosphere in there. It's never crowded—health food doesn't seem to be that important here in Riverside yet—and it has that herby-spicy-minty smell you only find in health food stores. They also make the best homemade vegetable soup in the world. I always get a cottage cheese and date sandwich, and a green drink to go with it. I have no idea what's in the green drink, but it's about as green as green can get. I do know that when I walk out the door after eating that particular lunch I feel like a million bucks. It's probably all psychological, but that's okay. Apparently the human psyche can actually work behind the scenes to help cure whatever ails a person, so if I just think something enough in my head, maybe it will start to come true. I've tried it on my asthma, and so far, it hasn't worked. I'm not ready to give up on the theory yet, though.

I was sitting at my favorite table in the back corner—for some reason, I feel compelled to sit in a restaurant where I can have a full view of the place. Anyway, I was savoring my lunch when two of my yoga students, Jeff and Nellie, entered the store. I hardly ever see one without the other so I have always assumed that they are a couple. Jeff is a short, stocky guy with longish black hair and olive skin—he could be Mexican or Mediterranean. I've never seen him wear anything besides shorts and t-shirts, even in winter. Of course, winters here in Riverside don't amount to much. He makes wooden flutes. They have great tone and are quite nice. He is actually able to make a living selling them. He gave me one last year that I still haven't learned how to play. It looks cool hanging on my wall in The Hole, though.

Nellie is a little taller than Jeff and very thin, with shoulder-length red hair that she ties back in a ponytail. She never wears makeup, but she doesn't really need it. She's one of those girls who has perfect skin, a glowing complexion, no zits, and just a hint of a tan. I don't know if she uses some sort of oil on her skin, or what, but it glistens, even indoors and out of direct sunlight. She is pretty in a classic, rather Victorian way, with thin pink lips and a long finely-chiseled nose. Her bright green eyes are striking even though they're relatively small and close set. When she first showed up in my yoga class, I thought that she was Scots, based on her appearance combined with her slight accent. I learned later that she and her family hail originally from somewhere up in the Lake District where, like Scotland and Ireland, red hair and green eyes are not uncommon. I guess I have a lot to learn about the various British accents.

I love to see Nellie show up anywhere. In addition to her red hair, her clothing brings a splash of color that livens up any scene. She doesn't act or dress in any way the part of a Beat, but more along the lines of something different that's been popping up here and there, something more colorful and just a little bit kitschy, involving beads and chains and large medallions, and girls with strange, tightly-woven hair—braids I guess—and dresses and shirts with bright colors and wild patterns, and much of it comes from India.

It seems that India and all things Indian are the up-and-coming thing right now. Even here on the bulletin board at the market there are several notices advertising local meditation groups around Riverside that claim to have their roots in India. At least Nellie doesn't have the strange braids in her hair; I like the ponytail look. She does, however, wear loose fitting shirts made of Indian fabrics, long dresses made of the same, and like most of the other yoga girls today, it's quite obvious that Nellie never wears a bra under that thin Indian cloth. What's with this braless thing? I don't remember it being a "thing" a year ago. Lots of things are changing rapidly in the girl department. Riverside was never like Mayberry, and the girls were never really prim and proper, but not many girls at this time last year would have even thought about seducing a guy before he seduced them, like what's been happening to me lately, and almost no girl ever considered going braless. It just wasn't done. I don't get it. It's all very sudden.

Jeff and Nellie looked around and saw me right away and waved.

"Hey, DH," Jeff said as he headed for the lunch counter to place their orders. "Mind if we join you for lunch?"

Nellie continued toward my table, her face lit with her ever-present, wide, toothy smile. "Wow! What a treat to find you here," she said as she sat down next to me. "Jeff and I were just talking about you."

"I thought my ears were burning." I felt my own face smiling in response to her infectious grin. "I hope it was all nice talk and nothing bad."

"Of course!" Nellie laughed. "We were just saying how great it is to have you teaching around here. There are only two other yoga teachers that we know of, and they're so damned pompous we don't like to go to them."

"Yeah," said Jeff, as he returned with their food. "And they force you into those ungodly postures the human body was never built for."

I nodded in sympathy. "Nazi yoga." I think I first heard that term from Mam when she and Abby came over and spent the night with me.

"Yeah!" Nellie giggled. "I so like that label, Nazi yoga."

"Not to worry," I assured them. "I will never teach Nazi yoga in my classes. To me, yoga is all about healing. If a person comes in and gets injured by the very postures that are supposed to be aiding in the healing, then what good is it?"

"Right on," Jeff said. "That's how I feel about it, too."

"So, what are you two up to on this lovely summer's day?" I asked.

"Shopping," Nellie announced with delight.

"Spending lots of money," Jeff grumped. "If Nellie's parents weren't loaded, we'd be at home watching TV."

"I buy you things, too, Jeffie boy," Nellie said.

Jeff smiled apologetically at her. "I know you do. I'm just not into all that Indian stuff you buy. That shirt you're wearing doesn't look normal and it cost a fortune."

"But it isn't meant to be a normal shirt," Nellie protested. "It was made in India."

"Whoopie," Jeff said sarcastically.

"I think it's pretty," I told her. Jeff grimaced and shook his head.

"Thank you, DH." Then she looked pointedly at Jeff and said, "At least one man in my life has good taste."

I thought Jeff looked a little pained when he looked back at her. It was an odd thing for her to say, though. At least one man in my life — does that mean she considers me a part of her life?

Changing the subject, I asked her, "What do your parents do for a living,?"

Jeff sat back in his chair and spread his arms. "You're lookin' at it," he said.

"What?"

"They own this Health Market!"

"You're kidding," I said. "So that's why I see you here so often, Nellie."

"I come in and work sometimes when the hired hands can't make it," she said. "I don't mind. It's actually kind of fun." I get the feeling she treats most everything she does as kind of fun.

"Is there really that much money in a market like this? I hardly ever see anyone come in here."

"This isn't all they own," Jeff said, rolling his eyes.

"Really?"

"My parents also own D&B Liquor over by the mall," she explained.

Now I am impressed. "That's the biggest liquor store in town. "Not being twenty-one, I've never shopped there, but it's huge. It looks like the Disneyland of liquor stores."

"It is," Jeff said. "And they do a multi-million-dollar business."

"What can I say? People like to drink," Nellie said. "Since you're under age, I guess you don't drink yet."

"I drink wine," I confess. "I have some good friends who keep me supplied with Red Mountain. That seems to be the preference among art people, which is what most of them are—either art lovers or Beats."

"Well, now that I know you like Red Mountain, I'll see to it you never run out." Nellie grinned big time.

"Don't get the wrong idea," I said quickly. "About the only time I ever drink is when I'm having a party or at someone else's party. I don't just sit around guzzling wine every day. I still live with my parents and I doubt that they'd go for that."

"Probably not," Nellie agreed. "I'm glad I don't live with my parents. I moved out on my twenty-first birthday. My dad bought me my own place out near La Sierra."

"She's got her own swimming pool," Jeff interjected. "And lots of interesting furnishings in her house," he added, rolling his eyes.

"Let me guess," I said, falling into a Carnac the Magnificent pose. "Your furnishings are from India."

"Bingo!" He grinned as he pointed his finger at me.

"What have you got against India?" I asked.

"It's a weird place. Too crazy for me," he said.

"I don't know, apart from the dusty, smoky air there, I think it's interesting. I'd love to visit someday," I said.

"I've been there twice already, and I want to go back," Nellie said.

"Really?"

"You're right about the dust and smoke. Everywhere I went, I thought I was going to choke to death. But the people are so nice that they make up for it."

"I guess being an asthmatic, I need to cross India off my travel list."

"You wouldn't make it through one day there," Nellie agreed.

"That's really too bad. I love the Indian culture and I'd love to see where it all began. Have you ever heard of Paramhansa Yogananda?" I asked.

Jeff wrinkled his brow and asked, "Who?"

Nellie, however, became quite animated. "Yes, of course I have," she said. "Do you belong to the SRF?"

"The what?" It was my turn to wrinkle my brow.

"Self-Realization Fellowship," Nellie explained.

"Never heard of it. I came across a couple of pamphlets by this Yogananda guy and they kinda tripped my trigger."

"SRF is the spiritual organization he founded in 1920 for the purpose of sharing Indian spiritual philosophies with the Western world, and to bring spiritual awakening to individuals who are in any way interested."

"Really? Does it have a headquarters or someplace where you can visit?"

"Yes, the Mother Center is in LA. I've been there many times."

"Why don't I know about this Yogananda guy?" Jeff said peevishly.

"Because I know you aren't interested in anything that has anything to do with India. Besides, you'd hate the ashram."

"The what?" Jeff asked.

"The Mother Center. Some of us call it an ashram."

"I know what an ashram is," I said. "I've always wanted to live at one, at least for a while."

"You can't live at the Mother Center unless you're a monk or a

nun—they call them Bramacharyas—but you can visit there just
about any time. It's such a peaceful place. They have a big, rambling, wooded park that you can get lost in. I sometimes go there
to meditate and don't come out for hours." She closed her eyes and
sighed deeply, lost in the blissful recollection.

"How cool is that. You'll have to give me the directions so I can
drive in one day."

Nellie opened her eyes and smiled at me. "Maybe we can go
together sometime."

"Ahem." Jeff waved his hands at us. "I'm still here."

"Don't worry, Jeff. We could all go together," Nellie told him
somewhat dismissively, then she turned her attention back to me.
"So, what did you think of the pamphlets, DH?"

"I'm not really sure. They were just little meditation
moments—things to read to put one's mind in the proper place
for meditation. A lot of stuff about the Divine Mother and devotion
to God and Guru. I'm not all that sold on gods and gurus, though."

"You ought to pick up his autobiography. It's a fun read and it
will put the stuff in the pamphlets into context. He talks about his
early years growing up in India and all the saints and holy men he
came in contact with. He introduces the reader to his own guru
through that book, Swami Sri Yukteswar—I loved reading about
him. There are some other books by Yogananda that you might like.
I'll bring a couple for you to the next yoga class."

"That would be very nice of you," I said.

"No prob. I have a ton of his stuff at home. They fill a bookcase
I had shipped back from Delhi when I was there last year.

"So, you collect quality Indian art?" I had spent much of the previous few days alone and I was enjoying the conversation. I didn't
want it to end too soon.

"Yes, I do. Everything from statues to paintings to incense burners
and posters. My kitchenware is also from India, and so is everything
in my bedroom. My bedroom has slatted doors and windows, and a
large sliding glass door that opens onto the patio by the pool. You

should come over sometime and check it out."

"She's never invited me into her bedroom before," Jeff grumbled.

"My bedroom is where I meditate. I can't have anyone in there who hates India and everything Indian. What kind of energy would that produce?" Nellie seemed a bit short with him. What's with these two?

Turning to me, Jeff said, "She has a giant statute of some Indian guy in the living room. I can't remember who he is, but it's pretty spectacular. It looks like solid gold, but I think it's brass."

"It's bronze, and the Indian guy you refer to is Shiva."

"The god of yoga," I said, pleased to show off my limited knowledge.

"Right," Nellie affirmed, pleased that I knew.

"I'm pretty well read on India, especially the stuff concerning yoga. I have a little Shiva statue on my desk at home in The Hole."

"The what?" Jeff asked.

"The Hole. It's a room my grandfather built for me in the garage so I could have privacy from my brother. It's a long story."

"Let me guess." This time, Nellie was Carnac. "You shared a room with your brother who's older than you and you guys just don't have enough elbow room to be the guys you both want to be. Your brother's the tamer of the two, the more responsible, and you're the younger guy who wants to jump into the ocean even though you can't swim."

I laughed and told her, "You must be psychic. That about covers it, except that my brother and I are real close. I'm not moving out because of any problems, I just want my own separate space. The only drawback is that he has a private bathroom now and I don't. I have to go into the house to shower, go to the bathroom, and all that. Sometimes late at night, though, I go out in the back yard and stand on the edge of the grotto and do it there so I don't wake up my parents."

"The grotto?" Nellie's green eyes sparkle with interest.

"It's more like a drop-off into a little depression or valley behind our yard, I just call it a grotto. It has a beautiful view, though."

Nellie smiled, imagining the scene. "I'd like to see that someday. I love grottos. I was raised Catholic and one of my dreams has always been to visit the grotto in Lourdes where the Our Lady miracles occur. I love places that have an energy to them, *a feeling*."

"Speaking of peeing," Jeff said as he pushed his chair away from the table. "I gotta find the head." With that announcement, Jeff stood up and went to find the restrooms.

"You'll have to excuse Jeff," Nellie said. "He can be pretty rude and opinionated at times."

"That's alright. I don't mind."

"And he doesn't ever like anything I buy to wear. I just bought this shirt today and he hates it already."

"I was thinking it's really lovely. That's an intricate design on there. What's it made out of?"

"It's a fine, soft cotton. It's called, Madras, because it's spun, dyed and woven in Madras, India, and the towns around there. Feel how soft it is."

Before I knew what she was doing, Nellie grabbed my right hand and placed it firmly on her left breast. "See?" she said as she rubbed it all around her breast.

"Ah … Yes …" I stuttered. "I think it's one of the softest I've ever felt."

Still pressing my hand to her breast, she grinned wickedly and asked, "When can I come over and see your grotto?"

"Well, I'm not sure," I replied honestly.

I don't get it. I really don't understand what the heck is going on in my life. I mean, how many girls — women — have I met so far this summer, and how many have I begun to develop some sort of relationship with, and how many of those relationships have ended with the girls taking off and leaving me? Is this normal? I suppose it isn't so unusual that I should be able to attract a girl or two; I'm not that bad looking, and I have a good personality. I also like to talk about things that some girls find more interesting than the things regular guys usually talk about. Most of the girls have been from my yoga classes, and I've known for quite some time that some of them were interested in me. Even though it boggles my mind a bit, I can understand the ones that are close to my age being interested in me, but the older ones—where does that come from? The thing that really baffles me is that so many girls have come on to me in such a short period of time. Is that normal, or is it just the way our society is going? I mean, it wasn't that long ago that Lucy and Desi weren't even allowed to sleep in the same bed on TV. Now, any girl—every girl—seems to want to jump right into the sack, and based on my recent experiences, there doesn't even have to be a sack. How many girls have I been with so far in the past few weeks? Four or five? Diane's only been gone a few days, and now Nellie seems to be coming on to me. I just don't understand.

And what about the part where they all had to leave and move to another city or state? That really screws up a relationship. I mean, if Abby had stayed here, chances are I would never even have met some of these other girls. Abby and I would still be together, and everything would be normal. But what's normal any more? Let's say I take Nellie back to The Hole, or better still she takes me to her house so I can see all the cool stuff there. What then? Is she going to suddenly get a phone call informing her that one of her aunts, or cousins, or whatevers is dying of toe warts and she needs to hop the next bus outta Dodge? Is that the way it's going to be? And when Nellie dumps me, what then? Another girl comes along, we get to know each other for a week or two and then she has to leave? And then another? And another? And another? Is that the way my life is going to be from here on out? Are women becoming that free and easy that all a guy has to do is say, "Hi," and the next minute she's tearing his clothes off?

To be honest, part of this is just fine. Part of it is really exciting for a young guy just starting to feel his oats, but there's a part of it that's kind of disturbing. The old ways and morals are comfortable and familiar to me, and that makes me question these new ways and lack of morals. Having been raised as a Southern Baptist boy, I have the fear and the guilt messages deeply seeded in my conscience. But why is that? What is there to fear? And why should I feel guilt? I've tried to be the perfect gentleman with every girl I've been with. I've never done anything to entice them into anything. In fact, it's been the other way around! So, what guilt should I be feeling?

And now here's Nellie—pretty redheaded Nellie—who is into some of the same things I'm into and that none of the other girls were into, especially the yoga and the India stuff. I've loved India since I was a kid, and now I meet a girl who has actually been there. Twice. A girl who belongs to an organization that I might want to join, that Self-Realization thing in LA. A girl whose house is filled with Indian treasures that I would love to look at, to pick up, and study.

On the other hand, taking these women back to my place is getting kind of old. We go there and do the same things every time. It could also get risky. What if I take Nellie back to The Hole and we start kissing and I call her Diane by mistake because I forget who I'm with? Or Mam? Or Abby? Or even Mrs. Collard—Jan. Speaking of whom, maybe she's the one I really ought to be hanging with. She's mature, well-settled here in Riverside, and not apt to take off to Arizona or anything like that. She's not that much older than I am. And she's drop-dead gorgeous. She's also an alcoholic, but we could work on that.

Maybe I should have just finished my sandwich there at the Health Market and left without giving Nellie the time of day. But I didn't do that. I thought it would be rude to leave early without talking to her. I also entertained the possibility that maybe I had Nellie all wrong. Maybe she wasn't coming on to me. Maybe she meant for me to feel only the Indian Madras cloth on her breast. Maybe I just imagined that she pressed my hand firmly into her left boob and moved it all around slowly, pausing for a bit on her hardened nipple.

I asked Nellie, "Aren't you and Jeff a couple? I see you guys together all the time."

"You are kidding, aren't you? Me and Jeff?" She laughed. "He's like a puppy dog that follows me around everywhere I go. I don't know why he insists on doing that because he and I don't even like the same things."

"I just thought ..."

"I know what it looks like, and maybe he would like to be having a thing with me, but no way, Jose. I don't even like talking to him, let alone doing anything more than talk, if you know what I mean."

"He does seem a little —"

"Dense?"

I smiled at that. "As good a word as any."

"So, can I come see your grotto tonight?" Nellie asked.

It was tempting. I was a little bit lonely. For weeks I had been looking for some kind of companionship besides Manny, but ...

"I'm sorry Nellie. To be honest, I just ended one relationship with a girl and I'm not ready to start a new one just yet."

"We aren't getting married I just want to see your grotto." She gave me what was supposed to be an encouraging smile.

"I know, but I'm a bit down right now and I'd rather be alone this evening. I like you a lot, and you're one of the prettiest girls I've ever known, but I need some time."

"I understand." She smiled again, wistfully this time. "But I think I could help you get over the girl you just lost. Anyway ..."

"Maybe we can get together sometime later on down the line. I would like to see those Indian treasures of yours." I left the door open.

I looked up and was relieved to see Jeff returning back from the restroom. I was getting a bit nervous being with Nellie without a chaperone.

"Well guys," Jeff said as he approached the table. "What shall we do? It's kinda boring just sitting around here."

"I don't know about you, but I think I need to check on my parents," Nellie said. "The last I heard they were having trouble staffing the liquor store."

"I thought we could maybe spend the evening doing something," Jeff said, looking back and forth from Nellie to me.

"Sounds good, Jeff," I said. "But I have a lot of things I need to do this evening. I'll have to take a rain check."

"Too bad. We could have had a lot fun." Jeff smiled, but his disappointment was obvious.

"Yes, we could have," Nellie said, looking directly at me.

Nellie stood up, and the two of them walked out of the Health Market and into the sunset. My first thought as I watched them walk away? Simple: What in the world is the matter with you? Have you lost your head? I had a beautiful woman who was in the process of seducing me, practically begging me to come to my place and spend the night. Temporary insanity, it's the only explanation. For a few minutes I just went nuts. But it's too late. I already kissed her off. She probably won't come back to yoga now, either, because she'll be too embarrassed by her failed attempt to get me to take her back to my place. Damn. Or maybe I made the right move. I don't know. Regardless, I'm going to be alone again tonight, and maybe for many nights to come.

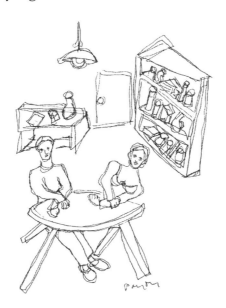

◎ ◎ ◎

So, why am I sitting here alone on my bed in The Hole, writing in my journal after 3 AM? I can't sleep, that's why. After leaving the Health Market I came straight home. I didn't feel like going anywhere in town or seeing anyone in particular. I thought that if I went home maybe Manny might call and he and I could get together, drink some wine and talk about nothing. But he never called. I didn't call him, either.

I got out my sketchpad and started drawing fairly early in the evening. I think I also held out hope for the unlikely possibility of a phone call from one of the girls who had moved away. Since they were all hundreds of miles away, I felt it would be a good thing just to talk and not play around like we would have done if they were here. I thought about who I'd rather have call me — Abby, June, or Diane — but to pick one over the others would mean that the one I picked would be my favorite out of the three, and in all honesty, I don't have a favorite. I like all three pretty much the same. The big question that I've been hesitant to answer for a long time is, I like them, yes, BUT do I love one of them more than the other two? Am I in love with one of the three? The answer to that is complex. I like each one for different reasons. They each have certain qualities that are unique to each alone and that I really like. I thought about putting all three names at the top of a piece of paper and drawing lines down between them, then listing the attributes of each one in their separate boxes. I've done that kind of thing before when trying to make decisions like which school to go to, which course to take, etc., but I've never applied that method to picking a girl out of a crowd. And that's why I didn't do it. I didn't want to cheapen any one of them by boxing them up like that, picking one, and throwing the others away. Damn it! The truth is, I like all three of them a lot. I don't know how I could pick one over another. And that's why I'm sitting here wide-awake writing in my journal and not sleeping like a baby.

I was still hungry when I got home since I hadn't really finished my lunch at the Health Market, so I cooked a pot of linguini, made a simple little sauce, and ate it with great relish. That, of course, reminded me of Diane and it made me terribly sad because I had been really happy hanging around with her. For some reason, being with Diane made me feel a little more … masculine? Grown up? I don't know. It could just be because Diane is thirty and I'm only eighteen, but I don't think it's that simple. I think it has more to do with the fact that Diane has been around the block more than anyone I've ever known, and while she was with me, I was able to share her experiences and make them my own. I could live in NYC vicariously through Diane's memories. I could even be up in San Francisco with Diane in my imagination. It's hard to explain, but I loved that about being with Diane.

After I ate, I decided I wasn't going to just sit around and mope all evening, so I went out to my makeshift studio in the garage and started looking through my art supplies and the few paintings that I've completed. That, of course, made me think of June. June, the fairly successful LA artist with dozens of her paintings leaning up around her studio, and who now has a big show coming up soon in Taos, New Mexico, one of the major centers for art in America outside of New York and LA. While I stood there filled with thoughts of June, my gaze went to the shelf where my father keeps some of his camping gear. The sight of a brown tarp sitting there brought up memories of the evening June and I spent sheltering from a thunder storm at the beach—the two of us making love under the tarp and drinking wine in the rain, her fear of the thunder, her naked bottom inches from my face when she peeked out of the tent. Whatever creative juices I had going into the garage studio suddenly ceased flowing.

I decided that I would read instead. I have fairly large and eclectic collection of books in The Hole, but it exists as a haphazard arrangement of piles on the shelves of my little bookcase and along the back of my desk. I picked one at random without looking at the cover, flopped down on my bed, and began to read. It turned out to be On the Road, which, of course brought thoughts of Abby into my head. I laid there with the book on my chest while I remembered all the fun things we did together, and the great talks we had about the Beats, jazz, and life in general. Then I remembered that I will never see her again, so I did the only thing I could think of doing — I threw the book as hard as I could against the wall, which didn't really do much of anything since it was a paperback. Then I did something I've never done before. I went to my closet, pulled out a gallon of Red Mountain, and began to drink it down like it was water and I was dying of thirst. Right out of the jug, no cup, just glub glub glub, I love you jug. Jug — one jug, two jugs. Speaking of jugs ... a vision of Mam swam into my head, followed by a vision of Jan, then a rhyme:

WHAM! Slam! Mam! Jan! ...

It was crazy and stupid. All I could do was sit on the bed and think about all that stuff without being able to do much of anything that didn't remind me of one or more of the girls I've dated recently. Crap ... and the winner is ...

Not the one I have decided that I love, but the one who seems to be popping in my head the most

NO, it isn't Abby or Diane or June ...

it is ...

Wait for it ...

DRUM ROLL ...

Jan Collard, my alcoholic English teacher from high school!

What the heck is that all about? She left my house in disgrace after admitting to me she was an easy drunk, while all the other girls only left because they sort of had to leave because of extenuating circumstances.

At that point in the evening I did what any guy would do who had been going through the mental anguish I'd been going through. I decided that there must be a reason why I couldn't stop thinking about her. Then I remembered that she'd written her number on a piece of paper. I spent about an hour tearing The Hole apart from floor to ceiling looking for that little piece of paper — but nothing. So, I drank more wine. And I started sketching again. It was while I was trying to sketch Jan from memory that the thought hit me, What the hell are you doing? All you do is think about girls all the time. Look at you! Look at what you just did to The Hole — it's a mess! You're outta your mind.

But then I thought, Of course all I think about is girls! Who do you think I am? I'm eighteen, for cryin' out loud. It's what eighteen-year-old guys do! They think about girls. All across America, right now, nearly every eighteen-year-old guy is thinking about girls!

I'm not a grown up yet. I don't have to start thinking about car payments and house mortgages and problems at work yet. I don't have an adult mind yet. What else is there for me to think about? Girls! And I don't think about them all the time. The only reason I spend so much time on the subject now is because it's summer. When school starts, my mind will be occupied with school work, passing tests, making grades. There won't be time to think about girls. But for the three months of this summer, I'll think about them all I want.

And if you don't like it, tough!

You? You who? I'm writing to an imaginary friend, I guess. I think I'm going crazy.

And another thing — I don't have girls over to my house every day and every night. That just doesn't happen. For that matter, I can go weeks at a time without ever seeing a girl, especially during the school year. It's just that I don't record all the mundane activities I suffer through daily in my journal. I don't want to waste my time thirty years from now reading about those boring things. I just want to read the highlights. The only things I ever record in my journal are the meaningful times in my life. I'm stuck here alone most days with just I, myself, and me, doing virtually nothing. I sit and read books, and maybe go inside the house and watch TV, but I get tired of those things. I've read just about every book I have, and there isn't much on TV worth watching in my estimation except maybe *Lost in Space*. I kinda like *Lost in Space*, even though it's a little silly at times. Maybe that's why I like it. Some of the scenes are almost slapstick, and the costumes, space ship, and other props are a bit—ok, definitely—cheesy, and I think all of the outdoor, other-planet scenery was filmed in front of painted backdrops. Even though the rocks and plants are obviously fake, and you can clearly see the seams between the panels of the backdrops, the whole thing is very imaginative and creative in a kitschy sort of way. Judy and Penny, played by Marta Kristen and Angela Cartwright, are cute, too, but what's with the chimpanzee? Anyway, it's a fun show. I like Dr. Who, too, for many of the same reasons. The girls are not only cute, but really different. There I go with girls again. What am I talking about? Just shut up!

So here I am. It's now nearly 4 AM, Saturday. I need to think of something to do today that will take my mind off everything. Girls and art and Beats and museums and health markets and yoga—everything. What could it be? I'm gonna take a blanket out to the edge of the grotto now and I'm gonna lay it down on the ground and I'm gonna drink wine till I fall asleep. The hot summer sun will wake me up when it wants to, and then I will get up, shower, eat a little breakfast and plan my day. Maybe I'll dream of something I can do that will take my mind off all the garbage I've been chewing over for the past several hours.

13 SATURDAY

I woke up when I felt the sun begin to burn my face. I picked up the blanket and the half-empty wine jug—I'll never do that again—and headed back to The Hole. As I passed through the breezeway, I heard the phone ring, so I detoured into the house to answer it. It turned out to be Elvis, and you're not gonna believe what he wanted me to do. In fact, he didn't just want me to do it, he insisted that I do it, and that's why I'm now sitting in a comfy chair in the living room of a home belonging to a University professor here in Riverside, listening to some pretty cool Hindu music. It's being played by a real live Indian guy on an Indian guitar that Elvis called a sitar. He is accompanied by another Indian guy playing a drum called a tabla, and two pretty Indian girls in flowing Indian dresses singing some chants. It actually sounds kinda neat.

It's odd that just yesterday I ran into Nellie at the Health Market and found out that she's into Hindu stuff, and then Elvis calls and asks me to go with him to a satsang at his professor's house. Coincidence? Last night I was hoping for something to happen today that would get my mind off girls and everything else, and I think this experience just might do the trick, although the two chanting girls down there on the floor are not helping much.

I've wondered for a long time about the Hindu religion and I've read a lot about it. I've never gone to a Hindu church or whatever they call it or attended a satsang before, either. I'm enjoying this experience, though. If I close my eyes, the music takes me into another place. I'm not sure where or what that place is, but it's nice. The only distraction is the tabla player. He gets a little carried away at times and starts wailin' on his drum. I mean, this ain't a big auditorium, it's a room in a house. That little drum is pretty darned loud and high-pitched, and in my opinion, it sort of ruins the mood. Now and then, just when I'm getting lulled into a state of near bliss—at least I think it's bliss-ish—the tabla guy starts improvising on his little drum like he's doing big jazz up in The City. That bites my nerves a bit. I'm surprised it doesn't shatter the windows like in those commercials when that fat lady sings those high notes and the wine glass pops.

The music wasn't playing when we first got here. We came in and just sort of wandered around, drinking wine and chatting with the other people who were here for the event. I was surprised to find the gathering was a Hindu thing. Elvis has been into Zen for a while—he's always going up to the Mt. Baldy Zen Center to get beaten by sticks—but I never knew he was into Hindu stuff. Finding myself rubbing elbows with a bunch of Hindu folks with Elvis there at my side was almost surreal. Of course, just about anything I ever have done with Elvis has been surreal. He's an odd duck, but that's what makes him one of my favorite friends. He's unpredictable. Go figure, here's a Jewish guy who attends a Zen center and also hangs with a bunch of Hindu people. It wouldn't surprise me if he started wearing a crucifix just to give equal time to the Christians.

So, why am I here? Why did the stars line up just right to bring all this Hindu stuff into my life all at once? Is it a sign? Does this mean I shouldn't have kissed Nellie off yesterday, that maybe I should have taken her home with me and spent the night with her? Who knows. Another odd thing is that several of the people here belong to that SRF group Nellie told me about. They're what Elvis called devotees of Paramhansa Yogananda, which doesn't mean they worship him, it just means that they are students of his teachings. They call Yogananda, Master, as a form of honor, but in Hinduland, that just means teacher. Yogananda is the teacher and these guys are his students. Elvis seems to be so into this new Hindu interest that he's now threatening to become a devotee himself. But then, Elvis changes his interests in life on an almost weekly basis. Last week he was a Buddhist, this week he might become a Hindu, and next week he might start doing Cherokee rain dances. I never know from week to week just where Elvis stands in his latest endeavors to "find God," as he puts it. I've told him over and over again that he might as well just be a Jew. I reminded him that he was born a Jew, and was used to being a Jew, and advised him that he should just be the best Jew he could be. He says he's not ready to do that yet. He wants to experiment with all the religions in the world before he decides to devote his time to just one of them. I told him that there are thousands of religions, so he'd better get started. I guess this satsang thing is a part of his journey.

Elvis's professor, the one who is hosting this event, is rather attractive. Of course, she's dressed in all the Hindu garb—I think it's called a sari. Her yellow outfit has two pieces, a skirt and a top. The soft, intricately-patterned skirt is long and made from that Madras cloth Nellie told me about. The fabric is wrapped around her waist with an end left free to drape over one shoulder. The short-sleeved, low-cut top is plain yellow. It fits snugly and is short enough to leave her midriff bare. She's also wearing gold chains around her neck and seven or eight colorful bracelets from elbow to wrist on each arm. She isn't an Indian woman—she's a blonde and as white as I am, and that's pretty darned white—so she's more of a wannabe Hindu than the real thing, but she looks pretty hot in that outfit. She looks to me to be about forty to forty-five-years old. Her body is what I would call mature, meaning that she has a bit of a tummy hanging over the top of her skirt. Also, just for the sake of the record, she has very large breasts. Actually, what I find most intriguing about her body is not her breasts, but her bottom. That soft cotton madras stuff her skirt is made of clings tightly around her butt cheeks, clearly highlighting her assets. She either doesn't know that's happening, or she does and doesn't care. Or maybe she planned it that way. When she first greeted us, she told me that Elvis had told her about me the other day.

"I'd like to visit with you more before the evening is over," she said as she continued to hold my hand in hers after the initial handshake. I think she's fishing for new devotees.

"How long does this little ceremony last," I asked, thinking it would be over early, like around 5 PM or so.

"It usually goes on late into the night. The actual satsang, with the music and chanting and such, usually wraps up around five," she explained. "After that, the general chit-chat and socializing can go on for hours."

"What do they chit-chat about at one of these Hindu confabs?" I asked.

"Oh, some people like to talk shop, that is, they talk about the life and teachings of Yogananda. A lot of the members are employed by the university, so issues there are a frequent topic. Occasionally, a few will talk politics. We try to keep that to a minimum, though, because talking about politics usually starts a fight, and fights are never good, especially at religious gatherings. Mostly people just like to drink wine and chat about things in general."

The music has stopped and the musicians are all headed over to the table with the food and drinks, so it looks like it might be an intermission of sorts. Elvis has already zeroed in on one of the singers and is casting his line of flirtation at her. The girl is smiling at him, but I'm laughing. The tabla player just told Elvis that the girl doesn't speak a word of English and has no clue to what he's saying.

Elvis looked at the tabla player, then back at the girl. Looking back at the drummer, he said, "Well, I guess that explains it then." The tabla guy put his hands together, smiled, bowed, and walked away, and Elvis is looking around for another girl to flirt with.

As near as I can judge, it looks like there are about fifty people at this gathering. Most of them are white Americans, with a sprinkling of actual Indian folks. I don't know much about them, but I have met a few people from India in my life, and I've found them to be a lot more interesting than the Americans I know, at least at parties. Most of the people I go to parties with are highly predictable. I suppose that could be because we all have so much in common and do the same things together. The Indians I've met talk about things I've never considered before. Again, that could just be a cultural difference. Everything I've read about India and Indian culture leads me to think that, over all, they're pretty bright. A lot of things we take for granted in science and medicine and such actually originated in India.

From where I'm seated, I'm able to catch snippets of conversations from around the room. Much of what is said is just the usual party patter, but the Indians, most of whom are professors or researchers, are on a higher level. They are discussing things like atomic energy, agricultural development, astronomy, and physics. Conversations like that usually leave me in the dust, but the Indians are so nice about it. They seem to be able to modify their language so that I can understand what they're talking about without having been made to feel dumb. They really come across as kind people. I like that. Kind is good.

Elvis just plopped down in the chair next to mine. I guess he's taking a break from his efforts to chat up one of the girls. He watched me finish a sentence in my journal before asking, "Do you have to bring that journal with you everywhere you go? How can you enjoy a conversation while writing in that thing all the time?"

I gave him a deadpan look. "Who said I enjoy conversations?"

"Funny," he responded. "So, what do you think of all this?" He spread his arms wide to indicate the gathering.

"It's different, I like it. Even the music, except for that crazy drummer."

"The tabla is a big part of the meditative quality of the music," Elvis explained seriously.

"I couldn't meditate with that playing. I need total silence."

"I didn't know you meditated."

"I don't. It's never silent," I said flatly, then grinned when he just looked at me blankly.

He shook his head. "There you go again."

"Are you going to become a disciple of this Yogananda guy?" I asked.

"Not disciple, devotee," he clarified.

"Pretty much the same. Disciple means learner, devotee means student. I don't see much difference."

"Whatever," he said. "I'm not sure yet. It has it's good points and it has it's bad points."

"I'm listening."

"On the good side, it isn't as complicated as the Zen teachings, and Yogananda wrote some really good books that are actually fun to read. The Zen stuff's a bit boring."

"And the bad?"

"Those girls don't speak English," he said ruefully, then he got up to take one more pass around the room before he gives up and leaves.

Elvis can spend an entire evening plotting and planning the conquest of a woman to take home for the night. I get a kick out of watching him work a room. He's like an eagle waiting patiently for a little mouse to pop its head up out of a hole, then he swoops down, lays on the charm, and usually within minutes he's left the party with at least one girl in his car. I'm watching him now as he surveys the room. He seems to have given up on the singing Indian girls, but there aren't a lot of other girls that fit his style here. Elvis likes them young, pretty, and just a little bit wild. Most of the girls here are older women, not what he would consider pretty, and the Hindu influence seems to have had a taming effect on most of them. Elvis just might go home alone tonight.

I learned from experience not to go to parties with Elvis without my own transportation, so that even if he leaves early I can hang around for a while. I'll eat a little Indian food, drink some wine, and enjoy this comfy chair. If I go home now, it's gonna be whatever I can get on the boob tube—reruns of Dr. Who, if I'm lucky, or old movies if I'm not. We only get three channels clearly at my place—four if the weather is right—so there isn't a lot to choose from. Speaking of boobs, our hostess, the lady professor is coming this way.

"Hello again. Mind if I join you?" Without waiting for an answer, she sits down in the chair just vacated by Elvis. She extends her hand to me and says, "I don't think I properly introduced myself earlier. I'm Jennifer Hamblin. Everyone calls me, Jenn."

I took her hand rather awkwardly and replied. "I'm DH. Everyone calls me, DH." Jeez, that was stupid.

"You look like a busy young man," she says, pointing at my journal.

"It's my journal. I like to keep track of where I've been."

"How can you write so fast and talk at the same time?" she asks.

"That's not the first time I've been asked that question. I don't know, I just can. I did it all through high school, too. I used to infuriate some of my teachers because I wrote down just about every word they said, even the dumb jokes, and they were afraid I'd show my notes to the principal. But they got used to me."

"Well, it's certainly a talent. Are you going to be a writer?"

"Maybe, I have no idea."

"What do you think of the satsang?" Jenn gives a wave of the arm around the room.

"I'm finding the music very nice, except maybe for that loud little drum. It kind of gets on my nerves, but the guitar sounds cool."

Jenn laughs. "I've never heard it called a guitar before."

"Well, I've never really heard that instrument before."

"I suppose you've heard of Yogananda? she asks.

"Yes, I have. All of a sudden he's popping up all over the place."

"I'm not surprised."

"Why's that?"

"He has a way of doing that."

"What do you mean?"

"Yogananda has a way of popping up in the lives of people he's trying to get to know."

"I thought he was dead."

"He died in 1952, but he is still fully aware of his work down here and he constantly tries to build upon it."

"You mean his ghost?"

"I prefer to call it his spirit. Don't you believe that when one of your loved ones dies their spirit goes to heaven, and even though they're up there they can still keep an eye on you down here?"

"I suppose I do."

"Well, Yogananda keeps an eye on his organization and all the people in it, plus he continually visits the lives of many others in the attempt to bring them into his family."

"So, you think that's what he's doing with me?" I ask.

"I do. I've seen it before many times. And even if you don't join with us now, at some point Master will return and he will become even more obvious in your life, and you will join then."

"Seriously?"

"You may not believe me now, but one day you will." Jenn smiled and got up.

"Wait a minute," I say as she starts to walk away. "I'm not disbelieving anything you just said. It's just very strange to me because I've never heard anything like it before. I never throw anything out until I study it a while." I smile in a way that I hope will convince her of my sincerity. It must have worked, because she returned to stand closer to me.

"All I ask is that you study this a while, but keep your heart and mind open to it. Don't study as a skeptic," she says gently. "Maybe for tonight all you should do is just listen to the music, eat some of that delicious Indian food over there, and chat with some of these nice folk. They aren't all SRF members, you know. Incidentally, the older gentleman playing the sitar has been a devotee for many years. I think you would really enjoy talking with him. He came over from India right after Master began the SRF back in 1920, and he's been with it since then. He has a wealth of knowledge. You might learn something."

"I just might strike up a chit-chat with him before the night's over. Thanks for the tip."

"You're welcome," she said. She smiled then, and I was surprised and somewhat dazzled by what it revealed. "And maybe you and I can talk again later."

"I hope so," I said.

So, here I am in the comfy chair, wondering what to do next. I haven't talked to many people. Maybe that's because I've mostly been sitting here observing and not mingling with the others. The old sitar player has been swamped with people wanting to talk to him. It wouldn't be polite of me to elbow my way past the crowd, so I'm just sitting here bringing the journal up to date while I wait for an opening.

I haven't seen Elvis for a while. I last noticed him about an hour ago on the other side of the room chatting up a woman. She didn't quite look his type, but I think he left with her. I guess he had to pick one out before the evening ended. I don't know why he didn't go for Jenn. Probably because she lives here and wouldn't be free to take off with him like that.

This house is lovely. The large living and dining rooms are arranged to create one long room. The long back wall is mostly windows that look out on a nice backyard. A big sliding glass door provides access to the yard, which contains a small lawn as well as a patio and a swimming pool. There also appears to be a small orchard on the far side, maybe orange trees — this is Riverside, after all.

It's getting dark now, and the lights out back have come on. Jenn has strung tiny white Christmas lights in the trees and bushes around the yard. They make the place look like a faerie world. The pool is lit by a blue flood lamp at the bottom which gives the whole scene an otherworldly look.

Jenn is walking back toward me. I think I'll close the journal now and give her my full attention.

14 SUNDAY

The Hole • 1 AM

Jenn rejoined me and we chatted for a few minutes before she offered to take me on a tour of the backyard and the rest of her property. It really was beautiful. The swimming pool was big enough to indulge in some serious swimming, and the water was the clearest I've ever seen. The dim blue light at each end of the pool gave it an ethereal glow, seductive almost to the extent of drawing a person into the water without his permission; literally enchanting, like the Siren's song.

As we strolled around the perimeter of the pool, Jenn told me about how she got into the Self Realization Fellowship and of her experiences in the organization. She's been with it for a long time, about sixteen years, and currently holds the position of Regional Representative for the Riverside area.

She joined just before Yogananda died, and was shocked and saddened the night she learned of his death. Yogananda had been attending a banquet where he was one of the speakers. He gave his talk, finishing up with a poem that he'd written about India, then he dropped peacefully to the floor. He died of a heart attack right there at the table. How odd is that? Why didn't he die on the way to the party, or while he was eating? Why didn't he die a week later? Why then, right after reading his poem about India? It makes me think that maybe there was something crucial about his having to read that poem. Maybe something in the poem needed to be heard by everyone. Or maybe not. But there is something strange and alluring about this Yogananda fellow. I doubt that I'll think about him much after tonight—I'm not ready to devote my life to anyone or anything right now—but I'm going to be really spooked if he pops up at some point in my future.

The trees out behind the pool were, indeed, orange trees. Jenn owns about ten acres right up next to the foothills, with about five of those acres in orange trees. The night was beautiful; the moon was big and high in the sky so that we could see our way as we walked among the trees. When we came to the bottom of a steep hill on the far side of the orange grove, Jenn asked if I wanted to climb to the top and see the view.

"What about rattlesnakes?" I asked. To me, the hillside strewn with warm boulders looked like the perfect neighborhood for rattlesnakes.

"I've been up there on many nights just like this and I've never had a problem with snakes. But if you're afraid to try it—"

"No," I said, just a little too quick and a little too loud. "I'm not afraid. I'm game if you are." That statement was not entirely true. I was afraid, and I didn't want to become prey for the snakes, but off we went, trudging on up the hill. I let her lead the way so that if anyone got bit, it would be her. I know, not very chivalrous. Mainly I wanted to watch her butt bounce with that Madras cloth wrapped around her cheeks as she hiked up the hill. Much better than sitting at home watching Dr. Who."

Jenn was right about the view. It was spectacular. I don't know just how high that hill was, but it was high enough to see the entire valley from Mt. San Jacinto to the Santa Ana Mountains.

We stood there for a moment, catching our breath and taking in the sight. Then Jenn said, "I told you."

"Yes, you did, and you weren't kidding."

"Every tiny spot of light down there is someone's universe," she said.

"What an interesting thing to say."

"When I first started coming up here, I used to look out over that sea of lights and see nothing more than porch lights and street lights. Then I began to read Master's writings. He says that everything, including people, is made of energy. Now, when I look at the view down there, I am aware of the aura of the energy that people emit. I can not only see it, but I can feel its makeup, and whether it's good or bad."

"You mean you can tell what kind of people live in which house? Bad guys or good guys?"

"No, but I can feel how things are in this world simply by coming up here and feeling the energy released from all those buildings and houses. When people think thoughts, those thoughts are released as energy into the air. When you combine the millions of thoughts being produced down there in that single town, it all contributes to a generalized feeling representing the dominant emotion of everyone down there. If there is something bad going on in the world and the people are aware of it, they release that awareness into the atmosphere, and it accumulates and collects. It becomes like a blanket over the city, a blanket of energy that I can feel."

"Interesting. I'm impressed."

"I don't mean to impress you. But I do mean to intrigue you and lead you to read some of Yogananda's books. They're filled with these kinds of ideas."

"You're the second person in two days to tell me that." Now I truly am intrigued.

"Really? Who else do you know who knows of Master?"

"One of my yoga students, Nellie. Her parents own the Health Market downtown."

"I know that market quite well. I go in there all the time, but I've never met Nellie. You say you teach yoga?"

"Yes, I do."

"I've always wanted to take a yoga class. Yogananda spoke of Hatha yoga, but he didn't push the physical as much as the spiritual aspects of yoga. He taught more about Bhakti yoga than Hatha."

"That's the aspect of yoga that focuses on worship, correct?"

"Yes, it is. It's practice leads you to the realization that the physical world and all it has to offer is only an illusion in the mind of God. When you reach that awareness, your mind turns more to Him, and you begin to worship the Presence of God rather than the presence of things."

"I can see the importance of that, but the Hatha postures also have some tremendous benefits for the physical human body don't they?"

"That is true, and there's nothing wrong with that. A person can do both. In fact, I would love to have you teach me some Hatha postures."

"Any time," I offered. "I have four classes a week—"

"How about right now?"

"On top of this hill?"

"Why not? It's a beautiful night. We have the light of the moon above to see by."

"The ground here is a little rocky and not very level, so some of the postures might be a bit awkward to do."

"Teach me the ones that aren't so awkward."

We were able to find a spot that was relatively level and where the gravel was a little more like sand. I took her through pretty much the same routine that I teach in my classes, making allowance for the uneven footing and the hard ground. Since we owed this night to the light from the moon, we started off with Chandrasana, the moon pose. I demonstrated the pose first, then Jenn attempted to copy what I'd done. Her balance wasn't very good, so I had to steady her a few times through all of the standing poses. She was able to accomplish them all fairly well, though. The hardest one for her was what I call the jackknife pose, a forward bend. The only light was that of the moon, which was not all that bright. The dim light combined with the slope of the hill made balance difficult and she had a hard time bending forward without falling over completely. Even I tend to lose my balance in the dark, but I think that most of Jenn's problem was that she is top-heavy. Her large breasts add to the total weight of her upper body, so that when she made the bend, she was pulled off balance even more. I assured her that with practice she would find her center for stability. In the meantime, she had me stand behind her and hold on to her hips so that she wouldn't topple forward.

We were able to do a few of the floor postures on the coarse, sandy ground. As with the standing postures, I first demonstrated the pose, then guided Jenn into the proper positions. She quickly gained confidence and was soon able to do the entire routine on her own. We ran through the routine one more time, then took one last look at the valley below us before heading back down the hill.

By the time we got back to the house, the rest of the guests had gone. Jenn walked out to my car with me where we said good night. I thanked her for her hospitality, she thanked me for the yoga lesson, and I drove away.

I have to say that my time spent at the satsang was mostly enjoyable, even restful, since I didn't have the extra burden of having to socialize as much as I would have at any other gathering. I was largely ignored by the other attendees, so I was free to indulge in one of my favorite pastimes, observing other people. The only real interaction I had with anyone during the evening was with Jenn. Her background and the knowledge she shared about SRF and Yogananda were interesting and thought-provoking, and the yoga class on the hilltop was peaceful and relaxing, with no commitments made for future lessons — or anything else for that matter. She and I just had a nice time doing yoga in the moonlight. I suppose it could have turned into something more romantic in nature, but I sensed that Jenn wasn't looking for anything like that. Quite frankly, neither was I.

It's now 1:30, Sunday morning, so I guess I'll turn in and try to get a few hours' sleep before I see what the new day brings.

The summer has flown by and I feel like I've just watched it go. It won't be long before classes start at RCC and I hardly feel ready for it. Maybe I'll take the little map my high school counselor gave me and head on over there later this morning. I could ramble around for a while and get familiar with the campus. I can use the exercise and it might help put me in the right frame of mind for getting back to school. There won't be a lot of people around since today is Sunday, so I should have the run of the place. I'll see how I feel when I wake up.

The Pit at RCC • 11 AM

I got here at about 9 AM and after spending the past couple of hours roaming around the campus and checking out the areas where some of my classes will be held, I managed to find my way down to The Pit. Most of the buildings are shut up tight and the whole college is pretty much a ghost town—it is Sunday, after all. I probably should have waited until tomorrow when the buildings will be open. This close to the beginning of school, there will likely be teachers here making preparations for the big day, too.

Today though, I'm not even sure I know which buildings are which, even with my little map. The only ones I can nail for sure are the art buildings. When I was at RCC last June for the visitation day they have for high school seniors, I spent most of my time exploring the art department.

Most of the art classes are held in three or four of the little old houses across the street from the Quad. The interior rooms are set up as studio space and storage room for works in progress and supplies. The back yards are full of stuff too big or messy for the indoors. There are several kilns for ceramics, and areas to work on sculptures of carved wood or stone, or welded metal. There is also a furnace and all the other equipment necessary for casting metal sculptures. I'm looking forward to trying my hand at that. I'm not sure what I'll make—I'm not sure what a person can make out of metal. From what the instructor told me on visitation day, the only limitations are the imagination and skill of the artist. It takes several steps to produce the finished piece, but it sounds like a fun thing to do. Who wouldn't want to create little statues of things? A little Marilyn Monroe statue would be nice. Heck, maybe even a life-sized Marilyn. I'm not sure how big a project the sculpture yard can handle.

The atmosphere on campus today is kind of eerie, as I seem to be the only person here in spite of the warm and sunny day. Or maybe because of it. After all, who wants to spend one of the last days of summer in town when it's a perfect day for the mountains or the beach?

Someone who looks like he might be a janitor just appeared at the top of stairs to The Pit. I guess a janitor's work never ends, and the best time to get stuff done is when the campus is closed, although I wouldn't expect that kind of activity on a Sunday.

I can't tell much about him from down here. He appears to be older, but not really that old, short, and a little plump but not fat. I would think that the job of janitor is a pretty active one that burns calories and works off fat. Still, this guy looks like he could lose a pound or two. Maybe he's not a janitor. I haven't really seen him clean anything, although he did pick up a piece of trash at the top of the stairs. Maybe he's a hobo who just wandered into the quad to see if he can find any food left on the tables. The train tracks are not far from here, and there's always a few hobos hanging around the outskirts of the downtown district. The poor guy does look pretty unkempt. Part of the tail of his old blue shirt is tucked in, but about half of it is half hanging out over his high-water pants. It's hard to tell from here if the white spaces between the bottom of his pants and the top of his shoes are his socks or his bare ankles. Whoever he is, he's seen me and he's slowly making his way down the stairs toward my table. If he's a hobo, I bet he'll hit me up for some cash. If he's a janitor, he'll probably ask me to leave. There are probably rules about being on campus during off days—insurance and all that.

Wait a minute, I recognize that guy. He's not a janitor, he's the guy who's going to be teaching my English class—Huntington, or something like that. I met him on visitation day. We chatted for a while and he told me about the courses he teaches. I'll be darned.

He sure looks like a janitor.

He's reached the bottom of the stairs and is waving and smiling at me as he crosses the floor of The Pit. "Hello, young man. It's DH, isn't it?"

How in the world did he remember my name?

"Yes, it's DH." I return his smile as he grabs my hand to shake it.

"You remember me, don't you? Bill Hunter."

I knew it was Hunt-something. I've had so much going on this summer it's no wonder his name had slipped my mind.

"Of course, I remember you," I said. "We had quite a conversation about Beat poetry and contemporary literature."

"Yes, we did." He takes a seat on the bench on the other side of the table. "And you remembered that as well."

"How could I forget? You told me things that really got my mind working. I'm looking forward to taking your class."

"We always have fun. I think you will find my classes are unlike any others you may have had in the past."

"I hope so."

"I see you are still writing in your journal," he said.

"You even remember that?"

"Yes, I do. I am quite impressed by those who take life so seriously that they feel it necessary to take notes throughout their day."

"It is kind of silly, isn't it?"

"No, it is not silly at all. Most young men your age spend their days staring at one of two things, the television set, or their feet as they walk along, never seeing what life truly has in store for them. You, young man, are at least looking upward at the scenery as you go forward."

"I like to think so," I said. "But I'm not so sure."

"Oh, but you don't have to be sure." He grins, his pale blue eyes twinkling behind his black-rimmed glasses. "You're much too young to be sure of anything yet. The only thing you need to concentrate on is the exploration of life. There is much to see and even more to ponder, my young friend. Life can be very complicated, but if you remain calm and collected, and approach all of life as an observer and not a reactor it will make all the difference in the world."

"Interesting," I say, nodding my head. "I do like to observe."

"Yes, you do, and keeping that journal is a very good idea. I wish I'd have done that myself when I was your age."

"I'm afraid that a lot of what I write down is just hot air. Sometimes it doesn't even make sense when I go back and read it."

"That doesn't matter. It's the act of writing it down that's important. Every day a thousand experiences come our way and we remember only those that hurt us the most. Keeping track of the good things is a wonderful thing to do. One day in the distant future you'll come back and read what you have written, bringing back all the good things while most of the bad will have been forgotten. The bad can sometimes overwhelm us, but in the long run, it is the good that is eternal. The bad passes away in a whimper."

I am silent for several heartbeats as the full weight of his words sinks in. "I never thought of all that. That puts this journal writing stuff into a new light."

"Never forget, young man, it's when you are young that you lay the foundation of who and what you will become. Never waste a moment. Every minute is a page in your autobiography, every year, a chapter. That little journal you are keeping might well become a best seller one day."

"Or a flop," I add wryly.

"If it flops, you have only yourself to blame," he says, pinning me with his remarkable blue gaze. "But in all my years I've never known one person who truly flopped."

It's been quiet in the quadrangle, but at that moment an even deeper silence falls over The Pit as I respond, "I hope I'm not the first." I feel like I'm taking an oath.

"You're off to a very good start," he says as the twinkle returns to his eyes and birdsong returns to the quad. "You seem to be doing everything right at this point in your life."

"That's only because you don't know me yet."

"And what could there possibly be about you that would cause me to shudder even in the least?"

"How about my goals in life? I don't really have any. I don't know whether I want to be a writer or an artist. And I can't seem to make meaningful friendships or start up solid relationships with girls—actually, that's not true. I can start them, but they always come to a screeching halt in a matter of days."

He looks at me with mock sympathy. "Tsk, tsk," he says. "Such complicated drama for one so young. No one makes long term friendships at your age. You haven't been alive long enough. And relationships with girls? Same thing. You haven't been alive long enough to make a meaningful relationship with a girl yet, and if you do in the next year or two, I would tell you that you're being foolish and to slow it down a bit. These young adult years you find yourself in are among the best you will ever know. You have the freedom now to do as you please, to experiment, to try new things, to meet new people. You will go through dozens of lesser girls in order to know how to recognize the one that will be truly meaningful to you. As for your major here at RCC, you don't really have to declare it just yet. When I was your age it took me five years to figure out that I wanted to be an English teacher, and even then I wasn't positive about it. Writer? Artist? Why not be both? But I must say that writing is the more economical of the two." He grinned. "In the long term it may be your wisest choice. In the meantime, take as many art courses as you can while this wonderful college agrees to pay the expenses for you. Art materials are not cheap."

"You're the second person to tell me that." I smile, remembering that June had given me the same advice the first day I met her.

"That other person must have been very wise indeed to agree with me."

"She was."

"One of your lost loves?" he asks gently.

"Not sure yet. She's in New Mexico right now."

"Really?"

"Yep. I got one in New Mexico, one in San Francisco, one getting ready to go back to New York or maybe San Francisco ..."

"Oh my," Mr. Hunter sympathizes. Then with kindly good humor he says, "Have you thought about starting a travel agency?"

"Funny," I respond wryly. "It seems to be the story of my life — I date them for a week and then they're outta here."

"Did they all have reasons for going?"

"That's one thing I can hang onto at least. They all had legit reasons for leaving town, and they all promised to keep in touch with me, except maybe for Abby. She's in some sort of witness protection thing ..."

"What?"

"It's a long story."

"Perhaps it's best I don't know."

"Probably." I shake my head and look down at the table top. Recalling all the girls has made me a bit out of sorts.

"Oh dear, you look sad now." Mr. Hunter puts is hand on my shoulder. "Perhaps we should think of other things to talk about."

"Not too depressed, really. Just feeling stupid."

"I have an idea. Why don't we go take a look at your new English classroom? Maybe you won't like it and you'll decide to take something else instead." He smiles, knowing full well I won't drop his class.

"Not on your life, Mr. Hunter. Your class would be the last one that I would ever consider changing.

"Well, one thing has to change, whether you like it or not." He has suddenly become quite serious.

"What's that?" I hope I haven't said something wrong.

"You have to stop calling me Mr. Hunter. We don't do that here in grown up school." The now-familiar smile and twinkle return. "I'm just plain old Bill here."

"Boy, that's gonna take some getting used to."

"No, it won't. After a week or two it will seem quite natural."

"Plain Old Bill, huh?"

"That's right."

"So, do I call you, Plain, for short?"

"I'm going to have to watch you aren't I, young DH." He looks at me with those piercing, yet kind, blue eyes of his. "I'm afraid you just might be much smarter than I was at your age."

"Right." I shake my head, knowing that ain't possible.

Manny's Back Yard • 1 PM

I put my journal away and followed Bill into one of the buildings surrounding The Quad. The buildings are the oldest on campus, and Bill's classroom is up on the second floor. The room itself is of average size, but the high ceilings and tall windows make it feel large and airy. About thirty student desks were arranged in rows facing a large, well-used teacher's desk, and a large green chalkboard that filled the wall behind it. There was a row of coat hooks on the wall by the door which were probably filled with coats in the winter. This morning, however, they held three shirts identical to the one Bill was wearing. All three had plastic pocket protectors filled with pens, pencils and pieces of chalk, and all three were smeared with chalk dust as if Bill had leaned against the board and used his body to clean it. What an odd little man. I'm not sure eccentric is the word I'm looking for, but for now it will do.

After a few minutes in the room, Bill suggested that he and I go have a quick lunch somewhere, so I suggested the Royal Scot. He had the deep-fried shrimp and I had fried chicken, and he insisted on paying for it all. That bothered me for about a minute, but since he's the guy with the job and I think I only have about five bucks in my wallet right now, I got over it.

As usual, my chicken was as good, and Bill enjoyed his shrimp, but the best part was the conversation. We talked about everything except English — Bill said there would be plenty of time for that when classes start. He seemed to be pulling up a wide range of apparently unrelated topics in order to test my reactions and to find out how my mind works. I got the feeling that most of his students are pretty transparent to him and that he has them figured out as soon as they walk into the room and introduce themselves. I think I confound him just a little, and that seems to be a good thing. He told me that in all the years he's been teaching, he's never socialized with any of his students. This was a first for him.

After spending just a few hours with Bill, I feel like I've known him all my life. I hope this marks the beginning of a new and long-lasting friendship. I feel there is much I can learn from the odd little man who looks like a hobo but has the heart of a saint and the brains of an Einstein. Well, that description may be a little over the top—I am, after all, young and impressionable. Still, it may not be too far from the truth.

Bill and I went our separate ways after lunch with promises to do this again sometime. I went home to The Hole intending to spend the rest of the day reading or drawing, but the previous hours of stimulating activity and conversation had left me too restless to settle on anything. For lack of a better idea, I called Manny to see what he was up to. He told me that the new band was there practicing all day and that I was welcome to come over and mess around. I got here about a half hour ago and listened to a couple of tunes from the new guys. They sounded really good, but for some reason I just wasn't into it, so I came out here to the backyard where I've been bringing the journal up to date and scribbling little drawings in the margins.

It's a beautiful day. The summer sun is bright and there's just enough of a breeze to take the edge off the heat. The neighborhood around here is quiet and still except for the noise coming from the garage. I was hoping to see Pet at the band practice. Manny had told me that he's talked to her and he thinks she'll be joining up again. She had tried working with Burt and Paul, but they were so nasty and bitter about Manny breaking up the band that she left halfway through the first rehearsal. Apparently, they were more interested in dragging down Manny than in making music. Every other word was some kind of profanity, and Manny was always, That Motherf---er, and she just couldn't dig that. Pet has a pretty colorful vocabulary, and when she does let loose, it's usually all in fun or for a very good reason. I've never heard her drop the f-word. She and I are both of the opinion that only lowlife's use the f-word. I've only ever heard it used by hard core nasties in the news who have just been arrested for rape or murder. I've never actually heard a normal person use it, so if Burt and Paul are using it, they must have sunk pretty low.

I just realized that I really have to pee. If I were at home, I'd just go into the house or out to the grotto, but I don't think I can get away with that here in Manny's back yard. I really don't want to go inside. Hester's in there somewhere and I don't want to run into her. Every time I see Hester, it seems like she's coming onto me. I am a young guy, though, and pretty naive about older women, so it could just be wishful thinking on my part. It's laughable when you think about it. Why in the world would a woman twice my age be flirting with me like that? I'm probably just reading her wrong and blowing things all out of proportion. After all, she really is a nice person. I've never heard her say a bad word about anybody. She's a hard worker and she's had a few bad lumps in her life, but she's bounced back every time. She's managed to raise Manny in spite of the obstacles, and that ain't bad. If Manny's a reflection on Hester's sense of ethics and whatever, then that should be good enough for me. Manny's about the best person I know. I'm going to go over there and knock on the back door and ask her if I can come in to use the head. She'll probably just say sure, then disappear into the kitchen to do her chores.

The Hole • 2:30 PM

So, I knocked on the back door thinking that Hester would come and let me in to use their bathroom, but nobody answered. I knocked a little louder, but still no answer. I thought then that maybe Hester was no longer in the house. She sometimes takes walks around the neighborhood, and she could have gone out the front door and I would not have known. I really had to go, so I mustered up the courage and walked in. I didn't think anyone would care.

The back door opens into a small mudroom which doubles as a laundry room. Beyond the mudroom is the kitchen, and past that is a dining room joined to the living room. The hall on the other side leads to the bedrooms. Hester's is at the near end, and Manny's is at the far end, with two other bedrooms, one of which is Shanie's, and a bathroom in between. They refer to the fourth bedroom as the guest room, but while it is used for many different things, it hardly ever houses guests. Well, I walked through the kitchen into the dining room and made my way across the living room to the hall. Just as I started down the hall, I heard some faint sounds coming from the guest room. Was that someone crying? Hester? I've known Manny long enough and spent enough time at his house to almost feel like one of the family. Now, though, I felt like an intruder. What should I do? I stood frozen in the hallway. She seemed really upset about something and I'm sure she would be embarrassed if she were to find me out in the hallway listening to her cry like that.

I'm sure she hadn't heard me come in, but her crying had become quieter and I didn't know if I could make my escape without being heard. I could find a spot to pee behind the house if I had to, but I had to avoid the squeaky board in the hall floor first.

I decided to wait where I was a little longer. If Hester stopped crying and discovered me, I could pretend that I had just gotten there and had heard nothing. If she started up louder again, then I could make my move and sneak out the back. Sure enough, she started up again, but as I listened more closely it didn't really sound like crying. It sounded more like she was gasping for air. Could she be hurt? Maybe she fell and hit her head and she was lying there half conscious, waiting for help to come. The bedroom door was open just a crack, so I decided to carefully peak in just to check on her. I would have felt terrible had I left and found out later Hester had hurt herself badly and I could have saved her had I only checked.

Carefully avoiding the creaky floorboard I approached the door to the guest room and maneuvered my head so that I could see through the two inches of space between the door and its frame. I had a clear view of Hester lying on the bed, the lower half of her body was covered with a sheet while her top half was fully exposed. She was moaning, but she wasn't crying. Her eyes were closed and there was a big smile on her face. Believe me, she was in no pain—those moans were from pure pleasure. Her hands were under the sheet so I couldn't tell exactly what was going on, but my imagination jumped in to provide the details. I held my breath—I really didn't want to get caught there watching her like that. By the time I had to breathe again, Hester's activity was more than enough to provide cover for any noise that I might make, so I turned around and made my escape.

If Hester was aware that I had seen her, or if she had heard me running out the back door, I can't be sure, but she made no attempt to chase after me. When I got outside, the need to pee was urgent. I found a secluded spot between the house and the fence and relieved myself as quickly as I could, then I returned to my lawn chair, picked up my journal and started drawing images of what I had just seen. I couldn't resist recording that sight for my own future enjoyment. It was the first time I'd ever actually seen Hester's completely bared breasts. My only regret about the whole incident was that I had to leave so quickly. I would have enjoyed standing there much longer.

I was still drawing in my journal about ten minutes later when Hester came out of the house carrying a small laundry basket. When she got to the clothesline, she set the basket on the ground and began removing items from it one by one, bras, panties, slips, that sort of thing. She reached down, picked one out, and held it up for inspection before carefully pinning it to the line. She repeated the process until the basket was empty. She picked up the basket, but before returning to the house she turned toward me. She let her eyes move from my face to my feet, then back again. Finally, the curve of her lips broadened to a smile. She looked straight into my eyes and said, "I'll sure be glad when you turn eighteen." Then she turned and walked back into the house. I guess Manny never mentioned that my birthday was just last week.

◎ ◎ ◎

I really have to get out of town for a while. I'm not sure where I want to go or what I want to do when I get there, but I need to just get the heck outta here, find some place I can be out in nature, ponder the breeze, think about things, plan some other things, make some decisions. I don't have to go far, somewhere within an hour or two's drive from here. A totally different setting where I can build a fire, roast some wieners, pop some popcorn, maybe even spend the night out under the stars listening to the pines rustling.

I've got it! Why didn't I think of this before?

Joe and Leona's Campground • 5:30 PM

This was a brilliant idea. As soon as I thought of it, I headed to the garage for my camping gear—an army surplus pup tent, a small camp stove, a lantern, a flashlight, and a small ice chest—and loaded it into my VW. The ice chest filled the tiny front-end trunk, and the rest of it went into the back seat. Next, I raided the pantry in the kitchen and came out with a couple of sacks of camp-appropriate food. The last stop was back in The Hole where I stuffed a change of clothes and my toothbrush, along with my journal, a sketch pad, and a book to read into an old knapsack. Before heading back out to the car, I paused to pull two jugs of Red Mountain from the back of my closet.

The campground is somewhere around 5500 feet in elevation, so the view from up here is truly magnificent, day or night. I had wanted to make it here before dark so that I could watch the sunset from one of my favorite spots overlooking the valley below. It actually took me less than two hours to get here, including a short stop for gas and ice, so I had plenty of time to set up camp before sunset. I wanted to be completely ready for the evening. I pitched my tent first, then I cleaned and repaired the rock fire circle and gathered some wood for a campfire, which brought on thoughts of how good the wieners were going to taste roasted over an open fire and eaten along side a can of pork and beans.

What I'm really looking forward to though, is the peace and quiet. Since it's Sunday afternoon, the weekend crowd has all gone home and there are very few people here. Most of the people who stay on through the week are here for the same reason I am—the solitude. I want this to be a spiritual retreat of sorts where I can be alone with my thoughts to hash over the events of this summer and make some decisions about what to do with my life going forward. I'm not sure how good I'll be with this spiritual stuff, though, never having immersed myself in such things before, but I'm gonna give it a try.

Sitting on a Boulder Overlooking the Valley

I finished setting up camp, locked up the car, and wandered up the hill and over the ridge to sit on this boulder which was heaved up out of the earth millions of years ago by the same forces that will one day be responsible for making California into an island. My family has been coming up here to camp for many years, and I had long ago claimed this ancient rock as "my spot." I've been taking in the scene below me for about thirty minutes. Off to my right—I think that's north—I can see most of Hemet, and a little slice of Riverside. Straight ahead, though, is almost all open space with an assortment of chicken ranches, alfalfa fields, fruit and nut orchards, and native scrub. There is a string of little towns at the foot of the low mountains on the other side of the valley, but they won't be visible until after dark when people turn their lights on.

The color of the sunlight is rapidly shifting from yellow-white to orange, and the brilliant disc appears to be increasing in size as it slides down the dome of the sky. Once the giant glowing orb slips below the western rim of the valley, it will get dark quickly, but that's what I'm waiting for. The night sky up on this mountain is always so beautiful. The dry air is crystal clear, and every star in the galaxy is a vibrant pinpoint of brilliant light — twinkle twinkle, on and off, green and red and icy blue. If I turn around I can see the glow of the moon as it begins to rise above the high peaks behind me. It's nearly full, so there should be enough light for me to find my way back to camp or to continue writing well into the evening, that is, if I have that much in my head to write about.

My brain is already filled with images and words and questions. Not necessarily what I'd call spiritual, but thoughts about life and things in general that I've been pondering for a long time. Well, maybe some of it actually is spiritual, but I'm not sure how I'm defining that word these days. Having been raised Southern Baptist, my idea of spiritual has been whatever that denomination defines it to be. Since I've been reading about other world religions though, my scope and definition of spiritual has grown beyond what I once understood it to be and has become more complex than the simplicity it once represented. It's so easy to grow up in a single faith and just let it take over your life, allow it to guide and shape you into what the culture of that faith has determined to be the ideal being, fully mature and whole.

That's another word I have a hard time with right now, whole — what does that really mean? What does maturity mean? When fruit is ready to pick, it is said to be mature. Is that what it means to be a grown up? You're like a fat, swollen, syrupy fruit getting ready to burst at the seams with knowledge and wisdom and all the stuff that comes with being an adult? But how is it that a fruit is able to ripen? It needs to be fed and watered, and even though a banana tree and an apple tree give different fruits they're basically fed and watered with the same nutrients. But that isn't the case with human beings. Humans are fed and watered with all kinds of different things from hundreds of different cultures and religions and opinions, and they end up like snowflakes — no two are alike.

I used to be a single-minded Southern Baptist boy. I was fed all the things that all other SB boys were fed and I was destined to grow into a SB man like all the other SB men out there. But then it happened. My diet changed. I didn't plan it that way. I didn't even want it to change, it just did. I read Greek Myths, the Egyptian Book of the Dead, parts of the Catholic Catechism, a little Zen, a little Tao, some Confucianism, and recently the writings of that Yogananda guy who, quite frankly, makes a lot of sense. But all those things are a long way from Baptist theology. My fruit may be getting fatter and maybe even sweeter, but it sure ain't focused on becoming just another Southern Baptist man in the crowd of all other SB men. My fruit is a confusion of flavors. The poor thing doesn't know if it's going to be a mango or a pear, a watermelon or prune.

So, what do I do with all this nonsense? Should I even care? That's the other question I ask myself all the time. What difference does it make, if it makes any difference at all? The ultimate purpose of spirituality seems to be to point you in the direction of God and the afterlife, yet according to every scripture of every religion I've read so far, neither of those things can be proven to even exist. The Bible raises two unanswerable questions: is there a God, and is there an afterlife? We're told to take the existence of both of those on faith alone, but faith can't be proven to be accurate, either. Which faith or religious teaching does one choose to build one's belief in the afterlife? Hindu? Christian? Buddhist (which is sort of no faith at all)? Baptist? Catholic? Choosing one is kind of like playing Russian roulette, except that instead of having one loaded chamber out of six or so in your gun, you've got hundreds — thousands if you count all the variations — in your religion gun, and they're all loaded except for one. You put your faith in pulling the trigger on the one chamber that won't blow your spiritual brains out. If you are successful, then you have chosen the correct religion to follow for your entire life. If you are not, then you're probably destined for hell or something like that depending upon which religion-bullet you blew your brains out with. Some religions believe in hell, others don't.

Does any of this make any sense? I hope not. That's why I don't like to even think about spirituality stuff, and yet it seems to be on my mind all the time here lately. But what does it have to do with the price of tea in China, or the price of rice in India? Or my own life and what it's become over the past few months, or what it will become in the next few? What does it have to do with all the girls I've met — there I go again, back to the girls. My retreat is going to turn into a romance novel. Pick a daisy, pull out its little petals one by one naming a girl with each petal. The one petal left is the girl I choose. Sounds like the Russian Roulette bit again, only with a flower instead of a gun.

So, what do I do about the girl quandary? School will be starting in a few days and I don't want to be saddled by a bunch of silly stuff when classes begin. I'm gonna be taking some pretty tough courses first semester and I might even have to study a little to pass them all, unlike high school where I did very little studying. The classes at RCC are going to be much harder and more time consuming and I can't be trying to solve complex issues while being weighted down with girl-drama. Maybe it will all boil down to the daisy petal routine — the last petal is the girl I'll concentrate on. Maybe that's where I'll have to leave the summer behind. Ha! How optimistic of me. There's always the possibility that none of the girls will ever call me again. They might all just forget about me. They might get so involved in their own little worlds and spiritual quests that I become a distant memory, or not even that — no memory at all.

The sky is beautiful. It's turning a dozen different shades of orange and yellow, fading into purple, violet, and ultramarine. Soon it will be dark, and all the little star drops will be flitting about the heavens. I think there's supposed be a meteor shower over the next couple of days and nights. That could be really spectacular sitting up here on this big rock. I'm starting to feel pretty good about being here. It's gonna be well worth the drive just for the feeling I get out of this place. It's so quiet right now. The only sound I can hear is the rustle of the pine needles in the forest behind me. The only odors I smell are the aromas of pine and sage carried by the soft summer breeze. The only sight I see is the cathedral of the sky right front of me, colored like stained-glass by the setting sun. I can almost touch the edge of the galaxy.

I've been watching a jet, make its way across the sky above the hills on the other side of the valley. I know it's probably moving at a speed of at least 300 mph, but from my point of view it seems to be taking it forever just to travel the short distance from Temecula to Riverside. There may be a couple hundred people on that jet. I wonder if any of them are aware of me down here looking up at them. Is there someone on that plane right now who's looking out the window just by chance and making perfect eye contact with me? Some guy in a suit on his way to a business meeting in some big city hundreds of miles away? Or a little kid who's bored out of his head by the long flight, even though it would take much longer if he was in a car—days or weeks, if he were traveling by wagon or stagecoach. Maybe there's a Catholic priest on board who is looking at me at this very moment while reciting his Rosary. He's on his fifth way around the beads and instead of focusing on whatever mystery he's supposed to be contemplating, the image of an eighteen-year-old guy staring up at him from the mountain slope below pops into his head. Sorry to blow your prayers, Padre, I really am. In fact, I kinda wish you were off that plane and down here on this boulder with me right now so you and I could have a little chat about all the questions I have. I do love Catholic priests.

Maybe it isn't a priest who is looking out the window at me.

Maybe it's Diane on her way back to NYC. Maybe things got too ordinary for her here on the west coast and she got homesick for her own wild kind back in New York. Wouldn't that be something? I mean really something? What if she really is up there looking down at me? Maybe that's the very reason I'm even thinking about it—her—some sort of psychic link has just occurred. I wonder if she can sense it? I wonder if she knows? I can dream, can't I? More likely the jet is filled with dog ladies on their way to a poodle contest somewhere. Diane's probably with her aunt at her trailer, the two of them drinking wine and watching Lawrence Welk on TV. And if there is a priest up in that plane, I doubt that he's thinking about this little Southern Baptist boy who's never stepped foot in a Catholic church.

Oh well, such is life. My life. Which right now consists of me sitting alone on this boulder while watching the sky get darker, and hearing the birds go quiet for the night in the forest behind me. Birds stop singing pretty much when the sun goes down. I wonder why that is? It must be a rule among birds going back eons. I think it has something to do with mating practices. I'm pretty sure that at least 90% of all birdsong is related in some way or another to attracting a mate, and since birds can't find each other in the dark, why try to attract a mate after the sun goes down? Your future bird-wife couldn't find you if she wanted. There may be some other reasons that birds sing. Maybe some of their songs are sung for purposes of territorial stakeouts, or for warning, or maybe a dozen other bird things I know nothing about. One thing is certain, though, when the lights go out at night, the birds hit the hay—except for owls, of course.

Most humans, unlike most birds, don't have the sense to pack it in early. They just party all night long when they're young, and then cut the number of parties in half when they get older, except in my case. I guess I'm what they call the exception that proves the rule. Even though I'm young, I'm not too hot on parties, at least not parties with large numbers of people. I like to get together with my friends one at a time, or maybe a small party with three or four people, but anything over that I'd rather not be bothered. Parties are a pain in the butt to prepare for and to clean up after, and all the time the party's going on you have to make the rounds and chit-chat with everyone so you don't hurt anybody's feelings. The difficulty is that everybody has different things they like to talk about. That means the host needs to be well-versed in a ton of things — or at least be able to pretend to be — in order to keep the party going. If you talk to the wrong person about the wrong thing, it can be really embarrassing. Or you might start a conversation about something with somebody who then starts rattling off like they're the only one who knows anything about it, and pretty soon you're really not all that interested anymore. It's hard to get a word in edgewise or to change the topic, and you can't just walk away without being rude. In other words, throwing a party is an art and a science — and at times, a nightmare.

Well, this is some party I'm having right here. I probably ought to stop writing and just lay back on my rock and listen to the breeze. When I write I can hear my own thoughts as if I'm saying them out loud, and that's disturbing the silence of my surroundings. But my thoughts are more productive when I write for some reason, so if I am truly intent on solving problems while I'm here, I should both think and write as much as I can. One of my teachers last year told me that he thought I was like one of those psychic characters that does what they call automatic writing. I sit down, open my journal, and just start writing. What comes out may or may not even be from my own head, but from the head of some dead guy who's trying to communicate with the world through me. He called it channeling. I mentioned the automatic writing thing to Bill Hunter, and he didn't deny it might be possible, but he also added his own two-bit theory. He called the kind of writing I do, stream of consciousness, meaning that I just let my mind flow and whatever flows out of it I write down. It's not from some dead guy, it's all from me. It's my relaxed, subconscious mind attempting to release ideas into my active conscious mind in order to … what? That's what I asked Bill. What? Why? Why would my inner mind be releasing thoughts to my brain? What in the world could I have buried deep down inside that would be worth pulling out and putting on paper? Bill didn't know what or why, but we had a good time talking about it.

Still Sitting on the Boulder • 8:30 PM

I decided that my meditations on my troubles and woes might go better with a little Red Mountain, so I hiked back down to my car to get a jug to bring back here to my rock. I also took time to put a note under my windshield wiper as to where I am. There's always been an unwritten rule at Joe and Leona's campground about leaving a note whenever you leave your camp site in case of an emergency. Just a simple, *I'm over the rise in back, sitting on the big boulder drinking wine,* will do nicely. There's never been an emergency in all the times my family has been coming here, but you never know.

The moon was indeed bright enough to write by, but I grabbed my little battery-operated lantern just in case. I was never a Boy Scout, but I always thought their motto, Be Prepared, is a good one for everybody. Just be prepared for anything that might come up.

I know I want to be either a painter or a writer, and the more I think about it, the more logical it seems to become a writer. So, what does that have to do with the Boy Scout motto? If I were to be suddenly inspired to paint something—like the magnificent view from this rock—it would be very difficult to do so at short notice. My Be Prepared list would have to include at least one stretched canvas, several paint brushes of various sizes, lots of tubes of paint, a bottle of linseed oil, a bottle of drying medium, a can of turpentine and a jar to pour it in, and a few rags to wipe up with. That's a lot of stuff to lug around. As a writer inspired to describe the scene, all I need is a pen and paper and maybe a lantern.

So, here I am, admiring the view from my lofty boulder-throne, swigging cheap wine straight from the jug—I am alone, after all—and awaiting the flash of inspiration.

"Hello?"

What the heck?

◎ ◎ ◎

I wasn't expecting to hear any human voices again until I drive back to Riverside in a day or two, so I was quite startled by a voice coming from behind me. I turned around to see who it was. There in the last glow of the twilight stood Abby's friend, Mamie—the Mam who had come to my house and tried to seduce me right out from under Abby's nose.

"How did you—" I stuttered.

"—find you? Totally by coincidence," she said. "I came up to visit Joe and Leona and maybe spend a night with them, but I saw your car while I was weaving up the road through the campsites."

"There are thousands of VWs just like it on the road. How did you know it was mine?"

"I didn't at first, but I remembered you telling me about coming up here with your family all the time, so I slowed down to take a better look. I saw a piece of paper stuck under your windshield wiper, and I remembered Leona's rule about people leaving a note when they were gone from their spot."

"And I signed the note, DH." I said.

"And how many DHs are there in VWs like yours staying at a campground I know you visit a lot?" Mam smiled smugly, pleased with her deduction.

"Very good, Sherlock," I said, but I wasn't smiling. I had hoped for my retreat to be a solitary one.

As if reading my mind, Mam said, "You look pretty content here all by yourself. If you don't want the company, I'll split."

"No. If you can crawl up onto this rock, I'll be happy to share my wine with you." What the heck.

She smiled and reached out her hand so I could help her up. "Sounds good. I brought a couple of gallons with me to gift to Joe and Leona, but I can give you one to pay you back."

"Not necessary," I said. "I have another jug in the car. You know, Be Prepared and all that."

"Huh?" Mam asked as she scrambled up the rock and sat next to me.

"The Boy Scout motto, Be Prepared," I explained.

"Sounds like a good one," she said.

"Yep.

I can hear her breathing heavily next to me. She's not a small woman, so the hike up the hill and over the ridge winded her a bit. I really don't know what to say to her. Yes, it's a coincidence that she stumbled upon me here, but I never really expected to see her again anywhere. Here least of all. The last time I saw Mam, she was speeding down my driveway after having tried to seduce me in The Hole. That image brought many thoughts back to my head.

"You warned me," I told her softly.

"What did I warn you?" Mam asked, but she knew what I was talking about.

"You told me that Abby would disappoint me."

"And she did, didn't she?" Mam grabbed the jug and took a long drink. "She disappointed us both. I don't suppose you've heard anything from her since she went on the lam."

"Not a word."

"She could be dead, for all we know. That fake stepdad of hers hasn't been back to Riverside since he showed up in San Francisco. Her house there in town looks deserted. Somebody's bein' paid to mow the lawn and keep it up, and every now and then a cop pulls in just to check on the place, but no one ever goes inside. I think the cops have it staked out just in case he shows up one day."

"No news is not necessarily good news in this case, Mam. Alive or dead, we may never know Abby's fate. She can't call us while she's alive and on the run, and if she dies we'll never be notified."

"That's how I figure it," Mam said softly. "Abby and I are pretty close. We've never been out of touch for this long before, even when she's up in The City we always talk on the phone at least once a day. But it's been weeks. I fear the worst."

I put my head down and sigh.

"You guys were getting pretty close, too, weren't you?"

"As close as we could in the short amount of time we had together."

"Well, life goes on. No use broodin' about it. It's a beautiful night." Mam smiled and took my hand in hers. "Let me know if you think I'm being too forward, but it seems to me that our being here together tonight is not a coincidence. I mean, go figure. What are the odds?"

"You may be right," I agreed. Indeed, what are the odds? I haven't seen Mam in weeks, in fact, I thought she was completely out of my life. Then I decide on the spur-of-the-moment to come up here to the mountains away from all possible distractions for a sort of spiritual retreat. As soon as I settle down for some serious introspection in what I have always considered to be my secret spot, Mam appears out of nowhere. What are the odds? She's either very intuitive and lucky, or she's an angel who has dropped down out of heaven just to keep an eye on me. Flip a coin.

"Can I hold your hand?" Mam asked softly.

"You already are," I replied.

"I can pull it away."

"No, leave it there." To be truthful, it felt good.

Mam takes another swig of wine from the jug then passes it to me. I take a large swallow before setting it down on the boulder next to me and looking up into the deepness of the night sky. It's fully dark now except for the full moon, and the stars in the incredibly clear sky are twinkling now like a bazillion little sparklers on the Fourth of July. When I turn to look at her face, I can see Mam's eyes reflecting the twinkling of the stars.

"So, what do you think, Mr. Writer?" she asked.

"Think about what?"

"Coincidences. Is it purely coincidence that I found you out here in this primeval forest?"

"It does seem a bit remote."

"The forest or the coincidence?"

"Both."

"A coincidence means that it happened totally by chance. I could see it if we were driving in our cars at the same time—you in Riverside and me in LA. The fact that we are both in our cars at exactly the same time might be a coincidence, a chance occurrence, but it wouldn't have any value. I mean, so what? We're both driving at the same time. Whoopie. But for two people to find themselves sixty-five miles away from home, not just in the same general area at about the same time, but in the exact same out-of-the-way place at the exact same time, that pretty much defies the laws of chance—if there are any laws to chance. It's a big world, and out of all the pinpoint spots on this world, look at us. Here we are in exactly the same spot where neither of us knew we would be an hour before we left home. Chance? I think not."

"Of all the gin joints, in all the towns, in all the world, she walks into mine," I muse.

"Huh?"

"Casablanca. I don't have a problem with that kind of thinking. I don't really believe in coincidences either, but I'm not sure I believe in fate or destiny. Just because something can't be explained by the laws of physics or whatever, that doesn't automatically mean it has something to do with spirituality or destiny. That always seems to be the answer in the human culture. If it isn't one, it's the other. If it isn't scientific, it's gotta be religious. If it isn't religious, it's gotta be scientific. But what if there's something else? Other governing forces with laws that haven't been discovered yet?"

"Maybe there are." Mam smiled. "But in the meantime, we're stuck with calling it all fate, and fate is as good a word as any."

"Why?" I asked. "Why can't we make up our own laws? You and me, right here on this boulder?"

"You mean totally navigate around the laws of science and religion?"

"Why not? After all, where did those laws come from? Other people sitting on boulders somewhere else? Or maybe on top of a sand dune, or under a tree? Who died and made them God? We have every right to make up our own laws, and I'll bet ours would be better than most of the ones those guys have stuck us with for all these centuries."

"I like the way you think, Plato." Mam squeezed my hand hard in hers. "And I'll just bet that the guys who made up all those laws way back then weren't nearly as smart as you."

"I'm sure they weren't." I grinned.

"So, let's do it!"

"Do what?"

"Make up some new rules — some new laws."

"Okay," I said. "Let's start with fate. Let's make it fact."

"Fate as fact?"

"Yep. Let's say that before we came into these bodies as little babies, we were alive somewhere else as spiritual grown-ups, and it wasn't just a random thing that we became who we are today. Somewhere up there, out there in deep space, there's some sort of Command Center, a Capitol City of the universe — call it Heaven if you want — and that huge city is where everything that goes on down here, and on every inhabited planet in the universe, is planned out. Babies aren't just random things, they're houses that spirit people come to live in when they want to live a physical life on a planet. They use the human bodies here like cars to drive around in. Let's say that you and I are actually eternal, and we live in that big Capitol City up in the sky. One day, eighteen or twenty Earth years ago, we decided that we'd like to come here to this planet and hang around for a few years, kinda like a vacation. As spirit beings we live forever, but it gets really boring if we have to stay in that big city all the time just floating around in the air doing nothing, so we have the ability to go live as humans anywhere in the universe, just by jumping into human bodies when they come out of their mama's womb."

"Wow…" Mam looks a little stunned, but I can see her mental gears working on the possibilities. Slowly, her smile expands, and she nods her head. "I like it so far."

"That could be what all this reincarnation stuff you hear about really is. It's just a race of aliens from millions of light years away on vacation. We do it all the time as eternal spirit people jumping into human babies, living out a life for as long as their human body lives. When the human body wears out, the aliens just jump out, go back up to the Capitol City, and hang around until they decide to jump into another baby, maybe not even here on Earth but on another planet somewhere else in the universe."

"So after floating around up there for a couple hundred years or so, you and I got bored, came down here, jumped into babies and then grew up, knowing full well that we would meet each other someday in our future?" Mam asked.

"Something like that. We would meet because it was all written into the plan. No coincidence, no fate. We set the exact place, date, and time, and here we are, sitting on this boulder exactly as we should be."

"Wow. That all sounds so logical," Mam said. "What if it's true? I mean, what if all that stuff you just said is actually what really is?"

"It just might be," I said. "After all, nobody really knows. Everything down here is just guesswork. All the laws and theories about things, especially things like heaven and the afterlife, are all just guesswork. Nobody has proof of anything because they don't remember anything about where they came from, and they certainly don't have a clue about the afterlife."

"So, your guess is as good as anything else anyone's come up with down here."

"Yep. People get all tied up in their heads about their religions and philosophies, but when you get right down to it, none of it is true because it's all just a big guessing game. I'm talkin' every religion on this planet and every theory and every philosophy, they're all in the same boat. None of them have proof of what they claim. And some of what they claim is a lot sillier than the ideas I've come up with."

"Your idea sounds a lot more logical than most of the religions I know, that's for sure." Mam looked at me and smiled. "You know, Abby warned me about you," she said.

"What?"

"She told me you like to talk about religion and philosophy all the time, that you ponder things like that for hours on end. Maybe you ought to take some philosophy classes instead of art classes when you get to RCC."

"That might not be a bad idea." I smiled.

"I like your thoughts, though," Mam said. "What if our sitting here tonight is indeed the result of a plan that we laid out years ago in that big city up there, and that you driving up here today had nothing to do with anything but the fulfillment of that plan? The same for me driving up here. It could be that everything that's happened in our entire lives has been for the sole purpose of getting us here tonight. None of it is coincidence. It's a part of a plan that has to be implemented exactly as it was laid out, and whatever we do right here and now is meant to be. From this moment forward, everything is out of our control. It's all under the control of the plan."

"So, how do you think the plan ends? What happens from here on out?" I asked her.

"I have no idea, but I think we ought to have fun trying to figure it out." Mam pulled me over and kissed me. "Abby's not here anymore to stop this. I guess she wasn't a part of our plan."

15 SATURDAY

It's 12:45 PM, six days since my last journal entry. I'm at home sitting in a lawn chair in the driveway out in front of the breeze-way having just finished a late breakfast of scrambled eggs, bacon, toast. It's a warm and sunny Saturday afternoon, technically it's still summer, but the subtle signs that mark the passage into autumn in Southern California are there — the air is a little drier, the quality of the light is a little different, the direction of the breeze has shifted — summer is nearing its end.

The last six days have been long, pleasant, and pleasantly busy. So busy, in fact, that I haven't written in my journal since I set it aside last Sunday up on the boulder in order to focus more on Mam. Actually, Mam hasn't let me write in the journal. Every time I picked it up to pen a few words, she snatched it away from me with words like, *no way, Plato*, or something similar. You might say I've been a willing prisoner kept under the spell of Mam's energetic aura of enchantment.

We finally returned to the campsite long after dark last Sunday. We built a small fire to warm a pan of pork and beans, and we roasted a few wieners, mainly just for the smell of it. We cleaned up after our dinner so that we wouldn't have a critter invasion, put out our fire so that we wouldn't start a forest fire, then crawled into my pup tent and spent the rest of the night getting to know each other better.

"You know," Mam confided, "I've wanted to do that ever since you and Abby and I spent the night on the floor in your parents' living room. I was really disappointed the next morning when you refused to give in to my advances."

"Really?"

316

x
x

"Yes, really. I was so frustrated that I couldn't think about anything else all the way home. It kept me awake all night, too."

"I'm sorry," I said. "I had no idea. I do think that I did the right thing, though, given the circumstances at the time."

"That's OK," she said. "I think at the time, it probably was."

Summer days are hot and dry up at Joe and Leona's, and the nights are chilly, but two grown people on top of a sleeping bag in the intimate confines of a tiny pup tent generate their own weather. The bag was a soggy mess by morning.

We spent two more days together at the campground. We talked about anything and everything as the thoughts popped into our heads and came out in a stream of consciousness. We visited the boulder each night, drinking wine and laying quietly staring up at the stars and watching the meteors whiz by. The meteor shower continued for all three of the nights we were at the campground. It was really something to see.

Wednesday morning we got into our respective cars and drove back to my parent's home where we picked up where we had left off up on the mountain. For the next three days, we talked, walked, laughed, cooked, and ate. The only difference was that instead of sweating the nights out on a sleeping bag inside a pup tent, we sweated them out on my little bed in The Hole.

Mam has turned out to be full of surprises. For one thing, she is a much deeper thinker than I originally gave her credit for being. When I met her that first night when Abby was here, she seemed to be a bit of an airhead. Now though, I think it might have been Abby's presence that caused her to act that way. I think that, in a way, Mam is intimidated by Abby. Abby's more a woman of the world than Mam is and she loves to experience things that might not be of an entirely safe nature. Let's face it, hanging around with Beats in San Francisco for any length of time might not be for everyone, and even though Mam has Beat leanings, I think she's uncomfortable about going all in with the Beat lifestyle. With Abby gone, Mam is a different person. From the first day of yoga classes, Abby was always the outgoing, flirtatious one in the front of the class while Mam was the quiet one in the back who hardly ever took her eyes off me.

"You know, I've loved you from the first minute I saw you," Mam told me that Sunday night at the campfire over beans and wieners.

"You're kidding."

For a moment, we looked at each other, then Mam turned her gaze back to the fire. I'm not sure if the rosy glow of her face was because of the firelight, or because of the embarrassment of her confession. "I'd never kid about that," she said. "Abby and I went over to RCC after that first class and sat in The Pit. We talked about you for two hours."

"Two hours?" I was astonished.

"At least," she said. "Abby's the one who started the conversation. She said she thought you were cute."

"What did you tell her?"

She looked at me and grinned. "I told her I'd fight her for you."

"You had to be kidding about that."

"Sort of. I'm twice her size, I could take her."

"But you wouldn't have really fought her, would you?"

"Naw," she said. "Anyway, I already knew that I didn't stand a chance."

"What do you mean?"

"Abby's a lot cuter than me and she's not fat., I knew that if she ever came on to you, you'd jump at the chance to get her into bed."

"You must think I'm pretty shallow," I said.

"You don't think she's hot?"

"To be honest, sex had nothing to do with my attraction to Abby. It was the things we talked about that got me interested in her."

"All the Beat stuff?"

"That was a lot of it. I've been fascinated by the whole Beat thing for a while, then along comes a girl who's not only fluent in the ways of the Beats, but she and her mother know some of them personally and pal around with them when they're up in The City. That's a pretty irresistible hook."

"I can understand that," Mam said ruefully. "And all I have to offer are my miniskirts and big tits."

"Don't sell yourself short, Mam. There's no comparison between you and Abby. First of all, physically you're way hotter than Abby can ever be, and second, you're just as smart as she is, only the things that trigger your intelligence are different from the things that trigger hers. Had I known at the time that you were in love with me, I might have been the one making a play for you and Abby would have never come into the picture."

"Seriously?"

"Seriously. I don't fall for girls easily. I date them like any other young guy. I even ogle them, but that doesn't mean I'm in love with them. It's not even about what is or isn't in a girl's head, it's more about how we get along. It's easier for me to fall for a girl if she and I can just be together for long periods of time without doing anything, just enjoying each other's company."

"You had that with Abby, didn't you?" Mam looked at me wistfully.

"Up to a point. But to be honest, my relationship with Abby seemed to be more on her terms rather than our terms. We had fun together, but we didn't necessarily agree on everything. In the end, the final outcomes were of her doing. It's not that I have to be the boss all the time, because I don't believe that. It's not a her thing, or even a me thing. It's an our thing—a mutual understanding and respect in all things. Does that make sense?"

"Perfectly. And that's just one more reason why I'm in love with you." Mam smiled, and this time her smile was warm and contented. Then she hugged me to her and put her head on my shoulder. We were quiet for a long time after that.

◎ ◎ ◎

So, here I am sitting in the driveway, contemplating the remainder of the day. I feel as if my life has come full circle over the past few days. I'm still in a quandary about what I'm going to do and who I'm going to do it with. Mam left yesterday afternoon to check on her house and to run a few errands. She promised she would be back today to spend some more time with me.

"Don't worry, I won't bug out on you!" she yelled as she backed out of the driveway. Then she laughed and drove away.

Mam's not going to run out on me. She's not going to leave town, ditch me for something or someone else, go into witness protection, or whatever. She assured me that she was just going to take care of some stuff at home and that she would be back on Saturday, today. In fact, as she was getting into her car, she told me that she would be here at exactly 1:27 PM. She told me to be in the driveway at 1:25 PM so that I would be ready to hug her and kiss her the very second she got out of her car. It was pretty cute of her, although a bit far-fetched, to specify an exact time like that, but I truly believe that if anyone can pull off something like that, Mam can. I'll just have to wait and see. My past experiences with women don't inspire much confidence.

What's my real problem, then? Simple — my original questions still haven't been answered. Even if Mam really is in love with me and she does come back today, what does that mean? Is that all there is to it? What do I do with my thoughts and memories of Abby and Diane and June and Jan? Do I erase those women from my head and move forward with Mam at full speed?

Something is missing. This can't be all there is. It just doesn't feel right yet. Will it ever feel right? What does the future hold for me? When exactly does the future begin? And who will be in my future? I don't mean just the girls I've met this summer, but all the people I've grown close to over the past few years, like Manny and Elvis. Will Manny and I still be friends five years from now, or will he and his band ride off into the sunset? What about Pet?

Where the heck is she? What new acquaintances will I make at RCC and how deep or shallow will those relationships be? Will they become friends? Will I make any friends at RCC? The way I'm going, I wouldn't bet on it. I seem to have a way of chasing people away, and for the life of me, I can't figure out why. I'm not a bad person. I don't try to run the show or boss my friends around. Quite the opposite, in fact. I'm usually the one who sits back and listens to all the commotion and nonsense that any friendship creates. I try not to react but to remain the observer, like the Zen monks teach at that monastery Elvis goes to. I try not to be too judgmental with anyone, which can be difficult as people have a tendency to act irrationally or silly at times. I don't like silly. I try not to do silly.

There is one person at RCC who I'm sure I'll be able to count on as a friend, and that's my English prof, Bill Hunter. We seem to have hit it off pretty well, so I hope I don't blow it with him. I think I'll be learning a lot from him, both in and out of the classroom, and if his classes are anything like his conversations it should be a whole lot of fun in the process.

So, here I sit at 1:23 on a Saturday afternoon, in my little nylon lawn chair at the center of the only universe I know, contemplating a mysterious future. Yes, I realize that finding the right girl should not be at the top of my list of things to do right now, but the experiences I've had with girls over the past few weeks make the issue hard to ignore. I know that I must find some sort of resolution or I won't be able to concentrate on anything else. Maybe the flower petal game really is the best idea. Just pick the petals, naming a girl with each one. The name left for the last little petal pulled from the flower will be the name of the girl I'll concentrate on building a relationship with.

Maybe it's completely out of my hands. Maybe there's some sort of mysterious force working in another dimension that's controlling everything I do. Maybe I don't need to concentrate on that last name at all. Maybe it really is fate, and someone or something somewhere else has manipulated my flower to give to me the name that pops up last. Maybe it's all set in concrete after all.

Maybe the name will be Abby! If that's the case, then I'll know it's out of my hands since there is no way on Earth that I could control anything about a relationship with her. I don't even know where she is, or even if she is alive. Even her best friend, Mam, doesn't know. The same is true with June. At least I know she's alive and well in New Mexico, but she may have another boyfriend by now, or she may be so caught up in her art world that I'm no longer even a distant thought to her. In fact, it's the same with all of the girls. I have no control over any of them — not that I really want to. In fact, the more I think about it, the more I like the idea of fate. Let the universe decide. After all, life ain't nothin' but a slow jazz dance.

It's now 1:26 PM, and I hear a car coming up the road. When it pulls up in front of my chair, it will be exactly 1:27 PM.

Made in the
USA
Middletown, DE